KING OF SAVAGERY

PIPER STONE

Published by Stormy Night Publications and Design, LLC.
www.StormyNightPublications.com

Stone, Piper
King of Savagery

Cover Design by Korey Mae Johnson

PROLOGUE

*S*avannah

"You don't want to do this," I managed, choking on the words as soon as I'd said them. Of course he wanted to end my life. I'd betrayed him in the worst way possible.

I'd lied.

"Moy krasivyy, greshnyy malen'kiy krapivnik."

My beautiful, sinful little wren.

There was rage as well as sadness in his deep voice, but I sensed he was close to a dangerous edge. I wouldn't survive.

I'd also stolen from him, a cardinal sin in any language. but in his, punishment was issued by way of death warrant. While nothing of value, at least not in the world of such a powerful, dangerous man, it had been precious to him, to me as well. What I'd taken had been very personal. I'd managed to crawl past his thick armor, gaining his trust.

There was also so much more.

Lust.

Need.

Love...

Was it possible the brutal Russian could remember his love for me?

"Why is that, Savannah?"

"Because it's not you. You're not a killer." I shifted in the chair, keeping my eyes on him the entire time. I'd never seen him so angry, the terrifying gleam in his eyes keeping me shivering. I twisted my bound wrists, my skin chafed from the thick rope. The harsh burn was nothing like the terror that had swept through me the moment I realized he'd learned the truth.

The smile on his face had faded, the ice blue of his eyes changing color. And his features had hardened as he'd studied me.

"That's where you're wrong. You don't know me very well at all, my beautiful little bird. I once told you I'm a very bad man," he said quietly as he turned to face me. "Unfortunately, you'll soon learn exactly what I meant. You lied to me. You betrayed me. Why?"

I couldn't tell him the truth. "I had no choice."

"We always have a choice, my beautiful little wren. Now, your choices belong to me. Whether you live or die, experience pain or pleasure. You are mine from now until the end of time."

As he yanked me off the chair, wrapping his hand around my throat, I gasped. He pushed me against the wall, holding me in place as he lowered his head. "The things I still want to do to you. Would you like that? Do you crave my rough touch, the way I make your body feel?"

I couldn't stop shuddering, my mind a blur. I wanted him. I needed him.

He knew it.

As he pushed himself against me, I wanted to shove him away, but even if I weren't bound, he'd know I wasn't capable.

"Yes," I managed.

"Damn you. Damn you for making me do this." Anger flowed through every syllable, his face twisting in rage, but everything we'd shared hadn't been a lie and he knew it.

His hot breath tickled my skin, his closeness exciting me as it had always done from the first moment we'd met. I couldn't stop shaking and as he dragged the tip of his tongue along the line of my ear, sliding it into the shell, I trembled all over. He had no recourse but to kill me, ridding himself of the traitor.

Just like his father had faced, betrayed by someone he'd trusted.

I was sick inside, but as I tried to hate him, both my body and heart had something else in mind.

"Maxim. Please."

"Please what? Have mercy? Do you deserve it after what you did?"

"I..."

He brushed his lips across mine, drinking my essence. I arched my back involuntarily, longing to be closer. As he fisted my hair, pulling me into a kiss, the taste of him had never been sweeter. I was lost in the moment, almost pretending that we weren't enemies. As he swept his tongue inside, images of what we'd shared rushed into my mind, spilling over into my senses. I could feel every moment of passion we'd shared, every darkness that he'd introduced me to.

Pain so intense that I'd thought I'd lose my mind.

Pleasure so extreme that I finally learned the true meaning of ecstasy.

He controlled me. My wants. My needs. Every emotion.

Yet I'd broken through too many layers, exposing the man underneath, and he hated me for that most of all.

And still, I loved him.

"The things I will do to you," he added, the gruffness of his voice keeping my pussy aching. He rolled his other hand down my neck, following his dancing fingers with aggressive kisses, finally biting my lower lip until he drew blood. Then he raked his hand down my dress, ripping it into with ease.

I couldn't make a sound, even if anyone could hear me. As he yanked the two parts aside, my body betrayed me all over again, shoving aside the anger and fear, leaving only desire in its wake. He took a deep breath, issuing a dark, furious growl before twisting his finger around the thin elastic of my panties, snapping his wrist. I defied him as I'd done so many times, refusing to show him any fear.

Maybe that's because I didn't believe he wanted to hurt me. There was too much emotion between us. He took a step away, allowing his gaze to fall. "Why?"

I closed my eyes. There wasn't an answer that would soothe the beast. "Because I had no choice."

"As I said, we always have a choice."

He'd continually used the same words I'd thrown at him before, and I cringed inside.

"Do you want me, little wren? Do you hunger to have my cock thrust deep inside?"

"I..."

"Answer me!"

"Yes. Yes..." Why lie? He'd only know it like he now knew almost everything else about me.

"Mmmm..." He squeezed my breast, taking his time to pinch my nipple between his thumb and forefinger. "Perhaps I'll indulge you one more time, but not before you're punished." He pulled me away, shoving me onto the bed, shoving the remnants of my dress aside then yanking my arms up over my head.

I didn't dare move. There was nowhere to go, no place I could run to for safety. I was his prisoner.

And he was mine.

As he pulled the belt from his trousers, his eyes never left me. There was such hunger in them, a brutal fix that only I could fill. My body. My kiss. My touch.

My heart.

After he rolled me over, I closed my eyes, holding my breath as he snapped the leather strap against the floor. When I sensed him right behind me, I fisted my fingers around the comforter, opening my legs wider without command.

For him

Because of him.

Because of us.

Fear and desire coursed through me and as I looked over my shoulder, I was still captivated by the man who'd driven me away from the light.

And I wanted him. God help me but I did.

As he exhaled, twisting the belt in his hand, his dazzling eyes pierced me once again. There was no anger in them, just resolution.

Without hesitation, he brought the belt down several times in rapid succession, the pain blinding. Within seconds, I was released from a sense of anguish, floating into a sublime state, just as he'd taught me was possible. I sucked back a cry, biting my lip until I tasted the blood he'd drawn. As he took several ragged breaths, I rested my cheek against the covers, finding a way to smile. Maybe this was our destiny after all.

I took several gasping breaths, fighting the tears that threatened to give away my emotions. He was brutal in his actions, adding strike after strike, every action methodical.

I couldn't stop shaking, the ache in my stomach worse than any round of discipline.

He brought the strap down several more times, the heat and agony building to a precipice. When he stopped, peering down at me, his shifted his eyes back and forth and rolled his fingers from one side to the other. Then he tossed the strap aside, reaching down and fisting my hair. As he yanked my head at an awkward angle, he crawled onto the bed, leaning down.

His whisper was harsh, filled with coldness, but the heat of his body was not to be denied.

"Prepare to give up your old life, Savannah. You belong to me in every way. You always have."

We'd once shared so much, passion that knew no bounds. But I'd crossed a line, one that I couldn't recover from even if I was saved.

Now there was nothing left but sorrow for either one of us.

CHAPTER 1

*M*axim

Two weeks earlier

The footage was clear. There was no sense in denying the obvious any longer.

"Fuck, boss. The informant was right," Ricardo Diaz said from behind me. He was a loyal member of the Bratva, a good friend, but I'd never considered him family and it had nothing to do with the fact he'd been born and raised in Puerto Rico.

The man in the video I'd considered a brother, someone I could look up to and count on as I'd earned my stripes in preparation for taking over from my uncle. I said nothing at first, but my rage increased as the video continued to roll. Watching the man I'd admired for his loyalty to the organization spill his guts to the Feds was enough to turn my stomach.

In the world of the Bratva, there was no right or wrong, just destruction when necessary, bloody violence that painted the streets in crimson.

There was no moral ambiguity, no second-guessing decisions made.

No guilt.

No remorse.

Absolutely no acceptance of betrayal.

And when it was exhibited in one of your own, the consequences necessary were savage.

I moved away from the table, noticing every man in the room was staring at me, waiting to see how I'd react.

"He knows everything," one of my other soldiers said, although he kept his voice low as if worried he would anger me further.

At this point, nothing could.

I'd almost beat the lowlife informant to death when he'd come to me with his accusations. Then I'd had Sergei trailed. Now I knew the truth, yet it was difficult to swallow. Hell, it had been widely known that if I hadn't been Vladimir Nikitin's nephew, Sergei would have been honored by being given the nod for Pakhan when Vladimir retired or perished.

I moved toward the bar, the realization of what was necessary weighing heavily on my mind. The Feds had been breathing down our backs for months, doing everything they could to derail our operations.

The only possible saving grace was that I'd shifted Sergei's attention in another direction, feeding him false information. However, he knew enough that the men had every right to be concerned. I could only imagine my uncle's reaction at this point. With an enemy breathing down our necks at the same time, determined to slide into our territory, this was the last thing we needed.

"What are you going to do, boss?" Ricardo moved behind me as I poured a hefty amount of bourbon. "You know this can't stand."

"Don't tell me what can or can't happen, Ricardo. That won't bode well for you." The tension in the room was high. The soldiers were used to my quick reactions, refusing to listen to a single excuse from anyone. Mistakes were handled with extreme punishment, and that's the reason I'd earned the respect of every soldier who'd pledged their loyalty to me as I began taking over from my uncle.

"I'm sorry. I didn't mean any disrespect."

"I know what needs to happen." I made the statement for all of them to hear. I had a reputation to uphold and if it were any other man, I'd have already left the building, hunting him down. I was a merciless leader, which had earned me the title of the Angel of Death. There would be no mercy for a rat. "He needs to die."

"Do you want me to handle it?" Ricardo asked, keeping his distance from me.

I took a swig, swirling the liquid in the glass immediately afterwards. "He dies by my hands. No one else. Is that understood?"

I'd been trained from an early age that showing emotion of any kind was a weakness. That had been easy, my entire life stripped away in the blink of an eye long enough ago that I considered myself dead inside.

Now this.

I considered myself observant, easily able to catch anyone in a lie, but this, this... I couldn't find the right words but there was no other recourse. I wouldn't give the man time to defend himself. There was nothing he could say that would counter what he'd done. All that was left was to clean up the mess.

"Shut down all operations until further notice," I said over my shoulder.

"We have the shipment coming in," Ricardo reminded me. "Do you want me to back it off?"

The shipment of drugs was large, more so than I typically allowed to come through Miami's ports. Up until now, I hadn't worried because we owned a good portion of law enforcement in the city. But the Feds were different. They'd tried placing men in my organization three times before, failing every time.

While I kept to myself, my personal life completely off the grid, Sergei had lived every day of his life as if it was his last.

He'd been an easy target to manipulate, but that didn't matter in the least. Betrayal had an ugly stench just like terror.

"We're not abandoning the shipment. Period." Not unless it was absolutely necessary. I'd lose millions if I did. I polished off my drink, the glass thudding against the wood as I sat it down. When I grabbed my jacket, Ricardo seemed surprised.

"Do you want me to go with you?"

I slipped my arms into the sleeves, yanking out my weapon and checking the ammunition. Then I made certain my dagger remained in my pocket as well. "Not necessary. This I'll handle alone. Make certain every other soldier in the organization knows what sentence was doled out. There are consequences for every action, most punishable by death."

* * *

We were all different as soldiers. Some men had families that they cherished, keeping them far removed from the life. Others preferred to live like playboys, fucking everything in a dress. I chose neither, spending my off time in a house in South Beach, usually very much alone. Tonight, I stood on the deck of Sergei's house, which was only a few blocks from mine. How many hours had I spent staring at the ocean in hopes of finding some answer or maybe divine intervention?

Enough to know I wouldn't find any.

I'd made myself at home in Sergei's absence, pouring another bourbon. He always had a penchant for the best of everything, spending his money on toys and whores. At least he'd enjoyed himself during his nearly forty-three years of life.

I heard movement behind me and unbuttoned my jacket. It wasn't unusual that I stopped by his house. There'd even been a few times I'd crashed on his couch after a night of drinking and playing pool. Those had been good times. Now they seemed like a distant memory. I didn't want to think of him as a traitor, but he stopped being my friend a long time ago or he wouldn't have betrayed the family.

"Hey, Max. What are you doing here?" Sergei thought nothing of my appearance. I sensed he was making himself a drink.

"Just in the neighborhood." It was the same thing I'd said every time I'd shown up unannounced. It had become a joke between us. Perhaps later I'd remember those times fondly. Not for a long time.

He joined me on the deck, keeping his distance and for a few seconds, remaining quiet.

"What's up?" he finally asked as he shifted against the railing, studying me intently. "You seem tense."

"I am." I took another swig before turning toward him. In my hand was my weapon.

He slowly lowered his eyes then exhaled, returning his gaze toward the ocean waters. "How did you find out?"

"Does it really matter?"

"I guess not." He stared into his glass then polished it off in one glug. "If it makes you feel any better, I was forced into talking with them."

"You were forced?" In the waning afternoon light, I noticed his eyes first. They were haunted yet held fear. And the stench of his terror wafted into my nostrils.

He wasn't the kind of man to beg for his life. He'd made fun of the assholes we'd killed for doing so, mimicking them after the fact. He'd used a line every time he'd pulled the trigger or wielded the knife he always carried.

Time to meet your maker. Have a great time in hell.

I'd heard that first when I was sixteen and he was twenty-two, witnessing my first extermination. I'd admired his coolness, his lack of emotion. I'd wanted to be just like him instead of my uncle.

The betrayal of our friendship was like a dagger shoved through my heart.

"They promised immunity if I provided information. I gave them crap, Max. I promise you that."

Now he was getting nervous.

"What exactly did you tell them, old friend?"

"Does it matter, Max? You're going to kill me anyway."

"Yes, I am. However, I would think you'd prefer clearing your conscience before meeting your maker." I tossed the glass over the railing, holding the gun casually. By all rights, I should cut out his organs while he was still alive, making him suffer as long as possible.

PIPER STONE

"Nothing of importance."

I nodded several times, allowing myself to watch him squirm. He deserved the sickness of anticipation like I'd experienced the horror of his treachery. There was no reason to care why he'd met with a federal agent. None. In my position, I couldn't afford to be emotional or have any second thoughts. Still, the burn of not knowing had already begun to haunt me.

"Why?"

"Why?" Sergei repeated then laughed.

"You taught me everything I know, Sergei. You sat with the family at Christmas dinner. You protected my cousins for years, ensuring that no monster would hurt them. And you were my friend. Did none of that matter to you?" The anger and hatred in my voice was evident.

The waning light didn't diminish the single flash of pain and regret in his eyes.

It just didn't matter.

"I didn't have a choice, Maxim."

Chuckling, I took a deep breath. "We all have choices, some more difficult than others. However, when trust and respect are involved, there's only one choice to make."

"You just don't understand."

Did the traitor actually think I cared at this point?

"Who did you turn over?" When I asked the question, I sensed he had no remorse for what he'd done.

"No one."

"Bullshit. Who?"

When I realized he was gloating, I raised my weapon, taking two steps forward. Then I smashed the cold steel against his cheek hard enough I heard his bones crunch.

Of all the things he could have done, he had the nerve to laugh.

"*Vremya poznakomit'sya s vashim sozdatelem. Priyatnogo vremyapreprovozhdeniya v adu.*"

Time to meet your maker. Have a great time in hell.

That's the moment I pressed the barrel against his forehead, pulling the trigger.

Then I walked out of his house for the last time.

* * *

It was rare that my uncle was quiet. He was a brooding man who was either enraged, every word out of his mouth and every action taken brutal, or he was driven by lust and greed. His manic personality was often overbearing. Tonight he was quiet, so much so I wondered whether he'd heard me.

The tension was high.

There was no one else in the room, no one to hear the words stated or the emotions presented. We still had a reputation to uphold. Damage had been done but with my swift and deadly actions, a message had been sent.

We would not tolerate a traitor of any kind.

"*Kogda predatel' ryadom, bol'she nikomu ne doveryay.*"

When the traitor is close, trust no one again.

While I understood the sentiments, had questioned every soldier's loyalty, we had a business to run.

He walked to the bar, pouring a tall glass of vodka, gulping a portion before turning to face me. "The damage?"

"Yet to be determined."

"You need to assess every aspect of our business. Make certain the collections are handled promptly."

"That's already being taken care of as we speak." I'd sent soldiers out to the various businesses we were protecting for their weekly payment. Once the FBI discovered Sergei's absence, they'd likely try to use what information they'd already gained for several arrests. My men were prepared to take a fall, knowing our attorney would easily get them off.

Or so I hoped.

"The shipment is the concern."

Vladimir eyed me carefully. "It's important we provide to our clients."

"Understood. Measures are being taken to keep it on track."

As he walked closer, he continued studying me as he'd done for years. He'd toughened me up, never going easy, beating me for the smallest infraction. As he'd told me more than once, his savage behavior and lack of compassion would help make me a great leader. "You need someone you can count on."

"I have Ricardo. I trust him."

"Do you really?"

I had to think about the truthful answer. "Enough to know he can't hide things from me."

Snorting, he swirled the liquid in his glass. "Not good enough, Maxim. You know that as well as I do. We have sharks in the water waiting for chum. We're not going to feed them."

"Absolutely not." Once word got out on the street of the betrayal, even our weakest enemies would swarm like locusts, waiting for our complete downfall.

"I'm reassigning Damien to your command."

"Fuck. Damien? I wouldn't trust him to make a goddamn collection." He was a younger soldier my uncle had recruited years before, once a lowlife criminal but he had technical savvy, which had allowed Vladimir to come out of the dark ages. I loathed the man, my gut telling me it was just a matter of time before he did what he could to sell us out.

"He is trustworthy!" Vladimir snapped.

"You'd trust him with your life or those of your daughters?" I could tell the question wasn't an easy one for him to answer.

"Enough. The decision has been made."

I gritted my teeth but said nothing. At least with the man under my command, I could keep an eye on him.

And I wouldn't hesitate to put a bullet between his eyes if he crossed me.

"Fine." There was no reason for any further discussion. I did what I'd come to do. As I turned to leave, Vladimir spoke again.

"Did you know Sergei had a daughter?"

I stopped short, the news hitting me hard. "No."

"She's only six. He doted on her. Her mother is very poor and without Sergei's assistance, they'd be homeless."

My jaw remained clenched, my heart racing. Fuck. "I'll have them both taken care of."

"See that you do. No child should suffer because of the sins of the father."

I almost laughed at this sentiment. He hadn't given a shit about my suffering since he was the one responsible for the death of my parents. While it hadn't been proven, I knew it in my gut.

Sins of the father. I would bring no child into a world of violence and blood. That was the single promise I'd made to myself years ago.

And I planned on keeping it.

CHAPTER 2

 avannah

Fruit.

I was sick to death of eating nuts and berries. What I wanted was a juicy cheeseburger. I hated being good, which is what I'd been since I could remember—the good girl. The one who followed the rules. The girl who never got into trouble. The idiot who never let herself experience anything outside the box.

As I adjusted the volume, I gritted my teeth and shoved the plastic container out of my reach, promising myself I'd purchase that juicy-lucy thick quarter pounder with double cheese, thick mayonnaise, and three slices of bacon on my way home. I'd grab a nine-pack of chicken nuggets at the same time as a surprise. Grinning, I pulled my diet beverage closer and tried to get comfortable in the chair. That was the daily issue, trying to find a comfortable spot for the long haul.

I'd begged for a new chair, but I might as well have been asking for a big-screen TV. I was in a shitty office with a single window, the heating system never working right. At least I could wear comfortable clothes, which saved money. I didn't look great in suits anyway.

Now it was just a matter of waiting, which is what usually happened for extended periods of time. The big wait.

Then nothing.

On the occasion I did get something, it was usually pointless, nothing of value to offer. But I sat in the same seat five days a week for eight solid hours listening. If only the hours were nine to five, but that wasn't possible in the world of criminals. They handled their business during the dark, when the parties were in full swing, and lovers were masking themselves as someone else.

Listen to me. I'd suddenly turned poet now? That's what happened to someone who spent all their time listening to dead air.

For some reason, I was frustrated more than usual, antsy to do something different. I'd studied and mastered six languages, for God's sake. One would think I'd manage to find a job that entailed traveling to luxurious locations, wining and dining with powerful, influential people. Wearing expensive clothes and jewels, traveling first class. Those had been my intentions when I'd earned my degree in two things I'd loved. So much for dreams.

Who was I kidding? I was an analyst and would be until the day I died.

Not cut out for field work. At least that's what had been stated on my last review. I sensed my boss had wanted to add to the bottom line that I was too naïve. Maybe I was, but I studied every scrap of information that I could find on whoever I was listening to. I knew their likes and dislikes, their weaknesses and all about their enemies.

So what?

I eased the folder I'd put together on the Nikitin organization in front of me. I'd studied the major players as I did at least once a day. I wanted to be certain who was talking. The photographs allowed me to interpret vocal inflections, which I'd gotten very good at, but I wasn't supposed to interpret emotions.

Yet I did anyway. Maybe I was a rule breaker.

Ricardo Diaz—lieutenant for the Bratva, party of the security group.

Sergei Sokolov—part of the elite group, Maxim's best friend and mentor.

Damien Pavlov—sometimes soldier but usually for Vladimir Nikitin, a man considered the Pakhan but not for much longer. Both the man's age and failing health had pushed his nephew into the limelight years before. Damien was the wildcard, a man Maxim obviously didn't trust.

There were dozens of other players, but none as prominent.

Maxim Nikitin was the center of it all, a brutal soldier that had earned his way into becoming the next Pakhan. He was the nephew, adopted when he was very young by Vladimir and his wife, but not before suffering in a Moscow orphanage for a couple of years. Even so, he'd been treated no better than the other soldiers coming up through the ranks.

Maxim was considered one of the most notorious, savage men on the East Coast. As second in command of the Russian Bratva, his merciless tactics in handling his enemies had earned him the moniker of the Angel of Death. I'd heard too many stories about what he supposedly did to his enemies, but he never talked about the details and there was no evidence he was directly responsible for the dozens of murders he had supposedly committed.

The world of the Bratva was fascinating as well as dangerous. And I'd made a bet that Sergei was betraying Maxim. I'd sensed it after a single conversation I'd overheard between him and Maxim. They were supposed to be best friends, even growing up together, but Sergei was definitely hiding something from Maxim.

As I stared at Maxim's picture, the same tingling sensations I'd had since the day I was assigned to listen coursed through me. The man kept me hot and bothered, his dark, curly hair and ice blue eyes along with his muscular physique the thing fantasies were made of.

Down, girl. Down.

Laughing softly, I closed my eyes, sucking on the straw as I thought about birthday presents instead of kinky sex. I also reminded myself that I needed to ask for the day off for the party. This year was going to be special, and I refused to allow work to interfere. I pulled my feet onto the edge of the chair, rocking back and forth.

Then a dark voice entered my realm, and I snapped open my eyes.

Maxim…

"My ne mozhem dopustit', chtoby ocherednaya partiya isportilas'."

We can't let another shipment get fucked.

As I heard noise coming from the other end, I pressed the headphones closer to my head, straining to hear what was being said. The ambient noise was terrible. I'd been told the computer geeks had a way of drowning it out. Maybe I was last on the list with everything. I was shivering, far too excited since listening in at the casino was usually bust. I'd recognize the voice anywhere, so smooth that every time I heard his rich baritone, I couldn't stop quivering for several minutes.

Butterflies took off in my stomach, my heart thudding like it did every time.

Good, Agent Parkins. That's the way you should be thinking about a brutal criminal.

His tone was gruffer than normal, his anger heightened. But to me, he was the sexy voice on the other end of the line.

And it was rare that I was given the opportunity to hear it.

"Grebanyy predatel'."

Fucking traitor. Maxim's anger was evident, more so than usual. Who was the traitor? Sergei. If I was a gambler, I'd bet a million bucks.

"I know, boss. The trickle-down effect ain't good," Ricardo Diaz snorted, a man with an illustrious former life in the military. Why he'd gravitated to a life of crime was unknown.

I shoved everything in front of me aside, concentrating on what I was listening to. As Maxim continued to talk in a hushed tone, it became apparent that he was discussing an internal issue with his second in command. I started making notes, jotting down Ricardo Diaz's name alongside Maxim's. Diaz was an interesting character, a man born in Puerto Rico but also a linguist, mastering four languages in addition to Spanish and English. That made him invaluable to Maxim's operation.

Or at least so I thought.

As they continued speaking in Russian, I tried to take copious notes, but Maxim was enraged, snarling out details and tossing out threats toward the Colombians as well. But as he continued, more details came to light, and I began translating their conversation into English quickly and easily.

"Do you want to consider stalling the shipment now, boss?" Ricardo asked. "I don't like the vibe on the streets. We had trouble with collections, some of our customers acting as if they had a right to deny payment."

"*Vy ikh nakazali?*"

Did you punish them? I found it interesting that Ricardo spoke Russian. Most of their conversations were usually held speaking the language for security purposes. But Maxim was different today, angrier than I'd heard in a long time.

Ricardo laughed. "With pleasure."

I could hear Maxim's heavy breathing. He was an angry man in general, every interaction I'd transcribed out of fury, but it seemed he was ready to explode. I pulled up the last file in my computer, studying Maxim's picture. He was an insanely gorgeous man, the kind of man who took the time out of his busy schedule to keep his physique in perfect condition. I knew that because I'd discovered that some of the best conversations for gathering useful information had been when he was in the gym that he frequented in his own resort.

The find had given me atta-girl points. If only it had led to an increase in salary. I rolled my eyes. How many times had I heard the term 'budget constraints' during my annual review?

Still, it was rare to find him spouting off this kind of information, which meant Maxim was beyond furious.

"We are not halting the shipment!" he snapped in English. "Two weeks. Period." His snarl sent another wave of shivers down my spine. As he switched back to Russian, I struggled to keep up with him. Could the man ever learn to slow down?

A shipment. This was the first time I'd heard any kind of date. Maxim was usually overly cautious about sharing any details. That was one reason he'd never been brought up on charges.

"*Golovy poletyat!*"

Heads will roll.

I imagined his face and the lower half of my body throbbed.

What is wrong with you? This is no time for attraction.

The conversation continued for another four minutes and thirty-two seconds. Then Maxim shut it off, ordering Ricardo to have their people sweep the streets of Miami in search of any hidden informants for the Colombian. He never called the leader of the Colombian Cartel by his name, which I found unusual.

Then all I could hear was Maxim's heavy breathing as he pumped iron.

I sat back, reading my notes then switching off the recording equipment, capturing the audio and sending it to my boss. As I read over my notes, I realized what I'd overheard was exactly the kind of thing the FBI had been searching for. I gave myself a mental high five and bounded toward Special Agent Christopher Reynolds' office. He almost always used his full title, which irritated everyone in the department.

"You have something, girl?' Sheila asked as I flew by her desk. "I can tell because you're unusually excited."

"I get excited about things," I told her, giving her a pouty look.

"Since when? Oh, yeah. When the vending machine finally had Oreo cookies again."

"Very funny." But sadly true. I knocked on Christopher's door, excited enough I was shifting my weight from foot to foot. At least this would give a push to get my day off, which seemed rare to come by these days unless planned months in advance, which Brittany couldn't do. She'd just sprung it on me what she wanted to do two nights before.

"Come," he barked, his voice harsher than normal.

I peeked my head in, planting a grin on my face. "I sent you an email."

"Okay?" He barely threw me a look.

"It's important. So I think."

He appeared exhausted, the job obviously beating him down. He had quotas to fill just like everyone else and the criminals were getting damn good at either discovering our listening devices or bypassing situations where we could listen in altogether. After a few seconds, he beckoned me in, immediately searching his computer.

As he started to play the audio, I was forced to repeat most of the words in English. I'd transcribe the information into English later. When the few minutes were finished, I realized he was staring at me.

"That is something. Isn't it?" Oh, my God. I couldn't believe how meek I sounded.

"Jesus Christ. That might just be the break we're looking for." He jumped up from his desk, more animated than I'd seen him in a long time. As he moved from behind the small area, pacing the floor, I wasn't certain whether to interrupt his thinking process.

"So that's good. Right?"

"Agent Parkins. What you listened in on could mean we all get a goddamn raise for a change. Where'd you get that?"

"The gym at the hotel."

"I'll be damned. You were right. Okay. Go back and transcribe then keep listening. If he's in the hotel, track him as best you can. I need to let my boss know."

"Yes, sir." It was the first time I could remember him this excited. Contrary to what my sister had tossed in my face less than a week before during our once a year conversation, maybe I was good at this job.

After work, I was definitely bringing home fast-food treats in celebration. At least the little things still made me happy.

* * *

"What in God's name are they arguing about?" Sheila said as she met me at the coffee machine the next morning.

I glanced at Chris' office again and shook my head. He'd been in with the assistant director for a full hour, at least half of it with raised voices. "I have a bad feeling it's about me."

"Why?"

"I just do." I took a sip of coffee and almost choked. That's the moment Chris took long strides toward his door, throwing it open, his eyes scanning the area. When they locked onto me, I shrank back.

"Parkins. In my office. Now." He didn't exactly slam the door but everyone in close proximity jumped.

"Jesus. What crawled up his ass?" Sheila muttered.

Chris was the kind of man who didn't like to be told what to do. Especially from a woman. He immediately shut the blinds on his all glass office walls.

Exhaling, I took another sip of coffee before tossing it out.

"Good luck."

I gave Sheila a look and rolled my eyes. A perfect way to start the day. When I walked closer, I took another deep breath before knocking, opening the door just a few inches.

"You wanted to see me, Chris?" I asked then stuck my head inside. For some reason, I was lightheaded.

I'd gotten very little sleep the night before, my curiosity about Maxim and his world keeping me sitting in front of the computer until two in the morning. Somewhere in the back of my mind, I knew my fascination with the Miami Bratva was a bit ridiculous, but Maxim lived the kind of life most people could only dream about doing. Exciting. Dangerous. In the lap of luxury. And he was gorgeous, checking off every box.

The big boss, Assistant Director Katherine Helms, was sitting in a chair in front of my boss's desk, her expression bland. She had a reputation as a woman who never lost an argument. Given the expression Chris wore, I had to guess today was no exception.

"You heard me," Chris said. "And close the door after you."

I did as he asked, feeling small in the big world of the FBI. Sometimes I had to remind myself that they'd recruited me for the job.

"Assistant Director. It's good to see you again," I told her, although I wasn't certain I liked the woman.

"Please, titles drive me bat-shit crazy. Call me Katherine. Sit down, Savannah."

Every part of me stiff, I did as she asked, watching as Chris sat back in his seat, a smug look remaining on his face.

"Chris supplied me with the recording of what you overheard, Savannah. Excellent work. Your diligence with regard to the gym has proven to be spot on. How did you know Mr. Nikitin would ultimately let his guard down at the location?"

As Chris shifted in his seat, I tried not to let him make me uncomfortable. "That's the only place where he's able to be himself. He works out like he does everything else, with a vengeance, but he's different. He listens to music. He seems relaxed. Everywhere else it's like he has a spotlight on him at all times. When he gets angry, he goes to the gym. I knew one day he'd take his business there."

Katherine gave Chris a look then smiled. "Astute. What do you know about the Nikitin Bratva, Maxim in particular?"

"Maxim is thirty-seven, adopted by his uncle and brought to America when he was five years old. His parents were gunned down in Moscow where they were visiting friends. Given Vladimir Nikitin has no male children, only three daughters, Maxim is slated to become the Pakhan when Vladimir retires. That is said to be any day."

"That's not what I asked, Savannah. That information is located on the file for any agent to see. What do you know about him, the man, the way their organization is set up?"

I chewed my inner lip as I shifted into the personal file I kept on him in my mind. "He's an introvert, preferring not to deal with people. When he does, he'd almost always angry with them. He's rarely with a woman but when he is, he frequents BDSM clubs in either Miami or New Orleans, but never more than once, then the woman disappears from his life. He enjoys the finer things in life, but usually spends more time alone than with anyone. He's a rock music lover, prefers red meat, and wouldn't be caught dead drinking a cup of tea." I wasn't certain what she was looking for, but I'd gleaned the snippets about his life after two years on the job. "Oh, and he's also in something called the Brotherhood."

Chris jerked up in his seat. "What did you say?"

"Yes, the Brotherhood. I don't know much about it but from what I've gathered, it's an alliance of several prominent leaders from different crime syndicates across the country."

"For what purpose?" Katherine asked, her excitement building.

"He's very cautious about mentioning it. I overheard an argument Maxim had with Vladimir, his uncle, about it earlier this week." I could tell by the looks on their faces I should have come to them about the alliance.

"Go on," Chris encouraged.

"If you're asking if they plan on taking over the world, no. I think their organization is about keeping the peace, but I really haven't heard much about it." I noticed Katherine was practically salivating from the news.

"Who are the members?" she asked.

"He's very cautious about that. I don't know for certain other than one is in New York. That's it."

The two looked at each other again in a silent discussion and I hated it.

"That could prove more useful than anything," Katherine finally said.

"Maybe," Chris countered.

"Oh, I knew I was right."

What was she so right about?

"And their organization?" Katherine prodded.

"They're well organized, Maxim very cautious about providing details. They have several legitimate businesses, but their bread and butter is in illegal drugs, their products high quality. They trust very few dealers, none of which have been caught in any illegal activities. They cater to the rich and famous, the money laundered through their movie production company."

A wry smile formed on her face, and she sat forward in her seat, resting her forearms on her knees. "Let me tell you what isn't detailed in the dossier on him. He's a brutal man, responsible for at least twenty murders, although there's never been enough evidence to charge him or any of his associates. He's very protective of the men in his employ, and they are willing to die for him. You're right in that he's very sadistic, said to brutalize women. Yet again, not a single woman has come forward accusing him of assault."

"Why are you telling me this?" A knot had formed in the pit of my stomach.

"Because we need your help."

Chris gave her a hard look. "Katherine. She's not ready. Period."

"I decide when and if she's ready and I can tell you with certainty that she is more than ready for this."

"That man will eat her alive," Chris threw at her.

She snapped her head in his direction. "She'll have backup."

"That Maxim will see a thousand feet away. You know exactly what happened to the last agent we put in undercover."

I cleared my throat, which at least got their attention. "What am I *not ready* for and what happened to the agent?" I looked from one to the other, uncertain either one was going to tell me the truth. "What?"

"The agent was found impaled by steel rods on a construction site of a building owned by the Nikitin family."

I could feel a heated flush burning my skin. "And that wasn't enough evidence to arrest him?"

"He fell off a building nearby that wasn't owned by a member of the Russian Bratva," Chris said dryly.

"What about the traitor he mentioned?" I asked, glancing from one to the other. They both looked uncomfortable as hell.

Chris took a deep breath. "While not through this department, we'd finally been able to nail a single member of the Bratva, a man considered to be family. Upon threat of arrest, he was more than helpful in providing details to another agent. Sergei Sokolov was high ranking within the organization, considered family."

"Maxim found out." No wonder Maxim had been livid. "I sensed it." I wanted to give myself a high five, but the thought was ridiculous.

"What do you mean you sensed it?" Katherine asked.

"I can tell by inflections when people are being deceptive. Sergei was nervous, although he did a damn good job hiding it."

The two of them looked at each other.

"Yes, well, Mr. Sokolov disappeared," Katherine added, dismissing what I called a gift.

No, he'd been killed. "The Bratva are tight, their loyalties stronger than most crime syndicates. They live or die by the oath they make to the organization. Why would a trusted almost family member turncoat? He'd do his time in prison then be considered a hero."

When neither one of them responded, I sensed whatever the man had been threatened with had been very personal.

"Sergei has a child, a six-year-old girl. The agent used her as a bargaining chip." Chris didn't sound happy about how Sergei had been turned.

"You used a child against him?" I snarled. "That's disgusting."

"This is a criminal organization responsible for gunning down men and women, Savannah. They don't deserve the same respect that you or I do." Katherine was gloating about the lengths the FBI had gone to.

I remained disgusted. Maybe I was too close to Maxim in a strange way. I certainly understood him better than most people.

"Okay. So what about me?" Was her statement supposed to make me feel comfortable or terrified of the man? I didn't know the violent side of him, other than what I read in the papers. I'd heard other things, a few very private details about his anger and fears because he didn't think anyone else was listening to. I almost felt guilty about it.

"The director would like for you to go undercover for the FBI." Katherine said the words clearly, without inflection, but it took me several seconds to process them.

"I'm sorry. What?"

Chris appeared more uncomfortable than before, his entire face pinched. "You would be promoted to a field agent in order to do this, of course," he said.

I narrowed my eyes, finding it somewhat difficult to focus. "Oh, of course. What exactly would this mean?"

"It would mean that you're going into the belly of the beast." Katherine searched my eyes, smiling at me warmly. If this was some kind of FBI talk, I had no clue what she was trying to tell me. "Not so dramatic as that but you would be getting closer to Maxim than anyone has ever been able to. At least that's our hope. He can sniff out an agent unlike anyone we've tracked before."

"And he kills them." I swallowed hard.

"Not all of them." Her response seemed trite, as if laying my life on the line wasn't a big deal. "Is there an element of danger and risk? Of course, but there will be an extraction team close by at all times."

"I have responsibilities that preclude me from leaving the area."

"And I'm certain you can manage them. This is important. This is the first time we've gotten so close. This could mean taking down his entire operation, perhaps a second one as well."

I was no fool. The possibility of that happening was slim to nil even with my involvement. "Look. I appreciate the opportunity, but I'm not trained."

"You've had weapons and self-defense training. You speak his language and a half dozen more. You're intelligent, cunning, and observant. Plus, you're his type." Katherine's words didn't have as much meaning as I'm certain she wanted them to.

"His type?" I sounded like a damn parrot.

"Yes, your look is exactly what he's been seen with. However, don't make it seem like you're too interested. Make him want you. Be sassy, which I know is not necessarily your personality, but I have no doubt you can do this. Challenge him."

I wasn't certain whether to think of her words as a compliment or a slight. Whichever it was, her statement left a lump in my stomach.

Chris jerked up from his chair, heading toward his window. "This is a bad idea. If he makes her, she's dead. Plus, I'm not going to have my agent seducing a fucking monster."

"We're not going to allow that to happen and if it takes her seducing him, then that's what she needs to do."

"And you're not going to force one of my employees to go undercover. It's not going to happen, Katherine."

"Hold on!" I snapped. "I am sitting here in front of you. I get to decide." Didn't I?

Suddenly, it got very quiet in the room, both shocked at my outburst.

Exhaling, I closed my eyes. "What would I need to do?" When neither one of them answered immediately, I was ready to lose my temper. "Would one of you give me the details? Please?"

"You're a chef. Right?"

Katherine suddenly seemed like an entirely different person. "What does that have to do with anything?"

"Because there's a position open at one of his restaurants in Miami. It's an excellent place for you to meet him completely under the radar."

Miami. That was a world away from Atlanta and my comfort zone.

"My skills are rusty," I insisted.

"I'm certain you can adapt," she countered.

"Stop pushing her, Katherine. I am not going to allow you to do this." I'd never seen Chris so angry.

Katherine leaned over the desk, her eyes narrowing. "As I said before. You have no choice, Agent Reynolds. It's out of your hands."

"This is fucking bullshit."

I was exasperated from their arguing alone. "Let me hear what we're talking about." As soon as I made the statement, Katherine seemed pleased.

As I listened to her idea of what could happen, I thought how excited I'd been to get into culinary school, longing to become a chef. I'd been okay, graduating and finding what I'd thought was the perfect job. Only then had I realized how much I hated the profession. Of course, I'd also been involved in an abusive relationship, which hadn't helped. When the suggestion that I learn another language was presented to me, I realized that maybe I could salvage all the money I'd spent for culinary school by getting a job overseas. The world of food and eateries was entirely different. Or so I'd read in books, never having experienced another country myself.

Then something had happened, and I've fallen in love with languages, still determined to live carefree in another country.

My dreams never came to be. First my mother got sick, Jessie refusing to help take care of her. Then I'd dealt with the aftermath of kicking a horrible man out of my world, forced to take him to court. The big surprise had been the mitigating factor, but I wouldn't change the outcome for anything. Finally, I'd found another reason to stay in the States, a joyful one that kept me busy all the time.

When Katherine finished, I thought about everything she'd told me, uncertain I could pretend I was anything but me. "I don't know." It had become painfully obvious to me that whatever either Chris or I said wasn't going to matter. Why did I have a terrible feeling there was a lot more at stake than just arresting the second in command to the Miami Bratva?

My skin crawled at her flippant attitude.

"Of course, we'll need to update your look a bit, a little makeover for your sacrifices. And you'll need to push yourself with this. Maxim is cunning. You need to remember that. He's charming and debonair but don't let him fool you."

As I turned my head toward Katherine, I realized how sick to my stomach I was. Did I really look that bad? Granted, I barely wore makeup, didn't have time to do anything but shove my hair into a ponytail and certainly couldn't afford glamorous clothes. When I shifted my gaze toward Chris, I could swear the man was turning green.

"Yeah, he's a cold-blooded killer," Chris muttered.

Debonair. I'd spent months looking at his picture every other day or so. He was gorgeous, but it was easy to tell even in photographs that he had no soul. I wasn't born yesterday. Katherine was asking me to throw myself at him, only in subtle ways. My head ached, my mind a blur but I had to make a decision.

"What do you think, Savannah? Will you do it?" she asked, her tone now as pushy as before. "We have limited time so I will need to know your answer. I did forget to mention that you'll receive a thirty percent increase in your salary."

Thirty percent? It meant the difference in being able to afford treats and excursions out versus watching the same DVDs that were two years old before I could afford to purchase them.

"Stop fucking pushing her," Chris demanded.

"I have no choice. You heard the damn tape," Katherine retorted.

As they started arguing all over again, my mind shifted to the strange but electric attraction I had to Maxim Nikitin. It didn't matter that he was supposedly a brutal killer. Just the sound of his voice made me crazy. He didn't know me at all, but I felt like he'd captured a portion of my soul. "I'll do it."

CHAPTER 3

 *avannah*

"Mommy. I don't want you to go away."

A part of me died inside from hearing her little voice, the pleading sound that always broke my heart into teensy pieces. We were all each other had and the thought of leaving her for a day let alone an undetermined amount of time made me sick to my stomach. Tears formed in my eyes, and I was thankful the sun was starting to set so maybe my little girl wouldn't be able to tell how unhappy I was.

It had been over five days of preparation to become an entirely different person. I was still Savannah Parkins, but most of my past had been wiped out. I was a low-level chef who needed a job, moving to Miami with nothing but the clothes on her back and a few hundred dollars in her bank account. My family had been wiped out with the exception of using one bit of truth. That I'd taken care of my ailing mother through her battle with cancer, depleting her bank account then mine to try to afford the drugs.

All reference to my work with the FBI had been erased, and I'd been reborn as a sweet, vulnerable girl who could allow herself to fall for a monster. I'd been promised that Brittany would be watched out for even though she would be staying with my sister, an estranged family member who'd reluctantly agreed to take her. But I knew Jessie too well. She'd get sick of being hampered by a child after a week max. I had no other choice.

Even though I'd be close by, I'd been forbidden to see my little girl even once. If I was successful with the first phase of the operation, Maxim would take a keen interest in me, likely checking out my story. That could include being followed.

While I'd also been provided with a contact person, the meetings would only occur in the beginning. It would be too risky if I was lucky enough to find his favor. That was the goal. To have him fall for me, bringing me into his private domain until the shipment went down.

Ten days tops, I was told.

As long as everything went according to plans.

I'd also spent hours listening, gleaning little else regarding the shipment. Maxim had been unusually quiet, which had continued to concern Chris. He'd tried three times to pull the plug, but no one was paying him any attention. The possible arrest was too important, my services far too valuable. I wondered if the words would be put on my gravestone when Maxim shot me between the eyes.

A cold shiver banked down my spine. If I was this nervous now, how could I expect to fall into such an important role?

"Baby, we talked about this," I said in as comforting a voice as possible.

She whimpered slightly, curling her arm around her favorite teddy bear, the one she never went anywhere without. I was broken inside, uncertain I could pretend to be anything but a haunted single mom. I love her with all my heart and I'd give anything up in order for her to have a better life than I'd been able to provide. At least I'd been able to take her on a little road trip from our home outside of Atlanta to Ft. Lauderdale where Jessie lived, spending some time in a couple of small amusement parks. I'd broken the budget with ice cream stops and souvenirs, another new stuffie and far too much fast food, but she deserved to have a beautiful little holiday.

I was terrified I'd never see her again.

Oh, real good, Savannah. Just keep thinking that way.

I shoved aside my inner voice, trying to put the pieces of my heart back together.

"I know, Mommy. How many nights will you be gone?"

"Less than ten. You can count to ten. Right?"

She nodded emphatically. There were times she seemed so much older than her four years. As she started to count, I took a deep breath, making the last turn to the lovely house my sister lived in with her husband, a man I barely knew. He was rich, which allowed Jessie to stay at home, lounging by the pool. While I'd never forgive her for not providing a single dime of money to care for our mother, she was my sister. I did love her.

Maybe there really was a fine line between love and hate.

"You did so good, baby girl. Now, remember what I told you. You need to obey your Auntie Jessie."

"I don't know her."

"I know, baby. But she loves you and is so excited!" My damn sister better love my little girl with all her heart, or I'd rip hers out with my bare hands when I returned. "She has a pool."

"Really?"

"Absolutely. That's why we bought you a new little swimsuit." I reached over, pressing my finger into her tummy. God, this was going to be so hard. A lump had remained in my throat for days. Even though I'd been pampered—a new haircut and color, gorgeous new clothes and a manicure, new lingerie and heels—I felt like a fake. I wanted to turn around and go home, curling up with my fluffy purple robe with Brittany, eating popcorn and watching a silly movie. I was no femme fatale, but I needed to learn quickly, or I'd be outed in minutes.

As I pulled into the driveway, I grabbed her little hand. "You do know how much I love you. Don't you, my sweet angel?"

"Of course, Mommy. Love you bunches back."

After cutting the engine I hesitated before climbing out. Jessie's house was four times the size of mine. It was difficult not to be envious of all the pretty things she had. We'd grown up so poor in a small town in North Carolina. We'd both said we'd never return. At least she'd kept the promise she'd made to herself. It had taken me months to convince my mother to leave her broken-down house and move in with me.

"Come on, baby girl. An adventure awaits." By the time I grabbed her things out of the trunk, Jessie was standing in the doorway, a sour look on her face. At least when she noticed Brittany she grinned, bending down to my child's level.

"You must be Brittany."

She nodded while reaching for my hand.

"You're adorable. Now, I have a plate of fresh cookies hot out of the oven. If you go through the door right there, you'll find the kitchen."

Brittany peered up at me longingly. I never let her have sweets before dinner, but this was a special occasion. "Sure, honey. Go grab a treat. But just one."

Jessie folded her arms as she stared at me.

"You bake now?" I asked. My sister had been the cheerleader, the pompom girl in college, the homecoming queen and even won a couple of pageants. I was the studious one with glasses, the ugly kid sister.

"Not a chance. It's a roll but at least I put the cookies on a baking sheet."

"That's something." The awkwardness between us was worse than before.

"She's precious."

I lit up as I always did when someone talked about her. "She's my whole life."

"You need to get a man."

"The last thing I need is a goddamn man. I had my fill." I wasn't going to add in after dealing with Brittany's loser father.

"I'm sorry you had to go through that."

I almost spit up. She sounded genuine. I bit my lip to keep from doing so. "Thank you for taking care of her. I put books and toys in her suitcase, stuffed animals and all her clothes are clean."

"Don't worry. I have a housekeeper who'll make sure she has everything she needs."

"She needs her aunt. She's never been without me for longer than a few hours, not days."

Jessie's eyes held the same fire mine always did, but she chose not to start a fight at this point, which I wasn't certain I could handle.

"I promise I'll take good care of her, Savannah. She is my niece."

Like that had mattered to her for one minute. She'd never tried to come visit or send a single birthday card. I was crazy to think my sister could handle something so adult.

"Where's Ken? Working?"

She got a funny look on her face and sighed. "Ken's staying at a hotel. We're not sure we're going to make it."

This was husband number three, and she was only thirty-four years old. "Well, maybe you guys can patch it up."

"He wants a kid."

And I care why? I didn't say it. "Well, this will give you a good chance to see if you want one."

Was I bargaining here?

"That's what I thought."

"I need to get going. I want to say goodbye." As I bypassed her, heading inside, I sensed she was watching me closely.

"I like the haircut. You look sensational, not tired like you used to."

That was the only compliment I'd likely ever get out of my sister. "Thanks." As soon as I was finished with the godfor-saken operation, I planned on altering it, tossing the clothes.

Maybe.

"Hey, Savannah," she said, her voice entirely different.

"Uh-huh?" I didn't bother turning around.

"I'm worried you're doing something dangerous. You know, deadly?"

Great. She was worried that she would be required to take care of Brittany. "Don't worry, sis. You wouldn't be called on to watch her forever. She'll be well taken care of by a friend of mine." At least Sheila had agreed reluctantly to care for her. I would have preferred leaving Brittany with her during the mission but couldn't risk the FBI connection.

"That's not what I was going to say. I just… I just worry about you. You've always been so strong, but you can't take on the world. You know?"

"I'll be just fine." Very few things shocked me any longer, but her words did, and I believed her. Sadly, I wasn't certain I believed mine.

I would never forget something my mother told me when she was close to her death, and it struck me hard.

"I'm not afraid of dying. I'm terrified of the journey getting there."

* * *

Maxim

I took a deep breath and held it, slowly letting it out as I pushed my feet against the weights, finishing the reps. After feeling the burn, I hopped off the bench, immediately grabbing a towel. The workout had been brutal, but not enough to squelch the continued rage. As I wiped my face, my thoughts drifted to Sergei's little girl. The email Ricardo had sent with the grainy picture had heightened the fury that was spinning out of control.

The man I'd once considered my best friend had betrayed me for a tiny blonde-haired creature who had no clue how dangerous her daddy was. As Ricardo walked in, I tossed the towel and pulled a bottle of water from the fridge, cursing Sergei for forcing my hand.

"They're here."

"Bring them in and stay by the door. I don't want a single interruption."

"Absolutely, boss."

Ricardo disappeared for a few seconds and when the door opened again, I realized there was a part of my job that I loathed. I'd lost men, my soldiers forced to tell their families that they while their partner died, they'd be well taken care of.

But I'd never been asked to deliver the news I'd brought down the wrath of God in their lives. I wasn't a good man, and had no understanding of humanity, but when the nervous young woman walked in, her face ashen, for a few seconds I was humbled.

I kept my gaze locked on her eyes for a full ten seconds before allowing myself to gaze down at the little girl dressed in all pink. I'd accepted a long time ago that if there was a God, my soul would burn in hell. Today, I was reminded why.

"Victoria," I said quietly.

The woman nodded, her lower lip quivering, but in a moment of strength, she managed to address me. "Mr. Nikitin. Sergei spoke of you highly. This is Emily, our daughter."

Our daughter. The words hit me hard.

"Say hello to the nice man," Victoria told her.

The little girl continued to cling to her mother's dress, staring at me with the same deep blue eyes of her father. When she waved, offering a little giggle, I wanted to feel something more than anger, but it was impossible at this point.

"Hi, Emily. You have a beautiful dress."

"Thank you." Even her voice somehow reminded me of my old friend.

The little girl fidgeted, her attention drawn to the exercise equipment. I'd learned that before Sergei had found out he had a daughter, Victoria and Emily had barely made ends meet, living in a rat-infested shithole of an apartment, the owner charging her twice what the place was worth. As a result, Victoria had worked three jobs just to try to put food on the table.

Unacceptable.

I grabbed the present I'd purchased from the gift store downstairs, chastising myself for not taking the time to buy her something special. As I hunkered down, Victoria flinched. "I have something for you, Emily." I gave her mother a single nod.

Victoria had daggers in her eyes, already told what had happened to the man she'd cared for, but she encouraged the little girl to come to me. Emily giggled when I handed her the package, looking back at her mother for approval to open it.

"Go on, honey. Mr. Nikitin and I have some things to talk about."

Emily skipped toward another part of the room, tearing at the package. Victoria approached, her jaw clenched. She was beautiful, albeit worn down from years of experiencing a rough life. When she slapped me hard across the face, I closed my eyes. Normally, my anger would be unleashed, retaliating without thought or question. But with her, I let it slide.

"How dare you take a father away from a child."

That was the moment I realized she'd remained in love with him despite his philandering ways. I felt sorry for her, which was something new for me.

"It was necessary."

"Necessary. Someone will need to explain to me why murder is ever necessary." Victoria's words were biting, and she had no fear of what I could do to her.

"You're Sergei's family. You and your daughter will be well taken care of by the Bratva."

"I don't want your blood money. You can rot in hell."

I closed the distance, keeping my voice low so Emily wouldn't hear my harsh words. "Don't be a fool, Victoria. Sergei did everything in his life to protect you, including betraying me. He died because he loved both of you. While I cannot forgive what he did, I do understand his reasons. I've paid off the mortgage on the house Sergei bought for both of you. I've established a trust fund in Emily's name and the savings account he regularly deposited money in will continue being funded. More important, I will keep your identities safe."

"Safe?"

"There are many enemies as well as men I employ who would enjoy destroying anything having to do with a turncoat. You have my word neither you nor your daughter will ever be harmed. Should something happen, you can always come to me."

She studied me intently, her lips pursed. "And you think that allows you to remain guilt free for what you did?"

I thought about her question, the ache remaining from the loss. "No. It doesn't. But it's the right thing to do and I will honor Sergei's commitment to his family. That does mean something."

The way she searched my eyes was an indication she was trying to see if I had a soul.

While I hated to disappoint her, she shouldn't bother.

A man like me had no soul.

CHAPTER 4

*S*avannah

"Get your ass in gear. We don't have all night to wait for your station!"

I looked up from the sauté pan, blinking as beads of perspiration stung my eyes. The kitchen was oppressive, which apparently the chef didn't care about. At least he was barking about someone else. I resumed my duties, trying to keep my eyes in the swinging door. I had a bird's-eye view of part of the dining room, but I'd yet to catch a glimpse of the man I was here to observe.

As well as entice.

You can do this. You can.

If the butterflies in my stomach were any indication, I'd fail on my first day of the promotion.

"You need to remember that. He's charming and debonair but don't let him fool you." Katherine's words chimed in my mind for the tenth time since I'd walked into the kitchen only a few hours before. I almost laughed thinking about the fact I was trying to pass myself off as a chef while undercover. Ugh. Even after boning up on my skills, they were still rusty.

Shuddering, I tried to resume cutting more vegetables, nicking my finger in the process. As blood flowed, Chef Salinger walked by, the horrid man cursing in French.

"Get the hell out of my kitchen and clean yourself up! What is wrong with all of you?"

The chef's bellow was likely heard throughout the posh dining room. How could the man still be employed? I rushed toward the side door leading to the bathrooms, grabbing a paper towel along the way. My blood pressure must be sky high given the way my finger was bleeding, soaking into my pure white chef's coat. I burst through the door, trying to wrap my finger at the same time.

Then I hit something rock solid and gasped.

"Whoa." The single word was husky, soft like velvet with rough around the edges.

I lifted my head slowly only to gaze into the most intense pair of ice blue eyes I'd ever seen. Long, dark eyelashes highlighted his sculpted cheekbones, and darkened stubble covering his angular jaw adding to his mysterious as well as dangerous persona.

"I'm so sorry," I muttered, unable to recognize my voice. I hadn't anticipated running into Maxim Nikitin this way if at all. I was stunned at the turn of events.

"No reason to be sorry." His gaze was glittered with amusement, but there was also a hint of something primal in nature, as if a hunter had just tracked down his prey.

The thought was totally unfounded, yet my instinct told me I was right.

The light Russian accent was as enticing as the tone, but his smile was magical. He was taller than I'd thought, every muscle sculpted to perfection, something his tailored suit was unable to hide. His pictures hadn't done him justice.

"I wasn't paying attention where I was going." He still had a firm grip on both arms and as he allowed his gaze to travel from my face further down, offering a brief but intimate appraisal. A heated shiver coursed through me from the way he was looking at me. I wasn't supposed to be attracted to him, but it was impossible not to notice every chiseled feature. He was tall, strong, and painfully handsome, but the dangerous quality was the most attractive. Weren't all women into bad boys? If so, he was the poster boy of a dark alpha.

"Not to worry. You've cut yourself." He backed away, lifting my arm. "Do I need to call for an ambulance?"

I laughed with ease, some of the tension releasing. "Oh, no. I've been through much worse than this."

At that moment, the door was tossed open, Chef Salinger barging into the hallway. "What the hell is taking so long?"

"*Rentrer a l'interieur!*" Maxim snapped in French, his tone dark and ominous. Go back inside.

I glanced over my shoulder, noticing the chef had turned bright red. I made note that Maxim also spoke French.

So did I.

"Of course, Mr. Nikitin." The horrid chef gave me a nasty glare before turning on his heel, bolting back into the kitchen. Almost immediately I heard something being tossed, the clanging sound followed by heavy cursing.

"He's not a very nice man," I said, the words just slipping from my mouth.

"No, he's not," he said under his breath, but I heard the anger laced through every word. "I'm very sorry you had to experience such a ridiculous tantrum."

"I'm used to it. The chefs I've had the displeasure of working with have been pompous pigs who have a very high opinion of themselves. My guess is that their arrogance was comparison for their lack of performance under the sheets." The only time I blurted off something like that was when I was terrified or furious.

I was both.

I sucked in my breath as I looked at him. "I'm sorry. That was uncalled for."

"As I told you before, no apologies necessary. Now, please take the time you need to clean and dress your wound. If you need any further assistance, I'll be just outside in the dining room. No one as beautiful as you should ever bleed."

"Thank you. I don't even know your name."

He eyed me carefully then smiled. "Maxim. And you are?"

"Oh, you're the owner." My entire body was on fire, so much so breathing wasn't second nature any longer.

Chuckling, he had more of a boyish grin than I'd antici-pated. "I don't always admit it, but yes." He lowered his head when I didn't answer his question immediately. "You are?"

"Oh," I said, laughing even though I was only acting. I wasn't this doe-eyed over any man, no matter who they were. "Savannah."

"A lovely name for a beautiful woman. Please take care of yourself, Savannah." As he backed away, his nostrils flared, his eyelids half closing. If I didn't know better, I'd say he was undressing me with his eyes.

Pure carnal need roared to life inside of me. I'd told myself I'd never get caught up in finding another man attractive. Then Maxim had disrupted my quiet little world with his sexy voice and dangerous demeanor.

What are you doing, Savannah? You're out of your mind.

When he was gone, I leaned against the wall, trying to catch my breath. I wasn't cut out for this, not by a longshot, but I'd made a commitment and was determined to follow it through. Maxim Nikitin was a venomous snake and nothing more.

At least that's what I needed to try to convince myself of.

I was also right about the chef, and I stood by my words, even though I needed the job. I'd been warned about the powerful, dangerous owner but no one had said anything about the jerk I'd be forced to work beside for an undetermined length of time. It was a good thing I carried sharp knives with me.

Ten minutes later, I was second guessing whether I was cut out for this profession or any other after setting a pan on fire. My nerves were getting the better of me.

You can do this. Breathe and work. Remember the goal.

Goal. I couldn't imagine seeing Maxim behind bars.

"Jesus Christ, you incompetent pig. Get out of my kitchen!" Chef Salinger yelled.

I'd known from the first moment I'd returned to the noisy establishment that the chef had it out for me.

Ordinarily given my personality, I'd walk out with my tail between my legs. Not today. I wasn't the same girl, which gave me permission to be anyone I wanted to be.

Including one with a backbone.

As I unbuttoned my jacket, I walked closer, feeling the oppressive stares of everyone else in the kitchen who'd backed away out of fear. "You know what? There's something I've wanted to say to you from ten minutes after walking into this kitchen. You're an asshole, not just as a chef but also as a man. You don't deserve to be wearing the white coat under any circumstances."

The gasps in the kitchen fueled the fire burning in my core.

The chef puffed up like a blowfish, his face red as the blood he'd caused.

"How dare you!" he snapped. "You are a worthless bitch. I'll make certain you never work anywhere else again in this town."

I closed the distance with a single long stride, putting my index finger in his face. "Go ahead and try it. Then you'll face my wrath." The harrumphing sounds were louder and I could swear the rest of the oppressed crew was going to burst into cheers when I tossed my chef's coat in his face, grabbing my roll of knives, holding up the butcher knife for the pompous son of a bitch to see. After twisting it several times, I shoved the sharp blade into the roll, throwing back my head before turning around.

That's when I realized that not only had the door been left open by a curious member of the waitstaff, but also Maxim had been a party to the entire gruesome scene.

So had a good portion of the dining room.

Embarrassed, I did what I could not to run past him, but by the time I hit the hallway, I was jogging toward the exit, tears threatening to form. I'd fucked it up. I'd been inside the kitchen for less than four hours and I'd been fired.

What the hell was I supposed to do now?

I fled out the door, tears already slipping past my lashes. I had no idea how to salvage the situation. None. This was all or nothing. As I headed for my car, something made me stop, turning toward the gardens that I'd admired when walking into the gorgeous casino and resort. Somehow, I found my way to the stunning fountain, vibrant lights shimmering across the water.

This was crazy and I couldn't breathe. I sat down on the stone surrounding the fountain, curling my knees under me as I stared at the colorful fountain. After a few seconds, I placed my knives next to me, fingering the canvas case then rolling it open. The metal blades had a vibrant glow in the neon lights. I thought I'd never use them again. I'd taken out all my meager savings, purchasing the best of what I could afford. Maybe it was time to finally get rid of them. At least I'd been given the opportunity to feel like a chef one more time.

What could I say at this point? Or think? I'd allowed my temper to get the better of me. I closed my eyes, still shivering from the rush of adrenaline. At least I'd been able to tell the asshole off. A lot of good it would do. I'd put that on a resume.

The sound of running water was only mildly soothing. I couldn't sit here all night long, but I would until I figured out how to rectify my fuckup. Groaning, I dropped my head into my hands, hating myself for how everything had gone down.

"God. I need this job. I need this job so badly. Stupid girl. Stupid girl." I'd certainly gotten a chance to see a huge group of celebrities because of the movie premiere, even running into Brad Pitt just outside the restroom, but I doubted that would do me any good at this point.

When I felt a presence behind me, I reacted or maybe over-reacted, jerking up and around, grabbing one of the knives on instinct. Then my eyes opened wide. Oh, shit. Now I'd really done it.

"It's not often that a beautiful woman is prepared to drive a knife into my gut while being offered a glass of wine." The entire night sky seemed lit up from the vibrant lights surrounding the resort. The neon shimmers also highlighted Maxim as he stood holding two glasses of wine in his hands, his eyes twinkling.

I'd been unprepared to see him before, floundering my way through an awkward conversation. Now I was positively petrified to the point my throat was closed off. I lowered my arm, trying to laugh it off. "I'm sorry. I guess my defense training classes remain in the back of my mind. A girl can't be too careful." My hand shaking, I slid the boning knife into its slot, closing the roll.

"You are very astute, but I hope you don't think I'm the boogeyman." He lifted the corners of his lush lips, the smirk full of amusement.

"I don't know. Are you a creature that slinks out from underneath beds in the middle of the night?"

"Hmmm… That is a loaded question and one that can only be answered over a glass of wine." He held one out, obviously not willing to take no for an answer.

I accepted, accidentally touching his fingers. The quick soar of heat and electricity was startling, but I didn't react other than giving him a slight nod. Jesus. The man was magnetic, far too much so.

"I'm terribly sorry for my bad behavior. I hope I didn't upset your guests."

"I couldn't care less, but no, you didn't, Savannah. The man deserved a small taste of your wrath." He seemed amused, his stern features softening. "I enjoyed the show tremendously."

The wine was incredible, but nothing was going to calm my nerves. "Still, I usually don't behave in such an atrocious manner." We stood in silence, and I was surprised I didn't feel more uncomfortable than I did.

"I hope I'm not crossing too many lines, but I am curious. Why do you need the job so badly?"

Exhaling, I hated the rattling sound of my voice, the weakness that I knew he could hear. "I'm sure you're heard the same sob stories your entire life. I have so much debt that I'd drowning in it. I've tried for months to get more than a part time job doing what I love, but no one's hiring back home. When I accepted this position, I moved away without thinking it through, selling what little crap I owned in my hope for a new start. I'm staying in a shithole motel in a rundown city that I've never been to before. Now this. Maybe you don't know this, but Miami is a tough city to try and make a living in."

"Yes, so I've heard." His expression was one of amusement. That shouldn't piss me off, but it did.

"Aren't you glad you asked? Some people weren't born with a silver spoon in their mouths." As soon as I shot off the statement, I bit my lower lip.

He smirked, cocking his head.

"That was shitty of me."

"Nonsense. You spoke your mind and you're right," he admitted. "I'm a very lucky man. From what I've already seen, you won't have an issue getting another job."

"I hope so. I really do. I like it here. Kind of." I laughed nervously, trying to keep my eyes on the massive building in front of me.

Maxim moved beside me, following my line of sight. "What do you think of my hotel?"

"I wasn't given a grand tour, and this was my first day."

"Still, from what you've seen. What are your impressions?"

I tried to think of the right words. "It's a majestic hotel that creates a festive atmosphere, allowing every guest to feel pampered."

He chuckled then pointed to the area where I was sitting. "What do you really think?"

The man was challenging me. Fine. Why not tell the truth? "I think it's gaudy, overpriced, and the interior designer must have been on crack. All you need are dolphins, and you might as well run a kiddy park."

When he nearly spit out his wine, I started to laugh in spite of myself.

"A kiddy park. It's extremely rare that any woman has the nerve to tell me the truth."

"Why is that?"

"Because they're afraid of my reaction. You have no fear of speaking your mind."

"Which is the very reason I'm sitting on this cold stone instead of suffering in a kitchen that needs a much better exhaust system." I took a sip of wine, trying to calm down. I'd been prepared for various scenarios but nothing this personal or intimate.

At least so soon.

I'd memorized everything I'd been handed, formulating scenarios in my mind with perfect answers to hundreds of questions. This wasn't what I'd expected, but I had to admit that it was much more fun.

"Duly noted. Just who are you, Savannah?"

"A girl in need of a job."

"Mmm... Unfortunately, I've learned through the years that it's in my best interest to stay out of human resources. However, that doesn't mean I won't make a few calls. I do know some people in this town."

"Oh, no. I didn't tell you my sob story to try and garner a favor. I understand and would never suggest that you interfere. But I will ask, what do you do to make those millions of dollars?" I was surprised how easy it was to be around him, my nerves slowly abating.

He seemed genuinely surprised I'd asked him that question. "That's honestly something I ask myself far too often but to give you a fair answer, I run several businesses including this one. I handle the marketing and some aspects of real estate development. I also own a movie production company."

"Ah, yes, the reason for this party and all the fabulous celebrities."

"None of which you admire." He made a statement, the second flash of his smile making me woozy.

Shrugging, I glanced toward the stars. "I prefer more natural entertainment."

"Very interesting. Unfortunately, my work keeps me far too busy to enjoy much of anything."

"Then you must love what you do."

He lifted his eyebrow as he tipped his head in my direction. "To be honest with you, the people I work with are difficult, arrogant, and often don't have any common sense."

"Then why don't we toast to winning the lottery and moving to an island paradise where the sky is always blue, the clouds are white and puffy, and the sand is warm beneath our feet. I'd toss in a permanent cabana boy as well."

"What if I'd prefer a cabana girl?"

"If we won the lottery, we could have anything we wanted." I held up my glass, giving him a mischievous look.

"That sounds like something I would thoroughly enjoy." He studied me as he'd done before, allowing his eyes to roam across my jaw to my shoulders, falling to the way too tight tank top I'd worn underneath the jacket.

"I would as well."

"Is that what you're wish for, Savannah, to win the lottery?"

He motioned toward the fountain. There were thousands of pennies and other coins in the water. "Truthfully? If I had any change I could toss in, I'd wish for something else entirely. While winning the lottery sounds fabulous, I've heard of too many people who gambled or spent their winnings immediately, falling into additional despair, others realizing that money really can't buy happiness." While I was playing a role, I meant what I said.

I noticed he'd reached into his pocket and when he opened his hand, he had a palm full of change. "Please, make that wish."

After staring him in the eyes for a few precious seconds, I selected a polished-looking penny. Then I brought it to my lips, pressing it lightly against both before tossing it into the pool. It was the same wish I'd had for almost five years, and it would be the same one I'd have for years to come.

The perfect Prince Charming.

"What did you wish for?" he asked, his voice deepening.

"If I told you then it wouldn't come true. Somehow, I have a feeling your penny was exactly the luck I needed."

I thought I'd lost him as he took several sips of his drink. Then he stood, extending his arm. "Would you like to have dinner with me, Savannah?"

I used the glass to hide behind for a few seconds before rising to my feet. "I'd love to, but the location of choice will have to take me as I am. Scruffy."

He took a deep breath, holding it for a few seconds. Then he inched closer, towering over me, his prowess creating a wave of desire burning deep within. His scent was just as powerful as the man, his aftershave sandalwood and citrus, both fragrances enticing my senses. As he raked his eyes down to my bright red tennis shoes, a smile curled across his face.

"I have just the place in mind."

CHAPTER 5

 axim

Very few people surprised me, except those who'd been stupid enough to betray me over the years. But this woman was... I couldn't find the right words. I employed hundreds of women in my casino and resorts, more in the corporate offices, but none had been so bold as to tell me their unabashed thoughts about the garish hotel. Let alone the way she'd given Chef Salinger a piece of her mind had been priceless.

If only I had more like her in my employ, I could rule the world.

However, by inviting her into my private suite at the resort, one I frequented rarely and was typically used for meetings or other less attractive actions of business, I was setting a precedent that could come back to haunt me. If it did, I'd handle it. In the meantime, I'd enjoy some private time with a beautiful woman who'd found herself down on her luck.

I wasn't into giving handouts, but my anger toward Salinger continued to increase. The girl was just trying to make a goddamn living and as usual, he'd acted like an arrogant prick, likely because she was the kind of woman who wouldn't fall for his tricks in an effort to get her to suck his dick.

As I guided Savannah through the hotel to the private elevators, I sensed all eyes were on us, including several of my soldiers. It was rare I was seen with a woman on my arm, including to commercial functions that required me to bring a date. I wasn't the kind of man to follow anyone's rules.

The passion she exuded matched mine, desire that could light the entire city of Miami on fire. I hungered for her, more so than I should, but her defiance had put me in a good mood. I needed it after the shitty few days I'd experienced. Every soldier remained on edge, some with far too much testosterone, which had forced me to delve into the middle of situations that were beneath me.

But to prevent blood raining in the streets of Miami, my interference had been necessary. That had only added waves of discontent between our regular buyers and our usual dealers, let alone those paying hefty taxes for protection. Eliminating Sergei had done little to begin repairing the rip in the atmosphere surrounding us.

A distraction was necessary to keep me from going off the rails. There was nothing better than interacting with a beautiful woman.

She said nothing, but I sensed she was questioning where I was taking her. When we stopped in front of the bank of elevators, she finally tilted her head, allowing me to catch a lovely vision of her long neck. "This goes to the upper floors."

"That's correct."

"There are no restaurants on those floors."

Allowing a smile to cross my face, I enjoyed watching her brows furrow, her luscious, plump lips pursing. But it was the fire in her eyes I coveted more than anything. I could tell she had no idea just how beautiful she truly was. Even with stains on her light gray trousers, and her hair strangled in a creative, yet wild bun on top of her head, everything about her made my mouth water. "You are correct again, but you seem to forget we have room service, even if my hotel is garish."

"Are you going to keep reminding me of that?"

I moved closer, inhaling her scent, a light floral fragrance that managed to cut through the odors of the kitchen. My cock was uncomfortable, my need to drive it inside of her tight pussy increasing. "It doesn't seem you mind."

"Mr. Nikitin. While I appreciate the gesture, I don't think accompanying you to your suite is professional or the best protocol."

She was firm, her conviction another reason I longed to strip away her tank top, revealing her voluptuous breasts. It was getting impossible to resist her. While she deserved a taste of the finer things in life, I sensed her increasing needs, coming close to matching mine. The connection was combustible.

"I get to decide."

"Oh, you do, huh?" she asked, her defiance increasing.

As the elevator doors opened, I guided her inside, pressing my thumb against the keypad. "You're headed up to my suite alone. However, I promise you that I won't be long. I have one small business activity to handle."

She pressed her hand against my chest, and I was surprised by the heightened level of electricity we shared. Her eyes opened wide and for a few seconds, she reminded me of an innocent lamb.

Then I had to remind myself that lambs were usually meant for slaughter.

"This is my hotel, Savannah, which means everyone follows my rules. Including you. I do get what I want. Please make yourself at home. I have a well-stocked bar so you should be able to find something to your liking."

When she started to press the point, I placed my finger across her lips, my hunger increasing. I could tell the moment she acquiesced, her entire demeanor changing.

That was all I could tolerate.

I wasn't used to losing control under any circumstances but in the limited time I'd spent with her, I'd lost partial sense of myself. I pressed my thumb against the keypad again, locking down the elevator.

"What are you doing?" she asked, already losing her breath with anticipation.

"Taking what I want." I advanced, more a predator than anything else. When I planted my hands on either side of her, she immediately pushed her palms against my chest, but she wasn't trying to drive me away. She'd already wrapped her fingers around my shirt, holding me in place.

"This isn't a good idea," she whispered, arching her back as she tilted her head.

"Probably not." I crushed my mouth over hers, immediately thrusting my tongue inside. The taste of her was sweeter than any single kiss I'd had before, but my needs were too intense to bother with much foreplay. I'd never wanted a woman this much.

Every sound she made, every moan that erupted past her lips drew me in, the need spiraling out of control.

I lifted her off the floor and she threw her arms around my neck. Within seconds, I'd yanked off one of her tennis shoes then the other, tossing them aside. She wiggled against me, the scent of her desire wafting between us. I sensed she was hot and wet, ready for my hard cock. As I started to yank down her pants, she threw one arm behind her back, tugging on the material. I ran my fingers down the crack of her ass, rolling the tips under the thin lace of her G-string.

She murmured under her breath, fighting with me to get them down and off.

The luscious woman didn't want me ripping them off. That enticed me even more.

When she was freed of the tight confines, I shoved her body against the elevator wall, fighting to slide my hand between us.

I shouldn't have bothered. She broke the kiss, panting as she fumbled to unfasten my belt. I pressed my forehead against hers, savoring the scent of her perfume as it filled my nostrils.

The moment my cock was freed, I rolled onto the balls of my feet, impaling her tight pussy with a single thrust.

"Oh, God. Oh… my God." Savannah pitched her arm over her head, slapping her hand against the steel panels.

My cock continued to throb and the way her pussy muscles clamped around the thick invasion sucked the breath from my chest.

"So fucking tight," I growled, pulling out and plunging into her again with enough force the entire elevator rattled.

She laughed, her eyes wild with lust and she gripped my shoulder with one hand, digging her fingers into my jacket. I'd never done anything this impulsive, but it felt damn good. Exhaling, I developed a rhythm, fucking her like a crazed animal. As the sound echoed in the small space, she lolled her head against my shoulder, her moans like sweet music.

Savannah's breathing remained ragged as she pressed her knees against me, bucking hard against the savage carnal act. I pushed her up even higher, switching the angle until I was crazed with desire, unable to stop thrusting brutally.

She tossed her head from side to side, barely catching her breath. Within seconds, I sensed she was ready to come, her entire body shaking.

"Oh. Oh, God. This is so…" She closed her eyes, her body convulsing as an orgasm rolled through her.

"That's it. Come for me." I no longer recognized my voice, the deep husky sound filled with twisted need, my mind rolling from the filthy thoughts of what I wanted to do to her. Everything was a fabulous blur as I continued taking every inch of her, gasping for air as beads of sweat rolled down both sides of my face.

I pulled her away from the wall, turning and slamming her against the one beside it, chuckling darkly from her surprise.

"Such a bad man," she mewed.

"You have no idea."

"Yes, I think I do." She nipped my lower lip as her body continued to shake, another climax sweeping through her.

The scent of sex was raw and delicious, and I wanted her entire body covered in my cum. I wanted her tied and ready for my feasting, prepared for me to take her in every hole. Every part of me craved defiling her in the filthiest ways.

And I would.

As I spun her around again, her eyes were even more wild than before. She gasped for air, raking her nails down the back of my neck as I rolled my hips, driving even deeper inside. The heat between us was intense, the passion we shared creating a firestorm. I couldn't breathe or think and that was just fine with me.

She tangled her fingers in my hair, still taking sweeping breaths as she finally lolled her head on my shoulder. Only then did I allow the sweet peace of release.

My body shaking, she sensed I was ready to erupt and squeezed her pussy muscles. That was all I could take. As I filled her with my seed, several thoughts came to mind.

"*Odnazhdy ya budu vladet' toboy.*" As soon I said the words out loud, I almost laughed. I'd never wanted anyone enough.

I eased her to the floor, and a warm flush swept over her jawline. She tensed, her trembling continuing. The moment I backed away, she scrambled to grab her pants and thong, turning away as she struggled to get into them quickly.

Meanwhile, I took my time sliding my cock back into position, zipping then fastening my belt. And all the while I thought about what her rounded bottom would look like with stripes from my thick leather strap. Perhaps that would come later. Once her tennis shoes had been shoved onto her feet, she folded her arms, still trying to control her breathing.

I casually moved closer, and she tensed all over again. "Relax, Savannah. Call it animal attraction and nothing more."

"It can't happen again."

After taking a deep breath, I answered, "Then it won't."

She nodded twice without saying anything else.

I raked my hands through my hair, intoxicated from her scent. The woman standing in front of me had no control. She would learn that soon enough. After adjusting my jacket, I pressed my thumb on the keypad, keeping my eyes on her as I backed into the lobby once again.

At the same time, she backed further into the elevator, leaning against the wall, her eyes never blinking as the door slowly closed.

At that point, I had a feeling she was going to become a personal issue, but for the first time since I could remember, I was looking forward to the company of a woman.

And tasting every inch of her, especially her sweet pussy.

However, first things first. I was finished dealing with Franco Salinger, the slimy bastard hassling far too many employees. But that wasn't the only reason it was time for me to take out the trash.

The man was a snitch, what little information he believed he'd gleaned from working in my organization going straight to the Colombians. He'd been sly about it, coming in under the radar, and I'd planned on feeding him a line of crap until he'd hassled Savannah. His behavior was inexcusable, and I would enjoy feeding him to the sharks.

There was a large deal on the table, one I was already hesitant about. It was scheduled for a week from now and I had no intentions of scrapping it unless absolutely necessary. I'd lose millions in the process, something that would fucking piss off my uncle. Right now, we were already at odds. Additional tension wouldn't serve me well.

I pulled out my phone as I strode through the lobby, dialing my chief of security, who answered on the first ring.

"What do you need, boss?" Ricardo asked, the noise in the background indicating he was on one of the casino floors. The man enjoyed the perks of being in charge of the resort a little too much in my opinion, but he was loyal without question, one of the most valuable traits to have in an employee.

"Bring Chef Salinger to the private conference room."

"When?"

"Now." I heard the angry growl in my voice and smiled. My uncle had told me I enjoyed killing our enemies entirely too much. The taste for blood was ingrained in my system, the brutality of our world an everyday occurrence.

As I headed to the front desk, I was confronted by several tourists, wanting their picture taken with me. Usually, I shied away from such frivolous activity but tonight, I was in a good mood.

"Certainly." I posed for the camera, placing my arms around two women who acted as if they'd just met the Prince of Wales. Sometimes, it was good to be me. While the photograph was being taken, I scanned the perimeter of the lobby, noticing some lurkers, which usually meant cops sniffing around to try to discover improprieties. Not in my hotel.

The squeals of the women brought me back to the moment and I kissed one of them on the cheek.

"Oh, Mr. Nikitin, I've been longing to meet you," one of them said, her eyes sparkling in the hotel lighting.

"The pleasure is all mine." I kissed her hand, prompting another set of admiring yelps. Christ, I smelled like sex, but if the women noticed, they didn't react. "What room are you staying in?"

"Four seventy-two," the second woman said.

"Good to know. Ladies. Have a wonderful night." I backed away, still watching everything that was happening before moving to the front desk.

"Mr. Nikitin," Sherry said, her smile as wide as those of the two women. "Is there something you need?"

"Send a bottle of our finest champagne to room four seventy-two and have a filet and lobster dinner sent to my suite. For two."

"Yes, sir."

I had no doubt Sherry would be efficient, the food arriving in less than twenty minutes. It would provide all the time I needed to handle business. I took my time, swinging through the main casino floor, observing every dealer. There was nothing out of order. Then I headed to the private conference room located on the main floor. It was an auxiliary location designed and placed next to an exterior door no one else used but my personal staff. It helped in cases such as what would occur within moments.

By the time I walked inside, Ricardo and another one of my soldiers was already inside, keeping the chef company.

I closed the door with a soft click, unbuttoning my jacket before approaching the tired-looking chef.

"What is the meaning of this?" Chef Salinger demanded. "I'm in the middle of dinner service."

"Contrary to what you believe, you have an extremely competent staff, even if you recently fired a valuable employee."

He narrowed his eyes, already starting to sputter, his face turning red from anger, indignation, and... fear.

He knew he'd crossed the line, his behavior likely resulting in termination. He simply didn't know what that meant but he would soon learn.

"She was an idiot!" he insisted, further boiling my blood.

"No, she was perfectly within her rights to call you an asshole." I moved closer, taking my time and enjoying the way apprehension was settling into the man's brain. "Because you are. You're also a snitch, which is something I won't allow in my organization." I allowed the information to settle in.

That's the moment all fury left his system, replaced with cold-blooded terror. "You're wrong."

"Am I?" I glanced at Ricardo who chuckled. He'd been the man to bring it to my attention, receiving a nice bonus in his last paycheck. "I don't think I need to remind you who you work for. Or should I say worked for? I wonder how much the Colombians enjoyed the bogus information?"

I allowed him to ponder a few seconds longer. Then he started begging, which I loathed more than anything. The men who took their punishment like a trooper were given a pass, exterminated quickly. But those who pleaded for their lives I took a special liking to.

"Mr. Nikitin. They forced me," he insisted, his chest heaving.

The usual answer. They forced me. If I had a dime for every time I'd heard that, I'd be a richer man. I grinned at the thought. "They did, huh? With what? You have no family. You have no friends. What could they possibly use to make you turn against the man who supplied you with a house, a job, and a hefty bank account?"

His blubbering continued.

He couldn't come up with a decent answer because there was only one.

Greed.

Sighing, I debated how I wanted to handle the situation. Sadly, I refused to keep my beautiful dinner companion alone but for so long. It would seem my enjoyment of tormenting him would only be in my mind.

Yet I punched him in the face, waiting as he tried to right himself. Then I added two more powerful blows, knocking both the wind out of him and his body against the wall. The hard thud was like music to my ears.

"If that didn't piss me off," I said, grabbing him around the throat and slamming his head down on the table, "the way you treated your employee did." I repeated the move, my rage increasing. "But I'm going to rectify the situation right now. Chef Salinger, you are terminated."

"Yes, sir. Yes. Sir. I'll leave immediately. I'm sorry, sir."

"Yes, you will. If only you could provide Savannah with an apology. Alas, you won't be able to, but I'll make certain and do that for you." I yanked out my weapon, pointing the barrel at the back of his head. Given the room was sound-proofed, I didn't need to worry about exciting the guests. "Your one minute's notice is accepted." I pulled the trigger, taking a deep breath as soon as I did. Then I backed away, shaking my head. There were times all the fun was taken out of my job.

Ricardo huffed, immediately pushing Salinger's body to the floor. "What do you want me to do with him?"

"Dispose of him in Colombian territory. That'll give them a message I won't be fucked with."

"You're hoping it heads south of the border to Santiago."

I laughed, the sound as evil as the man I'd become. "Absolutely."

"Yes, sir." His grin was wide, the happiness on his face as twisted as usual. When he continued to stare at me, I lifted an eyebrow.

"What?"

"Nothin'. Just you smell like sex."

I rubbed my eyes. "Let it alone. What have you learned about the Colombians' activities?"

Ricardo snorted. "They're laying low right now. Maybe they thought their boy here would bring them something juicy."

Like information on the upcoming shipment.

The men who worked in Miami were mostly low-level soldiers, waiting for orders from their omnipresent leader Emmanuel Santiago. However, that didn't mean they hadn't been disruptive to my operations the last few weeks. I was vaguely concerned the aging Colombian was considering coming into the country, something he'd promised not to do before. Maybe he was hoping to come in through the back door before making his way to LA where he had family.

"I guess they underestimated me. Make certain and leave a love note with the body."

"Sure thing, boss."

"Unfortunately, my uncle had taken it upon himself to assign Damien to our ranks."

Ricardo raised his eyebrows. He knew how much I loathed the man. "To watch over us?"

"To ensure I have enough help."

"What a crock of shit," he said then immediately gave me a sheepish look. "I mean no offense."

"We'll have a meeting later regarding the additional details."

"Good deal. So, who's this Savannah? I mean, if you don't mind me asking, sir."

I eased my gun into my jacket, buttoning it once again. "A much needed distraction and nothing more. Handle the floor for a few hours. I have other business to take care of."

"Have fun."

Fun was a word that wasn't usually a part of my vocabulary but tonight was different.

The scintillating Savannah hadn't realized she'd waltzed into the lair of a monster, but she'd soon learn that predators were everywhere.

And I was the kind who refused to take no for an answer.

The lovely creature had become my prey, my pet.

And my possession.

avannah

"One day I'll own you."

That's what Maxim had whispered in Russian after we'd finished... fucking. And I could tell he'd meant the words.

"Oh, God," I whispered, my throat still threatening to close permanently. I was such a fool. I'd lost myself and disobeyed my orders on the very first day of my undercover work. Or had I? Katherine had anticipated this would happen. I should have known. Maxim's type. How would she know? He was rarely photographed with women, which had to some unscrupulous speculations on the part of the press. There were fabricated stories about a woman who'd betrayed him, and he'd been forced to kill her. All fiction.

Or was it?

When the elevator doors opened on the top floor, I almost panicked, trying to figure out what the hell I was doing here.

Insanity.

This was nothing but raw, pure insanity. That was the answer. I was alone in a suite owned by the most dangerous, notorious man in Miami. And he'd taken a liking to me. Liking? No, I sensed he planned on devouring me inch by inch.

Again.

Bad little girl. Bad. Bad. Bad.

That wasn't strong enough. I'd allowed him to fuck me just out of the gate. No, I'd practically encouraged him. I needed to call my contact. No, I couldn't do that, not unless it was an emergency.

Even worse, I'd been completely aroused by the man, still shivering from his closeness, the scent of our combined sex. Being attracted to him was a detriment.

I hadn't anticipated the extreme heat between us, an electricity I'd never experienced before.

Or losing my mind in the middle of a stopped elevator. It was easy to tell the man enjoyed exposing vulnerabilities, which is exactly what he'd done with me almost as if he'd profiled me.

Everything about him was dangerous, including his good looks. A cold shiver trickled along my arms and legs at a rapid rate, the images of our carnal sin rushing past the forefront of my mind twisted in every way.

I wrung my hands as I walked further into the room, anxiety tearing through me. A private dinner.

A gift. That's what you need to think of this as.

Maybe so, but I was ill equipped to handle the situation; I needed to figure out how quickly or I'd lose everything I'd come to achieve. *Put it behind you. You enticed him. You did what you came here to do.*

I had, but that didn't mean the night was over. Not by a long shot.

As I walked into the middle of the main room, I was struck by the surroundings, everything I'd expect from a man considered one of the wealthiest on the East Coast. I'd learned as much about Maxim as had been detailed, but there was very little about his background before coming to the United States.

The top floor suite overlooked Miami, dazzling lights from other buildings creating a shimmering glow coming from every floor-to-ceiling window. The main room consisted of several lounge areas, a baby grand a centerpiece. I moved closer, running my fingers across the keys, shuddering from the tinkling sounds.

Then I turned in a full circle. There were several adjoining rooms; that much I already knew. I'd memorized as much of the floor layout of the hotel as possible, but there were supposedly hidden passages, rooms not located on any plans. This suite was different than I'd expected, glamorous and posh. Everything I had zero experience with.

I ran my fingers down my neck, feeling disheveled. Feeling freshly fucked. Then I ripped at the clip holding my long hair kind of in place, moving quickly down one of the two hallways in search of a bathroom. As soon as I walked inside, flicking on the light, I almost had a panic attack. I was so out of my realm that my chest was tight, my pulse racing. Somehow, I had to find a way to control it.

After turning on the water, I grabbed a towel, using it to wipe dried perspiration from my neck and chest. Then I ran my fingers through my curls, the humidity creating a wild look even for me. I was the unruly girl who never took time for her appearance, preferring jeans and tops, and some-times sweats at work. They served a purpose, including being comfortable since I sat for several long hours at a time.

When I was satisfied I was as presentable as possible, I gripped the edge of the sink, staring into the face of a girl I didn't recognize. The color of my hair was different, the cut allowing for a softer vision of my face. At least I was wearing waterproof makeup, enough so the eye shadow allowed for a smoky effect.

This would have to do. I took a step back, tilting my head, falling into the pretense of a girl I'd never wanted to be. I was confident I could make the man swoon.

Oh, who was I kidding?

One thing I couldn't deny about my reflection was the glow of my skin. From being fucked by a monster. Oh, God.

Butterflies threatened to swarm and stay in my stomach for all eternity.

After turning out the light, I glanced toward the front of the condo before heading further down the hall. I likely had a few seconds to scan the area. While I kept the lights off, every window was wide open, allowing the shimmer of the various marquis signs and other lighting to provide just enough I could make out every item in the room. It had to be his private bedroom. I felt like a thief, even though I'd been sent to his penthouse.

There was nothing out of the ordinary, but I opened a couple of drawers, feeling inside. I wanted to get a sense of him. Even if I had no clue what I was looking for. There were clothes inside, socks and underwear. The nightstand held nothing unusual except for a weapon. Swallowing hard, I started to get jittery. He'd be back soon enough.

I tentatively returned to the living room, taking several deep breaths then deciding to turn on a few lights. The bar he'd mentioned drew my attention. A drink wouldn't hurt. Maybe it would even calm my nerves.

There was a wine cabinet attached to the gorgeous, ornate wooden structure and I selected a merlot, one that cost more than what I made in a week. My fingers were shaking as I opened drawers, finding a wine opener. Once I removed the cork, I laughed softly to myself. This time a week ago, I'd had no idea I'd be forced into becoming an entirely different person.

At least I could have fun with it.

I poured a glass, retreating toward the windows. The city was dazzling in every way, electric and alive. Just like I'd felt being around Maxim. Was it okay to be attracted to the man I was supposed to challenge? The question wasn't one I wanted an answer to.

As I sipped the wine, I allowed myself to become mesmerized by the twinkling lights in every color of the rainbow. This was how rich people lived, whether they made their money legally or not.

Only a few seconds later, I heard a sound and tensed, refusing to turn around. The footsteps weren't heavy but created by a man. Then I noticed his reflection in the window.

Maxim stood several feet away, studying me without saying a word. When he finally approached, I could see a pensive look on his face.

"Did you find what you were looking for?" The question seemed leading, as if he was already suspicious of who I was. His eyes were laced with coldness, but he radiated heat.

"The wine is exquisite, hints of raspberry and a light tannin, just a touch of citrus. My favorite kind."

He studied me for a few additional seconds then seemed to relax.

"You have excellent tastes." When he crowded my space, his deep velvety voice cascading around my bare shoulders, my mouth was suddenly dry. Then he removed the glass from my hand, taking a sip, his eyes never leaving me.

I sucked in my breath, trying to erase the fear. I was no longer the woman who'd arrived.

"A perfect selection." When he handed it back to me, our fingers touched as they'd done before, the instant jolt of current like the start of a wildfire that would never be controlled. "I took the liberty of ordering something for dinner. I hope you'll approve of my selection."

As he walked away, I allowed my gaze to follow. He was sophisticated, yet I knew underneath the expensive façade was the heart of a true savage, a man capable of murder without hesitation or remorse. I'd never admit it to anyone else, but the dangerous aspect about him was exciting as his extreme good looks.

He should be on the cover of a magazine instead of on the most wanted list.

I watched as he removed his jacket, tossing it across the back of the couch. Then he turned toward me as he unfastened the sleeves on his shirt, slowly rolling them up past his elbows. Every action he performed, every mannerism was subtle yet provocative, adding to the allure. "I'm going to hang up my jacket. There will be no other business this evening."

"Of course." When he walked down the same hallway where I'd been, I closed my eyes briefly, an icy chill tingling all my senses. I tried to take a few sips of wine, but I almost choked. When he returned, I stiffened yet plastered a seductive smile on my face as I turned around to face him.

"Now, we can enjoy our time together," he said, his tone gruffer than before. I could swear the man never blinked and the way he was studying me held an air of possession. My nipples ached from the thought of having his full lips wrapped around them, sucking until they were sore.

I bit my lower lip, admonishing the ridiculous thoughts. "You don't know me."

"I know everything I need to know in order to decide to spend time with you. You're feisty, self-assured, intelligent, tough, and beautiful. What else do I need to know?" He walked closer and that's when I noticed specks of blood on his crisp white shirt. I couldn't stop my eyes from lingering and I sensed he realized what I was staring at, lowering his head as if looking at his shirt the way I was.

My pulse was even higher. He'd just hurt or killed someone. My God. The man was an animal. My self-doubt crawled in, clawing at my mind and skin, trying to rip apart what little confidence I'd managed to instill in me.

No. No. I wouldn't allow this to happen.

"I'm pigheaded and impatient most of the time."

"Aren't we all?" he said, chuckling darkly. "I'm curious what you think you know about me."

"You're arrogant, powerful, dominant, and most important, lonely." I caught him off guard, his mask falling just enough I could see I was right.

His laugh sent a shower of tingles dancing down my spine. "Lonely. No one has ever said that to me before."

And lived.

"It's true. You have everything you need in life, all the trinkets and toys in the world, except for the one person to keep you on your toes."

"Are you that person?"

I offered a smile, laughing softly, but my eyes dropped to the bloodstains for a second time. They were small, mere specks but I knew exactly what they were given the ruddy color. "While I'm up to the challenge, I'm afraid I'm not looking for a significant other. I've sworn off relationships, perhaps forever."

"Hmmm…" he muttered as he crowded my personal space as if he had every right to do so, close enough goosebumps appeared on my arms. His sudden nearness was suffocating, my stomach doing flip-flops. Just by glancing in his eyes I could tell he had no intentions of letting me go until he was finished with me based on his terms. Even the cruel twist of his voluptuous lips was a clear indication of his lurid thoughts.

Or was I hoping his intentions were carnal?

"I'm certain there's a sad story somewhere behind your statement. But I suggest we concentrate on the here and now, our combined enjoyment. Fair enough?" he asked in a way that indicated he'd already determined how he wanted to move forward.

"Fair enough."

"If you would like me to change shirts before dinner, I'm happy to do so." He was issuing another challenge.

"Not necessary, especially given the way I'm dressed."

"Natural beauty is far more attractive."

Why did his deep voice managed to penetrate my soul? I was still fearful that he was doing nothing more than playing a game before vanquishing my life, but there was no violence in his gaze, just the sadistic desire that I'd learned existed.

"I assume you were handling business?"

A smirk rolled across his face. "Yes, the type that shouldn't concern you."

"What will you do with the chef? If you don't mind me asking." My hackles were raised.

He took a deep breath before answering, "Unfortunately, I had to let him go."

"Why?" He'd killed the man. My gut told me that. Oh, God. What was I supposed to do?

"Because I can't have anyone hurting one of my possessions."

Maxim's eyes were lit like firecrackers as he awaited my reaction. His possession. Jesus. This was unexpected. I faltered for a few seconds, uncertain what to say or how to react. But I sensed my face reddening, the heat creeping across my clenched jaw. "I don't know what to say."

I couldn't get over the realization that he'd killed for me. He'd ended a man's life because the asshole had been rude to me. Who did that kind of a thing? I couldn't wrap my mind around it.

"You need say nothing, *malen'kiy krapivnik.*"

He'd called me his little wren.

"What does that mean?"

Everything about him was oppressive, the darkness he exuded terrifying yet thrilling. "It means little wren."

"Why do you call me that?"

"Because you're delicate, breakable yet strong."

Swallowing, I realized my hand was shaking enough he had to sense it. I blinked several times, allowing myself to smile. "That's beautiful."

"It suits you perfectly. Perhaps I'll need to protect you in a gilded cage."

"But birds are meant to fly free, enjoying the light."

"Yes, but there are many predators, hunters who will stop at nothing to crush the beautiful creature if for no other reason than to enjoy watching their life drain away. I can't allow that to happen."

There was such a hidden meaning in his words that I was completely frozen, trying to keep my heartrate in check. This was nothing like what I'd expected. He was so much more. Now my pussy was clenching, so wet my panties were damp. "You'd be surprised, Mr. Nikitin, how well I can handle myself."

"No, I would not be, but this is a dangerous world you walked into, Savannah. And please, since we're going to become very close, you should call me Maxim."

The man was in control of everything. That now included me. "Close." I don't know why I repeated the single word, but it seemed to amuse him.

He now stood only a few inches away, his eyes roaming over every inch of me. His expression was easy to read, the desire he felt the same as mine. When he reached out, brushing his fingers down my cheek and neck, I held my breath.

As he lifted my chin with a single finger, his intoxicating aftershave created a dizzying effect.

"*Strast' okhvatyvayat t'mu.*"

"You have an advantage over me. I don't speak another language unless you count bad Spanish." His lips were suddenly dangerously close. The kiss in the elevator had been a blazing wildfire. The saying was unusual for the situation but tempting nonetheless. He had many layers, which I'd been warned about. But beneath it all was the violence he'd been born into, his upbringing close to abusive.

"Passion embraces darkness. It's something my father once said."

"Was your father a poet?"

He shook his head as he slowly lowered it, his breath skipping across my face. "No, just a man trying to survive in a brutal world." When he captured my mouth, I swayed into him, the move completely involuntary.

As soon as I fisted his shirt, another chill coursed through me, thoughts about the man he'd killed floating into the front of my mind. The taste of him was unlike any other man I'd shared a kiss with, as if the richness of the merlot had melded with several exotic spices. I was thrown by how easy it was to fall into his arms, parting my lips to allow him to dominate my mouth.

He did so without hesitation, sweeping his tongue inside. When he slid his arm around me, wrapping his long fingers around my neck, my instinct was to pull out of his grasp. But he was too powerful, creating the kind of desire that only existed in fantasies and books.

His hold was possessive, as if he'd never let me go. The rush of adrenaline from the hard hammering of my heart brought echoes in my ears and as he crushed his full weight against me, the fact he was hard as a rock forced a moan from deep within my system.

He'd already ignited a fire inside. Now I had to learn how to control it.

When he pulled away, his chest rising and falling, he lifted his head.

"I'll be up front with you, Savannah. I'm not a good man. There isn't a person in this city who will try and tell you otherwise, but I am a man of passion. However, my needs are too sadistic for some."

"Is that so?" I managed.

"But I sense you're not a typical woman by anyone's standards." He took a deep breath, holding it as his nostrils flaring. Easing away by a few inches, he continued his exploration, trailing his fingers between my breasts. My nipples were hard, poking through the thin fabric, my pussy aching for his touch.

This was bad, so very bad, but no man's touch had ever made me feel so alive. Yet I refused to give in to his method of seduction. That wasn't what this was about.

So I took a decided step away from him, breaking the connection, giving him a haughty look before turning my attention to the city around us. While I acted as if he'd just annoyed me, hiding behind the wine and taking cautious sips, my entire mind was foggy from trying to figure out just how far he was prepared to go.

He took a deep, exaggerated breath, backing away from the window. I sensed his annoyance, as well as his mind processing why I was turning him down. I watched as he sat down on one of the leather chairs, crossing his long legs, studying me intently. He was quiet, so much so that I was fearful his next move would be to pull out a weapon.

The strange sensations coursing through me were so unexpected that I couldn't think clearly. There was nothing about this that was acceptable or right, but the connection we shared was strong enough I couldn't walk away. And he knew it.

"Come here, little wren," he commanded, his voice little more than a growl.

When I hesitated, I sensed his increasing fury. I had to push him to see what he would do.

"Do not deny me, Savannah, or I'll need to teach you a lesson."

"Why? I thought this was just about dinner."

"Then you'd be sorely wrong. You see, I take what I want. And I've decided to take you for a second time." The level of hunger on his devastatingly handsome face left me powerless to ignore him.

I took another sip of wine then turned to face him, heading in his direction. The look on his face had changed, morphing into something more feral, his eyes drifting into a terrifying level of darkness.

But I refused to allow him to make me sweat.

When I gingerly placed the glass on the table, I gave him a seductive smile. "You really don't have a sense of who I am, Maxim. Let me be very clear about one thing. I'm not for sale."

CHAPTER 7

axim

Another surprise.

Or should I say an annoyance?

Others in my employ might say a danger, but I'd handled all three before and would do it again.

In addition, my desire had cracked through the surface. When had the longing for anyone been at this level? However, there was something about her that was almost too good to be true, an innocent flower in the wrong place. Was it possible she was hiding something beneath her doe-eyed persona? My criteria for trusting anyone had reached a new bar, one so high almost no one would be able to rise to that level.

Maybe I was far too jaded at this point in my life, but women had used the art of seduction far too often in history, stabbing their partners in the heart the moment of climax.

With an entire empire to lose, it was vital that I remained cautious. Especially since it would seem the Colombians would stop at nothing to sabotage as many operations as possible. In my mind, they were little more than Neanderthals, using their brawn instead of brains. Sadly, I'd been forced to face the fact they'd moved into the electronics age, using experienced hackers to extract information that had led to several of our drug and gun shipments being hijacked.

I'd wondered if Sergei had made a play long before the FBI got their hands on him.

After the discovery, I'd put extra security measures in place, hiring the best professionals, including a staff of hackers myself. With that avenue now cut off, they'd be forced to use more creative methods of stealing from me.

That could include the use of the oldest trick in the book.

Even if that was the case, there were few women who enticed me, but none had ever ignored my command, acting as if they were going to reject my offer. Given I was a man with little patience in matters of business or pleasure, I was surprised that I was enjoying the banter as much as her continued resistance. Our connection had been obvious, the same desire that kept my balls tight creating the kind of electricity that I found rare.

My little wren wasn't exactly who she purported herself to be.

She'd been inside my room searching through my things.

That wasn't necessary a huge red flag, nor would anyone else have noticed. But being extremely observant in my business was one of few ways to remain alive. The precocious woman had taken it upon herself to open a few drawers. What had she discovered? I resisted chuckling. I'd also learned a long time before never to leave anyone in a room where incriminating evidence of any type could be found. The suite had nothing but clothes, my favorite liquors, and a few sadistic toys.

Whatever she was looking for had little to do with business. Anyone connected to my enemies or law enforcement would know better than to think I'd keep anything of real value inside a suite I rarely frequented. What else could she have been hoping to find? She wasn't law enforcement. I could see through a Fed or DEA agent from a significant distance, including the few women they'd sent my way over the years. She also didn't appear to be an assassin as her acting skills weren't that good. Then who and what was she?

It was entirely possible that Emmanuel Santiago had ignored the deal I knew had been made with the Santos crime syndicate in LA, the two leaders a part of the alliance I was involved in called the Brotherhood.

We were kings in a world full of organized crime, rivals in a dangerous game of supremacy. We were also ruthless predators who would stop at nothing to get what we wanted. The Brotherhood had been created to keep the peace between six powerful crime families. There was no question we were monsters, every one of us a bad man with a penchant for violence. However, we were determined to do things differently than our forefathers who started wars where blood rained in the streets. That wasn't our style, change continuously necessary.

While completely independent of one another, we would come to the aid of the other if necessary. Perhaps a call to either Dante or Diego was in order, finding out if they'd experienced any unusual activity within the Santiago clan.

My thoughts returned to the lovely redhead, becoming more curious about her true identity. The timing could be coincidental, but her firing hadn't been planned, at least not that I could tell. Still, coincidences were unusual in my business, normally portending another attack. Perhaps she was Emmanuel's lover, sent to defile me in the worst way possible. While that wasn't Santiago's usual method of handling business, the brute into violence, not seduction, he likely suspected that my alliance with the Santos Syndicate would be detrimental if he attempted an all-out war.

I was no fool and if she believed I was, then she would soon learn that playing with the devil would do nothing more than leave her with scars. Then I'd ship her back to Cartagena in a box.

But not without a taste or two of the merchandise.

I was adept at the art of torture, but tonight I'd handle my interrogation in an entirely different manner.

I'd break down her walls of decency, providing a taste of my world in a manner she likely didn't expect.

Then I would devour her inch by inch until I'd had my fill. For now, I'd bide my time, doing nothing more than exposing her to the darker side of passion. Perhaps I'd be surprised again and she was nothing more than a pleasant shift in my ordinary activities.

Perhaps...

Her heated stare remained, her eyes full of questions.

"You wouldn't be here if I considered you a high-priced call girl." My words seemed to surprise her.

"Then what are we doing?" Savannah asked, the spark in her eyes more enticing.

"Enjoying what you might call foreplay."

"What would *you* call it?"

I took a sip of my wine. While I enjoyed the taste, the hint of fruit, I had no doubt she'd taste much sweeter. As I placed the crystal stem on the table, she continued backing away. She was playful, obviously not realizing how dangerous I was.

Or perhaps she didn't care.

She continued to intrigue me to the point I didn't mind playing with her, but that would need to end soon. She'd pushed to the point of no return. "Come here." It was obvious she was debating my command, shifting those same pointed eyes down the length of me.

"No." The single word was stated with conviction.

Then she bolted for the elevator door, the sound as she smashed her hand against the keypad both amusing and irritating. "You can't go anywhere without my permission."

"So I'm your prisoner? Is that how you get your women? You lock them away?"

"I didn't say you weren't free to go. However, you will need my assistance. The elevator is only operable with the use of my thumbprint."

I heard her exhale, even cursing under her breath.

"Then are you going to let me out?"

"Is that what you really want?" I remained where I was, confident she was testing me and nothing else.

After a few seconds she returned, her glare as harsh as some of mine. "No. I'll stay but under one condition."

"And that is?"

"That you remember I'm not one of your escorts."

"Fair enough."

She relaxed, reaching for her wine.

As I sat studying her, memorizing every inch of her luscious body, my cock continued to swell, becoming entirely too painful as it pressed against my zipper. I leaned forward quickly, surprised when she jumped just enough I almost gathered a scent of fear even though she was fighting it.

She was doing everything in her power to defy me, ignoring her desires that had exploded before. Maybe it was out of embarrassment for what we'd enjoyed in the elevator. But the fact she had the nerve to push my buttons heightened the ache furrowing into my system. If this was a game, I was enjoying it entirely too much. When she'd placed her drink on the table, telling me in no uncertain terms she wasn't for sale, my hunger had almost exploded. However, she wasn't the kind of woman I wanted to force into anything just yet. Something about her was far too special.

However, that would change in time.

"Do I make you nervous, *malen'kiy krapivnik?*" She truly was like a little wren, far too delicate to be a part of my world.

But taking and tasting her was entirely different.

"Nothing makes me nervous," Savannah replied. "But I meant what I said. I've worked too hard in my life to allow anything to be taken away from me. I hope you understand."

"I have no intentions of taking anything away."

"But you've planned out the evening, which has me at a disadvantage."

"Then please tell me how you would prefer to handle the time we spend together."

Her defiance only made me want her that much more.

No one said no to me.

At least if they wanted to live.

While I'd never harm the beautiful creature if she was merely a former employee, she would soon learn that trying my patience wasn't in her best interest.

"Sharing wine and enjoying the picturesque vista is a wonderful start."

I never blinked as I remained quiet, enjoying an entirely different view. Then I rose to my feet, shoving my hand into my pocket. "Very well. Are you afraid of heights, my little wren?"

"Why?"

The nervousness in her voice was a clear indication that she was.

"I'd like to show you something."

Her eyes shifted to the window, and she pursed her lips. "Where?"

"Trust me, Savannah. While I already told you I was a bad man, I'm not going to allow anything or anyone to hurt you. That much I can assure you." Easing my drink to the table, I pulled hers away, setting it down. Then I held out my hand, waiting to see how she would react. I wondered what she would say if she knew that the good chef wouldn't be able to bother her again?

She was guarded, debating the odds that I had plans on tossing her over the balcony. Anyone who accepted a job in my organization knew of my reputation, few ever having any real interaction with me. When she came forward, pushing aside her fears, I was further impressed.

I clasped my fingers around hers, pulling her close. As before, the same jolt of current rushed through both of us, the kinetic energy a powerful moment. Then I led her to the door leading to what was one of my favorite locations, one of the few places where I felt peaceful.

This was entirely different.

Her face was pinched from the moment I opened the door. While eight-foot glass covered the majority of the oversized balcony, the wind was still able to rattle the enclosure, which made her skittish. I understood why she couldn't trust me under any circumstances, and I didn't blame her. Perhaps I was testing her resolve. While the little wren was fearful, the same fire in her eyes sparked the savage beast buried deep inside of me even more.

I'd never been this hungry, the pretense and mockery of who and what I normally was already growing thin.

"I don't think I can do this," she said, but there was defiance in her voice.

"There is no way to fall, especially if you're in my arms." Very slowly, I moved behind her trembling body, wrapping both arms around her small waist. "There is no other way to see what I'm about to show you unless you walk toward the railing. There is no danger."

"There's always danger, Maxim. While many people keep their blinders on, I have an instinct about such things."

"And what does your gut tell you about me?"

"That I should be very afraid but not for the reason you think."

"You have me curious."

Tilting her head so she could look into my eyes, the same smile that had drawn me in the first place crossed her face. "Perhaps one day I'll tell you."

"I'm looking forward to it."

She shuddered audibly but allowed herself to trust me enough so I could walk us both toward the edge. "What am I supposed to be looking at?"

I pointed through the glass to a special area below, enjoying the feel of having her in my arms more than I should.

After she narrowed her eyes, her laughter was a sweet reward. "Really? Dolphins? Here? I was just kidding before."

"Yes, here. The tank was installed only a few months ago on the suggestion of my marketing staff. Perhaps I do own a kiddy park."

"I've insulted you."

"Nonsense. I'm not insulted easily." I had to laugh. If only she knew how thick my skin truly was.

"Then I'll confess. I adore dolphins."

"Why does that not surprise me?"

"When I was a little kid, my parents didn't have much money, but one year they took me to a waterpark, and I got to swim with the dolphins." She turned around to face me, pressing her hands against my jacket and it was all I could not to strip away her clothing, which was only one of her defenses. I wanted to know who'd hurt her in the past, the man an obvious pig. "I'm sorry. A child's stupid memory. You just surprised me and that's rare." She looked away, her face pensive.

"Not stupid at all and I'll enjoy sharing the experience with you sometime."

"A busy man like yourself enjoying something so frivolous?" She laughed again, the slight nervous tic in the corner of her mouth endearing. "I find that hard to believe."

"I always make time for what I want, Savannah." The swell of need was too intense. While I should have my mind on business, the various upcoming acquisitions far too important for distractions, it was impossible to resist her. The sadistic man inside of me had been dragged to the surface. He wouldn't be satisfied until I'd marked her, tasted her.

And fucked her in every hole.

"Dolphins? I would have believed you to be more of a primal man like lions, tigers, and bears."

I cupped her face, pressing my fingertips into her skin. She was soft, her chiseled features unblemished, the light surrounding her like a beacon of goodness.

Meanwhile I was marked as a sinner for all eternity. Perhaps a taste of something so pure would ultimately do me some good. The only trouble was the previous kiss cemented what I already knew to be the truth.

Savannah was mine.

"All forms of entertainment interest me, especially when it involves luscious creatures."

"Am I a creature to you?"

"You're many things, Savannah. That's easy to see."

"You've only just met me," she whispered, the throaty sound of her voice keeping me fully aroused. Lust remained in her eyes, a hint of embarrassment as well. That accentuated her level of vulnerability. Maybe I was a lion, the ultimate predator.

"Perhaps, but I'm an excellent judge of character." As I lowered my head, prepared to indulge, she shivered in my arms. The woman was a sheer delight, igniting the fires deep within. I wouldn't be able to keep my hands off her. I crushed my mouth over hers and wrapped my hand around the back of her neck.

She shuddered again, gingerly pressing her hand against my chest. While I'd originally detected fear in her actions and words, there was none of that left, just a furious curiosity about who and what I was. That was an answer I couldn't easy provide.

As she yielded to me, arching her back, I took full control. Just the taste of her was enough to awaken the beast dwelling in the darkest places of my mind, my lurid thoughts turning sadistic. Should I warn her that she'd fallen into the lair of beast? No, let her find out on her own. By then it would be too late.

Her subtle yet powerful purrs filtered into my eardrums just like the taste of her sweet mouth had awakened my senses. I pressed the full weight of my body against hers, my cock throbbing. There was no doubt she knew what she did to me, but unlike others I'd been with, this wasn't about financial gain or power and influence. Our connection was much more primal.

I dominated her tongue, sweeping it back and forth as she undulated in my arms, shifting her hips. I wanted nothing more than to drive my cock deep inside, taking her brutally, but I also had other desires, longing to see how far she was willing to fall into my world of chaos and pain. Then I'd provide the kind of pleasure she deserved.

Savannah wrapped her hand around my shirt, clinging to me as I squeezed my fingers into her skin. If she believed she was in any kind of danger, it wasn't evident.

Just as I was ready to expose her to my world, the less than subtle beep of announcement that someone had requested entrance assaulted my senses.

"*K chertu preryvaniye*," I snarled. When I saw the amused look on her face as I passed her, returning to the suite, I stopped briefly. "I don't like interruptions."

"Apparently not. Is there a way I can get the dinner you ordered without needing your thumbprint? Of course, I could just cut it off."

She made me laugh as she'd done so many times. I pulled out my phone, checking the camera briefly to ensure I recognized the server. Then I allowed them entrance, the elevator doors opening slowly.

"So you lied to me," she said as she sauntered by me, heading toward the entrance. "All I need to do is steal the remote from you to gain my freedom."

"Yes, I did, and yes, if you managed to get the remote away, you'd find yourself in the lobby. But I assure you that my men would bring you back to me. You see, I never lose in anything."

"I'll keep that in mind." When the elevator doors opened, she spun around, pointing her finger at me. "However powerful you might be, don't lie to me again. I can tolerate many things, Mr. Nikitin, but lying isn't one of them."

"I'll take that under advisement, Savannah, but you should know that I don't take orders from anyone."

"We shall see." Her eyes flashed in sheer defiance as well as the same pronounced hunger that I'd felt around her all evening. If only she knew what I had in mind for soothing the same dark beast that resided inside of her. She was cut from the same cloth, her needs pronounced yet she'd never been able to find anyone who could fulfill them. Tonight would begin something incredible.

At that moment, I realized that I hadn't longed to introduce anyone into the life I preferred living in years. And that had only happened once, the end result abominable. Savannah was different, much stronger, and I wanted to devour every inch of her. That would start tonight.

Whether she liked it or not.

As the waiter brought in the massive cart, she darted her gaze from the young man back to me, a sly look crossing her face. She believed she'd gained control. She was dead wrong.

I walked toward them, nodding toward the only employee who was allowed to bring anything to my suite. He knew better than to ask any questions, leaving as silently as he'd arrived.

When the doors closed, she lifted one of the lids, dragging her tongue across her lips. I approached, my mood darkening. Tonight, she'd experience the driving hunger of a powerful man.

"Amazing," she whispered, her scent of desire increasing.

"Lower the lid, Savannah."

She glanced in my eyes, darting hers back and forth. "Why?"

"Because I told you to. Do not make me tell you again."

This time she obeyed me without hesitation, turning her body toward me.

When I reached out, she acted as if she was going to pull away. I took a single long stride toward her, snatching her arm and dragging her against my chest. Then I fisted her hair, yanking her onto her tiptoes. My patience was all but gone. "You can deny what you feel all you want, but that changes nothing."

She pressed her hand against my chest, her long eyelashes skimming her cheeks. "What does that mean?"

"Exactly what I said. I take what I want."

* * *

Savannah

. . .

Something had changed. I was certain of it, although I couldn't put my finger on why. He was attempting to entice me into his lair, baiting me with his possessiveness, as if I was a fragile fawn in the wild and he was a wolf. Our first round of passion was meant to lure me in and in truth, it had. But I wasn't oh-so vulnerable like he believed.

My instinct told me he was already suspicious of who I was. I took several deep breaths, able to keep it together. But how long would that last?

The man had a high opinion of himself, the kind of asshole I'd normally shy away from, but everything about Maxim excited me, more so than I'd expected. That put me at a serious disadvantage, possibly in danger, but there would be no way of getting away from him.

Even if I wanted to.

Did I?

As he pulled me into his arms, wrapping one around my waist, my breathing was already shallow. Yet as his after-shave drifted into my system all over again, I was intoxicated, more lightheaded than I should be. Maybe I was drunk on the adrenaline instead. This I hadn't expected. He cupped my face as he'd done before, but his hold was more possessive.

He rolled his lips across my jaw, his hot breath tickling my skin.

I couldn't resist, sliding my hand between us, offering a fake, shy smile as I rolled my fingers up and down his cock.

"Such a tease. Aren't you?"

"Always." I wrapped my fingers around the bulge, stroking up and down. His eyelids were heavy, half open as I toyed with him, his breathing more labored than before.

"What do you want, *malen'kiy krapivnik?*" he breathed, his tone deep and guttural.

"Everything."

"Then that's exactly what you will have."

The desire on his face was intense, so much so my heart fluttered. He rubbed his fingers across my skin, his actions more possessive than before. I had a feeling he was a man who didn't like to be touched, but he allowed me to share in the intimate moment. As I brushed my fingers down his face, he issued a series of intense growls.

I wanted this man. I understood the consequences, the raw fear that I should have being inside this room, but I wasn't afraid. No, I was exhilarated, shocked that I wanted him as much as I did.

He slid his hand to the back of my neck, digging his fingers into my skin as he held me. And as he lowered his head until our lips were almost touching, I fumbled to release his cock.

"Tsk. Tsk. You aren't in charge," he muttered, his voice dripping with innuendos.

"No fair."

"You have no choice. This isn't a democracy. Now, go to the window and close your eyes," he commanded.

"Why?"

"You'll need to trust me. Can you do that? Can you free yourself of the chains that are wrapped so tightly around you that you're suffocating?"

How had a complete stranger been able to read me so well in such a short time?

I continued trembling, several thoughts racing through my mind, some of them disturbing. But at the center of it all, I was completely aroused, longing to taste what he was offering. "Yes."

"If you want everything, you'll need to obey my commands." He cocked his head, trailing a single finger down my neck, rolling the tip around my pulse of life. He was challenging me, seeing how far he could go with tempting me into his darkness.

"I do trust you, although I'm not certain why." Even so, my throat was tightening, the suffocating sensations having little to do with what he was asking of me.

"It's an instinct. Learn to always follow it. Tell me, my little wren. Do you enjoy pain?" He backed away from me, walking around me in methodical steps, studying me from head to toe.

"I don't know."

"You've always indulged in a vanilla life."

"If by that you mean with men, then yes. Is that a problem?"

Chuckling, he brushed my hair from my shoulder, running his fingers all the way down my spine. "Of course it's not a problem. Always tell me the truth, Savannah, and I'll do the same with you. I want you to learn to trust me."

"I have nothing to lie about, Maxim. I've lived a simple, albeit boring life."

"Perhaps it's time for a change. I can tolerate many things in my life, Savannah, but lying is not one of them."

"I understand. I won't accept it either."

"Then we will enjoy the time we spend together. Go to the window and remove your clothes."

This I hadn't expected. When I jerked my head over my shoulder, he gave me an admonishing look. "What are you doing?"

When he smacked his hand across my bottom, a shiver trickled through me. "The first rule is that you will do as I say without question."

"Are there additional rules?" The nervousness was creeping to a frenzy, but I was proud of myself for not reacting.

He shifted slowly, facing me once again, sliding the same finger down to my tank top, cocking his head as he swirled the tip around my pronounced nipple. I held my breath, startled from the number of goosebumps drifting across my skin. "Several. But first things first." He yanked down both straps, exposing my breasts, his chest rising and falling. "Without pain there can be no pleasure." When he lifted his gaze, I was shocked at the difference in his eyes. It was as if he was two entirely different people.

119

"Okay." I wasn't immune to what he enjoyed, nor was I as innocent as he might believe. Yet when he pinched my hardened buds between his fingers, twisting them painfully, I couldn't hold back a surprised gasp. "Oh. Oh…" He continued the harsh actions, the hard ridge of his cock pressing against his trousers an indication inflicting pain ignited his hunger.

A smile crossed his face, and he lifted his gaze, studying me more intently than before. When he moved his hands, cupping my breasts from the bottom and squeezing, my body swayed. His touch was powerful, electric, and I was shocked how my body responded, betraying me instantly.

Without saying anything else, he lowered his head, immediately taking one of my aching nipples into his mouth. As he swirled his tongue back and forth, the discomfort quickly drifted into a subtle yet amazing moment of bliss. As my body continued to sway, I gripped his arms, closing my eyes more out of embarrassment than anything else.

He rolled his lips across my chest to my other nipple, taking his time flicking the tip of his tongue back and forth. It was difficult not to moan, my mind a complete blur from his controlling hold. I was certain I'd fall if I wasn't clinging to him. I concentrated on the ink on his arms, noticing the inside of one forearm had a crest, a jeweled dagger driven through a bloody black rose. It was unique, beautiful in a macabre way, but also terrifying.

He chuckled softly, noticing my pointed gaze. "It is a Cossack Khanjar dagger used by my ancestors." He fisted his hand, which seemed to make the jewels more prominent.

"Do you own one?"

"I have several in my collection."

"Beautiful."

"You have an affection for knives, little wren?"

"I also have a collection, one of the few items I have belonging to my father."

"I would enjoy seeing it one day. Weapons are to be revered, given their proper respect as they are often used in the wrong way." He exhaled, lightly brushing his fingers down my cheek. "And the sharp edge of a knife can do more damage than any firearm, especially to beautiful, sensitive skin. There are men who excel in various methods of torture that leave only a few scars, but the pain can last a lifetime."

"I understand."

As he narrowed his eyes, the singeing heat we shared became more intense. "I'm certain you do." He backed away, loosening his tie. "Yes, I'm almost positive you do. It's your choice, little wren, whether or not you surrender. Tell me. Are you ready to share every inch of yourself?"

I stood in the same place for a few seconds, mesmerized by his insanely good looks, but his words were as haunting as they were exciting. Yet against my better judgment, I backed away, ripping off my tank top.

And for some reason, the answer was easy. "Yes, sir."

CHAPTER 8

axim

The greatest deception men suffer is from their own opinions.

The quote from Leonardo da Vinci suddenly appeared in my mind, something I hadn't thought of in years. It was something my uncle had told me within the first week of coming to live with him in America. Granted, he'd spoken in Russian since I knew few words in English. Later, he'd made me recite them, one of many tools he used in order to shape me into becoming the future Pakhan. I'd never asked him what it meant or cared, learning early on that if I didn't follow my uncle Vladimir's rules, I would be severely punished.

Only through years of training had I begun to understand what he'd meant. He was a brutal man, merciless in almost every action, but he was a constant observer, only forming an opinion when he gathered all the facts. Then he exacted the necessary revenge. When I'd finally asked why he was so careful, it had been one of the few times he'd smiled. His answer?

That was the only way to alleviate any concept of remorse, for feeling guilt would become a significant weakness to be used by our enemies.

Today the words held the same meaning, yet for an entirely different reason. I would not be quick to judge such a beautiful woman, and one who was willing to place her trust in a monster. If she had an ulterior motive, then she had nerves of steel. As Savannah moved toward the window, I could see her face in the reflection, her gaze remaining locked on me.

I yanked the tie from my collar, taking a few seconds to revel in her beauty. She was unaffected by wealth or title, or so it seemed, preferring to enjoy things in life I'd never bothered to pay attention to. I'd been force fed all the expensive toys money could buy on a silver spoon, my forced upbringing preventing the kid from Russia from enjoying the simpler things in life. Only I knew the silver was tarnished from years of bloodshed.

When she was completely naked, it was all I could do not to close the distance, driving my cock deep inside her sweet pussy. For a sadistic man who had difficulty getting off unless significant pain was involved, this was refreshing, although I had to remind myself this could be nothing more than an illusion.

When I was within a few inches of where she stood, she stiffened, her breathing shallow. She had no way of knowing what I was going to do. In truth, I'd yet to decide completely. But at least one of her senses would be cut off entirely. I wanted her completely vulnerable, succumbing to my needs blindly. When I lifted my tie over her head, she followed the trail with her eyes, her face pensive.

"Full trust should be blind trust. Don't you agree, Savannah?" She didn't answer right away, allowing me to ease the silk over her eyes first, even placing her hands against the material, keeping it in place while I tied the knot.

"It's rare."

"Yes, which is the reason so few relationships last."

"Is that what you want, a relationship?"

Half laughing, I gripped her shoulders, leaning down to whisper in her ear, "No one could handle me but for so long."

"The right woman could."

"Mmm… A remote possibility." I backed away a few inches, waiting to see what she'd do. She turned her head to the side, listening for my footsteps. "Remain where you are. I'll return shortly." I retreated further, my footsteps echoing on the wooden floor. Then I grabbed my glass of wine, watching her reaction to the blindfold.

I'd interrogated enough people to gauge reactions quickly. If Savannah was here to collect information, she'd take the opportunity to glean what she could in my absence. That would require her to lift the makeshift mask. If she was a hired professional of a different nature, she'd wait for another opportunity, which meant she'd remain where she was without any sign of reservation.

But if Savannah was nothing more than a beautiful woman who'd decided to enjoy a night with a beast, then she'd second guess herself.

I shoved one hand into my pocket, doing my best to find a small amount of patience. Fortunately, within seconds it paid off. She started to tremble, constantly floating her hand to the blindfold. Her nervousness gave me a sense of comfort, at least enough to leave the room, heading for my private bedroom, my balls so tight it was painful.

After flicking on the light, I moved straight for the cabinet I'd had brought in, the specific piece custom built. As soon as I opened the double doors, I yanked out my phone.

"Yes, boss?" Ricardo asked, answering on the second ring.

"When you're finished with our illustrious chef, I need you check the employment records. Find Savannah's application and have her checked."

"Do you know her last name?"

"I have no clue. Find it. And I want an in-depth report."

"Do you need support?" he asked.

"Not necessary. Just get me what you can as soon as possible." After ending the call, I dumped my phone on the dresser. Then I cracked my knuckles before returning to the cabinet. I'd amassed several collections of implements and bondage equipment over the years, my savage tastes requiring sessions of kink every so often. Although I realized it had been a while, business keeping my attention.

If we were in my house in Boca, I'd keep her locked away in my playpen for an extended period of time. What I stored in my suite left much to be desired but was adequate for tonight's purposes. A smile crossed my face as I opted for cuffs, squeezing the leather between my fingers. A gag could prove useful, but I longed to hear her call out my name. That would happen soon enough.

I selected a flogger, one I'd use on a new submissive, rubbing my fingers down the thin straps of leather. Although my cravings were much more intense, I'd bide my time. If she was simply a girl in need of a job, let alone a new life, she might be provided with the opportunity to become something much more in my world.

Before I left, I ripped off my shirt, tossing it in the laundry. Then I took my time returning to the living room. By now, her anxiety level should be high. As I walked closer, Savannah tensed, her heated breath already creating a ring of fog on the window.

"Put your arms behind you," I commanded.

She was more tentative than before, the blindfold giving me the advantage. I was prepared for sass, but by the way she was twisting her lips, it was obvious she was having difficulty fighting her personality. She deserved an explanation.

"I'm going to bind your wrists. As I said before, you'll need to trust me. I will remind you that I'm not in the business of harming beautiful woman, only traitors. The leather cuffs will help heighten the experience."

Her arms were shaking but she did as I asked.

I almost dragged her down to her knees to suck my cock, my hunger roaring off the charts. Pain before pleasure. That's what I'd been taught early on in life and had adhered to the sentiment every day.

She'd fisted her hands, her shoulders rising and falling as I snapped the binding into place. As I mover her long hair away from her shoulder, she shuddered audibly. I raked my finger down the back of her neck, moving from one side to the other. "Perhaps one day you'll wear my collar."

Savannah was quiet, her jaw tightly clenched. "I won't be attached to anyone. Ever."

"We shall see, my little pet." I moved closer, enough so the heat of our bodies resonated back and forth. I placed the flogger on the end table, rolling my hand over her shoulder, cupping her breast savagely. "It would seem you've been lying to me. Haven't you?"

Even the best undercover agents would always stiffen just enough. She didn't. Instead, she flinched from the pain, a single moan slipping past her lips. I crossed out that particular box. However, if she had nothing to lose, everything to gain, then she'd do everything it took to maintain her studied persona.

I tangled my fingers in her hair with my other hand, lowering my head and nipping her earlobe. "Have you lied to me, *malen'kiy krapivnik*? Do you have something to confess to your master?"

"Why would I?"

"Come now. Please don't insult me. You were in my room going through my things. You see, I'm a very organized man and you were less than tidy."

She had the good graces to swallow then drag her tongue across her lips. "I'm sorry."

"Does that mean you were?"

"Yes. I was curious how a man of your... stature lives. Nothing more."

"Is that so?"

"Yes. Why else? What are you insinuating? That I'd want to steal from you? I might be desperate, Mr. Nikitin, but I'm no thief."

I wrapped her hair around my hand, tugging with enough force she gasped. Then I pressed my lips against hers, opening her mouth with mine. As I slipped my tongue inside, she didn't fight me, although her tremors had returned. She was still playful, sweeping her tongue against mine, the creaking leather an indication she was already fighting her bindings.

When I was finished tasting her, I kept my hold on her hair, sliding my arm around her waist. As I opened my fingers, crawling them down to her smooth pussy, she sucked in her breath. "Then exactly who are you, Savannah?"

"I already told you. I'm sorry I invaded your privacy. It was wrong. That's not my normal behavior."

"It would seem you're having a few of those experiences tonight. As with all bad behavior, there are consequences. That will need to be handled."

"Okay."

I yanked her head again. "Respect is the first thing you need to learn."

"Yes. Sir." The fact she issued the two words I was looking for through clenched teeth was a good indication she wasn't used to surrendering to anyone. Training her would be delicious.

"Good girl." I couldn't help myself, sliding the tip of my index finger around her clit. She immediately whimpered, the electricity already shooting between us increasing. As soon as her breathing became ragged, I pulled my hand away. "Before there can be pleasure, there will be punishment." I grabbed the flogger, sliding the six tails between her breasts all the way to her legs. "Do you understand me?"

"Yes, sir."

"Mmm…" I repeated the action, taking a few seconds to swish the tawse back and forth across one nipple then the other. When I cracked the leather strips against her breasts, she gritted out a slight yelp, stifling it immediately. She was a fierce little bird, determined not to let me in. That would soon change.

I repeated the action, enjoying the moment. She was moving her fingers, involuntarily rubbing them back and forth across my cock. The girl was going to drive me crazy.

After two more strikes across her breasts, I pulled her away from the window, using her long hair as a leash as I guided her toward the back of the couch. I was somewhat surprised that Savannah said nothing, struggling to a point but not enough to indicate she was terrified. Perhaps the sadistic side of me wanted her to be afraid, which would make her even more vulnerable, but then again, my arousal only increased because she wasn't pleading for her release.

When I tossed her over the couch, she threw her head over her shoulder, taking several gasping breaths. I kicked her legs apart then adjusted her bound hands against the small of her back. "I'm going to spank you, my little wren. You will not move or try to run. If you do, I assure you that you won't like where this punishment will go from here."

She bit her lower lip but nodded.

"I need to hear you say you understand."

"Yes, sir."

"Excellent." It had been a very long time since I'd used a tawse on anyone. Tonight I would enjoy every moment, especially exposing her to my world. She'd wanted to learn more. This was the best way. I dragged my finger down her spine, shifting over her bound hands to the crack of her ass. When I rolled the tip between her buttocks, she jumped. She was a virgin to the joys of anal sex. That only enticed the monster inside of me even more.

I took a step back, allowing the anticipation to increase for another few seconds. "Keep something in mind, my beautiful creature. No one fucks with me. Not even someone who seems innocent and beautiful. Consequences will always be necessary. The sooner you learn that I'm a man who refuses to tolerate betrayal, the better."

"Is that a threat, Maxim? I've done nothing to you. You invited me here, remember? Maybe I should leave."

As I'd done so many times, I savored a few seconds of observation, studying every nuance and slight tic, every heartbeat to see if she was lying to me. When she shifted away from the window, attempting to remove the blindfold, I snapped my hand around her wrist. "I would never threaten you, Savannah. I don't need to. You're an honorable woman. But I do make promises. And you're not leaving."

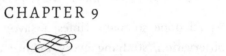
 avannah

His last few words were stated with emphasis.

And yes, they were a warning.

Danger.

It swept around me like a wildfire, ready to sear my skin, but as crazy as it seemed, I knew Maxim wasn't going to hurt me, at least not in the ways he did with those who defied him.

Or so I hoped.

Maxim wasn't exactly threatening me, but I'd been careless going into his room, searching through his things. Now I was paying the price of irresponsibility. The fact I was excited, my pussy aching appalled me.

Even the intimate touch had been breathtaking, awakening all my senses. I was still shaking from being commanded to remove my clothes, but I'd had no other choice.

A man so powerful wouldn't take no for an answer.

As he brought the flogger down, striking it across my buttocks four times, I sucked in my breath. Seconds later, I felt a series of stinging sensations, none of which were as bad as I thought they'd be. But as he continued, bringing the implement down time and time again, the pain began to build.

The blindfold was just as alarming, my lack of vision amplifying the experience. I could swear every smack against my skin was more sensualized, every sound of his wrist as he snapped it, bringing the tawse down was increased in volume. But being bound, unable to move or flee if necessary was absolutely terrifying. If I'd said no, would he have listened?

He issued a low, husky growl as he caressed my bottom, the heat already building on my skin. I wiggled, shifting back and forth but did my best to maintain my position. When he dared to roll his hand between my legs, I was thrown by the intensity of the pleasure. It was entirely different, every synapse in my body on fire.

Panting, even though I was blindfolded, stars managed to permeate my mind in vivid colors, dancing in spiraling formations as he drove his fingers past my swollen folds. He was rough in his actions, living up to his reputation as being a brutal man in every aspect of his life. But even as he murmured in Russian, the words floating up to my ears, I sensed something entirely different about him than I expected.

Just searching his eyes, I sensed a man with no home or family he could call his own. That shouldn't sadden me, but it did. He broke me from my pathetic trance, jerking his hand free, brushing his slickened fingers across my bottom. Then he delivered six more, one coming right after the other, shifting down to the tops of my thighs.

A blistering amount of anguish tore through me, but even though I bit back a scream from the pain, I was so aroused it was insane. I hung my head, fighting the bindings even if I'd likely receive more. I'd never been tied up before, a feeling of claustrophobia rushing in, a fear I didn't even know I had. And no one had ever tried to spank me before.

He was unforgiving of my misdeed, cracking the flogger down harder. Faster. But something told me he wasn't just marking my body because of my behavior. He was doing so as a statement that I belonged to him.

I was petrified and thrilled, the combination just as repulsive. But there was no turning back the clock, no ability to alter the future. I was his for the taking and he knew it.

Two turned into six, my body shaking.

Another four and a single bead of perspiration trickled between my breasts. I was lightheaded, filthy thoughts drifting through my mind, every cell in my body on fire.

When he stopped a second time, I heard how labored his breathing had become and when he touched me, I sensed his arm was shaking from adrenaline. I shifted back and forth, my legs wobbly.

"You defied me." His statement was cool, the hiss afterward making me more anxious.

"Yes. I'm sorry."

After Maxim gave me four more, I heard him dropping the flogger. Then he pulled me away from the couch, wrapping his hand around my throat. "I know you are, little wren." He wrapped his arms around me, cupping my breasts. "You did very well. I'm proud of you."

Was I supposed to say thank you? I had no idea.

I wasn't certain what to expect, but when he pushed me to the floor, a surge of electricity shot through me.

"*Teper ty sosesh moy chlen,*" he growled.

"What does that mean?" I heard rustling sounds and knew he was removing his trousers.

"That means you're now going to suck my cock." When he gripped both sides of my head, I shuddered to my core, but the same rush of excitement and desire roared through me. "Open your mouth."

I did what he asked, my breathing shallow, struggling all over again with my bindings. I wanted to touch him, to wrap my hands around his cock, sliding my other hand between his legs so I could cup his balls. As he tapped my cheek, I darted out my tongue.

"Wider, little wren."

The moment I stretched my mouth as wide open as possible, he shoved the tip of his cock inside. I didn't need to be told to suck him, immediately clamping my lips around his thickness, swirling my tongue back and forth.

"You're one hot woman, Savannah. Eager. I like that." His voice was soft velveteen, sliding down my naked skin in the most comforting way.

As he shoved a couple more inches inside, I was shocked how large he was, my jaw muscles aching almost instantly. His fingers dug into the side of my face as he held me, keeping me from going anywhere. Every sound he made was exaggerated, his scent rushing into my system, enticing my senses. I was shocked how much I enjoyed the fact he had full control.

"Your mouth is so hot, so fucking hot. Take it all, my little pet. Every single inch."

I shuddered as he thrust the remainder inside, the tip hitting the back of my throat. When I gagged, he only pushed harder, taking full control. I took shallow breaths, trying to control my gag reflex, fearful I couldn't do this. But seconds later, he developed a rhythm, and I was able to relax my throat muscles.

But he remained brutal, driving into me relentlessly, as if he was furious with his life and not just with me.

"Fuck. That's good. So damn good."

I had no way of knowing how long he fucked my mouth, shocked when he pulled out. I kept my mouth open, prepared for more.

"I could erupt in your throat easily, but I'm not finished with you yet, my sweet little bird. No, I need to taste you before I fuck you, indulging in the experience this time. And I assure you that I'm going to fuck that tight pussy of yours all over again."

His gravelly voice and promise of defiling me sent a wave of heat into my core. I'd never hungered for a man in this way, the darkness he exuded a part of his power and the excitement. He pulled me to my feet, turning me around. I was surprised when I sensed he was unfastening the bindings, releasing my wrists.

But he wasn't letting me go, using my long hair as he'd done before, walking me to another location. When he eased me down onto all fours on something soft, I looked over my shoulder, wishing I could see what he was doing. He widened my legs, leaving me totally exposed.

To him, a man who I knew to be a brutal killer.

How had I gotten here in the first place?

"As I said, with pain comes pleasure." He kept his hand on my bottom and in the next few seconds, vibrations danced down every inch of my body as he blew across my throbbing pussy. I was so wet my juice had already slickened my thighs, the wafting scent floating between us. I was lost in a sea of pleasure almost instantly when he darted his tongue around my clit. My God, he was going to lick me from behind. I dug my palms into the soft material, arching my back.

I was rewarded with a subtle growl, his heavy breathing spilling across my wetness.

"Oh, God."

"There's no God here, my little wren, just your master, a man who will give you everything you need. If you're a good little girl."

His words continued to thrill me, my mind a raging blur as he thrust his tongue past my swollen folds. No other pleasure had felt this amazing or intense. I bit back a cry as my muscles clamped and released almost immediately. What he'd done to me in the course of thirty minutes was unexpected, pushing me to the height of bliss. It was crazy I didn't want him to stop.

And I sensed he had no intention of it.

As he added a single finger, driving as deep inside as possible, I started panting. I clawed the upholstery, crazed from the jolts of current. He made good on his promise, taking his time, licking up and down, sucking on my clit several times. When I started tossing my head back and forth, I could tell I almost slipped off whatever he'd placed me on.

He wrapped one arm around my leg, opening me even wider, burying his face into my pussy. When he plunged two more fingers inside, flexing them open, I couldn't keep a strangled yelp from escaping. I could sense I was close to coming. He brought me to the brink several times, Pulling back, barely licking me.

"This is... so..." I couldn't find the words or express how good it felt, my mind a complete blur. I wiggled my hips and he smacked his hand against my aching backside, sending me soaring into a moment of utter rapture.

When he started licking me in earnest again, I couldn't stop shaking. As he pumped his fingers, driving into me as deeply as was possible, I nearly lost my mind.

"My perfect little wren. That's it, little pet. Come for me."

Whether or not in doing so was about obeying him or not, I wasn't certain, but I couldn't stop the explosive climax. As it rushed into me, I opened my mouth to scream but nothing came out. But my body wouldn't stop shaking, pitching from side to side as a single orgasm jetted into a beautiful wave.

He continued to lick like a wild man, his guttural sounds like a primal beast. He was right in that every one of my other senses was intensified from losing one. I couldn't stop panting, my body shaking, colorful visions sweeping through my mind. I'd never experienced anything like this before.

Then I experienced another shock as he smacked his fingers against my pussy.

"What? Oh, God."

He chuckled darkly and I struggled to breathe. He repeated the action, the hard cracks pushing me into another climax. I couldn't believe it, my mind a complete blur.

"Oh. Oh. Oh. Oh… Yes…" I was exhausted but alive, stars spinning out of control in my periphery of vision.

"That's it. Good girl. My perfect pet." He cracked his fingers a few more times then resumed licking me.

I was too sensitive, trying to scramble away but he was having none of it, yanking me back so he could finish the evil deed. I laughed even though tears were in my eyes, and I was shaking all over. There was no way to describe the combination, but when he finally slowed, I hung my head, gasping for air.

He backed away and I slumped down, tingling sensations remaining.

There was no rest for the weary. He fisted my hair, yanking me back onto all fours. "Now I'm taking what already belongs to me."

The words were suddenly chilling because I knew he meant them. He was determined to make me his prized pet, a woman who'd surrender at his command. I wasn't certain I could do that, not for any man.

Then he thrust his cock inside and I was floating, no longer capable of thinking clearly. His hold was firm, yanking my back into a deep arc. As he powered inside, slamming into me with so much force it knocked my breath away, I bucked hard against him.

"My little pet likes it rough," he growled, digging the fingers of his other hand into my hip. He was so dominating, predatory in every way.

And I loved it.

Panting, I did what I could to meet every brutal thrust, clawing the material underneath my fingers, every sound I made ragged. My sight deprivation only added to the sensations tearing through me, leaving me hot and wet, my pussy aching and my breasts swollen.

He smacked my bottom several times and it threw me into a raging orgasm, vibrations jetting through every cell and muscle.

"Yes. Yes. Yes!"

"Such a bad girl, coming without asking."

I couldn't answer, my mind spiraling out of control, the pleasure so extreme I could no longer breathe.

And he refused to stop, driving savagely, taking exactly what he wanted.

Wiggling and pitching, exhaustion was settling in but my body continued betraying me, allowing another climax to sweep in unexpectedly.

"My perfect little wren."

When he whispered something in Russian that I couldn't understand, another edge started to build, the pleasure flipping to severe anxiety. I stiffened, holding my breath. Then I realized by his jerking motions that he was close to coming. I closed my eyes, praying that this wasn't the end of the game by his choice.

And as he erupted deep inside, filling me with his seed, a single tear rolled down my face.

* * *

Maxim

· · ·

My little wren stood in the same place she'd been when I'd begun peeling away the layers of armor, staring out at the city as if it could offer answers, a new life.

Or perhaps salvation.

I fingered my glass before tossing back the rest of my scotch, studying her intently. And my cock still ached. What was I going to do with my little bird? Sighing, I put my empty glass on the table, rising to my feet. Ricardo had texted, providing an indication that he'd followed my orders.

Savannah seemed to sense I was staring at her, turning around slowly.

"I should go. I need to spend tomorrow searching for a job."

I walked closer, taking the glass of wine from her hand, placing it on the coffee table. Then I cupped one side of her face. "Wait here for a few moments while I make a phone call."

She dragged her tongue across her lower lips, the seductive move matching the twinkle in her eyes. "Okay."

After rubbing my thumb across her lips, I shoved it into her mouth, curious as to what she'd do. She wrapped her hand around my wrist, immediately sucking on my thumb as if I'd offered her a perfect raspberry lollypop. I was mesmerized by the subtle yet powerful actions, the way her mouth moved as she rolled it up and down my thick digit.

She smelled of sex and passion, which did nothing but keep me tantalized. She was the only woman who could keep me off guard for longer than a few minutes. Every sound she made was that of a kitten drinking a fresh bowl of milk and my balls ached more than before from the sweet murmurs alone.

Shit.

The moment I pulled away, she pursed her lips, giving me a pouting look. Chuckling, I shook my head then purposely moved away before things went too far. When I was inside my office, I closed the door and immediately dialed Ricardo.

"And?" I barked.

"She's legit. Savannah Parkins is from some bumfuck town in North Carolina. She went to a culinary school in Virginia Beach. She's had some pretty shitty jobs from what I can tell. Nothing to note other than she doesn't have any family, her mother dying a couple years ago from cancer. The poor girl is broke as shit. I'm surprised she has a pot to piss in."

"You're showing your age, Ricardo." A moment of happiness rushed into my system from the fact she was who she said she was. I would hate to need to crush anything so spectacular.

"Ha. Ha. Boss, I don't think you got to worry."

"Any noise in the last few hours?"

"Nah," he said. "Pretty quiet night."

"Keep it that way." After pressing end, I thought about what I wanted to do with her. She was right about Miami, and I didn't want her employed in my resort in the city. She'd become a weakness then a target. That wasn't acceptable. However… there were a couple of options.

The bottom line was that I'd need to capture and cage her or keep her in close proximity. I wasn't going to let her go. At least for now. As long as she followed my rules, obeying my commands.

I was an evil fuck.

Laughing, I returned to the living room, pulling out a business card and pen. "I have a proposition for you, Savannah."

"A proposition?"

I scribbled down an address and a phone number of the person in charge of my resort in New Orleans. "Yes. There is a job opening in New Orleans."

She immediately shook her head. "I can't accept your offer."

"You haven't heard it yet." I closed the distance, admiring her tenacity. "You need a job. I need a qualified person in the kitchen of my resort that I can trust. And I assure you that the head chef is not like Salinger." I held out the card and at first, she acted like she was going to take it. Then she fisted her hand.

"I really enjoyed spending time with you, Maxim, but I told you before, I'm not a whore. I don't want payment for services rendered and I can't promise you that I'll want to do that again. I don't need complications."

Goddamn, the woman turned me on. "Understood and that's not what this is about. I've checked your qualifications, the shitty jobs you've had. You have the skills, and you deserve a break."

She laughed, raking her hand through her hair. "I'm not sure I have the money to get a hotel. Between gas of getting there and food, I'll have pennies left. I know that's not your problem, but I really don't want to live on the street."

"And you won't have to. As with my head chef, you'll be given a suite in the hotel. I require it because this job is not for the faint of heart. I entertain often and demand perfection. Now, if you're not up to the rigors of the job, I can understand. But if you're intrigued, then at least take the card. If you've decided to accept the opportunity, call this number within forty-eight hours. Otherwise, I'll assume you're not interested. Fair enough?"

She glanced down at the card several times before taking it. "Fair enough."

As she slipped it into the pocket in her sweatpants, another wave of desire settled in as a thought came to my mind.

I tak eto nachalos'.

And so it begins.

CHAPTER 10

$\mathcal{M}$axim

"My Russian friend," Diego Santos said, his laugh boisterous.

I glared into the iPad, noticing his twin brother had entered the room. While there were subtle differences in the two men, they weren't enough to keep Dante from fooling the world into thinking he was Diego for several weeks a few months before. "Friend, my ass."

Dante moved closer, giving me a harsh look. "You're grumpier than normal."

I stuck up my middle finger. "I need to ask you both some questions about your real father." I threw them a look, curious as to how they'd react. I'd insisted on a fucking

146

Facetime call, so I'd be able to observe reactions when I asked pointed questions.

They exchanged a look, which already irritated me. Brotherhood or not, I wasn't in the mood to play games. I'd just as soon rip off their heads. The shipment remained in jeopardy, the quiet lull of inactivity making me jumpier than normal. That usually meant something was hiding just below the surface, an attack being prepared or a war to end all wars. I'd heard Santiago was crazy enough. Maybe his two illegitimate sons could talk him off the ledge before I cut his head off with a machete.

Even if I had to travel to South America to do it.

Still, I was close to making the decision to switch venues, utilizing the port in New Orleans instead. It had its own share of risks but if I made the change in a careful manner, the authorities would be none the wiser. Plus, Santiago had yet to rear his ugly head in the lovely city.

I also had personal motives for considering the change.

"What do you need?" Diego was the one who asked.

"Are you aware he has plans on invading the beautiful south shores?"

"Miami?" Dante leaned over his brother's shoulder. After what the man had put Diego through, I was shocked Diego hadn't put a bullet in the man's head or worse. Blood or no blood, the shit that had gone down wasn't something I'd be able to tolerate.

"I'm not talking about Texas."

147

"We haven't been informed. I think you know better. We might be blood, Maxim, but that doesn't mean we're friends. We won't allow him to interfere with our business and I'm certain you won't with yours."

"Do you care to stretch the extent of our alliance?" I wasn't the kind of man to ever ask for help, but this was an entirely different situation. Their blood relations could prove to be helpful. Or a disaster. However, I did trust the two men to a point.

Diego sat back. "You want us to make some inquiries."

"If possible, without drawing any attention. I have far too much going on."

Both men seemed surprised that I'd ask for their assistance. I wasn't known for my generosity or camaraderie, which was fine with me.

"I think I can speak for my brother in saying we'd be happy to help you, Russian. However, there may come a time we require a favor in return." Diego grinned as he made the statement.

I gritted my teeth, my jaw clenched. I wasn't the kind of man who wanted to owe anyone anything. However, this was justified. "Fine. That can be arranged but also remember, Dante, you owe me."

"The meeting is in a few days. Will the timing do?" Dante piped in, his eyes reflecting memories of my earlier assistance.

I'd almost forgotten that the quarterly meeting of the alliance was set to be held in Miami. "That will be fine."

"Good. We'll see what we can find."

There was no need to extend the conversation. We weren't friends. We weren't business associates. In fact, I'd been shocked my uncle had suggested that I accept the invitation. He wasn't the kind of man who liked to share in anything, including knowledge. Then he'd suddenly changed his mind, chastising me for continuing. Being the rebellious kid, I'd continued serving the Brotherhood for that reason alone.

I sat back in the chair of my office, the corporate headquarters located in an all glass building in Miami Beach, the view of the ocean, restaurants, and nightlife spectacular. While I wanted a tall glass of bourbon, my adrenaline was pumping enough that I'd decided to head to my private gym. At least I could work off some steam.

I closed my eyes, curious as to whether my little wren had accepted the job. If not, I wasn't planning on going after her. At least not now. If our paths crossed again, perhaps the outcome would be different.

I heard voices outside my door and sighed. I'd never have a moment of peace. When I heard the slight rapping on my door, I finally lifted my head. Ricardo walked into the room, Damien Pavlov alongside him. That fact his presence had been required by my uncle would remain a bone of contention between us. I was certain Damien had been told to keep tabs on my activities.

"Gentlemen. To what do I owe this pleasure?"

"We have another issue, boss. I wanted to bring it to your attention right away." Ricardo walked closer.

"And that is?"

"Someone has been embezzling money."

I started to laugh. Of all the things I had to be worried about, now someone was stealing from me. "And do we know who?"

Ricardo acted as if he didn't want to tell me, which meant it was someone I trusted.

"That fucking accountant of yours," Damien said with glee in his voice.

"Tony?" I asked. Tony Sanchez had been with the Nikitin family for years, long enough the man was considered a part of the family. I didn't buy it for one second.

Then I thought of Sergei. Up until recently, there'd been no unrest in the ranks, but with Sergei's betrayal, everything had changed.

Ricardo seemed sheepish about it but nodded.

I found it interesting that Damien would be pushing the issue. He'd worked with Tony for years, both men under my uncle's reign.

"Do we have evidence?" As soon as I'd posed the question, Damien tossed a jump drive on my desk. While I picked it up, shoving it into my jacket, I had no intentions of opening it here. "You've brought it to my attention. I'll handle the situation from here."

"You need to handle the traitor now. If not, trust will be broken." Damien's bold words were enough to tip me over the edge. I was out of my chair, issuing several brutal punches to his face and kidney, finally tossing him against the wall. As soon as he started to slide down, I turned around. But I was no idiot.

He came at me again and I had just enough time to yank out the very blade that resembled my tattoo. The sharp jab from his momentum was enough to draw a trickle of blood.

"Whoa! Can we just take it easy?" Ricardo hissed.

I cocked my head as I stared at Damien. He'd challenged me before and I'd let it pass with a warning given he hadn't been my soldier. I wasn't going to do that again.

When Damien threw up his arms in surrender, I took a deep breath, but the rage inside wasn't going away any time soon. There was nothing worse than being betrayed, but I wasn't the kind of leader to accept the word of someone I didn't trust. "I'm going to say this once. If you have continued issues with remembering who you work for, I'll have no problem reminding you. Then I'll toss you aside like the trash you've become."

Ricardo muttered under his breath in Spanish, pacing the office as he did when he was irritated.

While Damien's eyes flashed, he grinned. I had no doubt he had plans on contacting my uncle. That would only add to the punishment I already had planned for him. "Fine. *Boss*," he said a few seconds later. "Just remember I was the one who found out about Tony's treachery." He shifted forward, allowing the blade to dig into his skin. I resisted shoving it into his jugular. That would serve no purpose at this point. "It seems to be going around."

That would serve no purpose at this point but one day, I'd finish what I'd started. "If your hard evidence proves to be reliable, then I'll remember. Not until then." I raked the tip of the blade down his chest, easily ripping a button from his pristine shirt.

"*Ne moy Pakhan,*" he muttered then moved toward the door, throwing me a vicious look before storming out, the door smacking against the wall. The man had balls.

Ricardo shook his head. "Not my Pakhan? Does he not realize you already are or will be in a few short weeks?"

I returned the dagger to the leather sleeve, trying to calm my fury. "Do you believe what he's insinuating?"

Shrugging, he planted his hands on his hips. "Let's just put it to you this way. If Tony isn't guilty, someone is fucking with you. Do you think Sergei had anything to do with it?"

"It's possible." I didn't want to believe Sergei had infected the core, but at this point anything was possible.

Exhaling, I moved toward the window, thinking about what he'd just said. I'd been challenged before, easily able to discover the asshole who believed they could get away with extorting money, but times were different, enemies coming from all sides. "Put a tail on Tony. I want to know every single thing that man does. Who he sees, who he contacts, where he goes to eat, and who he's fucking."

"He has a family out of town."

I couldn't help but laugh. "That means shit in this world, Ricardo. You should know that by now." Enemies used every weakness. If Tony had one, it was possible he was being blackmailed.

"I'll put a couple men on him now. I'll let you know what I find."

"Good." I remained where I was.

"Is there anything else you need?"

As I shoved my hands in my pockets, my thoughts continually drifted to Savannah. "I'm switching the shipment. It's going to come into the port in New Orleans."

He seemed stunned. "You really want to do that?"

"If Santiago is expecting easy pickings, this will throw him. Plus, I'll force him to show his hand."

"You're an astute businessman, boss. Does the seller know?"

"He knows and appreciates the security measures. He's headed for New Orleans. We'll have the final meeting there before it arrives."

"Good deal. I love New Orleans."

The man had a full lust for life, always with a beautiful woman on his arm, even while he was working the casinos. I couldn't care less as long as he did his job.

"I want only the necessary people to know. We'll use N'awlins' soldiers." When I turned and looked at him, I noticed concern on his face.

"Some of them are green."

"They'll do. I don't anticipate any trouble but have a security team sweep the warehouse before the shipment arrives. I wouldn't put it past the DEA to have set up shop since the buildings have been vacant for a few months."

"Good point. What about Damien?"

I pondered the question. "Keep him out of the loop until the last minute."

"You think he's turned. Don't you?" he asked, darting his eyes back and forth across mine.

"I can't rule anything out. I'll be heading to the Big Easy in a day or so." If Emmanuel Santiago was making a play, he'd need someone on the inside to plow the road before he came in. If Damien's plan was to throw suspicion on another member of the organization, attempting to derail my attention to the shipment, he really didn't know me that well.

He took a few strides closer. "The switch of venues wouldn't happen to partially be about Savannah Parkins, would it?"

"As I told you before. She's nothing more than a distraction. I'll likely never see her again, which is fine."

"If you say so but avoiding her isn't going to be easy." Ricardo knew me as well as anyone, although I was a private man.

"And why would you say that?"

"She accepted the job you offered her." He studied me carefully after relaying the news. If he thought I'd have any kind of reaction, he was sorely mistaken. I'd never removed my mask.

My uncle had made certain I didn't, especially if captured by an enemy. He'd had a brutal way of ensuring I kept my mouth shut even while being tortured, his tactics only slightly removed from truly savage organization like the Colombians. I had the scars to prove his methods were very effective.

I hadn't told him about the offer I'd made because at this point, it was none of his business.

"Don't make more out of it than it is."

He couldn't help grinning. "I'm not saying a word. By the way, it might be a good idea to draw Santiago out in the open. He's protected in his home country."

"Yes, not a bad idea. Then I can deal with him once and for all."

"Perhaps a distraction could be used?"

When I snapped my head in his direction, he reared back, holding up his hands in surrender. "If by distraction you're suggesting that I use the woman I just hired, then you need to back off." My words were caustic, far too aggressive. A jealous streak had ripped through me, which wasn't like me.

"I wasn't suggesting you use Ms. Parkins. I wouldn't do that."

"Good because if you were, we would have issues."

He nodded. "I didn't mean any disrespect."

Unfortunately, he had a good idea, although I wasn't the kind of man to use bait in a situation like this, no matter how tempting. Santiago had no issues destroying a creature of beauty.

I narrowed my eyes, surprised that he found it so amusing. "Gather together the men who'll be responsible for the shipment once it's back in Miami. Schedule a meeting at the warehouse tonight."

"Will do." He hesitated, his brow furrowed. "I'm worried about some of the men. They have loyalty to Damien. After what happened with Sergei, they're scared."

"What the hell do they have to be scared of?"

He shrugged. "The Feds have been pushing for almost a year, the DEA is sniffing around more and more. Then there's this shipment."

"What about this shipment?" I bristled at the suggestion that I wasn't the best leader.

"The timing is bad. When they find out the venue has changed, they're going to see that as a weakness. Let alone this woman you're seeing."

"I'm not allowed to have a private life?" I gritted my teeth, wordless fury spiraling.

"You know how much I respect you, Max, but with Sergei's treachery, they're worried they'll be arrested and you're not powerful enough to stop it. You know the crackdowns are only going to get worse."

Scowling I took several deep breaths then raked my arm across my desk, tossing everything from the surface onto the floor.

He exhaled, the sound exaggerated. "I thought you should know."

"Who?"

"Do you want me to run down a list?"

"Yeah, I do. Fucking *who?*"

When he did, my blood began to boil. To think the men I'd led, I'd nurtured were gunning for Damien to take over burned me to the core. By all rights I should execute every one of them, but that would destroy the organization.

"What else is on your mind?" I also knew him well enough to realize when he was holding back. Why not add fuel to the fire?

"Nothing you need to deal with, but I wanted you to know I've discovered a pincher."

The term was used for the low-level dealers who dared cross a line, sampling the product. "How bad?"

"Just chump change in the big scheme, but he's hosted parties, some with celebrities, but that's not the worst part. There was a death from an overdose."

"Goddamn it." I slammed my hand on the desk. That kind of shit wasn't supposed to happen. The fact my uncle continued to be in the illegal drug industry irritated the hell out of me. It was the quickest way to have several of our men land in prison. And there wasn't a cellblock within four states that hadn't turned into a warzone.

"It gets worse. I'm not certain but from what I've heard, he was cutting with some shit to make it more powerful."

"Who is it?"

"Paulo Martin."

"What the fuck is the man doing on our payroll?" Mr. Martin was a local celebrity. Part club DJ, part playboy, inheriting enough money he could have any woman in Miami he wanted. And he took advantage of it.

"Not my call."

"Damien," I growled, fisting my hand.

He nodded. "Initially I didn't care because Paulo has a huge entourage. He's the number one supplier for us in Florida."

Sighing, I shoved my hands in my pockets. "I don't give a shit. Pick him up. Take him to the playpen. I'll deal with his indiscretions tonight as well." It had been a while since I'd made certain everyone in my employ knew that infractions would be dealt with harshly.

"That's not going to win you any bonus points either. He's more popular than the freaking Pope if you ask me."

"Does it look like I give a shit?"

"Not at all, boss. I'll have it taken care of, but you need to know that there are unconfirmed reports some Colombians were at the party as well."

"Well, well. Then I guess I have something to talk to the man about."

"I figured you'd think so."

My thoughts drifted and a different idea came into my mind.

"Have Damien there as well as every man on the list you spouted off. I want them to know what happens to men who dare defy me under any circumstances."

Ricardo whistled. "Yes, sir, but you're certain you want them to know about the change in itinerary?"

"They're going to know one way or the other. I might as well be the one controlling it."

It was becoming more apparent that Santiago was using every avenue available. Well, two could play at that game. It should also give Damien something to think about. I stared at the mess I'd made, my rage remaining.

As with any transfer of power, there were always issues, but the fact Damien had gone behind my back, creating a wave of loyalty of his own couldn't be tolerated.

However, because the man was still in my uncle's favor, I'd need to handle this cautiously.

First the shipment.

Then I'd clean house.

* * *

"What the fuck do you mean you're switching venues?" my uncle barked from his usual perch in the hot tub, a cigar in one hand, a whiskey in the other. He wasn't aging gracefully, but that didn't seem to faze the three young women frolicking in the water with him.

Even though Vladimir was my uncle by blood, in my mind he'd become a liability, but he was still considered Pakhan, requiring respect.

"It would appear Emmanuel Santiago had taken interest in our fair city." While he might not mind spouting off aspects of business in front of his whores, I had no intention of giving anything away.

He snorted, puffing on his cigar as he moved to the edge of the tub. When he instantly pushed one of the girls between his legs, I looked away.

"What's wrong, boy? Does this kind of thing bother you?" He laughed, as he always did when he knew I was uncomfortable.

"*Skontsentriruyles na biznese*," I hissed. Concentrate on business.

He eyed me carefully, his lack of reaction acknowledgement that he'd lost his edge. "*Vam nuzhno ulozhit'.*" You need to get laid.

Snorting, I walked closer. "That's my business."

"You need to make it everyone's business, Maxim. You need to get married. That will squelch the opinions of the assholes who think you're not ready to lead."

It was an old discussion. "It's not going to happen. Business at hand."

"You work too hard. So be it. It will be your downfall. If only I had a son."

"Well, you fucking don't." And I certainly didn't have a father. I'd always believed Vladimir had ordered a hit on my parents, taking my father's rightful role as Pakhan. Perhaps my uncle had felt guilty for destroying my life. How many times had I stood over him while he was sleeping with a knife in my hand?

He eyed me carefully, swigging on his drink while the buxom blonde sucked his cock. I was more repulsed than usual. My aunt was sequestered away in her suite, ignoring what went on in her own house. The entire situation was disgusting and something I wanted no part of.

"Emmanuel is not strong enough to challenge us," he said after a full minute.

"You're wrong. He's grown much stronger." I was surprised he didn't curse the Brotherhood as he'd done so many times, blaming them for Santiago's increase in power.

"It is a bad move. Switch it back."

"There's too much heat centered on Miami right now." When he narrowed his eyes, I could tell he had no clue what I was talking about.

"Meaning what?"

"Paulo Martin. He's become a party man, and someone died using our product that he's been selling for our organization. He's under investigation for manslaughter. What I want to know is why Damien was allowed to make him a dealer." I decided to skip the information regarding some of the man's guests.

His face turned red within seconds, and he brutally shoved the girl aside, climbing out of the hot tub and walking closer. "Kill the motherfucker."

"Not wise. The heat is explosive."

"You do what I say."

"Why don't you take out your anger on the man that allowed this to happen?" I watched as his expression turned stone cold.

"Damien had his reasons."

"Oh, really? I'd be curious what those are." I closed the distance, planting a smile on my face. "I'll tell you this now, Uncle. If any of my men are arrested because of Damien's decision, I assure you that I'll be looking for a new lieutenant."

As I turned to leave, I heard him laugh. "You are coming into your own, Maxim. That's good to see. By the way, Viktor Romanoff has been placed on the buyer list. You'll need to inform him of the change in venue." He seemed pleased with his surprise announcement.

What the fuck?

The news shouldn't bother me, the powerful Bratva leader out of Russia someone my uncle considered a friend, but I'd always been skeptical of their continued interactions. I'd heard enough stories about Vladimir breaking ties with the old Bratva regime in coming to America that I would think he'd be cautious of the continuing connection. However, my uncle was still technically in charge, the reasons behind his methods of handling business never to be questioned. He'd made that perfectly clear as he'd promoted me through the ranks.

The timing was horrendous, so much so that my hackles were raised.

"Risky," I told him. Several factions of law enforcement would love to get their hands on him.

"I owe him a favor. He's coming to the States for a visit."

The admittance was a surprise. "How much?"

"Four hundred kilograms."

I felt my jaw clenching. The amount was worth well over a hundred and twenty million. "That will stretch us with our other clients."

"I'm certain you can handle it. He's willing to pay whatever is necessary."

Which meant Viktor was being squeezed. But by whom?

"Fine. I'll make the arrangements. After the shipment is in, Damien is out. Period."

I didn't give him time to respond, heading out of the house to my Ferrari.

I was leaving for the airport as soon as business was finished. As I jumped inside, starting the engine, I made mental note to dig into Damien's heritage as well as his past. Vladimir was far too attached to the man for my liking.

As I sped through the streets, heading for the warehouse, I made a call to my concierge at my New Orleans resort. And my cock was already aching to introduce my little wren to even darker aspects of my world.

"Francois. I have a new employee who will be staying with us for an indeterminant amount of time. Prepare the queen suite for her. Make certain the cabinets and refrigerator are stocked. I want the best of everything."

"Yes, sir. I'll have it taken care of. Your suite is already prepared for your arrival."

"Excellent. I'll be there later tonight. I also have a guest, flying in from Russia. Make certain Mr. Romanoff and his associates are provided with several of our smaller suites, preferably on the same floor."

"Any special amenities, sir?"

I chuckled, thinking about Viktor's tastes. He was a true Russian through and through. "Have a bottle of the Kors George V vodka placed in Mr. Romanoff's room with a card."

"Very good, sir," Francois murmured.

While I wasn't interested in playing hospitality games with the man, his close proximity would allow me to keep an eye on him. There were too many players in the mix, which would add to the complications.

As I tossed the phone onto the seat next to me, the discomfort I felt between my legs gave me a smile.

Fifteen minutes later I pulled into the parking lot of the warehouse. The location was mainly used as temporary storage for several of the organization's products, more secure than any of our other facilities. With twenty-four-hour guards, state of the art equipment and booby traps, we'd yet to have anyone attempt to break inside. While several of Miami's finest men and women of law enforcement were on our payroll or blackmailed into looking the other way, I never took security lightly.

After stepping out of the vehicle, I studied the area, ensuring I hadn't been followed before heading to the retina scanning device. Once inside, I moved directly for the playpen. It had become the term used to describe the room, something Vladimir had established when the building had been purchased. The various pieces of equipment as well as the soundproofing panels used in the walls and ceiling prevented excess noise going either way.

The six men Ricardo had listed as supporting Damien had reached the second highest tier in the Bratva. They each controlled a territory including all aspects of business and had soldiers they commanded. While the Bratva weren't as structured as the Cosa Nostra, there were hierarchies that had been in place for generations. In order for man to reach this level, he'd been required to demonstrate the ultimate in loyalty and sacrifice, willing to die to protect the Pakhan.

That part of the organization's structured system I valued, but it was the barbaric aspects of handling infractions that had always held my rapt attention. I had to give my uncle credit for his creative methods of acting on Hammurabi's Code.

An eye for an eye wasn't that simple. It was how the body part was harvested that made all the difference. Unfortunately, I didn't have the time necessary to enjoy the process. I had no intention of killing Mr. Martin. That would take all the fun out of the activity. Instead, he would serve as a representative for our organization that attempting to go against our strict guidelines would result in stringent punishment.

However, Paulo was second on the agenda, held tight in lockdown until I was ready. Was it risky bringing him here given the recent questioning done by the police? Yes, but I was all about taking risks.

What this would do was provide a trickle-down effect within the organization. Every one of the men standing in front of me appeared uncomfortable but Damien was smug, as if he'd already won a battle that would allow him to ultimately win the spot of Pakhan. I wouldn't play my cards completely, but it would put the fear of God into at least some of them.

"What are we doing here?" Damien asked, acting as if he didn't need to follow my orders.

"Business. What do you think?"

His sneer annoyed the hell out of me, but I allowed the charade to continue.

"Gentlemen," I started. "One of the largest shipments purchased within the organization is due into the Port of

New Orleans. The seller has been made aware of the change in itinerary. I need you to coordinate the dock activities as well as handling the transfer to our secured facilities once the ship has docked at midpoint. The men in New Orleans will handle it up until then. Do not under any circumstances mention this to anyone you are not using for the required actions. And if there's a single sight of a Colombian, shoot to kill."

They glanced back and forth between themselves, one stupid enough to look toward Damien for the go-ahead.

Damien stared at me smugly.

"Ricardo will go over the various details. You'll make certain we don't have an issue with the Colombians in my absence."

"You don't have the necessary protection in New Orleans," Damien added.

"I assure you that I'll be just fine."

As Ricardo started to hand out diagrams and other instructions, I thought about how I wanted to handle Paulo. I moved from one piece of equipment to another, lifting various saws and implements, standing in front of the chipper unit then to the cabinet of lawn equipment. The first time I saw a man killed, I thought it was horrible, the bullet put right between his eyes. I'd been eleven, my uncle insisting I watch.

He'd waited until I was thirteen to bear witness to an event that had caused me to have nightmares for months. He'd laughed in joy at the savagery he'd used.

However, the incident had helped shape a monster, a man with no conscience, craving the brutality as much as I did any other drug of choice.

With one exception.

My intense cravings for Savannah continued to stymie me, almost to the frustrating level. I checked my watch and returned to the group. "Bring our guest into the room. Gentlemen, make yourself a drink. This will be another lesson in how I deal with traitors or those stupid enough to draw attention to our organization." I headed toward the table saw, flicking the on button for a few seconds. The whirring sound as it started up was particularly pleasing.

Paulo was already whimpering when he walked into the room. I waited as he was placed on the infamous red X on the floor, my uncle's attempt at being humorous.

"Mr. Nikitin. Good to see you," Paulo said and to his credit, he tried to shore up his emotions.

"I wish I could say the same, Paulo." I flipped the switch again before heading in his direction, taking my time. "I understand you've been throwing parties, Paulo. I'm certain that keeps you the toast of the town."

He swallowed hard, his body trembling. He wasn't in shackles and I had no intention of beating him to a pulp. I didn't handle my business that way, at least normally or any longer. I'd changed my methods and found I enjoyed them significantly more. My thoughts drifted to Damien, wondering if he'd encouraged Paulo's activities.

"I didn't mean for that kid to die. I'd thrown him out, he and his buddies. He didn't leave." Paulo sucked at being apologetic.

"A true tragedy. You do understand that you won't be selling for my organization any longer. Correct?"

A look of relief crossed his face. "Yes, sir. I'm sorry. I made a stupid move."

"Yes, you did." I walked even closer. "Here's the thing. While your behavior was egregious, what concerns me the most is the report on several of your guests. Specifically, the Colombians."

He opened his mouth, but nothing came out. However, by the way he was trembling, I could tell he knew damn good and well he'd crossed another line.

"What I need to know, Paulo, is if there was any discussion on your part with these guests regarding my organization."

"No. No, of course not," he said with more conviction in his voice than I'd anticipated. However, when he'd glanced away for a brief second, I knew he'd realized the error of his ways.

"What did you tell them, Paulo?"

"I swear to God, nothing. They asked about the product and the availability. All I said was that it was plentiful. That's it."

I glanced at Ricardo who was eager to get on with it. There were times I believed he should have been born Vladimir's son. I patted Paulo on the shoulder. "I believe you and I appreciate you being honest with me. However, the fact you fucked with my organization isn't something I can let slide by. You will be punished."

There was no particular reason I was finished being civilized other than the anger I felt for Damien and the bullshit he'd pulled over the last few months. I'd yet to glance at the jump drive but was eager to do so on the plane. With my master's in business, I certainly knew a thing or two about financials.

"No. I'm sorry. I'm really sorry," Paulo wailed.

"There is nothing worse than betraying my trust. Nothing. For all I know, you've been talking to the Colombians on a regular basis."

"No!"

I rubbed my jaw before finishing. "I think the best way to handle this is to provide your new friends with a conversational piece. That way you can let them know that I will not tolerate anyone coming into my city. Is that clear?"

His eyes were wild, all color draining from his face. Perhaps the message I'd send would put Santiago on notice. I grinned as I turned toward Damien. "I'll allow you to handle the required punishment."

Damien's smug look finally fell, the slight hint he was disturbed about the requirement pleasing me. He glanced at Paulo then back to me. "As you wish."

I walked away, nodding to Ricardo. He was meeting me at the airport. As I headed for the door, I heard the sound of the saw being flipped on once again.

It was good to have toys.

avannah

There had to be some mistake.

As the valet rolled in the cart behind me, I was so floored I knew he'd asked me a question, but I hadn't heard a single word.

"Miss?"

"Oh, I'm sorry." I laughed, the anxiety getting to me and I hadn't started. "What did you say?"

He grinned. "Everyone had that reaction the first time. Where would you like your suitcase, the master bedroom?"

Jesus Christ. There was more than one? "That would be fine." I sucked in my breath, scanning the length of the room I was in. I wasn't the best at judging sizes, but the room had to be fifty by thirty. Easily. There were windows banking the backside, the view of Duval Street absolutely stunning. Given I was one floor under the penthouse, I also had a direct view of the ocean waters. This was crazy.

When I heard him whistling, I fumbled to get cash from my purse. I had some cash and a brand new bank account with exactly the same amount of money that I had in my real one. Everything had to seem on the up and up. I had no clue what I should tip the guy. As soon as he saw what I was doing, he held out his hand.

"The tip has already been taken care of."

"By Mr. Nikitin."

"Absolutely." The young man's grin was infectious. "If you need anything, just call the front desk."

"Thank you again." When he closed the door, the adrenaline rush I'd experienced while driving had already started to wear off. I'd used the time to try to meditate, listening to jazz music until I couldn't take it any longer, switching to Disturbed. Their metal music suited my mood much better. As a matter of fact, I planned on pumping it from my phone as soon as I took a look around.

I put my purse on one of the tables, running my hand across the smooth leather of the couch. There were four of them in the room, several other chairs as well as a bar and an entertainment system that I had a feeling would baffle me.

Exhaling, I headed to the right, finding an insanely gorgeous dining room. There were chairs for twelve. I didn't even know twelve people. Laughing, I rolled my fingers across the wooden surface before heading into a darkened room, struggling to find a light. When I did, I squealed. I'd been worried that even with Maxim's generous offer, I'd be forced to eat out or even worse, hotel food. But the commercial-sized kitchen was what dreams were made of.

I spun around in a circle, allowing the moment of shock to settle. People actually traveled like this. The suite had to cost thousands of dollars a night. Why was Maxim doing this unless he suspected something?

No, I couldn't think that way. Period.

I noticed a deck off to the side and walked closer. It was private, the ocean view even closer. Just looking outside made me nervous given the height. That much I didn't need to lie about. Unable to help myself, I opened the refrigerator, shocked to find it stocked with fresh fruits and vegetables, meats and dairy products. There was also water, juice, and wine.

At this point, I was almost giddy, moving to the pantry, even more shocked at the crackers and cookies, pastas and soups. And there was a wine cabinet for red wines. "Wow." The single word echoed. Oh, I needed music.

Laughing, I returned to the living room, moving to the other hallway. There were three bedrooms, the first two lavishly decorated in their own special colors. There was an adjoining bathroom that was bigger than my living room. When I walked into the master bedroom, I was stunned. There were windows on two sides, another amazing view of the city providing a glorious backdrop. The king-size bed had at least eight pillows piled on top, the bedding luxurious. They hotel designers had even thought of adding a bookshelf full of books. As I walked closer, I realized they were current.

When I moved into the bathroom, I wasn't certain whether I could handle taking a shower or get ready in the morning. Glamorous was the only word that came to mind. Between the marble used everywhere, the large television in front of a bathtub that could easily fit six, the surround sound and intimate lighting, all I could think about was taking a bath. Maybe that's exactly what I'd do to try to calm my nerves.

If that was possible. At this point, I wasn't certain.

After a few seconds, I moved toward the window in the bedroom, leaning against it. I hadn't even been able to bring a picture of Brittany with me. I'd thought about slipping one in, but I'd followed the rules.

I had driven onto Jessie's street, catching the two of them going somewhere. Then I'd spent the next hour crying. I wasn't cut out to be a field agent, but with the promotion, I didn't have a choice.

It was time to stop thinking about Savannah's old life. After the pep talk, I headed to the kitchen. Why not have a glass of wine? I wasn't going anywhere. So, it was only one in the afternoon. This was the only time off I'd actually get until the mission was over.

Even the wines were expensive, which almost made me feel guilty. Almost. After pouring a glass, I grabbed my phone and charger, finding an electrical outlet on one of the legs of the four coffee tables, plugging it in. Then I shifted to my favorite band Disturbed, comforted almost instantly since 'The Animal' was the first selection.

With the wine in hand, I kicked off my shoes, trying to get into the role by loosening up.

By the time the second song came on, I'd had several sips and was feeling better. Then I heard pounding on the door. Shit. Was the music too loud? I turned it down, biting my lip and heading toward the door. As soon as I opened it, my throat started to close.

Maxim stood on the other side of the threshold, leaning against the frame, his long, muscular legs crossed. The look on his face was dark, his eyes more luminescent than I remembered. As usual, he was wearing a suit, Hugo Boss this time, but just as perfectly tailored as the others.

And I was dressed in jean shorts that had seen better days and a red tee shirt.

"Welcome to New Orleans." He allowed his gaze to fall ever so slowly, stopping on the glass of wine I held in my hand. "And you've made yourself at home."

"Thank you, Maxim. I wasn't expecting this. I don't know what to say."

"There's no need to say anything. Your abilities as a chef will help make the resort shine."

I could swear there was something different about him, as if he had the weight of the world on his shoulders. "I'll do my best. I guess I should meet with the chef."

"You're not on duty tonight. But you are having dinner with me."

"Not unless it's very casual; I have nothing to wear. You see what my wardrobe consists of."

He cupped my chin so quickly I was shocked. His hold was forceful, bringing me closer. "I'll handle everything, little wren. I'll drop by at six. I do not like tardiness. Do you understand?" As he rubbed his fingers back and forth, I took a deep breath.

"I've told you before, Maxim. I won't be your beck and call girl. I have far too much self-respect."

I don't know what I expected in his reaction, and I realized I could be pushing my luck but when he seemed amused, I allowed fury to show in my eyes.

Yet his touch was soft, the way he was brushing the rough pad of his thumb back and forth across my lips forcing rippling sensations to crest throughout my body. There was no look of malice in his eyes, no sense of anger, but for some reason this seemed more real to me, no longer just a game of dress-up. I was a long way from my safety net, even if there was a team located somewhere outside the hotel waiting and watching.

"*Krasivoy zhenshchinoy nuzhno dorozhit', a ne ispol'zovat'*," he said in his deep baritone.

I cocked my head, playing the role, surprised at his words. "What did you say?"

"I said that a beautiful woman is to be treasured, not used. I thought it would be a wise decision and helpful for you to

177

taste some of the dishes served in the restaurant where you'll be working. There's no hidden agenda, Savannah. However, let me be clear. I am the owner of this hotel. While I didn't place conditions on your employment, I demand respect in every aspect during the time we spend together. I hope I've made myself clear."

At least he'd laid down the gauntlet. I considered that a slight win.

Shit. I'd overblown that one. "Then yes, I'd like to have dinner with you."

"I'm glad to hear it. I will see you at six. Wear the red."

It took me a few seconds to realize what he was talking about. "You don't have to purchase any clothes for me. I'll throw together something."

He bristled, but only for a few seconds. "We've been over this. Accept my gesture."

"I don't look good in red."

As he slowly lifted his chin, the icy look in his eyes almost caused a panic attack. "Six o'clock."

"Yes, sir." Why I'd felt the need to issue the two little words, I wasn't certain, but there was no doubt he was in charge.

Of the resort.

Of his organization.

And of every aspect of my time as well as my body.

He slid his hand to my neck, squeezing for a few seconds. His hold was possessive but not threatening. As soon as he walked down the hall, I closed the door, leaning against it, shuddering to my core.

"What did you get yourself into?"

* * *

The rule of playing dress-up was that you could be anyone you wanted to be. As I stood in front of the mirror, I could see it was working. I felt stronger, more in control than I'd felt up to this point. Maxim had sent up bags and boxes from at least eight different stores. There were dresses so exquisite that I was fearful of getting something on them. He'd thought of lingerie, the primal colors keeping me tingling as well as tense the moment I'd opened the package. There were heels so tall I knew I'd break my neck, but another feeling of true elation had swept through me.

As if this was real.

He'd purchased four red dresses. All I could think about was Katherine's insistence that I seduce him if necessary. I guess I'd done a good job already. Sighing, I closed my eyes briefly.

I'd been told that during long missions, some undercover officers became the person they were portraying, unable to return to their real persona afterward. I'd stood in front of the mirror, unable to recognize the woman staring back. She appeared harder than just days before, her eyes no longer shining as they'd once done. It was almost as if I'd aged several years overnight.

But as I stood in front of the door, trying to find the courage to open it, I allowed myself to feel beautiful. As soon as I opened it, the look in Maxim's eyes spawned a flurry of butterflies in my stomach.

He seemed stunned by my change in appearance, so taken aback that he didn't have anything to say for the first few seconds. Then he muttered in Russian, thinking that I wouldn't understand.

"She will become my weakness."

I smiled, locking eyes with his. "It's customary to say something in a language your date can understand."

"I said that you were the most beautiful woman I'd ever seen."

"Oh, really? A lot of words in English for what you said in Russian."

He laughed, but took a glance over my shoulder, as if expecting he'd find someone else inside. "You have managed to catch me in a lie. That is rare. I said that you will become my weakness. That's not good for a man in my position."

"Your enemies?"

"Yes, you do understand. You look stunning. Red is definitely your color."

"You knew my size."

As he cocked his head, his eyes slowly traveling to the high heels that were already hurting my feet, I sensed he was devouring me with them. "Yes. I did." There was no explanation, no romantic quip, just his usual arrogant certainty.

"Everything you purchased is beautiful. Please make certain and take the cost out of my paycheck."

His smile returned, but so did the dominating coldness in his eyes. "Sadly, you would need to work for me for many months before you could afford them. Consider the items gifts for coming to my rescue."

"You don't seem like a man who needs to be rescued from anything."

"Then it's apparent you don't know me very well. Shall we?"

"Of course." I grabbed the small clutch with my things, closing the door behind us.

"You seem nervous."

"Should I be?"

His laugh was subtle. "That depends on if you aren't who you say you are." His voice seemed strained, as if he'd dealt with the very issue recently.

"I'm no one special. Just a girl trying to make ends meet."

"Then you have nothing to fear."

I took a chance, one I hoped I wouldn't regret. I laid some of the cards on the table.

"I know who and what you are, Maxim. I do read the papers and of course, I did research on the resort in Miami before I accepted the job."

"As I've said before, you are very astute. It is wise to learn every aspect of your enemy when going into battle."

Exhaling, I stopped short, lifting my head. "Should I consider you my enemy?"

He backed me against the corridor wall, pressing the full weight of his body against mine. "A vulnerable woman should always consider anyone they meet an enemy, Savannah. Rules of the street." He lowered his head and I sensed he was observing my reaction. I didn't waver, didn't allow him the satisfaction of seeing he'd disturbed me in any way. When I tilted my chin, dragging my tongue across my lips, he took the bait, capturing my mouth.

In my line of work, there was specific training on how not to get swept up in any emotion involving the individual being investigated. But there hadn't been any classes on avoiding extreme attraction. My body betrayed me instantly, desire roaring through every cell and bone. I wanted this man.

His touch.

His passionate kisses.

His mouth on my sex.

His cock buried inside.

And he wanted it too.

We both got caught up in the moment, the intimacy we shared explosive. He swept his tongue inside, still crushing his body against mine. The way the hard ridge of his cock pressed into my stomach left me with butterflies, my heart racing. He was so powerful in all things, his sexual appetites keeping me close to the edge.

When he broke the kiss, he wrapped his hand around my throat, using his thumb to push my head back. A husky growl rumbled from deep within him as he dragged his rough tongue along my jawline, nipping my chin with his teeth then moving his mouth over my pulse of life. The passion ignited my entire core, leaving me breathless and incapable of thinking. But somewhere deep in my mind, I knew he was making certain I realized he had my life in his hands.

To fuck and feast and finish.

That made the game we were playing that much more exciting.

A hazy swirl formed around my eyes as I blinked, the sensations he was creating like licking flames. Soon, I would be consumed, and tonight was important. I couldn't get lost in the moment.

Or in the man.

He slowly raised his head, taking a single finger of his other hand, rolling the tip down my neck to the deep V plunge of my bodice. There was something enigmatic about the way his eyes followed the slow but deliberate trail, a sly smirk crossing his face.

"A girl who lives alone must be on her guard at all times."

"Yes."

We were suspended in time as he shifted his thumb across the material to my fully taut nipple, rolling it ever so slowly in easy circles.

My legs were trembling, the haze getting thicker.

"You will learn many things tonight, little wren, but you must open your mind. And you must place your trust in me. I'm the only man who can fulfill your needs."

My pussy muscles clenched and released several times, my panties damp and the scent of my raging hunger floating between us. I'd never been this keyed up, my throat threatening to close.

He lifted his gaze as he'd done before, his chest rising and falling.

"I do trust you." I wasn't completely lying. As long as he believed that I was his new chef, no harm would come to me. All the horrible stories I'd heard had to be exaggerated. He wasn't a butcher, just a man forced to take over a brutal empire.

"I'm very much looking forward to our explorations together." He broke the magic spell, pulling me away from the wall and pressing his hand on the small of my back.

In complete control.

As we walked, I tried to shove aside the attraction, returning to the job I'd been assigned.

"Are your enemies always looking for a weakness?"

"Any leader worth his salt will hunt down every scrap of information regarding their enemies to possibly use later. Blackmail. Extortion. Whatever it takes." He pressed his thumb against the keypad much as I'd done, programmed into the system when I'd checked in. The elevator door opened immediately, and another lump formed in my throat. As I eased to the back of the empty space, he moved toward me with the predatory look in his eyes, the door slowly closing behind us. "Yes, little wren. There are men who would enjoy eating you alive if for no other reason than to get to me. It's something for you to keep in the back of your mind."

"Does that mean I'm in danger?"

He took a deep breath. "That means you need to watch your surroundings. I'll have one of my men keep you out of harm's way."

"A bodyguard? Really? How can you live that way?"

Chuckling, he came closer, placing his hands on either side of me against the elevator wall. "My life isn't easy, Savannah, but it's all I've ever known."

"But it's dangerous."

He lowered his head, his lips coming dangerously close to mine. I found myself tipping my head, almost as if daring him to kiss me.

The way he hovered over me was devastatingly possessive and the same feelings I'd had before, the deep emotions he'd evoked that had left me wanting more resurfaced.

"Danger is exciting, a way to remind ourselves that we're very much alive," he said and brushed a strand of hair from my face.

"You make it sound like a game."

He seemed to concentrate on easing the piece of hair away, tucking it behind my ear before answering. "In many ways it is. A game of the fittest, the strongest, and the most cunning."

"It sounds like one you enjoy."

"In some ways, yes. In others, it gets old. But I've never lost anything, and I don't plan to in the future." As soon as he brushed his lips across mine, the slight ping of the elevator announcing our floor sounded in our ears. He sighed, cutting his eyes to the left before pulling away. "But I assure you that the excitement of winning is worth losing everything." He backed away by two steps, taking my hand and leading me from the cold box.

"Then you really are a bad man."

I was shivering and I sensed he knew it, gripping my fingers as if worried that our connection would be broken. If he cared that others were staring at us, it wasn't evident.

His laugh was genuine. "Yes." It was a simple admittance but one he felt comfortable with. "But don't believe all you've read about me. I don't hunt and eat babies for breakfast."

"Did someone actually say that about you?" As soon as he dropped my hand, I caught a glimpse of a weapon inside his jacket. This wasn't just dangerous. This was suicidal.

"You'd be surprised what has been printed, little wren."

No, I actually wouldn't.

I was as self-conscious as I'd ever been, trying to recognize faces from the photographs of known associates that I'd memorized.

"This hotel was heavily damaged in hurricane Katrina. I spend millions of dollars refurbishing it but initially a part of the facility was used as a refuge for those who lost everything. Our chefs worked round the clock providing meals since the kitchen was spared. It was important to give back to the community."

I wasn't certain why he was telling me this other than to negate the perilous aspect of his business. Or perhaps he wanted to paint himself in a light that allowed me to see something good inside. Whatever the case, I was pleasantly surprised, more so than I should admit even to myself.

When he led me into the dining room, there wasn't a set of eyes not watching. He was tempting fate. I'd been told I'd have a target placed on my head from the connection alone. I had weapons and ammunition, finding a suitable hiding place. But I hadn't been able to carry one with me tonight and that made me nervous, my heart in my throat.

He led me to a private dining room, a pianist already tickling the ivories. His smile had turned into a smirk and as he eased one of the two chairs out for me, I did everything I could to ignore my raging nerves. If I could pull off tonight, maybe it would get easier.

"I took the liberty of ordering several dishes as well as wine. I hope you enjoy my selections." Maxim was so formal in his actions, opening the wine himself. It would seem he was an expert at everything he did.

"That's fine. I'm excited to taste what you've selected." As he sat down, I allowed myself to enjoy being across the table from him.

He sat back, studying me intently as he swirled the wine in his glass. And when he spoke, another icy chill formed in my heart. "Then it's time to begin your training."

CHAPTER 12

"*If you know the enemy and know yourself, you need not fear the result of a hundred battles. If you know yourself, but not the enemy, for every victory gained you will also suffer a defeat. If you know neither the enemy nor yourself, you will succumb in every battle.*"

Sun Tzu—The Art of War

Maxim

I'd left Mother Russia with two small suitcases. Nestled inside one of them had been a watch box my father made himself, something I remembered seeing, at least from the perspective of a three-year-old. Then he'd given it to me as a gift when I was a small child, telling me that one day I'd wear the watch in remembrance of family, loyalty, and respect. The quote had been inside on a card, scribbled in his terrible handwriting. I'd been far too young to under-stand the meaning or appreciate the gift. However, the watch had been placed on my wrist the day I'd become second in command of my uncle's empire.

And it would need to be removed from my cold, dead body.

Perhaps there were several reasons why the quote had come to mind in the middle of having dinner with the divine Savannah. How many warnings regarding women had Vladimir given me over the years? Enough it was second nature to ensure that either the girl entering my life was there to fuck and reap monetary rewards or was a person of honor in going about her day-to-day life.

My little wren had passed the first test in Miami. As I'd grilled her about the food the chef had presented to our table, I'd asked her to comment on each dish, explaining what she'd do differently. In other words, I'd tested her credibility. Those skilled in the art of deception could easily represent themselves as anything they wanted with a few lessons. However, they always faltered when pushed.

She'd passed with ease.

While I was still partially thinking with my cock, I forced my brain and intuition to take over. She was a very special woman, albeit nervous to be tested in front of her boss. That was to be expected. Test number two passed. The third test would push her boundaries. If she was someone working to bring down my empire, she'd find an excuse as to why she couldn't participate in the upcoming carnal activities.

My mouth watered at the thought of forcing her to shed her clothes, completely exposed to a group of people, more vulnerable than ever. Then she'd learn what it was like to be completely under my control.

As she sat quietly in the seat of my Mercedes, her lips pursed, the tension remained high. I'd left the festive, touristy area of the city, heading to a club I owned. The location was private, by invitation only, and the members were vetted carefully. Once the dues were paid, members could enjoy any dark proclivity they hungered for, no matter how sadistic it might be.

It had been months since I'd walked inside, other than a brief check on the employees and how the establishment was being run the last time I'd been in New Orleans. I was usually all about business. Tonight I would enjoy the fruits of my labor.

"Where are we going?" she asked quietly.

"A club I own."

"A club?" Savannah tilted her head, studying me carefully. "Do you dance?"

Chortling, I made the turn onto the last street. "While there is a small dancefloor for relaxation, it's not that type of club."

"Oh."

Her whispered word allowed me an indication that she knew exactly what I was talking about. There was nothing better than introducing someone to the ecstasy and agony of the darkest kind of pleasure.

As I pulled into valet parking, she stiffened even more. I threw another look in her direction, the ache in my loins increasing. The moment I'd seen her in the red dress I'd specifically selected from a catalog of beautiful attire, my mind had wondered to all the filthy things I wanted to do her.

And I would.

Over and over again.

"Good evening Mr. Nikitin," Peter said as I handed him the keys. "Will you be staying long?"

"A few hours. Keep the vehicle close."

"Yes, sir."

I buttoned my jacket, hiding the weapon I always carried, scanning the parking lot as I moved to the other side of the Mercedes. With the shipment date this close, I couldn't rule out an attempt on my life.

As soon as I opened the door, Savannah swung her legs to the pavement, extending her hand as if knowing I'd never allow her to roam the rooms of Club Threshold alone. Once inside, there would be dozens of patrons curious to learn the identity of the only woman I'd ever brought to the club.

I kept hand on her back possessively as I walked us through the main doors, giving each bouncer a nod. They said nothing, but I knew they'd made mental note of the woman I'd brought with me. They'd been highly trained, capable of crushing the windpipe of anyone who attempted to destroy the sanctity of the club.

The music had a tribal vibe, the neon lights in the main portion of the club reflecting the eagerness of the members and their guests. It was a safe zone, more casual in certain ways than the exclusive training and exhibition rooms. Then there were the private rooms located on the top two floors, men and women paying an additional hefty sum for the use for one to four hours.

I'd yet to decide just how far I'd go with Savannah.

My private table was never invaded, the location on one of the balconies allowing me to overlook several hundred feet. She seemed to know instinctively where we were going, keeping her head held high as she walked up the slender curved staircase leading to the intimate space. While her outward actions provided an indication to those who didn't know her that she was used to a fetish club, I could smell her fear. The lingering scent had furrowed its way into my system, keeping my cock hard and my sadistic needs on the forefront of my mind.

Within seconds of sitting down, a waiter appeared from the shadows, presenting a bottle of Cristal champagne, pouring two glasses within seconds. It was at that point her expressionless face failed her, a look of amusement easy to read. She took a few seconds to glance around the perimeter of the club before shifting her body to face me.

"People treat you like a king," she said as she leaned over the table.

"It comes with the territory."

"And what territory is that, Maxim? The one where you rule over two cities, forcing men and women to obey your every command? Or the brutal one where blood rains in the streets if an enemy dares to cross your path?"

There were few people in my life who'd been so blunt, the questions accusatory. Ordinarily, instant anger would arise, my retaliatory actions predictable. Not with her. She was pushing my buttons on purpose, trying to ascertain just how much control I'd have over her.

And her rebelliousness kept me fully aroused.

"Would it surprise you if I said both?"

She laughed and wrapped her hand around the crystal flute. "Nothing with you surprises me any longer. You simply grew up with a silver spoon in your mouth, expecting to be catered to. It's understandable that you believe everyone around you owes you something. And if they don't pay their dues, you have no problem exterminating or destroying."

For a few seconds, she managed to accomplish something few people in my world ever did.

Made it difficult for me to think of a retort.

Her words were still biting, enough so as I leaned across the table, I wrapped my fingers around a thick strand of hair, yanking her forward. "From a woman recently employed by the monster you so aptly described, I'd categorize your statement as fascinating."

"I speak my mind, Maxim. You're not hiding who and what you are."

I eased back in my seat, unable to take my eyes off her. "True enough. I never intend on hiding from anyone under any circumstances."

Savannah lifted her glass, offering a toast. "Here's to both of us being true to ourselves."

As we clinked glasses, my fascination for her only continued to increase. While her words were said with conviction, no hint of deceit, I sensed she was hiding something from me. Something personal.

"I'm curious, Savannah. What makes you happy in life?"

"Is this a trick question?"

"You should know by now that's not my style."

She took a few seconds to answer. "Simple things. Movies on a Friday night when I can stay up as late as I want to. An ice cream cone after a walk in the park. Digging my toes into the sand by the ocean. Even building sandcastles." Her laugh forced my cock to throb even more, the ache building. "I know that sounds silly to a man who likely has every expensive toy in the world, but I don't need things. I just want to smile and be able to relax. That's what makes me the happiest. I'm curious, given everything you have, every-thing you could buy by making a phone call, what makes you the happiest? You know the kind of happy I mean, giddy and tingling all over."

It was easy to laugh seeing the joy in her eyes when she was prodding me. "I don't think I've ever been giddy in my life."

"Then you are missing out." She continued laughing as she lifted her champagne glass, hiding behind the tall crystal.

The luminescent lighting allowed me to catch a perfect glimpse of her reddening face.

At that moment, I wanted to shower her with all the finer things in life. Jewels. Cars. Trips. Whatever she wanted. But I knew without a doubt what I purchased wouldn't be received in the light I'd intended. "I'll let you in on a little secret. I've yet to find anything that truly makes me happy."

Her face instantly fell and without hesitation, she reached across the table, entwining her fingers with mine. "That is so terribly sad, Maxim. I'm so sorry. Beaches don't allow you to grin, showing off that dimple you have?"

I inadvertently placed my hand on my chin, snickering after doing so. "I can't say I've ever dug my toes in sand."

"Oh, my gosh. Add that to your bucket list."

When I narrowed my eyes, she rolled hers. "A bucket list?"

"You've been kept hostage somewhere. That must be the reason. A list of things you must do before you die."

I already had one, only the items on that list would terrify her.

Hunt and kill the assassin responsible for gunning down my parents.

Slice my dagger across my uncle's neck.

Eliminate every soldier loyal to the fat pig.

"Duly noted," I told her.

"Hmmm… You're a hard case. Licking dark chocolate off fresh strawberries?" she asked, squeezing her hand around mine. The electricity was extremely high, my hunger building to the point our conversation would need to be cut short.

"Nope."

"Taking a walk in the rain?"

"I've done that, but not because I had to."

"Making a snow angel?" I obviously had an odd expression from the way she laughed after asking the question. "That's where you lie in the freshly fallen snow with your arms and legs together at first then opening your legs and lifting your arms to shoulder level several times."

"Sounds cold," I teased, curious as to her reaction.

"Goodness. Where did you grow up and what did your parents do with you for fun?"

I hadn't realized my expression must have darkened until she recoiled.

"I'm sorry. That was rude," she said quietly.

"No, it wasn't at all. I grew up in Russia, at least until I was five years old. Then I was brought to America after spending two years in an orphanage that shouldn't be allowed to house wild animals. And I assure you my uncle wanted nothing to do with playing with a child he had no interest in." I hadn't bothered to explain my situation to anyone other than Ricardo, and even then, my statement had been full of rage.

Not sadness.

She blinked several times. "Oh, Maxim. I'm so, so sorry. I didn't mean to pry."

"You didn't pry. Let me guess, my little wren. You had the perfect Hallmark family complete with special holidays and birthdays." Now I knew that what I'd seen in her gorgeous eyes had been real. She had a secret she hid from the world and if I had to guess, I'd say it was a tragic of a story as mine. However, my instinct continued to dig at my subconscious.

"In my dreams, Maxim. My father died in a car accident when I was three. My mother did her best to take care of me, but we lived in squalor. However, we were happy for the most part."

"Is your mother alive?"

Her face darkened.

This time her laugh was bitter. "My mother developed cancer. She battled the disease for years. I tried to take care of her, using all my savings, but in the end, I don't think I did a good job of providing the care she needed. Our insurance system sucks. I have no extended family so in truth, I'm pretty much alone in this world." She shifted her gaze in my direction, pursing her lips. "You didn't need to hear my sob story."

Her performance was believable. I studied her face, taking several sips of my champagne. It was time to draw the line, forcing her hand. Maybe I was nothing but a wretched savage to use her apparent difficulties, but I couldn't afford to be wrong.

"Boyfriends?"

She rolled her eyes. "I was the geeky kid with glasses that no one wanted. I'm not worldly like you're used to."

"Come here," I commanded.

"Why?"

"Because I told you to."

Savannah glanced at me, her lips pursed so tightly I sensed she wanted to bolt, which is what I suspected she'd done with everyone who'd gotten close in her life. We were two damaged souls on a collision course for a violent death. She rose from her chair, walking closer. As she peered down at me, the myriad emotions running through my heart should be troubling.

At this moment, they felt freeing.

But caution was necessary.

I took her hand, rubbing my thumb across her knuckle. Then I pulled her into my lap. There was no gasp of surprise, no pushback or caustic words spewed from her mouth. When she seemed to relax, leaning against me, I made the decision that as of right now, she belonged to me. I might not be able to provide the happiness she was so obviously seeking, but I would give her what she needed in the way of protection and encouragement.

Even if I wasn't capable of love.

I also wasn't the kind of man who gave compassion or praise easily. But this woman didn't need placating. She'd forged a way in this world despite what she'd been through. She needed structure, discipline, and a strong master.

When I wrapped my hand around her throat, yanking the back of her head against mine, she dug her fingers into my knee, her breathing ragged. I caressed her skin, running my fingers up and down the length of her neck. "Pity the fools who couldn't understand they had a beautiful gem hiding underneath a haze of grit and dust. Lucky me who made the scintillating find. As of now, my *malen'kiy krapivnik*, you belong to me. No one will dare cast you aside again."

Savannah said nothing, but I felt her continued fear.

"However, I need to make something very clear to you, Savannah. You need to listen to me carefully. If you are here to try and uncover information about my organization, hoping for an arrest and conviction, then you need to understand that's not going to happen. Because I believe you're in over your head, I'll give you a single gift in allowing you to ask to leave. Then you'll check out of my hotel, and I'll never see you again."

"I told you who I am. How dare you act or think otherwise." Her jaw was clenched, but there was anger in her words. "How dare I?" I laughed in her ear, nuzzling against her neck. "I dare because I *am* a dangerous man capable of heinous acts of violent and retaliation. Now, if you're who you want me to believe you are, then you already know that I am a possessive man. That being said, you need to prepare yourself for what I will teach you."

"What is that?"

She was definitely a defiant little one. "You'll be required to submit to me and me alone. As of now, no other man will touch you ever again. As with all things, there will consequences for disobedience, punishment doled out as necessary. Is that something you think you can handle, my little wren? Do you think you can accept the darkest part of yourself, accepting the need to surrender to me body and soul even as fear of the unknown continues to furrow inside of you?" I wasn't certain if she'd answer me or not, but when the two breathless words floated from her mouth, a switch flipped deep inside. I meant what I said. She was mine.

"Yes, sir."

"It would seem you can be trained, which is a very good sign. But I will ask you this and I want a truthful answer. Would you prefer that I let my little bird fly away from her gilded cage, back to the cackling henhouse hungry to destroy my entire world? It is your last opportunity to fly free."

"You're wrong, Maxim. I need this job. I want this... us."

Us.

Her conviction was strong and very real. There was no denying the connection of the current as it seared through our combined skin.

The second I lifted the glass of champagne toward her mouth, she parted her lips without being asked. She trembled in my hold, which added fuel to the sparks that jetted between us. I poured some of the bubbling liquid inside, several beads trickling from the corners of her mouth. The moment I released my hold, she shifted on my lap, lowering her head and staring into my eyes.

Then she pressed her luscious lips against mine, encouraging them to open. The crisp, cold liquid flowed into my mouth, quickly followed by her tongue. As she wrapped her arms around my neck, she wiggled enough to create a wave of friction. The kiss became powerful, our desire off the charts. She had no way of knowing what she was doing to me, the filthy thoughts no longer an option but a requirement.

When she pulled away, I instantly grabbed her jaw, holding her close. "If you're a very good girl, I'll teach you the art of pain and pleasure, the combination the only way of experiencing true ecstasy."

"What if I'm bad?" Her heated breath washed over my face, tickling my senses.

"Then you won't like the painful experience, Savannah. That's something for you to keep in mind. One pass. That's all you'll get."

As a rush of adrenaline flowed into my muscles, I realized the hunt had already ensued and she was my prey.

Only she didn't know it yet.

I would tempt her with my darkness.

Taste her.

Train her.

Fuck her.

Then own her.

And if she betrayed me, I would destroy her. My cock was aching all over again.

"I don't need a pass." Savannah pulled back even further. "I want to learn."

I cocked my head, taking a deep breath before easing her off my lap. She truly didn't understand she'd entered into the realm of a beast. She would learn soon enough that there was no escape. "Then come with me."

CHAPTER 13

 avannah

Thump. Thump. Thump.

My heart was slamming against my chest, my throat so tight I wasn't certain I could catch my breath. Several ugly words flashed through my mind.

Fear.

Excitement.

Treachery.

The last word held more meaning tonight than it ever had before.

Maxim was onto me, just like I was told he'd been with so many other undercover operatives. But I wasn't a field agent. I was a translator, for God's sake. What the hell was I doing here trailing behind a man who'd just as soon snap my neck and toss me into the dumpster as honor the free pass he'd given me? Although strangely enough, I believed he meant it.

Maybe I wasn't the best judge of character, but I'd seen his eyes when he'd told me about his parents. He was full of rage and the need to seek revenge, but there was also such sadness inside that it was eating him alive. At least that meant he wasn't just the cold-blooded killer I'd been led to believe.

Or maybe I was as wrong about my assessment as it seemed I had been about far too many things in my life. Somehow, I had to push my fears aside or I'd crumble under pressure, which is what was happening. He was still testing me. The man was using our attraction as a measure of my loyalty.

I was in a kink club, for God's sake. I was no prude, but I'd never been inside one. The pictures I'd noticed on the internet were enough to make me terrified of stepping foot in one.

Now I had to pretend like I liked being tied up and... flogged.

As my mind shifted to when he'd flogged me before, a strange set of sensations rushed through every muscle. A part of me had been eager to accept this job, excited because of the attraction I'd felt from studying him online. Who had I been kidding with acting cavalier about this when the man carried a gun with him wherever he went?

His hold remained tight as he pulled me through the crowd of people, leading me up a set of stairs. I was surprised how elegantly the men and women were dressed, the men wearing tuxedos, the women long gowns. However, there were those who left little to the imagination, women in corsets and thongs, a thick leather or jeweled collar around their necks with a leash attached. A few were even nestled at the feet of their masters.

I wasn't certain whether I was titillated or terrified. Maybe a combination of both. Suddenly, he was taking me down a hallway, the noise from the center of the club starting to fade. He slowed his gait, finally looking over his shoulder. I must look a fright to him with huge doe eyes and a twisted expression.

When he stopped in front of a closed room, I sucked in my breath. He moved behind me, not touching me but his presence was oppressive anyway.

"I'd going to allow you to become a voyeur for a few minutes, observing as couples engage in impact play. You're to remain quiet and you're to stay by my side at all times. Is that understood?"

There was no doubt what a man like him wanted, respect without question. For now, I'd give it to him. "Yes, sir."

"Good girl." He reached around me, opening the door. I wasn't certain what to expect. The room was nothing like I'd anticipated, the posh leather sofas and chairs set up like a movie theater. Smack in the center of the room were several apparatuses, some made of wood, some created from metal of some kind.

There were at least forty people in the room, most of which were staring intently at a couple who was front and center.

The man was dressed in all black, his muscular physique reminding me of Maxim's. In his hand was a thick paddle, the piece of wood appearing to be huge from where I was standing.

The woman was completely naked, her body bent in half, her wrists and ankles shackled by thick pieces of leather. When he fisted her hair, yanking her head up at an awkward angle, I could see a ball gag in her mouth. Weren't these places required to force the use of safe words?

Maybe during impact play it wasn't required.

My entire body was trembling and as the man lifted his arm, prepared to strike her bottom, a series of involuntary shivers coursed through me. As the master started to bring the thick board down against her buttocks, her moans escalated.

And the crowd loved it, nodding appreciatively at first then murmuring through the round of discipline. After a full two minutes, maybe longer, I couldn't watch any longer. I tried to turn away, but Maxim was having none of it, wrapping one arm around my waist, the other around my throat. Then he nuzzled his head against my neck, whispering in my ear. The tone of his voice was even more dominating than before, creating a wave of excitement coursing through me.

"You will follow my orders, my little wren, or you will be punished. Watch and learn. You need to accept that you will obey."

Why was it that his statement kept me fully aroused? I shuddered as he kept his hold, and even though a part of me wanted to close my eyes, I obeyed him. Obedience. The word reverberated on my tongue, and in my mind. The draw to him was more powerful than before, his controlling actions setting ablaze a darkness that I'd had for as long as I could remember. It was as if he'd read me, all of me, able to draw out my need to taste pure sin.

As the man brought the paddle down again and again, suddenly I wanted to be her, to experience the feeling of shame from being spanked like a bad little girl in front of strangers. It was shameful, but I'd never felt so excited in my life even as a knot formed in my stomach.

Maxim eased back from his hold and almost immediately, I found myself moving closer. As I imagined being the one in her place for a second time, I sensed how wet I'd become.

"Come. We have more to see," he said as he pulled me toward the door.

I wasn't certain if he wanted me to react, but I remained quiet, the fleeting images of being the girl surrendering impossible to shove aside.

He led me down another hallway, half-open doors allowing me to glance into several other rooms. I remained surprised how many people were watching, some being guided in obvious training classes, but most were simply enjoying the carnal activities.

When he stopped in front of another door, he turned me around to face him, his expression unreadable. "I'm an observant man, Savannah. I notice almost everything. Every nuance. Every tic. Every desire. You are a very bad girl in need of attention and care, someone who will take the time to train and nurture you. Only then can you free yourself from the tight chains you've placed around yourself for years."

"You think you're that man." I heard the edge of defiance in my voice, but he seemed amused, not offended.

"I know that I am, if you'll only let go." He'd had such a powerful effect on me since the beginning that standing here in the middle of a fetish club seemed almost normal.

But the longing that continued to spiral out of control wasn't.

He led me into another room, still keeping us in the back near the wall. I was immediately drawn to the girl hanging from the ceiling, her body twisted from the thick rope holding her in place.

"This is Shibari," he said, as if I knew what he was talking about. "Japanese bondage."

I swallowed hard as she was spun around, the front of her forced to face the crowd. I didn't need to be any closer to notice how wet and excited she was. While blindfolded, her moans were easy to hear.

My vision was suddenly foggy as the master selected something from a table near the swinging rope. As he brought it forward, I strained to see what it was. It looked like a small flyswatter. He wasted no time, bringing it down against her exposed pussy lips.

People in the crowd moaned their appreciation.

I yelped as if an injured dog.

"Oh, come now, my little wren. You can't tell me that you aren't imagining the one being tied in position, waiting for me to provide you with the pain you crave."

"No, I…" But in attempting to answer, I knew I'd only be lying. Every time I moved, my nipples shifted back and forth across the material of my dress and the sensations became almost too much to bear.

"Don't lie to me." As if knowing my body well enough to realize I was in distress, he slid his arm around my abdomen, pinching my nipple through the material.

I bit back a moan, my entire body shaking. And in the next few seconds, I could see myself as the mysterious woman, my pussy being whipped. When the man dipped down, rolling his tongue up and down her pussy several times, I slumped against Maxim's hold.

And I wanted to be her more than anything.

There was a strange series of vibrations that found its way into every cell and muscle, tugging at the good girl inside of me. But I couldn't surrender to him, not so easily, even if every part of me wanted to.

The pressure of what I was doing versus the building need was petrifying, a sense of fight or flight kicking in. I chose to flee, racing out of the room, expecting Maxim to be right behind me. For some reason, the catacomb of the hallways became disorienting, making it impossible to find my way out into the main room. I made turn after turn, seeing nothing familiar. Then as near panic settled in, I stopped, backing against a wall and trying to catch my breath.

My mind must be playing tricks on me because I heard wails coming from inside one of the rooms. I'd noticed the soundproofing panels so how could I be right? I closed my eyes, my mind saturated from the sounds of passion. Then I felt his presence looming over me as it had done so many times before.

"You disobeyed me," Maxim said quietly. His deep voice resonated somewhere inside of me, echoing in my ears.

"Yes."

"You do know what that means, don't you?"

I licked my lips, hating the fact my throat was completely dry, my voice cracked. I nodded my head, but he crowded closer, an indication that my acknowledgment wasn't good enough.

"I need to hear you say it." His command was darker, more aggressive.

"Yes, sir."

"What is it that you need for your infractions?"

Blinking, I could feel tears of frustration forming. While my mouth might be dry, my pussy was aching and wet, the need continuing to build. I did what I could to control my nerves before answering, "Punishment."

"Good girl. You're correct. Pain before pleasure. Are you ready, my little wren?"

And I reacted without thinking any further.

"Yes, sir."

He held out his hand, squeezing as if reassuring me. I had no way of knowing where he was taking me, but when he headed into another one of the rooms, I could swear he'd set me up, knowing I'd disobey him. I wanted to be angry, to fight him off, but the longing to feel like the woman in the other room was far too enticing.

There weren't as many people inside, but enough that I was immediately self-conscious, my heart racing. Was he really planning on disciplining me in front of them?

When he led me to the front of the room, every inch of my skin became heated, the warm flush of embarrassment sliding up from my chest stifling my breath all over again. I couldn't look anyone in the eyes, but they were certainly paying attention to me. I could also hear their wheels turning as questions were forming, one after the other.

Who is that girl?

What is she doing with Mr. Nikitin?

Is she his submissive?

I closed my eyes, allowing him to lead me to whichever spot he was taking me. When he stopped, he lowered his head, whispering in my ear, "Remove your clothes."

"Is it necessary?" I almost told him I'd be a very good girl, even though I knew it wouldn't matter.

"Yes."

The single word sent a few bottle rockets off in my mind. I opened my eyes, gazing into his. Of course he was pushing my boundaries as I'd pushed his earlier, trying to determine whether his instincts were correct. I had to go through with this.

You want to.

No, I didn't.

Yes, you do.

The yin and yang of my emotions added to the sick rush of adrenaline that kept me panting continuously. As I turned away from the audience, I realized there could be nothing more embarrassing than what was about to happen. A tumble of guilt rushed into my system, clashing with the reason I was here in the first place. If I didn't pass this test, there was a good chance I'd end up dead, his ancient dagger used.

I used the adrenaline flow to push me forward, ignoring the fear and anxiety that had built to a suffocating level. My fingers were freezing, stiff as I tried to remove the dress, the selection he'd orchestrated preventing me from wearing a bra. A crazy thought drifted through my head that I only had to take off two pieces of clothing.

"Leave the heels on, baby." The words weren't said but tickled the back of my mind.

As I folded my clothes, I heard Maxim speaking to the men and women arranged to view my humiliation. While I wasn't concentrating on what he was saying, I assumed he was telling them what a bad little girl I was.

"Turn around, my little wren."

I'd never been the kind of girl to show off my body so when he commanded me to expose myself fully, the panic all but closed off my throat. Goddamn him for doing this to me. I wanted to hate him, to scratch his eyes out, but I continued to remind myself of what I was doing, the importance of having him arrested before he could hurt or kill anyone else.

As he led me to a table that had straps on the sides, more attached to the legs, I wanted to race away, but I was locked into this moment.

He didn't bother asking me to get into position, easing me over the edge of the metal platform, taking his time securing one wrist then the other. I was surprised when he didn't bind my legs.

"Don't do this," I said without thinking.

He moved closer, allowing me to see his face. "That will cost you five additional strikes of my belt. I've told you before that for every misdeed, there will be consequences. You admitted your wrongdoing so it's time for you to accept your fate."

Maybe he thought he was being kind to me by not shackling me the way the other girl had been or by not using the same type of wooden paddle, allowing the humiliation to drag me further into his sadistic world. But with knots in my stomach and wetness between my legs, I wasn't certain I could handle what he was about to do.

Because I also knew that the spanking was just the beginning.

He rolled his fingers down my spine and I sucked in my breath, resting my cheek against the cold, hard steel. In trying to keep my composure, I was tearing up all over again, hating myself for doing so. Yet until this man had dropped into my life, I'd never been spanked before in my life. Not once.

When he slipped his fingers between my legs, touching my swollen, slick folds, I couldn't stop a moan. Only seconds later, I was aware he was removing his belt, the sound alone keeping the knot swirling in my stomach.

I could also hear the creaking of seats, as if everyone had moved to the edge in anticipation. Why not eat popcorn at the same time? The thought was revolting but allowed me to concentrate on the hatred swarming my mind for a few seconds.

Then he brought the strap down and I was forced to bite my tongue, instantly tasting blood. The last thing I wanted to do was cry out, allowing the club members to hear. I tried to hold my breath as Maxim sliced the belt across both my bottom and my upper thighs several more times, shocked that I felt nothing.

Absolutely nothing.

Then he delivered dozens, his belt whipping through the air continuously. I was certain every person in the building heard my cry of anguish, even over the music. I did every-thing I could to keep the tears of frustration away, but as a single tear slipped past my lashes, I watched it fall in slow motion to the table. *Fade away. Think about something else.*

But the something was the very reason I was putting myself through this. Another tear fell. Then another. But as the sting turned into anguish, shooting down the backs of my legs, it was closely followed by another even nastier realization.

I was so completely aroused that images of Maxim's naked body formed an impenetrable block in my mind.

I bit my lower lip, furious with myself for not being a better actor. And for not hating him the way I needed to in order to survive.

The cracking sound of his wrist jarred my senses, a single whimper escaping. He leaned over, raking hair from my face before trailing his fingers across my shoulders and down my arm. "You're doing very well, my little wren. You will be rewarded."

Rewarded? What other humiliating experience was he going to force me to go through?

I could hear rumblings in the crowd of people talking amongst themselves, likely asking what I'd done to receive this kind of punishment.

Then I had to remind myself that this was a kink club, my round of discipline considered mild. Why were they even watching, to please the owner of the club and nothing more? That's what it had to be. He was mocking me, trying to get me to break down, confessing my sins. Well, the bastard didn't know what I was made of. He would never get a confession.

He resumed the spanking and I tried to force myself to shut down, ignoring both the incredible sensations as well as the agony tearing through me. Yet the longing I continued to feel for him churned deep within, spiraling almost out of control. I wiggled on the table, my breathing shallow.

I'd lost count of how many strikes he'd issued but my bottom was sore and aching, the red-hot heat searing every inch of skin. It became oppressive, crushing down on every cell and molecule in my body.

When he stopped, the only sound I heard was the rapid beating of my heart. He caressed my bottom, taking his time, his tender touches surprising me. I was shocked how much my skin was tingling, the ache slowly fading as another wave of desire coursed through me. I cinched my eyes shut as he opened my legs, brushing the backs of his fingers along the inside of my leg.

"You're such a beautiful woman. You could be a queen."

Was he dangling a prominent position in front of me, acting as if I could possibly mean something to him? Or was this just for show? I took several shallow breaths, still trying to fade away into something that would allow me to lose myself in a pleasant moment.

But the electricity shooting through every muscle dragged me back to the moment, my pulse racing.

He continued teasing me, sliding his finger up and down my quivering pussy. Then he walked away, the sound of his shoes on the tile floor all I could concentrate on. When he unfastened the shackles, I breathed a sigh of relief, praying the session was over.

Maxim bent down next to me, his expression carnal. Possessive.

He was a man preparing to take what he wanted without hesitation or remorse. What he believed he deserved.

All of me.

Inhaling in an exaggerated fashion, he glanced down the length of me before speaking. "Now, I'm going to shower you with the kind of pleasure you deserve."

"Why, because I was a good girl?"

The twinkle in his eyes was full of amusement, but as with every other aspect about him, the look on his face held an aura of danger. He wanted to keep me on edge, unable to find my center around him. So far, he'd been very good at doing so. I had to find a balance around him instead of spiraling out of control.

He stood, every move he made methodical. Then he returned behind me, driving his fingers past my swollen folds.

I pressed my palms against the table, pursing my lips to hold the moan of pleasure. Nothing could have prepared me for his next move, yanking me onto my back, lifting my legs. I was completely thrown by his actions, even if I'd suspected that he hadn't been finished with me yet. He was driving me to as uncomfortable a point as I could tolerate, hoping I'd submit or break.

There was only one choice.

As he spread my legs wide open, I lowered my arms to the cold steel, trying to control my breathing. The sexy smirk remaining, he rubbed both his hands on the insides of my thighs, rolling his fingers all the way to my pussy then backing away, teasing me relentlessly.

I kept my eyes on him, refusing to blink. His eyes were enigmatic, drawing me into the darkness. Waves of goosebumps popped along every inch of my skin, and I shifted my gaze to the LED lights pulsing in the ceiling. When he leaned over, blowing across my wetness, I wiggled just enough I was reminded of the harsh spanking. But as strange as it would sound to anyone else, the rush of excitement and the stinging sensations melded together into something so powerful I wasn't afraid of what he'd do.

I should continue to be ashamed, but my skin was seared from his intimate touch, filthy fantasies rushing through my mind, one after the other. The first swirl of his tongue around my clit made me shiver, the second creating a spark and the third allowing the fire to begin consuming me inch by inch. I could be anybody I wanted to be, enjoying myself without reservations.

He fell into a rhythm, licking up and down several times. I was lost to the sweet release, longing to have his cock buried deep inside.

Perhaps that would come later after I'd proven myself.

Maybe he was ripping off the armor I'd surrounded myself with. I turned my head to the side, concentrating on my breathing as stars floated in front of my eyes.

Maxim wrapped his arms around my thighs, holding me in place as he began to feast. While the audience remained, I managed to block them out, allowing his husky growls to keep me electrified. My heartbeat was in overdrive, butterflies swarming my stomach in a frenzy. I took shallow breaths, struggling to keep from moaning.

But when he sucked on my clit, several whimpers escaped my mouth.

"You're hot and wet, my little wren, and very sweet." His murmur filtered into my ears, but I barely heard him.

However, his exotic cologne created another rush, just like the adrenaline sweeping through me, both leaving me drunk on need and desire. I couldn't believe how much I was enjoying this, embracing the darkness that had always been there. He hadn't just awakened the woman inside. He'd ripped her from her cocoon, exposing her to another world, one full of rapture.

As he drove several fingers inside, flexing them open, I couldn't stop panting. My skin was on fire, my mind now mush. He was intense with everything he did, a brutal artist who tormented me by bringing me close to the edge then pulling back, leaving me panting. I was ready to beg him to allow me to come.

"*Moya ochen' plokhaya devochka*," he muttered. I was his very bad girl.

And for tonight, I was happy that I was.

I bucked against him, jerking up from the table as a climax jetted into me like wildfire. This was crazy, and I'd lost all sense of reality, incapable of separating reality from this incredible fantasy.

"Oh. Oh. Yes. Yes." I tossed my head from side to side, noticing the people in the audience but their figures were blurry given the ecstasy rolling through me.

He held me in place, keeping my legs wide open. Only when I stopped shaking did he roll his lips up and down the inside of my thigh before pulling back. "Open your eyes, little wren."

I obeyed his command, my vision still foggy.

"That is just the beginning of the kind of ecstasy I can and will provide."

If I remained a good little girl. He didn't need to say the words. I could tell by the look in his eyes that he was issuing another challenge, still ensuring that I had no plans of betraying him.

His chest rose and fell as he eased my legs down, planting his hands on either side of me.

"You will be enjoyable to train."

He narrowed his eyes, the look on his face even more possessive than before. Then he lifted his head, staring at the audience. "Please enjoy the remainder of your evening. This show has concluded."

I held my breath, both nervous and excited.

As the audience members immediately began to leave, he slowly lowered his head. "But you and I are just getting started."

CHAPTER 14

" *Hidden in each of us is a secret person, often unknown even to ourselves.*"

—*Dr. Jean Wolf*

Savannah

A secret person.

I was hiding the real person from Maxim, more convincingly than I'd believed possible. It had been easy to mirror myself yet live a lie, enjoying the time spent. The fact I adored the man should make me feel guilty.

But it hadn't.

Even worse, I'd been able to see how much I'd been hiding from myself, as if I had two personalities. The good girl who followed the rules and the one who'd been shown a taste of life that had kept me ignited, longing for more.

After our exciting night together, we'd shared an incredible partial day, Maxim showing me parts of the city.

Now, three additional days had passed with no engagement. I'd seen him several times, always conducting business, twice in the restaurant. However, since our passionate time spent together, he'd been distant. That made me nervous, so much so that I initiated contact with my handler. To hell with the rules. I'd learned nothing more of interest, although the amount of activity within the hotel, men coming and going from the private elevator leading to Maxim's penthouse suggested a change in the shipment.

He'd had roses delivered to my suite, three dozen red roses with a simple note.

Until another tomorrow.

It was cryptic and utterly terrifying. I'd constantly looked over my shoulder, sleep difficult. Even the few hours I'd gotten each night had been filled with filthy fantasies, my pussy wet every time I woke.

The fire was still ignited from the night of passion. He'd taken me three times that night, once in the club and twice in my bedroom.

Then he'd left without initiating another date or suggesting additional time spent at the club. Maybe he'd gotten his fill.

My stomach was in knots, every word he'd said to me that night playing over and over again. I couldn't make sense of what he was trying to accomplish with me, other than making me hunger for him even more.

I'd followed through with the duties I'd been hired for at the resort, finding a decent enough rhythm that I hadn't caused any undue recognition. Maybe Maxim had told the chef to take it easy on me, the man patient in answering questions, praising me several times. I'd remained a nervous wreck, trying to hide it as best I could. At least with being the new kid on the block, I had an excuse for my anxiousness.

As I headed to my car, I scanned the parking lot, a part of me anticipating seeing Maxim or one of his soldiers. No one seemed to notice me. After climbing in and closing the door, I sat still, trying to stop shaking. What I was doing was as risky as everything else. But it had to be done.

While the burner phone was untraceable, in my mind Maxim could trace anything.

A few minutes later, I located the coffee shop I'd been directed to, heading inside and purchasing a coffee. Then I moved around the facility, ensuring I recognized no one in the crowded location. I'd been instructed to sit at a table away from the window, bringing a book with me to ensure my cover wouldn't be blown. No one could see the table from the store window, but I was still nervous. It was ten minutes before a man approached, sitting down without saying anything initially. Then he leaned over.

I'd never met him before, had only been told his name and that he'd worked countless covert operations during his career, spending more time undercover than any agent in the business.

"Ms. Parkins." His accent was one I couldn't place, definitely Eastern Europe. That sent a red flag into my system. He was dressed in all black, which in and of itself meant nothing. Then why was my skin crawling?

I nodded, uncertain I could find my voice. "I'm sorry. Do I know you?" I was no fool. There was always a possibility that the team had been discovered, replaced with some of Maxim's people.

"Someone here to help."

"I don't need any help. Thank you. I just came for a good cup of coffee."

He seemed amused, finally pulling out a small wallet, flashing it open so only I could see. The identification was official, exactly like the one I had remaining in Atlanta. Every aspect of my job had been erased from my house, my daughter's identity as well. Thinking about it now, a wave of sadness tore through me. The importance of this mission was hitting me harder than before. Maybe I'd been in a bubble, and it had just broken, the reality of what could happen cutting through me like a knife.

Like a dagger. Maxim's dagger.

"Satisfied?" he asked.

"For now." Eli Parker. The name in and of itself meant nothing, but it didn't match his accent.

"You shouldn't have made contact."

"I know," I finally said, noticing the deep scar on one side of his face. He noticed my gaze, smirking as he shifted his coffee from one hand to the other.

"Then what is the issue?"

"Concern over the mark's sudden lack of attention." I wasn't allowed to use Maxim's name under any circumstances. And I remained cautious, my stomach churning.

"Not unusual. Why the concern?" He shifted in his seat, appearing completely comfortable and at ease.

But listening to voices on the other end of a recording line had somehow allowed me to notice all the little things. Inflection differences, subtle tics that might not be heard by those engaged in the conversation. I'd parlayed that into my observation skills. I studied the agent as he leaned forward, the sleeves of the dark Henley shirt he was wearing sliding up both forearms. When he moved again, one arm drifting to another position, I noticed a tattoo.

The markings were unknown to me, but the symbol represented something important. I was certain of it. Another red flag popped up in my mind.

"Because of his previous interest." Now I was choosing my words carefully.

He studied me, taking way too much time doing so. I was more nervous than before.

"Any news on the shipment? I know you've grown very close to him, enough so he should have confided in you by now." The fact he'd ignored my question left a bad taste in my mouth. I shoved the coffee cup aside, once again glancing into his eyes. There was something wrong. I'd been told to rely on my instinct. This man was an imposter.

Terror rushed through me, but I refused to allow him to realize it. "Nothing new."

"You're certain."

"Very much so. I think I was just nervous. I'm fine now." I moved to a standing position and as soon as I did, I noticed another man outside the window. He was also dressed in all black.

Terror slammed against my heart and mind.

I grabbed my purse, giving him a wide smile.

"You should sit down so we can finish our discussion," Agent Parker said before I had a chance to leave the table.

"I think I was overreacting. That's all. It's best I get back before I'm missed." I didn't give him the opportunity to challenge me. I also had no intention of becoming a victim of my own stupidity. I'd found the rear exit and as I moved through the crowd, I hoped that the people standing in line would hide my departure.

I'd only have a few seconds to get away. As I started running down the sidewalk, I didn't look over my shoulder until I'd reached the corner. No one was following me. Was it possible that I'd been wrong? While I wasn't certain, I wouldn't take any additional chances until I'd managed to find a secure way to contact Chris.

My stomach was still in knots and I drove too fast, ignoring the speed limit. By the time I made it back to the hotel, I needed to find the closest bathroom. Why had I been so stupid? As I rushed into the lobby, racing past the front desk, I heard my name being called.

"Ms. Parkins. Ms. Parkins."

I ignored the imploring voice, flying around the corner to the women's restroom. The cool air hit me only seconds before the various fragrances of perfume. I pushed my way through several tourists in search of an empty stall, accidentally knocking an older lady into one of the marble walls, her bag dropping to the floor. I heard dozens of items rolling across the floor.

"I'm sorry." That was all I could manage to say.

She looked pissed, cursing at me in a high-pitched voice.

I couldn't care at this point. I slammed the stall door, crowding onto my knees, expecting to lose what little breakfast I'd eaten. When my stomach didn't cooperate, I took gulping breaths, realizing I'd just come too close to experiencing a full-blown panic attack. That had only happened once before and under entirely different circumstances.

After a minute or five, I couldn't be certain, I sat on the toilet with my head in my hands, doing what I could to calm down.

I had no idea how long I'd remained in the bathroom, but I waited until I wouldn't make a fool of myself again. After staring at my reflection in the mirror, I washed my hands, uncertain what to do from here. At this point, contacting Chris was even riskier, but if Agent Parker wasn't who he purported himself to be, then the mission would need to be aborted.

Only then I'd never get the chance to see Maxim again.

* * *

Maxim

Politics.

Russian politics to be exact. My uncle had taught me the art of playing them, as if I needed a lesson in brutality.

That's all that those who still believed in the old ways were capable of. Viktor Romanoff was a legend inside Russia, an oligarch who controlled a huge regime in Moscow. He was also a true savage, incapable of showing mercy. He was considered a friend of my uncle's, the two growing up together, alongside my father. The three had been insepa-rable for years, running the streets at ten years old similar to the way both Vladimir and Viktor ran their operations now.

At least so I'd been told.

We'd done business once years before, the occurrence leaving me with a foul taste in my mouth. I'd warned my uncle that Viktor would attempt to force an alliance, in doing so making the combined Bratva the most powerful syndicate in the world. That didn't seem disconcerting to Vladimir in the least. He'd puffed up, giving it some consid-eration. Then I'd managed to talk him out of it.

It was my belief that Viktor held that against me, which means he couldn't be trusted.

I found it interesting that Viktor had initiated a large purchase, risky doing so in America given the number of warrants issued by several countries for his arrest. Then I'd learned he'd burned several sources, including the one I'd been using for the last couple of years. The pressure from Vladimir to make this happen didn't sit well with me on any level.

Even more curious, the merciless oligarch had decided to handle the monetary transaction himself. The man never left his comfortable estate where he was surrounded by a harem of women. My gut told me he had a hidden agenda. I'd need to determine what that was. He'd been delayed in getting here, his weak reason as to why striking a nerve. He needed to be watched at all times.

I grabbed my jacket, sliding into it. This was the final meeting prior to the arrival of the shipment. I'd had the manifest altered, a small ship coming in with movie equipment. If the Feds were onto me, they'd spent time searching the cargo ship finding nothing. The shipment of party favors was arriving much later, registered in another dummy corporation no one knew about. The bait and switch wasn't my usual method of operation, but I'd felt the decision was prudent.

"Gentlemen. Nothing can go wrong tonight. If you see any sign of Colombian soldiers for the bogus shipment, allow the Feds to do their jobs," I told them.

"And the party favors?" Ricardo asked.

"When they arrive, make certain the sharks are fed."

"Yes, sir," a few of them said before heading to the elevator, Ricardo remaining.

I adjusted my cuffs then moved to the small safe. Images of Savannah's face entered my mind. Rosy lips, soft as clouds. Deep green eyes that magnetized every male when she walked into a room. She was mine, whether or not she was aware. I grabbed my Glock, popping in a magazine.

"I'm using Ms. Parkins tonight at dinner."

Ricardo whistled. "You know I don't mean any disrespect, but there's already talk of your appreciation of the new employee."

"We've gone through this before, Ricardo. I'm not kowtowing to anyone, including those within my organization. Is that clear?"

"Yes, but you've told me yourself that when a weakness is discovered, it's exploited. I'm not trying to tell you what to do, boss. You know that."

"Don't. I'll cut your tongue out if you do." Since Sergei's betrayal, I'd been more aggravated than usual, but Ricardo was the only man I'd ever let talk out of turn to me.

"You're placing her in harm's way. Maybe she's nothing but pussy to you, but if not then you need to consider she will be used against you given the opportunity."

It was something I already knew. While I wanted to tell him it was nobody's business but mine, the reality was that she was more in danger away from me than she was with me. I headed for the elevator, the door opening automatically. As I stepped inside, my thoughts drifted to the time we'd spent together. It had been especially sweet. "There won't be an opportunity. Ever. She will prove to be useful with the pig coming to dinner."

"Oh. That's right. Viktor had a thing for redheads with curvy figures."

"While I don't need to explain myself to you, I will. When he's ogling my employee, he'll let his guard down." I leaned against the elevator wall, taking a deep breath.

"I get it," he muttered, but I didn't think he did. The air between us was thick, the man still nervous. "Boss, there's something else."

I glanced in his direction and as he scratched his head, I bristled. "What?"

"Tony Sanchez is gone."

"What do you mean gone?"

I'd done little more than take a cursory look at what Damien had provided, the man obviously using his hacking skills to get into the computer system since he didn't have access. I'd yet to decide how to handle his infractions, let alone the damning information provided on the drive.

"He just disappeared. I had a couple men go to his house. It looks like he skipped town."

"No sign of violence?"

"Everything was... pristine."

Uh-huh. That was code for swept clean.

I was smart enough to know that appearances could be deceiving. I'd secured the accounts, which meant he'd been unable to access funds without authorization. "Have him hunted down."

"I thought you'd say that. I already put the word out."

"Let me know the second he's found." It would seem the word treachery was high in the organization. The realization burned deep within me.

"You'll be the first to know. The cameras are in the prepared suites," Ricardo told me as we headed into the lobby.

"Good. Wherever he goes, keep men on him."

"Already dispatched. Dinner in the hotel?"

"Yes. Then you're going to show him and his men a good time in the casino." As I headed for the front desk, I scanned the area. "Make certain Damien is the lead on this."

Ricardo stopped walking. I sensed his discord, his hatred for Damien just as strong as mine. "I don't mean to second guess you, but are you certain about that? He's decided to take Sergei's place. That's not something I need to tell you, I'm sure."

No, he didn't. Chuckling, I threw him a look. "Trust me, my friend. I do know what I'm doing." As soon as I reached the desk, a grin popped on his face.

"You're just like your uncle. Cunning as fuck."

Yes, I was finding out just how loyal Damien was to my uncle and the organization or if he was out to help himself. One more blow would open the door for Emmanuel to slide in. I refused to allow that to happen. Viktor's determination to be a part of low-level deal added another dimension of concern. Having a woman with me wasn't just disarming for Viktor. It would send a message that I wasn't on edge. That could force him to play his hand, Emmanuel as well.

The ship was due into the port tonight and nothing could go wrong.

"I assure you I'm nothing like Vladimir," I told him, turning my attention to the girl behind the counter. "Cassie, were you able to find Ms. Parkins?"

The young girl blushed as she always did when I approached. "She's in the restroom around the corner, Mr. Nikitin. I didn't have the chance to tell her you were looking for her."

"Did she seem disturbed?"

"Yes, sir."

I took a deep breath, glancing around the perimeter of the lobby again, keeping my voice low as I spoke to Ricardo. "Have a sweep done three times a day."

"What are we looking for?"

"I don't know yet, but if there's any unusual activity in the resort, the casino, the parking lot or surrounding streets, I need to know about it."

"I'll take care of it."

As soon as he walked away, I sauntered toward the set of restrooms, leaning against the wall just outside the door. After at least five minutes I checked my watch. Finally, I'd had enough. Fuck courtesy. Something had happened to her. I would slaughter anyone who dared lay a hand on what belonged to me.

I stormed inside, several of the women squealing while others gave me a hard onceover. I took long strides, moving from one side to the other. When I rounded a corner, the sight of my little wren staring at her reflection in front of the oversized mirror brought relief as well as concern. I moved forward slowly, my figure drawing her attention within seconds.

She stiffened then tried to change her entire demeanor. "What are you doing in the women's restroom?"

"Looking for you."

Her mouth twisted and she grabbed a paper towel, drying her hands before turning to face me. "I'm allowed to do what I want in my time off."

She was jittery, her hands shaking. There was also a look of fear in her eyes. "Yes, you are." When I said nothing else, she tossed the wadded paper in the trash before approaching.

"Did you need something, Mr. Nikitin?"

Now she was formal. Business had kept me from engaging in additional carnal activity, which had obviously annoyed her. Little did she know I'd kept my eye on her. However, I hadn't resorted to following her, although that might become necessary. "Yes, I do." I took her by the hand and although she tried to object, I led her from the restroom toward the private elevators. She didn't object, but she remained tense, the look on her face harried.

Once inside the steel box, I crowded her space. "Did something happen to you?"

She opened her eyes wide. "No, of course not. I went out to see more of the city and grab a cup of coffee and a beignet. It didn't agree with me."

I searched her eyes for any sign that she was lying. Then I pushed forward with my necessary agenda, relieved that she seemed no worse for wear. "Yes, they're very sweet, far too much so for me. I have a dinner engagement at the hotel tonight and I'd like you to be my guest."

She knew it wasn't a request but a command. "But I'm working tonight."

"I've taken the liberty of ensuring that you have the night off."

While she narrowed her eyes, she nodded. However, she was pensive. "I'll be happy to join you. A special occasion?"

"A business meeting. You will help diffuse the testosterone."

Her lilting laugh was enough to force my cock to full attention. She had that effect on me every time I was in her presence. "So I supposed I shouldn't flirt with your other guest?"

I crowded her space, giving her a heated look. "If you do, there will be consequences."

"I wouldn't want to be a bad girl, now, would I?"

"Mmmm... It's your choice."

"It depends on what he looks like. What time?"

"Eight."

"I'll make certain I'm all dolled up just for you."

"I was hoping you'd say that." I inched closer, but as soon as I did, she flinched just enough I noticed it. The doors opened to her floor and she skirted around me. Before she had a chance to walk out, I grabbed her arm, yanking her against me. When I cupped the side of her face, the fire in her eyes that I'd coveted from day one sparked.

"Is there something else?"

"After my business meeting, I have somewhere I want to take you."

She swallowed then smiled as she'd done so many times before. "Another club?"

"Somewhere private." As her breath skipped across my face, I had the urge to lock down the elevator for additional privacy as I'd done before.

"That sounds enticing."

I allowed my gaze to drift down the length of her before responding. "I've thought of you often."

"Have you now?" She tilted her head, her eyes dancing back and forth across mine. "I thought you forgot about me."

"That's not possible, *malen'kiy krapivnik*. My life has its share of challenges."

"I'm certain it does. But you need relaxation." She toyed with the collar of my jacket, rubbing her fingers down the lapel then patting it twice, giving me a salacious look.

"Relaxation is not what's on my mind."

Her smile was genuine. "Then what do you have on your mind?"

"Let's just say that you need to wear another one of your red dresses." I lowered my head, capturing her mouth. While she slid her arm around my shoulder, there was a slight hesitation. Still, the fire between us became combustible almost immediately, the hunger insatiable. But only seconds later, she pressed her hand against my chest, and I allowed her to back away and into her suite.

I shoved my hand on the open elevator door. "I need to be able to trust you, Savannah. Can I do that?" I was pressing the point for a reason. I needed her to work tonight to distract Viktor willingly. He was a vicious dog who'd stop at nothing to get what he wanted. Why did I continue to believe the shipment was just the tip of the iceberg?

"Yes, you can. Should I have the chef prepare a special meal?"

There was a glimmer of mischief in her eyes. "Why not? Whatever you think is appropriate."

"Excellent. Until tonight."

I leaned against the wall in the elevator, crossing my feet. "Yes. Until tonight." Whatever she was hiding was crawling closer to the surface. She kept her eyes on me as the doors started to close, but the split second before they did, a look of relief mixed with the continued fear.

Not only was she being used, she'd also been threatened.

Once I found out who, their time on earth would end.

* * *

Savannah

After Maxim had left, I'd remained frozen for a full minute, finally collecting myself enough to walk into the kitchen for some water. Then I'd started shaking. I had a bad feeling about tonight, not just because of the way Agent Parker had acted.

If he was an agent at all.

But from the look Maxim had given me. He refused to cease the endless tests of my loyalty, still unsure I wasn't out to betray him.

But my gut told me I'd been the one betrayed.

Dinner could prove to be deadly.

I was still shaken from the experience at the coffee shop, and I needed to know if I was right in my assumptions Agent Parker wasn't who he'd said he was. I couldn't risk bugs in the suite and I definitely wasn't going to go out until I learned the truth. Plus, the fact Maxim had barged into the restroom didn't add to my comfort factor. So, I stood in the massive shower with the water running, using the burner phone to dial Chris' cellphone. He'd given me his private number, which I knew was against company policy. He'd been concerned about me until I'd left Atlanta.

Maybe he knew me better than I knew myself.

I was certain I'd get voicemail when he answered. "Chris. It's me." His scattered breathing suggested surprise.

"You shouldn't be calling."

"I need your help."

He hesitated. "I've been taken off your assignment."

"What?" A shiver coursed through every muscle and I crowded into the corner of the shower. "Why?"

His laugh was bitter. "Insubordination."

My gut continued to churn, my instinct telling me to pack my things and run. Chris was the best at what he did. He had more commendations than anyone in the FBI I knew. This was Katherine's doing. God, I loathed the woman. "But I need your help."

"Is something wrong?"

"No. Yes. I don't know." My words were jumbled together. "He's not acting like himself." Why was it that I felt like I was betraying Maxim when I was just trying to do my job?

"Is this line secure?"

"I don't know if there's anywhere that's secure, but no one can hear me."

Exhaling, I could tell he was closing his office door. "What's wrong? Slow down and tell me."

"Eli Parker. Real?"

"Yeah, a damn good agent."

"What does he look like?" I'd turned on the hot water, the steam already rising, yet I couldn't seem to get warm.

"He changes his appearance all the time. That's why he's so damn good," Chris said, the concern in his voice increasing. "What's going on?"

"I followed my gut. Does he have an accent?"

"Something else he alters. I've never met him so I can't be too helpful. What happened? You're scaring me."

I was scaring him? I couldn't breathe. My mind was foggy. I needed to get out of here. No one was coming to help. Irrational thoughts kept slamming in my mind, echoes of my sister's voice telling me how much of a fool I am for taking this job.

"They're just going to use you. You're a bigger fool than I thought you were."

No. Chris wouldn't hurt me. He was my boss, a man I trusted. I sucked in my breath, trying to figure out the best way to handle this. Think like an agent.

I almost laughed at myself.

"Talk to me, Agent Parkins." His gruff voice jolted me out of my pity party.

"Can you have him checked to make certain he's the real deal?" I asked, my voice shaking.

Every time Chris hesitated my stomach dropped. "Yeah, I can do that. I just need to be careful. Getting you the information is risky." He sounded haggard, more so than I'd heard him before.

I wasn't certain whether he was talking about no longer being allowed to be involved or the possibility the phone was bugged. Nausea rolled into my stomach.

What was really going on? There were so many questions I wanted to ask but knew I couldn't. I'd dropped into the lion's den with no lifeline.

Think. Think.

"Text this number and if he's the real deal, say the salmon is fresh. If not, say you don't have any."

"Okay. I can do that. Are you really okay?"

I closed my eyes, the question loaded. "As okay as I can be, I think the venue has changed."

"To New Orleans."

"Yes."

"I can still get into the notes. Let me check the manifests of the incoming ships. Stay focused. We're almost there," he told me, more concern in his voice.

"I'll try."

"But I need you to hear me, Savannah. If I text the word abort, you get the hell out of there. Do you understand me? Don't trust anyone else other than me."

"What's going on, Chris?"

"I don't know but I'm damn certainly going to find out."

Swallowing hard, the same cold shiver I'd felt while sitting with the agent swept through every cell and molecule. "Okay."

"I'll see what I can find. Hang tight."

Trust. The word weighed heavily on my mind. Maxim had commanded my trust and I'd given it to him without hesitation. He wouldn't do anything to hurt me. Or would he? His comment minutes before meant he was still unsure of my loyalty. Now Chris wanted my trust, but he was a part of a system that had used a child to get what they wanted. I thought about my baby, my precious girl. Did she miss her mommy? Was Jessie spending any time with her? Oh, God.

As soon as I ended the conversation, I slid to the tile floor, erasing any evidence I'd just made a call. Then I tossed the phone onto the bathroom floor before pulling my knees to my chest, wrapping my arms around them.

And allowing tears to fall.

Dinner with Maxim and an unknown guest. Perhaps I'd manage to obtain the needed information Katherine and the director of the FBI were looking for. The evidence they were going to crucify him with.

Up to this point, I'd spent almost no time with a man I was supposed to help bring to justice, yet I feared that in doing so, I'd lost a part of myself.

As crazy as it sounded, as wrong as it might be, I was worried I was falling for him.

If that was the truth, I would give him my heart.

But there was no doubt I'd end up dead.

CHAPTER 15

 axim

One of the first things I'd learned in the business of the underworld was that there was no such thing as coincidences. None. They were always the tip of the iceberg when a disaster was about to happen.

In the chase to be top dog, there could only be one winner. Greed and the lust for power were the motivating factors, pushing world leaders to their breaking point. Everyone toed the line of good versus evil, often crossing from one side to the other as a matter of convenience or out of necessity. It didn't matter whether on the side of truth and justice or within the trenches of criminal activity, everyone had a price for selling their soul to the devil.

In truth, I wasn't unlike everyone I'd profiled. Brutal. Heartless. Cruel. Within my realm there was also a fine line of decency and complete lack of it, which allowed me to kill without conscience.

Nothing mattered but the bottom line.

Yet tonight I felt differently.

Because of her.

A woman who had no business being in my world. Someone with the spark of innocence and enough humanity for the both of us. Even pledging to protect her, killing anyone who dared try to take her away from me wouldn't matter in the end.

I'd be the reason for her demise, crushing her spirit as well as her soul.

Then someone else would destroy her body.

That would start an all-out war that neither city needed.

I understood and accepted all the reasons why I should send her packing.

But as I led her through the dining room of my own hotel, her hair smelling like fresh peaches, my conviction to own her was stronger than before.

She'd become my kryptonite in a matter of days, yet as always business had to come first.

I'd spent years in my uncle's shadow, learning the trade as he liked to call it. From the time I was a little kid, I'd been fascinated with the idea of the Bratva. The family-like atmosphere. The close-knit group of men who protected the three girls I considered sisters. While a huge part of me hated Vladimir, I'd developed respect for him early on given the extreme loyalty I'd seen, including two men taking a bullet so Vladimir would live. He'd been generous to the families, much like I'd been with Victoria and her daughter.

That didn't make them feel any better. They'd never fully understood their spouses' drive for power, the lure of free money for their hard work. All they'd wanted was a normal life.

I had no idea what that meant. The only sense of normalcy in my world was violent death.

That was another reason I'd only become involved with a single woman years before, but her betrayal should have been a clear warning that I wasn't cut out for a relationship of any kind.

Which is why as I pulled out the chair for Savannah, I felt more uncomfortable than I had before. The two soldiers who were sitting with Viktor had risen to their feet out of respect for the woman on my arm.

Viktor hadn't bothered.

He was so much like my uncle that it sickened me.

They backed away, now standing against the wall. They were not to be included in the festivities. He had a drink in his hand, his expression one of anger.

"I was not aware that we'd have a guest with us this evening, Maxim," Viktor said coolly.

The entire situation amused me. I'd kept Ricardo away on purpose, requiring him to continue monitoring both the incoming shipment and the surveillance cameras. Surprises couldn't be tolerated.

"I don't need to clear my agenda with you, Viktor." I sat down and as expected, a drink was placed in front of me, a glass of wine for Savannah within seconds.

Viktor's eyes sparked with fury. "Then please have the courtesy of introducing us."

"I can do that myself. Savannah Parkins," she said as lifted her arm toward him, her eyes filled with defiance. She had no idea she was engaging with a monster, but I knew she could hold her own. "And you are?"

He took her hand, pulling it close, his eyes flashing as he lowered his head, pressing kisses against her fingers.

My little wren was very good at keeping her reactions to a minimum, but I could tell she was nervous.

"Viktor Romanoff. It's a pleasure to meet such a great beauty. Tell me, dear. Are you and Maxim involved?"

Her laugh was no different than when she was with me. "No, we are just friends. In fact, he's my employer."

"She is a new chef at the resort," I said absently, noticing the gleam in his eyes. As expected, he was interested in getting to know her better.

"Friends," he repeated, giving me a cautious look. "It's good to have friends. It's good to know you can count on them to watch your back."

His subtle threat wasn't lost on me, but Viktor wasn't known for tiptoeing within his words as he was doing now.

"Yes, always." She pulled her hand away seconds later, giving me a heated look before grabbing her napkin. "I took the liberty of selecting very special dishes for tonight's dinner. Maxim mentioned this was an important meeting, so I wanted to make everything perfect."

Viktor seemed pleased, although he was already questioning why she'd been invited to sit in. I enjoyed easing back in my chair, watching his facial expressions. He wasn't a man who could hide his anger or his distrust easily.

"*Eto ne sposob vesti biznes,*" he said gruffly.

Perhaps he was right in that this was no way to conduct business, but it was my way. "*Vy pereveli depozit?*" Have you wired the deposit? I casually swirled my glass back and forth on the table. His two soldiers had been required to leave their weapons with one of my men, but I suspected they had others hidden in less conspicuous places. Viktor trusted no one, which was understandable. He was a wanted man in several countries for various atrocities.

He laughed, surprising me when he spoke English. "You have no trust, my friend. That will make you an excellent leader. To answer your question, yes. The deposit as required. The rest when our business is concluded. How is your uncle?"

"Sadly, he's been under the weather." The lie was simply adding another layer of bait.

"I'm sorry to hear that." He took several sips of his drink, shifting his gaze toward Savannah. "There is no replacement for family, blood ties often the only thing we can count on. Wouldn't you agree, Savannah?"

"Unfortunately, I have no family."

"That is a shame."

I heard a slight chirping and realized my little wren was carrying a phone. "I apologize. There was some concern about a delivery arriving in time for tonight's dinner." She pulled out the cellphone, running her finger across the screen.

Only I would be able to notice her hand was shaking. The slight change in her breathing kept my attention. "Is something wrong?"

"Yes. The shipment of salmon didn't arrive. You'll need to excuse me for a few minutes." As she started to rise from the table, I grabbed her wrist, catching a quick glimpse of the screen.

The text was to the point and exactly what she'd said.

"Don't take too long, my little wren."

"Of course not." She smiled at us both before heading toward the door. When she looked back for a few seconds, I could see the same longing in her eyes that had captivated me from the beginning. But there was another wave of fear. I bristled, fisting my hand under the table. Tonight I'd find out what had happened.

Viktor shifted his attention in my direction. "She's beautiful, Maxim. It would seem you're settling down. Every leader needs a woman to stand behind him, cleaning blood from his body after battle."

Chuckling, I shifted my gaze toward him. "Is the point of your insistence in coming to America to handle a simple transaction or another reason, Viktor?"

"I thought I'd spend some time with an old friend at the same time."

"Let me be very clear with you. You're in my territory now. As such, you are my guest and nothing more. Should you disregard my rules, you'll learn quickly the friendship you have with my uncle means shit to me. Understood?" He would get a single warning and nothing more. If he thought he would use this as an opportunity to try to convince Vladimir to join in an unholy alliance, then he had another think coming.

Viktor smiled. "You were always one to go to the extreme since you were a little boy, Maxim. I was hoping you'd grow out of it."

How the fuck would he know anything about how I was? From what I knew, he'd barely mourned his friend's death all those years ago.

My phone rang, the interruption pushing a growl up from my throat. Seeing Ricardo's number meant there was a situation he couldn't handle. "Yes?"

"I'm in the communications room. We need to talk," Ricardo said, his voice breathless.

I returned the phone into my jacket pocket, immediately rising.

"Is there a problem?" Viktor asked.

"Nothing that I can't handle. I run a multi-faceted business and my presence is often necessary."

"Of course. Take your time." The man was gloating.

Fortunately, the communications rooms Ricardo was talking about was situated near the kitchen. I headed out of the room, taking long strides down the hallway, grabbing one of my other soldiers. "Keep an eye on the private room."

"Yes, sir."

As soon as I walked inside, Ricardo lifted his head, tension riding his face. "What is it?"

"We're in a shitstorm. You told me to sweep the entire facility and I did. Suspicious van. I wanted you to see it." He pulled up the surveillance camera located in one of the valet centers. "I checked the tapes. It's been there on and off for five days."

Five days.

The exact length of time I'd been in New Orleans.

The same timeframe Savannah had been in New Orleans.

"What are you trying to tell me?" He closed his eyes and I overreacted, shaking him hard. "What the fuck are you trying to say to me?"

"You need to hear something."

When he flipped a switch, I sucked in and held my breath.

Chris. It's me. Savannah's voice was shaky, but I'd recognize it anywhere.

There was a pause, her breathing disguised by the sound of running water, but I sensed she was a nervous wreck.

"I need your help."

I glanced at the video screen again, doubting she was contacting anyone inside. That's where she'd gone when leaving the hotel.

"What?" she asked, the tremor in her voice increasing. *"Why?"*

Another short pause.

"But I need your help."

I glanced at Ricardo, the rush of anger and adrenaline a dangerous combination.

"No. Yes. I don't know. He's not acting like himself."

He? She was talking about me.

"I don't know if there's anywhere that's secure, but no one can hear me." She was in the shower of her suite, the water running as she was betraying me. I fisted my hand, trying to control my breathing.

"Eli Parker. Real?"

Another pause. The name sounded familiar.

Ricardo lifted his eyebrows, immediately moving to one of the computers.

"Find out who that is," I growled.

"On it."

"What does he look like?" Savannah asked, her voice trembling more.

A longer pause.

"I followed my gut. Does he have an accent?" Savannah was insistent.

"Turn it off," I told him.

Ricardo did then took a deep breath. "She's working for somebody."

His statement hung in the air. I closed my eyes, resisting destroying everything in the room.

"I'm sorry, boss."

I sped the recording up by a few seconds, turning it on again.

"Text this number and if he's the real deal, say the salmon is fresh. If not, say you don't have any."

The text she'd received. That's why she'd seemed disturbed. Whoever she'd met with hadn't been who she'd expected. It confirmed she was being used, but by whom? Goddamn it. The woman had betrayed me. Fuck. Fuck. "After the shipment is secured, we're leaving town. Have the plane on standby."

"Okay. What about the woman?"

"She's coming with us."

"Max. You can't do that. If anyone gets wind that you're keeping her after what you discovered, Damien will steal every ounce of loyalty you have left."

"Have left, Ricardo?" I snapped. "Does that mean you too? Have you switched sides?" I was close to losing my shit.

Exhaling, he looked away. "You know that's not the case. I will remain loyal until a bullet is driven into my brain, but you need to think about this."

"I just did. She's coming with me. But I will find out everything she knows."

He nodded after a few seconds, not comforted in the least. The man knew me far too well.

I moved toward one of the cabinets in the room, pressing my thumb against the keypad, yanking it open after the light turned green. I'd insisted on keeping certain items inside, additional weapons and other useful tools for instances just like this. After grabbing a Beretta and several magazines, I snatched a thick piece of rope. I knew Savannah wouldn't come along willingly.

He exhaled. "What about the van?"

"Leave it. If it's the Feds, they're not getting shit. Set up a diversion when I leave for the port. Take 'em out of town."

"You got it."

"Get every man we have at the docks."

As I headed for the door, my anger off balance with the way I felt about Savannah, I heard a popping sound.

"Ah, shit," Ricardo exclaimed.

I spun around just in time to see flames erupting from the van. Within seconds, it was consumed by another explosion.

We'd been compromised.

"Goddamn it. Call the ship. Have them stall," I commanded.

"Police are going to be all over the hotel in minutes. There's no telling who's responsible. We need to get you to the safehouse."

"Not without my possession. Warn Romanoff. Get the fucker out of the hotel." I wouldn't mind if the bastard was killed, but at this point I didn't need any additional blood on my hands.

There was no time to waste. I rushed from the room, slamming open the door to the kitchen. My gut had already told me I wouldn't find her inside. She'd been warned.

But she was going nowhere.

I'd been handed two major blows and my authority had been undercut in a limited timeframe. That meant every shark in the wild would be hungry for blood. That was the way in the mob world. Perceived weakness meant death and destruction. The world I'd grown up in was about power and control, which is what created and kept respect.

Without either one, the walls would come crashing down, enemies no longer fearing what I was capable of.

I already felt them cracking.

Someone was out to destroy the Bratva, the candidate list far too long. It was time to regroup then strike.

And when I did, I'd slaughter every person who'd betrayed me.

* * *

Savannah

Panic.

I'd never experienced real panic until a few moments before when I'd seen the single word pop on the screen after learning the agent was someone else, a person with dangerous intentions.

Abort.

I'd shifted into what little training I'd been given, racing toward the private elevators. I'd left the keys to my car in the suite, which had been stupid. At least I'd packed a go bag just in case, one I'd hidden well for fear that Maxim would search my room. I tried to think about the escape route I'd mapped out quickly, allowing me to get out of the city, but everything was fuzzy in my mind.

With no time to waste, I yanked off my shoes as the elevator opened, flying toward the bedroom. I didn't have to change, but I grabbed my tennis shoes, flopping onto the bed and shoving my feet into them. Then I grabbed my duffle bag, and another pang of fear almost forced me to crumple to the floor. Breathe. Breathe.

I managed to secure the weapon, tossing the other magazines into the bag. I could do this. I had training. I knew how to shoot a gun. My thoughts shifted to Brittany, my heart so heavy I couldn't breathe.

The agony and panic kept my stomach in huge knots.

That wasn't the only emotion rolling through me. There was also angst in leaving, of possibly never seeing Maxim again. I couldn't think this way. He meant nothing to me. Nothing.

But as hard as I tried to convince myself of it, my heart was telling me otherwise. Still shaking, I stared at my phone, squeezing the plastic. I knew I was running out of time to try to get away. *Follow your instincts. Follow your instincts.*

The little voice inside my head was insistent.

So I did.

After dialing Chris' number again, I closed my eyes, saying a silent prayer. I put the weapon on the bed, staring down at the hard, cold steel. Would the people outside know there was an issue? Would they try to save me? No. There was something wrong, terribly wrong. I'd fallen into a trap. But who'd set it? The people I'd trusted or was the nightmare just a play of hand by Maxim? Everything was a huge blur, my heart racing.

Third ring.

Fourth ring.

"Are you out?" he asked as soon as he answered the phone.

"Almost. What is going on? I need to know."

"The real Agent Parker was found dead inside his home in Birmingham."

"So who the hell is the man who met with me?"

"I'm not privy to that information. I've been shut out completely." His voice was exasperated. I heard noise as if he was tossing things wherever he was.

"Why? Why would they do that?"

"Just get out, Savannah. There's something going on. You're in danger."

"What do you mean something? Tell me, Chris. Please."

Boom!

The noise coming from the other end of the line put the fear of God into me. I couldn't stop shaking, my mind a blur. "What's happening? Talk to me."

I heard loud voices, angry men shouting. "Listen to me. Agents have been compromised. Those sent to protect you can't be reached. There's something wrong. Bad cops. Bad cops…"

It sounded like a door was kicked. "Get out of there, Chris. Get out." Bad cops? Oh, dear God. Had someone working for Maxim infiltrated the operation, getting inside the FBI? No. No. No!

"Argh…" Chris huffed.

Pop! Pop! Pop!

"Chris. Chris!" I slumped to the floor, holding my breath. He'd been shot. I remained quiet, the phone still live. Then I heard a sound I'd never forget.

A voice.

"Get this place cleaned up. Now! Move in on the targets. Kill the fucking Russian. No one is to be left alive."

I couldn't process what I'd just heard, the person behind the voice I recognized. But they were coming after Maxim.

And they planned on eliminating every loose end in the process.

Including me.

Before I had a chance to react, another sound caught my attention.

Someone was in the suite. Oh, God. Oh, God. I jerked up, my head spinning. Was it Maxim they were after? Was this even real? I couldn't trust anyone. That's what Chris had told me. There was little I could do but continue to try to protect my identity. I dropped the burner phone, smashing my foot down several times until it was in pieces.

Then my world caved in, the door to the bedroom bursting open.

Maxim stood larger than life, his broad shoulders taking up almost the entire width of the door, his chest heaving from rage. His smile was just as I'd remembered in the throes of passion, but his eyes were dark and cold, highlighting the fury that forced his chest to rise and fall rapidly. He glanced around the room, his gaze settling on the phone by my feet.

Then he took two steps inside and for some reason I didn't retreat, instead grabbing the weapon. I held it in both hands, trying to keep them from shaking as I pointed it at his chest.

He seemed amused, his eyes lighting up. "Go ahead, Savannah. Shoot me. But if you do, I assure you that you will die."

"You're a monster."

"Am I? Is that what your body tells you when I'm close? Is the desire I see in every action you take just a lie?" He took two additional steps. I was sick inside, my hands shaking like leaves.

"Don't come any closer."

He held out his arms, taking two more steps. "Do it. If that's what you want, then go right ahead, but I think you know I'm the only man who will keep your senses and desires alive." He took two more steps.

"You're an arrogant prick."

"And you're a liar."

"Who the hell are you?" I managed.

As he laughed, tingles slid into every muscle, the longing to have him touch me, kiss me, fuck me searing my skin, electrifying my core. My mind was abuzz, my system threatening to shut down.

"I think the better question is who are you? I will find out but as of right now, I'm the only man who can keep you alive."

"You're crazy. You're a horrible man, a killer."

"True, but I'm not the one who torched a van full of people. I suspect the Feds or DEA. That means someone is coming after me and in turn will use you against me. You'll be captured then tortured for the information you have." He was closing the distance and I couldn't take a shot. What was wrong with me?

You love him.

No. God, no.

"What? What did you say?" The information finally settled. The people here to protect me were dead. All dead. "You killed them." But the nagging voice inside my head told me he had nothing to do with it, or with Chris' murder.

"No, my little wren. I did not. And I'm not going to kill you as long as you cooperate. We're leaving."

"I'm not going anywhere with you."

"You have no choice."

I straightened my arms, lifting the weapon so the barrel was pointed at his head. I should pull the trigger. I had every right to do so. He was my target, my mission to bring him in or... no. I'd been used.

As he advanced, I took several shallow breaths. There was no way I could kill him.

Maxim wrapped his hand around the gun, easing it from my hand. "That's a good girl." After shoving it into his pocket, he grabbed my arms, holding my wrists with one hand. That's when the desire to live kicked in.

I drove my knee into his groin and pushed away, lunging toward the door. He caught me in seconds, pushing me down, crawling his body up and over me as I struggled to get away. Twisting my body, I managed to get off several hard punches, but he was too strong, shoving my arms to the floor.

"That wasn't very nice of you," he gritted out, his jaw clenched.

"I'm not the innocent bird you think I am." I continued struggling, trying to wrench my body from under the full weight of his, but it was no use.

"Yes. Now, I can see that."

As he started to wrap my wrists with rope, all I could think about was my baby girl. Tears formed in my eyes, the emotion strong and biting. She couldn't be without her mother. I had to survive. I would find a way of getting back to her.

He yanked me to my feet, pushing me into the living room, tossing me down on one of the chairs. "Stay right there."

I could tell he was struggling with figuring out what to do. Was it possible he wasn't lying about the van, that he wasn't responsible? "What's going on?"

Maxim cursed in Russian, his voice too low for me to understand the words but I sensed his growing rage. "The betrayal runs deep within my organization, my little wren."

"I haven't betrayed you." I winced when I said the words.

"You are the catalyst. You were sent here. By whom?"

"Nobody. I swear to you. I'm just a chef."

"Bullshit." The sound of his phone caught him off guard. He yanked it into his hand, turning away from me.

"What?"

While I had no idea what was being said, my gut told me whatever was going on was a shock.

"Pust' soldaty okruzhat zdaniye," he barked. Have the soldiers surround the building.

He was anticipating an attack. Was this predicated by the man I'd met with? I fought with my bindings, the rope chafing my skin after a few seconds.

"No," he said. "We're leaving in a few minutes," Maxim continued. Then he turned toward me. After ending the call, he advanced.

"You don't want to do this," I managed, choking on the words as soon as I'd said them. Of course he wanted to end my life. I'd betrayed him in the worst way possible.

I'd lied.

"Moy krasivyy, greshnyy malen'kiy krapivnik."

My beautiful, sinful little wren.

CHAPTER 16

$\mathcal{M}$axim

Great leaders knew when it was time to retreat, gathering their forces, using patience as they prepared for a counter-attack. The venomous snakes would soon be out in full force, ripping apart pieces of my organization in their bids for power.

My power.

I couldn't allow that to happen. However, I would be ineffective in starting a war from this location. Returning to Miami was the best course of action. Getting there might prove to be a problem though.

I heard my uncle's words in my head as I studied the woman who'd become my possession.

"If you lose respect of your men, you'll never recover. You'll be forced to defend your heritage and mine for the rest of your life. Wars will start, blood running in the streets. And you will never regain control."

Fuck. While the statement might be the one thing he'd taught me that made the most sense, I wasn't the kind of man to go down without a fight. I would find out who was behind the treachery, and they would die a torturous death. The fact the cargo ship had been blown out of the water meant the upcoming war was escalating. Santiago had also taken out a smaller ship that had barely left the port in Brazil. He'd already initiated a takeover plan.

The plane had been taken too, which meant I'd need to find a place to hide out for a few hours. There couldn't be a worse scenario. I'd allowed myself to be drawn into a trap.

I needed to gather whatever intel she had, the reason for her meeting with the unknown source, but that couldn't happen here. I'd taken far too much time already in disciplining her for trying to get away.

As I tried to put the pieces together, the fact she was constantly enticing me was getting to the point of madness. She'd betrayed me. I'd allowed her into the inner sanctum of my world, and she'd lied to me. I couldn't think of her as anything but a source to be used and tossed aside.

Savannah squirmed in the chair, her face pinched as she stared up at me. "You'll need to trust me."

"I will never be able to trust you," she said in the same defiant voice I'd heard the night I'd met her.

I yanked her from the chair, pulling her into my arms. I'd ripped her dress to pieces. "You're going to change but be quick about it." She didn't object as I pushed her into the bedroom. But as she threw open the closet door, her eyes were full of fire and brimstone.

"I hate you."

"Yeah? Get in line. Hurry."

She wasn't selective, grabbing another dress that was hanging on the back of the door. Within seconds, she turned to face me, her brow furrowed.

I kept my fingers wrapped around her upper arm, leading her toward the elevator doors. "You're going to remain quiet as we leave the building, Savannah. I assure you that if you don't, your punishment will be much worse than what you just received." As the elevator doors started to open, I pointed my weapon at chest level.

"You're worried," she said.

"I'm cautious. There is a difference." There was no one inside and I shoved her in, my patience level faded as my anger increased. I couldn't help but believe the entire shit I was going through had to do with Sergei. Somehow. Some way. While it didn't make any sense, the concept of coincidences continued to play in my mind. I needed time to think, to process.

And to plan.

She continued to shiver, her lips white from gritting her teeth. There were so many emotions in her eyes that I knew

I could break her with ease, discovering all her secrets. But that would also take time.

"Where are we going?" she asked as the elevator neared the first floor.

I loathed the fact there were no underground garages because of the high sea level. That would put us out in the open for far too long. My gut told me a strike was imminent.

"Somewhere safe."

"You don't know who's after you."

Laughing, I glanced at her. Her rebellion was a turn-on but at this point sex should be the last thing on my mind. "There will always be unknown foes trying to invade from time to time. It's my job to bury them."

"You think you're so powerful. Don't you?"

"I know I am." As the doors opened, I had less than three seconds to react before all hell broke loose. My instincts had been right, a gunman waiting in the lobby. I pushed her down, firing off two shots. The assassin dropped like a rock but there would be more of them.

To her credit, Savannah didn't scream, only continued shaking as I yanked her into my arms, pushing her down the corridor leading to the rear exit.

We were only twenty feet away when two men rounded the corner. "Get down," I yelled, shoving her again as I jumped in front of her, firing off round after round. "Fuck this shit." The gunshots finally drew the attention of several people in the lobby, their screaming adding to the chaos.

Ricardo and several of my men appeared. His eyes were as full of rage as mine. "We need to get you out of here."

"How many?" Once again, I pulled her into my arms, her body sagging against mine.

"Two dozen, maybe more."

I continued racing down the corridor, the sound of gunfire all around me. There was no time to ask about identities. This was crisis mode, my need for revenge keeping me on edge.

Three more appeared from an adjoining hallway, one of my soldiers taking the brunt of the shots. I was forced to back her against the wall, shielding her with my body as I cut down one of them, Ricardo handling another. This had been well orchestrated, the pathway leading to the exit covered by enough enemies that I knew insider information had been used or the place had been cased long before the attack.

Savannah clung to me, her eyes wild with terror.

"Stay with me. I'll get you out of here." Whether or not she trusted me couldn't matter. I'd meant what I said. She'd be used in ways that even if she survived, she'd never recover from.

We finally reached the exit and another assassin lunged toward me, able to pitch me back by several feet. As the gun flew out of my hand, the assassin jammed his weapon against my neck. There was no doubt about his authenticity.

"Fuck! There's more of them," Ricardo snarled, his attention pulled away.

As I struggled, our bodies rolling as I tried to wrench the weapon from his hand, he reared back, taking a few seconds to gloat from obtaining the prize. I managed a hard punch to his face, pummeling him backward. Then I retrieved the weapon but not before he lunged toward Savannah, grabbing her by the arm, ready to pop a bullet into her brain.

As she screamed, reaching for me in a silent plea of help, I reacted instantly.

Pop! Pop! Pop!

The fucker slowly dropped away, and I grabbed my beautiful wren, pulling her against my chest.

"Oh, God. Oh, God," she whimpered.

"Don't worry, baby. It's going to be okay."

"Go. Go. Go. Stay with him," Ricardo directed the two soldiers.

There was no time for goodbyes. I bolted out the exit door, dragging her with me. I only had thirty feet to go before reaching the bulletproof car, but it was thirty feet directly in the open. We were within five feet when a group of soldiers appeared out of the shadows. I'd have one shot at getting her to safety.

The pinging sound as bullets hit the car finally broke through her haze of terror, her screams jetting into the night air. Every muscle was tight, but my mind was crystal clear as I started planning my method of revenge.

Pop! Pop!

I spun around, taking out two more then was able to shove her into the passenger seat, jumping over the hood then firing off several more shots before jumping into the car. With zero hesitation, I started the engine, slamming the gear into reverse.

Panting, she gripped the dashboard, yelping the second I backed over one of the fuckers.

"Stay down," I told her, jerking the steering wheel to a hard left, slamming my foot onto the accelerator. Then I roared through the parking lot, skidding when I hit the main road just as sirens blasted off all around us.

As I glanced into the rearview mirror, I took a deep breath. At this point, no one was following us.

"Untie me," she demanded a few minutes later.

"Not until we reach our destination."

"You have no clue where that is."

Her biting words should annoy me but instead, they reminded me of the reason I'd found her irresistible in the first place. "As I said. Somewhere safe."

"Is there any place on this earth that's safe from you?"

I thought about her question perhaps longer than I should. Then I gave her an honest answer. "Probably not." I wanted to forgive her, to take her into my arms and continue telling her that everything in her pitiful world was going to be okay. But I couldn't do that. Doing so would make me weak, unfit to lead the Bratva. I couldn't take a single additional hit to my reputation or to the organization or there would be zero hope of regaining respect.

So using her was my only option, forcing her to face the fiery breath of my wrath.

In doing so I would break her, but that couldn't matter.

"If you're going to kill me then do it," she said breathlessly.

"I'm not going to kill you, *malen'kiy krapivnik*. You're going to become the reason for my salvation."

* * *

Savannah

Salvation.

Maxim believed I could offer hope, maybe happiness. It was crazy.

But I continued to wish I could.

Darkness had never been my friend, less so after the horrible experiences I'd had with Brittany's father. When night fell, he'd become a different person, the change in his personality so different from the man I'd met that I'd been incapable of handling it. Then he'd sucked me into his brand of darkness, sick proclivities that had left me scarred both psychologically and emotionally. Then I'd gotten pregnant, and he'd acted as if I could never leave him.

Maybe that was one tiny reason my little girl was so precious to me. I used to believe my way of thinking was twisted, a sign that I was a horrible mother, but I'd learned over the years that she'd given me back a life I'd believed dead, allowing me to feel again.

During the long drive, I'd been allowed to think freely, to suffer in silence under Maxim's control. He'd saved my life, not only protecting me with his body but killing someone in order to keep me alive. Was the reason to torture me later? I didn't want to believe it but my mind was spinning out of control, fear and anxiety ruling. I'd chastised myself a hundred times for falling for the man, questioning how I'd been able to enjoy the filthy needs he'd awakened.

I wanted to hate Maxim just as I had my child's father, but they were entirely different men. Or were they? As the headlights flashed across the welcome sign for Panama City, I shuddered. He was taking me back to Miami. There'd been no additional gunfire, no monsters hunting us down, but I knew it was a matter of time before the war started again. My thoughts were never far from Chris' death. He'd tried to warn me, to keep me protected. He'd been used exactly the way I had. If only I hadn't listened in on Maxim's conversation. If only the timing had been different.

If only.

"We're stopping for the night," Maxim said after a few minutes. I sensed he was exhausted, likely not used to going it alone. I almost laughed at the thought.

"Why not." I had nothing to say to him. The tears I'd felt earlier had dried up, the realization that I was facing certain death an ugliness I couldn't avoid.

I heard his phone, watching as he yanked it into his hand, smirking then declining the call.

"Aren't you going to get that?" I chided.

"Not now."

"Are the police going to arrest you?"

He turned his head slowly. The darkness couldn't hide the savage look in his eyes or the smirk on his face. "I'm far too powerful."

I wondered if that was really true. The number of men who'd attacked his soldiers had surprised Maxim. I'd seen that on his face. But I doubted he was certain of who'd attacked him. After receiving the text, I'd wanted to eavesdrop on Viktor, but he'd already gone. There was something about the gruff Russian that bothered me more than the simple fact he was another Bratva leader. I hadn't heard a word about him, nothing, but it was obvious he was a long-time player in the game of illegal drugs.

Between that and what I'd heard from calling Chris, my entire system wanted to shut down.

Trust no one.

Chris' words continued to roll in my mind. Why was it that a part of me knew I could trust Maxim?

"Are you hungry?"

"Why do you care?"

"Because I need you to stay healthy."

This time I couldn't stop a laugh from erupting, the sound as crazed as I felt. "You must be kidding me. You're going to put a bullet in my head for no other reason than you can't control the situation. Why bother giving a shit if I'm hungry or not?"

The lights from several commercial businesses flashed through the windows, allowing me to notice his grip on the steering wheel tightened. "Because I do care."

While his tone was genuine, I no longer cared. "It's the middle of the night. There's nothing open."

"I'll stop at a convenience store."

Seconds later, he pulled into the parking lot of a gas station, a small store attached. There was no one else in the parking lot and the pulsing fluorescent lights indicating a fading bulb provided an eerie atmosphere. When he parked the car, cutting the engine, I held my breath.

"You're coming with me. If you say anything to the clerk, he or she will die. Do you understand?"

"Sure." I gasped when he reached across the console, gripping my chin.

"Listen to me, Savannah. There are some very bad men after us. They will hunt me down and in turn, take you as their prisoner. While you might not like my brutal tactics, I assure you that I'm not nearly as savage as the men chasing us."

"You still have no idea who they are."

"It doesn't matter. Come with me."

"You have blood on your shirt." I said the words so casually that it surprised me.

Snickering, he buttoned his jacket, trying to hide the scene of a murder.

He dragged me out of the car and into the small store. While a part of me was tempted to cry for help, I knew he'd make good on his threat to kill the older man standing behind the counter watching us intently.

"Pick anything you want," he told me as he grabbed a few items including a bottle of bourbon.

I watched him for a few seconds then decided to load up on junk food. Why the hell not? If I was going to die, I might as well do so with a smile on my face.

Maxim seemed surprised when I dumped the items on the counter, his eyes twinkling in amusement.

"You can't buy the booze. We're not one of those counties that allows it after eleven at night." The store clerk had no idea what risk he was taking.

Maxim leaned over the counter by a few inches, an icy grin crossing his face. "You will make an exception this one time."

He was used to getting what he wanted and I turned away, wishing I was repulsed by his actions but I wasn't. Since the first day I'd heard his voice, I'd been enamored by his prowess.

"Sure," the clerk said, ringing up all the items.

Maxim used a credit card, which surprised me. It could be traced. Maybe someone would come to my aid after all.

Don't fool yourself, Savannah. The people you thought you could trust are corrupt.

My throat threatened to close again.

Minutes later he'd parked in front of a typical small-town motel, this time leaving me in the vehicle as he went inside. The same threat applied and as I studied the pretty young girl helping him, I knew I couldn't take the risk he was telling me the truth. After parking where the car couldn't be seen from the road, he grabbed two bags from the trunk he'd taken from the hotel.

He pushed me inside, immediately locking the door then yanking the drapes. I folded my arms, wincing when he turned on the light. This was the beginning of a prison sentence. I eased the food bags onto the table, watching as he placed the bags he'd retrieved on the dresser. When he started going through them, I sucked in my breath.

There were enough weapons to start a war, at least one change of clothing, and a huge wad of cash. He'd been prepared for an attack. He noticed me watching and chuckled. "A requirement of the business."

"It's not a business, Maxim. You're a criminal."

He said nothing as he cracked open the liquor, grabbing two of the four plastic glasses provided as a complimentary service. My stomach turned. I was in a shitty motel room with one of the most dangerous men in the world and soon I'd be consuming junk food. The irony was ridiculous.

As he handed me a glass, I glared at him.

"Drink it, Savannah. You went through an ordeal. You're likely still in shock."

While I accepted the gesture, I almost tossed it into his face. "Shock? You mean because in the space of thirty minutes I was punished for an unknown infraction, almost killed not once but twice and kidnapped, and taken to a dingy motel room in the middle of no-fucking-where? Is that what you mean?"

"Cut the dramatics. We both know you were hired to provide assistance in taking down my empire. What I want to know is by whom?"

"You're wrong." My voice didn't sound very convincing.

He casually took several sips, his piercing eyes creating several waves of shivers. "I don't want to hurt you, but I will if necessary."

"Is that what you're all about, Maxim? You threaten everyone into doing your bidding, resorting to violence if necessary? Do you think that makes you more of a man?"

Every time I'd heard him laugh, the sound was bitter and angry, even more so tonight. I'd say he reminded me of a beaten man, but I knew better. He was doing nothing more than recharging his batteries, waiting for the perfect time to strike back. I had no doubt he would use me as a hammer, but how and why?

"You have no understanding of this life. You act as if you couldn't care less about what you've learned in the press, yet you reek of fear."

"I don't know about your life? Really?" I took a gulp of air then convinced myself to walk closer, finding courage I didn't even know I had. "You're a man who's lived his entire life in the shadows of family member you can't stand, someone so vile that even you can't tolerate his leadership. You've bided your time like a good boy, promised the entire kingdom when in the back of your mind you know your uncle is never going to allow that to happen. Even if you kill him in cold blood. And while you purport yourself to be a monster, deep inside you long for a life that you were given a brief glimpse of, one that haunts every dream. How am I doing so far? You might keep me in a prison forever, Maxim, but you're the one locked away for life."

I'd never been so impetuous in my life and as soon as I issued the words, I was certain he'd pull out his weapon.

The first time I'd met him, he had the look of a man who'd grown accustomed to violence, immune to the aftermath of his brutality.

Right now, at this very moment, everything changed between us, a line crossed that could never be redone.

His eyes never left mine, pools of lust that bore into me like a raging fire.

Possessive.

Dominating.

My nerves remained on edge, raw terror skittering through my system but the desire tearing through me only continued to increase. His silence spoke volumes, his need primal and unforgiving. I swallowed hard, refusing to back down.

"You seem to forget who you're talking to, Savannah. Just for the record. I am a monster."

My breath caught in my throat, and I reacted again, tossing the drink in his face, glaring at him with all the defiance I could muster.

After wiping his hand across his face, he casually eased his cup onto the table. Then before I could react, he had his fingers wrapped around my throat, shoving me against the wall with enough force I gasped, immediately clawing at his arm.

"You should be very careful what you say and do around me," he snarled, but there was no venom in his words or in his eyes, just continuing desire.

"I'll say what I want." The tension was palpable, the electricity crackling. I was slip-sliding straight to hell and I no longer cared. The ache in my heart was heavy, but I was consumed with longing, desperate to feel his naked skin against mine.

He took a deep breath, tracing my lower lip with his thumb before using it to press open my mouth, his breathing ragged. The moment of tenderness was surreal, catching me off guard.

I pressed one hand against his chest, taking shallow breaths as he slowly lifted his gaze. For a few seconds, all time stood still. Then he crashed his lips against mine, jerking one arm over my head. In another unexpected move, he intertwined our fingers, digging his nails into my skin.

His touch left a trail of searing heat and fire, igniting the embers I'd tried desperately to forge into armor of steel. Somehow, I knew I could never be rid of the hunger, a need that had become a drug I couldn't live without. As he devoured my mouth, thrusting his tongue inside, all the resistance I'd been determined to have crumbled.

As I wrapped my arm around his neck, tangling my fingers in his hair, I was aware his hand left my throat, traveling down my side, bunching the dress in his fingers. Using his knee, he shoved my legs apart, pushing aside my panties.

I moaned into the kiss, the hard thumping of my heart continuing a steady beat. When he stroked my pussy lips, I was certain I'd climax within seconds. I writhed in his hold, twisting the material of his shirt as he slipped a single finger inside, then another. I shouldn't want him the way I did. My body shouldn't be responding the way it was but as I continued writhing, he thrusted deep inside.

He took joy in ravaging my lips, acting as if I was the only person who could quench his thirst. I let him, opened up for him, hungered for more. The taste sparked dozens of sensations, my nipples aching as jolts of current shattered my last resolve.

There was nothing gentle about the man, but I didn't care. I didn't want him to be. I needed to feel every inch of him. As he added a third finger, my wetness coating the long, thick digits, I fought to breathe.

He broke the kiss, every sound he made husky and full of carnal need. Even though I struggled in his hold, I knew I was completely at his mercy.

And there was no place I'd rather be.

"Oh. God."

"Do you want more, my little wren?" he asked, his hot breath cascading across my chin.

"Yes." I had no reservations in telling him. He'd stripped away my ability to ignore my brutal yearning for him and he knew it.

"Say it. Tell me what you want."

His command had the same power over me as it had before. I was spinning out of control, no longer able to think clearly. I hadn't intended on falling into his spell ever again, but I couldn't imagine not being able to touch him, to give myself to him.

"Fuck me. Please fuck me."

It was as if my words had released the beast, allowing him to break free of the very prison I'd accused him of being locked in. He curled the tips of his fingers, the switch in the angle forcing me to tremble. I closed my eyes, the pleasure consuming every inch of me. I pulled him closer, longing for him inside of me, but he was bringing me to the beginning of rapture.

I gasped for air as he finger fucked me, driving into my pussy with enough force I was pitched against the wall over and over again. My mind was hazy, lust consuming me. I couldn't get enough of him, his scent earthy and provocative, like the mountains and the sea colliding.

He whispered words in Russian and I fell further into the lull as my mind translated them.

"You will forever be mine. No one will take you from me or they will die."

His words were harsh and frank, but I needed to hear them. I wanted to belong to him. Right or wrong, good or bad, I couldn't ignore what was impossible to drive away. I pulled myself closer to him, ripping at the buttons on his shirt, longing to have his skin sear my fingertips.

As I wrapped my leg around his thigh, I came hard and fast, so unexpectedly that I couldn't utter a single noise. He refused to stop, rolling the rough pad of his thumb around my clit as he thrust like a crazed man in need of a fix. I was his drug, the only possible way he'd gain salvation.

When my body ceased to spasm, he removed his fingers, sliding one across my lips before shoving them into his mouth. After yanking his fingers free, he tore at my clothes as I did to his, my fingers fumbling as I unfastened his belt. The desperate need was growing, spilling past my veins.

Once finished, he lifted me into the air, forcing me to wrap my legs around his waist. Never blinking, his breathing labored, he walked me toward the bed, lowering me onto the covers.

As he leaned over, planting his hands on either side of me, his expression darkened. Then he whispered an admittance only because he thought I couldn't understand. But I did and it would haunt me for the rest of my life.

"Ty moya slabost'. Skoro ty budesh' moyey smert'yu."

You are my weakness. Soon, you will be my death.

CHAPTER 17

*S*avannah

Maxim's stare was telling, the fight with himself to ignore his feelings as real and damning as mine. As he crawled onto the bed, I reached for him, a part of me hating myself. No longer did I feel the rush of embarrassment, the hint of shame. The longing was too intense, the need furrowing into what was left of my mind with every passing second.

He pressed the full weight of his body against mine, pushing my legs apart with his knee. This wasn't like before, the brutal savage taking what he wanted. This was entirely different, a tender moment that might never be repeated.

In the seedy motel room in the middle of a city where we weren't known, we could forget the ugliness if only for a little while.

He captured my mouth as aggressively as before, but as he swept his tongue inside, the tenderness he used singed every nerve ending. I rolled my arms around his shoulders, one hand clinging to his neck as I brushed the tips of my fingers up and down his back. It was the first time I'd felt indentations, scars from what felt like bullet wounds.

For some reason, I wanted to explore every inch of his body, touching everywhere he'd been hurt. Maybe I could heal his pain. As he swept his tongue back and forth, I shut out the noise from fear and worry, concentrating on the way he made me feel, the sensations tickling every muscle.

His cock was long and hard, cruelly curved, which pushed the tip against my G-spot every time he thrust. As he ground his hips back and forth, a wall of fire licked at my skin, my heart echoing in my ears.

The emotions racing through me collided with the desire that was burning me up inside. When he finally broke the kiss, he panted then bit my lower lip as he eased his arm under my leg, lifting and bending it at the knee. He pushed it against the bed then slipped the tip of his cock to my swollen folds.

I was wet and hot, the scent wafting between us. He stared into my eyes, never blinking as he pushed the entire length inside, filling me completely. I raked my fingernails down his back, shivering underneath him.

"You're safe, *moy prekrasnyy rebenok*," he whispered, his voice deep and full of angst.

"What did you say?" I hated lying to him, loathed how this had come to be, but even though the passion was real, I couldn't dare tell him the truth.

"My beautiful baby. My baby." He pulled out, driving inside again, finally rising onto his elbows. The stare never faltered, his eyes never closed as he fucked me, taking his time to fill me completely.

I wrapped my other leg around his hips, pressing it against his heated skin, the vibrations like bottle rockets jetting into my system. He rocked me to my core every time we were close but tonight was just the beginning of another chapter, one I feared.

And one that excited me.

There was no good reason, no understanding of how I could be thinking that way.

As he stroked my pussy with his cock, my muscles straining to accept his thick girth, I took several deep breaths.

"Maxim," I whispered.

"Mmm..."

"Fuck me. Harder. Take away all the pain." Finally, his eyes opened wide, as if a dam had burst open, the fire in them entirely different than before. I'd given him permission to take me brutally, to force me to surrender to his needs.

He pulled almost all the way out, teasing me with leaving just the tip inside. Then he slammed his body into mine, the bed creaking from the force. "You like it rough."

"Yes. God, yes."

A primal look crossed his lips as he repeated the action, every savage thrust knocking the wind out of me. I was breathless, tingling from the jolt of current that kept my pulse racing.

He fucked me long and hard, smiling every time I came close to an orgasm. The man was a master of knowing my body, bringing me to the very precipice of rapture then pulling back.

I tossed my head back and forth, beads of perspiration trickling between my breasts. My mind was a blurry mess, and I clawed his arms, half laughing as my body began to shake.

"Does my little wren want to come?"

"Uh-huh." I dragged my tongue across my lips and he growled in response.

The feel of him was incredible, pushing me closer and closer until I couldn't take it any longer. A rush of adrenaline jolted my system as an orgasm roared up both legs, erupting deep inside.

"Yes. Oh, my... Yes." I couldn't stop shaking, the explosiveness of the release sending a shower of stars in front of my eyes.

"That's it. Come again for me."

His deep voice was so commanding, drawing me further into the cataclysm of his world. My body responded almost instantly, the rush as another climax washed into me stealing my breath.

But I found my voice moments later, issuing a sharp scream. Moaning, I bit my lower lip to keep from crying out again, another wave of stars creating a beautiful display of color. He rolled his hips, controlling his actions as he continued fucking me. His stamina was unstoppable, the wry smile on his face cutting through the dangerous persona.

If only for a few precious minutes.

When he rolled me over quickly, forcing me on top, I pushed my palms against his chest, kneading his muscles.

"I'm not done with you yet," he told me, his tone gruff.

His tattoos drew my attention. I indulged, taking the tip of my finger and tracing the one on his chest figure by figure. He seemed fascinated at what I was doing. His cock continued to pulse inside of me, reminding me that he'd yet to come. But I couldn't help myself, brushing my fingers to his arm, studying the various characters in fascination. "Do they all have meaning?"

"Some. Others are a kid's attempt at looking tough." His admittance surprised me.

"How about this one?" I rolled my finger across the dagger laced in blood, remembering the one he owned.

"You know what that one is for," he told me, pulling my hand to his mouth, kissing my fingers.

"I know it's a representation of your weapon. But does it have a meaning?"

He thought about it. "For me it means leaving behind my childhood."

"What age?"

"Eleven, and I was lucky I wasn't younger."

"How sad." His cock was swelling, his needs intensifying. The scent of his hunger formed a haze around my eyes.

"The way of the Bratva, my little wren."

I slipped my hand from his, turning his arm over. As I continued my path, I felt his heavy gaze as his chest rose and fell. The colors were magnificent, although only done by a true artist. "They're representing stages of your life. Anger. Grief. Fear. No love."

He seemed more uncomfortable. "A way of expressing how I felt without doing so openly."

"Because you weren't allowed."

That's the moment he cupped my breasts, yanking my attention away.

"No more artistic renderings. I need you." He pinched my nipples between his thumbs and forefingers, his eyes narrowing. "And I always take what I want. Now, ride me." The darkness in his voice had returned, his command not to be denied.

Everything about the man was breathtaking, the power he exuded unlike anyone else I'd met before. I'd been drawn to his muscular physique and chiseled features from his photographs, but the lust had changed, emotions dragging at my soul. I tossed my hair against his chest, rewarded with a laugh, something he rarely did.

As I bucked against him, he twisted my nipples until I moaned, my breath skipping. Then he rose to a sitting position, fisting my hair and dragging me into a deep arc.

I was forced to grip his shoulders, staring up at the ceiling as he replaced his fingers with his tongue, licking and sucking first one nipple then the other. I was lightheaded, my mind pushed into another frenzy of thoughts.

He issued a series of husky sounds, more animal than man as he continued tormenting my nipples, biting then sucking. The combination kept me in a fog, the bliss incredible. When he finally let go of my hair, I slowly lifted my head, sliding my arms across his shoulders.

I took my time, lifting my hips up and down slowly, easily able to see I was driving him crazy. When he gripped my hips, digging his fingers into my skin, I sensed he was relieving me of my limited control.

He held me aloft, driving his cock inside, the look in his eyes devastatingly controlling. Nothing was going to stop him from taking what he wanted.

There was no way of knowing how long he fucked me, his control unlike anything I'd ever experienced. But as I sensed him tensing, his need refusing to be held back any longer, I squeezed my muscles. I could watch his face for hours as his balls filled with seed, his eruption violent as his body shook. He closed his eyes, his hold on me tightening.

"Fuck. Fuck!"

When he was finished, he slowly opened his eyes, and in the next few seconds, the roar of passion I'd seen in them faded, his expression now stone cold. He continued to hold me, aimlessly rubbing his thumb up and down my back, refusing to let me go.

He wasn't just looking at me. He was looking through me, deciphering just how much I'd betrayed him. I was no fool. Punishment would come.

It was the form he'd choose that sent shivers down my spine.

* * *

Maxim

The desire for her would kill me.

One day I'd lose everything because of this fiery woman who'd ignited every cell and muscle in my body. But today was not that day. As I peered down at Savannah, her long hair splayed out like a breathtaking fan of fire, I almost lost all control. By all rights I should spend hours interrogating her, using methods that she wouldn't be able to handle, but I couldn't do it. The need for her was more powerful than I'd originally thought.

The fact she almost died by the hands of a fucking Colombian pig had changed everything, awakening a need that would never be satisfied.

She was more nervous than she'd been during our round of passion, her eyes darting back and forth across mine seeking answers that I couldn't provide. In her surrender to the same need that had infused my blood, she'd known she was losing a portion of her innocence to a man she considered a monster.

She'd not only accepted what we'd shared. She'd wanted it.

Just like I had.

If I had any decency, I'd leave her alone, pretending she meant nothing to me. But I wasn't that man.

Maybe I'd accepted that I was no longer capable of separating love and hate. Once my soldiers learned that she'd also betrayed me, no matter the circumstances, the hit my reputation would take could be irreversible.

Unless I killed her.

I fingered my phone, wishing I would hear from Ricardo. While the police had gotten involved, I'd formed enough connections with law enforcement that no one from my organization would be arrested. However, the cleanup would result in a loss of business.

Sighing, I grabbed the cups, pouring both glasses full again. By the time I returned to the bed, she'd gotten under the covers, hiding her body from me. I sat down, handing her the glass. Then I ripped the material away.

She scowled, but the fire in her eyes would likely never diminish. I took a few seconds to brush my knuckles across her face then down her arm, angry with the life I'd been forced to live for the first time.

"Who are you, Savannah?"

"I already told you and I'm certain you had my background checked." Her words were clear, with no raw emotion like she'd had before.

Practiced.

That was the word.

"Yes, I did. However, I'm well aware that identities can be altered or removed by experts. Your arrival was too coincidental. That doesn't happen in my world."

"Who do you think I am, Maxim? A lover of your enemy perhaps? Viktor? If you think that then you're crazy. He's a fucking pig."

She wasn't lying, her disgust for the man real. "There is a man by the name of Emmanuel Santiago. He is a cartel leader out of Colombia. He has caused problems for me over the past couple of years. It wouldn't be beneath him to use someone in his employ to seduce me."

As her eyes narrowed, a slight look of hurt came to the surface. Then she tried to hide it, passing it off as indignity. "You bastard. After what we just experienced you act as if I'm faking it?"

I took a sip of my drink. "Women are much better at pretending." I caught her hand just before she slapped me.

"You fucking son of a bitch. You shithole of a human being."

"Such filthy words for a beautiful lady." I squeezed her fingers, giving her a stern look. "Do not do that again. I don't want to punish you at this point, but I will if I need to."

"Oh, my God. What is wrong with me?" She leaned back against the headrest, shaking her head. "Some crazy part of me thought you cared about me. You saved my life. You would have taken a bullet for me. You just made love to me, not just fucked me. Don't tell me otherwise. Yet you call me a liar and a thief."

"I heard the recording, the phone call you made to a man by the name of Chris."

Now I'd gotten her attention. I could see the difference in her eyes before she closed them. When she brought the cup to her lips, there was only a hint of nervousness. "You invaded my privacy. You didn't trust me."

I rubbed my eyes. "The truth is that I had a recent betrayal that changed my way of thinking. I'd hoped that my instinct about you had been right. Apparently, that's not the case. Who is Agent Parker?"

She laughed until she choked. "He's dead."

As I studied her, I realized what had happened. "The man you went to see was an imposter."

"Yes. And no, I have no clue who he is. But he knew you. I left when I realized when my gut told him something was wrong."

These were all truths. "Who are you?"

"Nobody but I'm not your enemy."

I rose from the bed, moving to retrieve my weapon. As I turned around to face her, the terror in her eyes had returned. "No, Savannah. I'm not going to kill you, although that's what I should do. That's what I'm required to do. You're exhausted and you've been through a terrible ordeal, which I don't think it's something you're used to. Get some sleep. We're leaving in a few hours. When we arrive in Miami, you will talk."

"If I don't?"

"Everyone has a weakness, my little wren, including you. I will find it."

As her eyes opened wide, I knew whatever I'd find was very important to her, enough to risk losing her life.

* * *

Miami Beach

Two days later

Savannah

Weakness.

The word was one I continued to mull over and had since being locked in a room, a beautiful, gilded cage with no way of escape. The room was incredible, the view of the ocean keeping me at the bulletproof window. I'd had food brought to me three times a day, none of which I'd been able to eat. I'd had clothes provided to me, all expensive and gorgeous. But I didn't care. I had no information, no way of talking to my little girl to find out if she was okay.

There'd been no harsh punishments, no threats made. Maybe they were implied, but I knew he was digging, doing everything he could to learn the truth regarding my identity. When he did, his fury would be boundless.

He'd visited twice, both times asking the same single question.

Who was I?

I was beginning to have doubts I knew any longer.

As I eased into the chair by the window, my mind continued to process the details of what I knew. It was nothing in comparison to what I should know. If I had to follow my instinct, I'd say I'd placed my trust in the wrong organization. Chris had died doing the same. But if I told Maxim the truth, would he kill me in the end?

Anxiety tore through me more than it had before. I sat back, reaching for the bottle of water. I was getting weak, nightmares plaguing what little I'd slept. I pushed the tray of food away, disgusted with the smells. Then I curled my legs under me.

When I heard the lock being turned, I bristled, my nerves reaching my throat.

The woman who'd brought my food arrived to take the tray away. She peered down at the uneaten items, finally looking me in the eyes.

"You need to eat, *señorita*. You must keep your strength." Her tone was full of worry, her thin smile indicating the same.

"I'm not hungry, Maria. Thank you."

"Please, *señorita*."

"Let me out of the room, Maria. Just for a few minutes. I need fresh air, a walk on the beach and nothing more."

She grabbed the tray, immediately backing away as if I'd hit her. "I cannot do that. Mr. Nikitin would be angry. You wouldn't like him when he's angry."

I didn't have the heart to tell her that I'd seen him angry. When I got up quickly, she tried to rush to the door, but I was too quick for her, darting toward freedom before I had a chance to think about what I was doing.

As soon as I dashed out the door, preparing to close and lock it behind me, I ran smack into Maxim.

Shit.

Frightened, I took two steps away from him, trembling as I peered up at him.

He had his hands in his pockets, shaking his head. Then he grabbed my arm, yanking me inside the room.

"Don't blame Maria. She's been nothing but kind to me."

"Maria. Please leave us," he told her as he released his hold, his eyes daring me to defy him.

"Yes, *señor*." She left quickly, giving me a harsh glare before doing so, closing the door behind her.

He said nothing for a full minute, his eyes darker than I'd seen them before. "You continue to be disobedient. I can't tolerate that."

"You've kept me cooped up here for two days. You don't talk to me. You aren't telling me what's going on or what you have planned for me. I can't stay in this room forever."

"You will stay here as long as I deem it appropriate. If that's a week, a month, or a year is entirely up to you." His tone was gruff, unforgiving.

Exhaling, I folded my arms, trying to keep him from knowing how scared I'd become.

"I will ask you again. Who are you?"

"You know who I am." I looked away but could sense his hard, cold stare remaining.

"Very well. Remove your jeans."

"Why?"

"Because I'm going to punish you."

I stared at him in horror. This time was different. There was no pretense of kink or anything remotely resembling sexual in nature. This was punishment for trying to escape. There was no sense in arguing with him.

"Do it now, or your discipline will be much worse."

Swallowing hard, I started to unfasten my jeans.

"Lean against the dresser. I'll return momentarily." There was no emotion in his voice, no inflection at all.

It was as if everything we'd shared was gone. Resigned, I started to slide the dense material down my hips as he walked out of the room, the slam of the door the only indication of his anger.

I was shaking all over as I complied, folding my jeans and panties, placing them on the bed. As I moved to the dresser, I couldn't stop shaking. I couldn't live like this much longer. He'd known how to break me. Not with violence but with loneliness and worry.

The girl staring back at me in the mirror wasn't the same one who'd left for Miami. She was hardened from the experience, jaded because of lack of trust. She was also aching inside, longing to share the same experiences with Maxim. It was crazy, but he'd been the only man in my life that I'd adored, the only person who'd broken through the walls.

What seemed like hours later, he returned, the reflection providing realization regarding the implement he'd selected.

A cane.

He was going to mark me, reminding me that not only was I his possession, but that I would also be held accountable for lying to him. As he walked closer, he locked his eyes on mine in the mirror. What shook me more than anything was the sadness in them. He'd changed, the experience of our passion part of the reason.

I held my breath as he closed the distance, longing for his touch. When he gave it to me, brushing his fingers down the side of my neck, I shuddered visibly.

"You are such an incredible woman. So brave. So strong. I admire your convictions."

"What's happening? Are you okay?"

He chuckled then rolled his fingers down my spine to my bottom, gently caressing one side then the other. "You're worried about me, *malen'kiy krapivnik*? I can take care of myself. You should worry about you."

"Maybe I care about you."

As he lifted a single eyebrow, a hint of surprise crossed his face before he hid it. "Do you now?"

"Yes. Very much."

Cocking his head, he allowed his gaze to fall then tapped my buttocks with the cane. "Then show me."

"That's not fair."

"Nothing in this world is fair, Savannah. The sooner you accept that, the better."

"No. I still believe there are good people in the world, a few I could trust with my life." I knew what I'd just said would seem ridiculous, but I was becoming unraveled.

He laughed and lowered his head, using his face to brush aside my hair. "My innocent flower. It's a shame that you'll be disappointed."

"It's a shame that you're so jaded."

The smug look on his face remained but I could easily tell my words had sparked something deep inside. He pressed his hand against the small of my back, forcing me to lean over. Then he took a step back, snapping his wrist and bringing the cane down a few inches away.

"Remember, my little wren. There are consequences for every infraction." The even keel to his tone bothered me. I could swear he was dying inside.

When he brought the thin wooden reed down, I wasn't prepared for the shock of the pain coursing down both legs.

I jerked forward, a heavy breath escaping my mouth. He cracked his wrist again, slicing it across my sit spot three times in rapid succession. The breath was knocked out of me, but I refused to give him the satisfaction of knowing how much agony it brought.

But as he doled out six, one coming right after the other, I was horrified that as I'd experienced before, my pussy was pulsing, desire outweighing the pain.

Maxim took a deep breath then began caressing my aching buttocks, rolling his fingers from one side to the other. "I love the marks you wear for me."

For him? Who was he kidding?

"I can sense your desire, my beautiful creature. You longed for a firm hand, a man who could give you exactly what you need."

I bit my tongue, trying to keep from admitting that he was right. As he slipped his hand between my legs, rolling a single finger around my clit, I dug my nails into the dresser's edge. He had always lit me up like a fire and even with the anxiety that wouldn't leave, I was wet, the scent of my desire floating between us.

"I could fuck you right here, right now," he said brusquely. "But only good girls get fucked in the pussy." As his emotions finally started to swell, his cock pressing against his trousers, a part of me wanted to beg him to fuck me.

But I refused.

He sensed I wouldn't give in and resumed the caning, issuing one after another. The increasing pain was matched by my growing wetness. After he brought the cane down a few more times, I was shocked that my pussy was clenching and releasing. My God, the man could almost make me come.

I bit my lip to keep from crying out, more rattled than I'd been before. My bottom was on fire, the ache increasing, but it was nothing in comparison to the need I felt, a burning need that continuously attacked my core. Panting, I dropped my head, trying to control my breathing. Nothing about this was right, but I wanted him. Oh, God, I did. That made me a horrible person.

After he delivered a few more, he took a step back, raking his hand through his hair. He was unsettled, his eyes reflecting the same brutal longing.

Then he removed something from his pocket, a pad and what looked like an inkpad. As he placed them on the dresser in front of me, I knew exactly what he was going to do. He was collecting my fingerprints. I recoiled, but he grabbed my wrist, placing the paper on the flat surface then opening the pad.

"Since you refuse to be honest with me, I'm forced to resort to this. I wish I didn't need to."

I wanted to fight him, but what was the point. He carefully pushed every finger and my thumb from my right hand into the ink, pressing them against the paper. All the while, he studied me, his eyes piercing mine.

Then he returned everything to his pocket. Almost immediately he turned away from me, heading to the door. Before walking out, he stopped short, tipping his head over his shoulder.

"I have a business meeting. Then you will join me for dinner tonight."

"Okay."

He acted as if he wanted to say something else then exhaled before he walked out, closing the door.

I slumped against the dresser, a single tear trickling past my lashes. I had to tell him the truth or I'd never see my little girl again. I was certain of it, my heart racing because of it. No, he wasn't the enemy. He was the only man who could keep Brittany and me alive.

Even worse.

He was the man I'd fallen head over heels in love with.

 axim

Pain tore through me, enough so my chest was heavy.

I'd seen the look in her eyes, the hatred she had for me. While the connection, the blast of electricity remained, she could never care for me anymore than I could place my trust in her. But I ached for her, longing to slide my cock deep inside her tight little pussy.

I'd taken a chance by returning to Miami, to the house I'd lived in for two years. While there were a dozen soldiers surrounding the property, that meant shit to a man like Santiago.

"Tony is dead," Ricardo stated as soon as I walked into the office.

I stared at him, taking a deep breath before responding. "Where and how?"

"He left his house, heading to a motel in Daytona Beach. It looks like he was running. Assassin's bullet. Clean. No mess. But whoever it was knew we'd find the body."

Fuck.

"Any indication of where he was headed?"

He shook his head. "None. But I can tell he wasn't heading to see his family. They live in Phoenix. Wrong way."

I knew Tony well enough to realize he'd felt the heat closing in and was trying to protect his family. Since I knew where they lived, that meant he wasn't as terrified of what I'd find as he was about someone else. Why did I have the bad feeling he'd become just another player in a game so devious that it had been planned for years?

"What did you do with his body?"

"Dropped in the ocean."

"Good." I didn't need any additional dead bodies showing up. The shit in New Orleans had brought enough heat even with the police trying to look the other way. The fact the van had been full of FBI agents didn't bode well for my reputation on any level.

"How is Savannah?" he asked, the tone of his voice indicating he couldn't give a shit.

"The same."

"Meaning she didn't tell you anything," he added, his smirk pissing me off. "She's a strong-willed woman."

She'd kept my senses awakened, my blood pumping and my cock aching from the moment she came into my life. Goddamn it, I wanted to spend every waking minute with her, but because of our involvement, my business was suffering, the organization close to chaos. As Ricardo had warned, the dissention in the ranks was high, soldiers questioning my leadership ability. With the shipment sitting at the bottom of the ocean, millions lost, the hit wasn't what I'd needed at this point in time.

And I was still trying to figure out how best to handle Santiago.

"How are you coming with finding the truth I need?" I asked.

"If you're talking about the woman, there's nothing new. I've used every source. If she's law enforcement, there's no additional backup coming for her. Doesn't that seem strange to you?"

Exhaling, I nodded. If she was, by now I'd have agents pounding down my door. Something didn't add up whatsoever.

I pulled the paper holding her fingerprints into the light. "I know someone who might be able to weed through the lies."

He lowered his gaze, snorting when he realized what I was holding in my hand. "That's one way of doing it, but you know Santiago likely wiped her identity if that's who she's working for."

I had doubts she had anything to do with Santiago, more likely a federal officer. However, I'd had enough experience with those attempting to move into my operation to know that she wasn't trained to go undercover. That was the sole reason I'd kept her alive.

Bullshit.

I'd locked her away in a prison of my choosing because she belonged to me. "My associate will be able to find the answers we need."

"Hmmm... Are you talking about the Brotherhood?"

While I didn't talk about my alliance with the men from other syndicates to anyone, Ricardo had caught me on a phone call, asking questions. It had been another test of his loyalty to keep his mouth shut. So far, he'd done so. "I have a meeting with them this morning."

My thoughts constantly drifted to Savannah, the ghostly sensations of having the cane in my hand tingling my skin. I fisted then flexed my fingers, longing to mark her entire body. That made me a very sadistic man.

"Your uncle called me late last night."

His admission forced me to take a deep breath. "And what did he have to say?"

"Nothing good. He asked why you were avoiding him."

I had my reasons. "Is Damien outside?" I'd wanted him close at all times, hoping he'd play his hand. I had no doubt he was partially responsible for the hit on the shipment as well as the attack on the resort.

"He's here. Not happy about it so I think—"

"I don't pay you to think and I don't give a shit if he's unhappy. Keep him occupied," I interrupted, hissing after losing my temper.

"Yes, sir, my *Pakhan*."

I gave him a look and moved toward the window, staring out at the ocean waves. "Was the deposit received from Viktor?"

"Yeah, but that's something else I need to talk about. The funds are being held. That's locking down all the offshore accounts at this point until it's settled."

As I turned slightly, I could tell by the look in his eyes that the situation was suspicious.

Just like everything else at this point.

"By the bank?"

"Yeah. I can't determine why, but I've seen this kind of shit before. The assholes from Belize are cracking down on unknown deposits, checking to see if they're counterfeit. I think they're getting heat from law enforcement from several countries. They're giving me excuse after excuse."

"Someone's pushing them since the money is dirty." With the offshore accounts down, several aspects of my business were on hold. Whoever was infecting my organization was hitting from all sides. Laughing, I rubbed my jaw. "Touché, motherfucker."

"Glad you're enjoying this nightmare. What do you want me to do? From what I can see of the transaction, the dollar amount for the deposit is correct but that doesn't matter worth shit if it stays frozen."

I thought about the angry conversation I'd had with Viktor the night before. While I'd tracked him back to Russia, I still needed to make good on the deal. That would add another layer of heat. A masterful plan, but the responsible party had underestimated me. "Nothing at this point. I'm going to force a meeting with Santiago."

"Really?"

"Yeah. I'm going to require him to tip his hand. Then we strike." It was time to end the charade.

"Just let me know where and when. I'm itching to get some payback."

"You always are." When I brought down the hand of God, I knew the walls of the Nikitin Bratva could come tumbling down, exposing lies and deceit years in the making. I'd bided my time with my uncle, my suspicions regarding my parents' deaths still weighing heavily on my mind. It was time to deal with the faded memories, the agony I'd suffered.

Either it would mean walking away from everything I knew or claiming what rightfully belonged to me.

Even in death, I would be vindicated.

* * *

The Brotherhood.

I'd been the one who'd remained on the outside even as a member. I'd never wanted to be involved, but it had seemed important at the time I made the decision. After the alliance had brought him nothing, Vladimir had laughed at my continued membership, telling me I was a fool in trusting them. However, even as jaded as Savannah had accused me of being, I was able to admit the limited assistance I'd received had proven helpful.

However, whether they cared to remember or not, Dante and Diego owed me more than just their allegiance given events months before. They owed me their lives.

I'd invited the group to the Bratva corporate offices, the location as secure as any other. With so much on the line, it felt as if danger was all around me. I'd dealt with it many times before, but somehow, this was different.

As I walked into my office, the other members had already arrived. This wasn't a social gathering, although two of them had drinks in their hands even though it was eleven in the morning. I was in no mood for alcohol.

Or anything other than getting down to business.

"The Pakhan has arrived," Constantine Thorn stated from his perch on the couch. He was one of the most powerful men in the room, his secure hold on Kansas City and the entire Midwest unrivaled at this point. While he'd had his share of battles over the years, his organization scarred from bad decisions, there was no denying his business acumen.

I snorted as I closed the door. "We shall see if that happens."

Brogan Callahan lifted an eyebrow as he studied me. "You're angrier than usual." Since taking over Chicago, the Irishman had prevented a war from ensuing in the streets. Perhaps his degree in psychiatry had proven to be helpful. Or the woman he'd fallen in love with had tempered him. He was the best at securing information out of all of us, which is why I pulled out Savannah's fingerprints.

I wasn't known for my charming attitude, my anger always prevailing, but today I needed to keep a cool head. I also wasn't the kind of man who asked for assistance, but at this point there was no other choice. I'd already heard rumors that Damien was escalating his move to take over as leader, several other soldiers giving the pompous piece of shit their loyalty.

"I need you to run these prints, finding out every scrap of information regarding the woman."

Brogan accepted the paper, giving me a curious look. "Is this the chef you hired?" He immediately moved to my desk, grabbing the briefcase he'd brought with him. I watched as he pulled out his computer as well as a personal scanner, not wasting any time handling my request.

Huffing, I was second guessing my pass on a drink already. "News travels fast in the underground."

"More than you know," Phoenix Diamondis said casually. As the leader of the Greek mafia out of Philadelphia, he knew better than the others about issues with shipments. He'd also been hit recently, losing millions of dollars of illegal drugs and weapons. Perhaps he had an insight as to who was behind the constant hijacking attempts. "The loss of that shipment sent shockwaves throughout the industry. There are few dealers from South America to Europe willing to risk sending product. A shipment I was expecting in a few days had been delayed."

"It's even affecting cargo ships coming into LA," Diego mentioned.

I'd heard as much, which didn't bode well for several of the Brotherhood. The trickle-down effect could last for months.

"Tell me something I don't know. The question is, are we together in eliminating Santiago?" I glanced from one man to the other, setting my sights on the twins from Los Angeles. Dante and Diego Santos were a formidable force, the men who'd grown up separately mending the fence after learning Santiago was their real father. They'd survived the aftermath of Diego murdering the man who'd destroyed their lives pretending to be their father, without further bloodshed. Their soldiers hadn't been given the choice as to whether they'd remain loyal. If not, they were eliminated.

Diego glanced at his brother before advancing. "I know you don't want to hear this, but it's not Santiago. There's been limited activity directly linked to his organization. Yes, he's still determined to come into America, but not by way of Miami or New Orleans."

"I don't buy that for a second. He is directly linked to destroying ships off the coast of Brazil," I told them.

Diego grimaced, glancing at his brother. "That's because the product originally belonged to Santiago."

"That's bullshit!" I snarled.

"I confirmed it," Brogan added.

Constantine could obviously tell how enraged I'd become. "Let's just say that's the truth; what conclusion did you get out of your investigation into Santiago's possible responsibility?"

"From what I can tell, he's determined to form an alliance with our empire," Dante added. "Which we're not allowing."

"That's garbage. He'd never consider that," I snapped. "It was his men who attacked the resort in New Orleans. They wore the tattoo of the organization." Carvings were often used when joining the ranks, the symbol allowing for instant identification. I could tell the brothers were surprised at the news, if not concerned.

"Shit," Dante growled. "Then he lied to us."

"Blood isn't always thicker than water, gentlemen," Gabriel Giordano piped in, although in his case, the accidental death of his brother, the Don of the Cosa Nostra had forced him into taking the helm. New York had seen its share of bloodshed in the last year, all thanks to several syndicate leaders striking after during the family's weeks of grief. The area was still unsettled, enough so he had his wife in lockdown, fearful of her abduction.

That's what I anticipated for Savannah at some point.

"True," I said in passing.

"Something doesn't add up. Blood or no blood to you gentlemen," Constantine said to the brothers, "Santiago isn't foolish enough to try and use the connection."

"He's right," Gabriel added.

While I continued to fume, there was some sense to what Constantine was suggesting.

"Fine, then I want a meeting with Santiago. The three of us," I told the brothers.

Diego took a deep breath, swirling the drink he had in his hand. "Where?"

"Here." My answer was succinct. It was far too dangerous to head to Colombia. "Can you arrange it?"

"Yeah, but he'll need assurance that it won't be a bloodbath," Dante stated. He'd considered the man his godfather while living in South America, the man protecting both him and his mother while never allowing the secret he kept to be exposed. Dante was still the man I had the most reservations about, his upbringing entirely different than the rest of us. He was one of the good guys, protecting the innocent, not destroying them.

"I'll provide that assurance, but it will be under my terms." It would be played my way. Period.

Diego nodded. "I'll make the arrangements. What is the purpose of the meeting?"

I'd thought about nothing else for the last two days. "Let's see if what you heard was correct. An alliance."

"That idea might come back to bite me," Constantine huffed, taking long strides in my direction.

"Having Santiago as an ally will prove helpful given his power, gentlemen. It could mean the roads for helping all of us." There was a twinkle in Phoenix's eyes. "Clever but you know it could backfire."

Nodding, I headed to the bar. One drink might clear my head, releasing the rage that continued to build. "I'm well aware of that. The alliance will be between all of us. That's the only way it will work."

Gabriel whistled. "You don't mince words or go slow with anything. Do you?"

"Never."

"What about your uncle?" Brogan asked as he lifted his head from the computer screen.

I poured a half glass of bourbon before answering, "It's time for him to retire."

"You're having issues within your own ranks. Yes?" Constantine asked. His directness and getting in my business would normally rile me to the point of violence, but I'd been forced to accept that there were reasons my men were close to betrayal.

"Yes." The one word answer was all that was necessary.

"You might not want my advice, Maxim, but you're going to get it. Deal with the treachery immediately. Don't allow it to fester any longer than absolutely necessary. If you do, you'll never regain control. You'll be chasing your tail, doing your best to avoid bullets. But you'll lose in the end." Phoenix was a brutal man hiding behind a wide smile and dancing eyes, using his boisterous behavior as a disarming tactic. And he was damn good at it.

"Agreed," I said, taking a swallow.

"This woman. A Fed?" Gabriel asked.

"Doubtful given I'm still a free man but I don't know for certain. However, if she is, she's been played."

"Meaning?" Brogan pushed.

I lifted my head, thinking about the question. "Meaning I think she was used by her organization to get close, not to have me imprisoned."

Diego narrowed his eyes. "You think the Feds are tied to Santiago."

"Maybe. It's happened before. Funds are frozen. My main accountant sold out. All orchestrated very carefully."

"Fuck. Then you're screwed, buddy," Dante chortled.

"She won't talk?" Constantine asked, his tone softening. He'd fallen hard for a woman who'd deceived him years before, almost sending him to prison after witnessing a murder. He knew where I stood, the dire consequences if I handled the situation badly.

"No. She's protecting someone. I'm certain of it."

"Then she's dangerous as fuck," Gabriel said, shaking his head. "But you won't get rid of her."

All I could do was shake my head.

"Well. Well. The brooding Russian had finally fallen in love." As Phoenix laughed, I snapped my head in his direction, ready to bite his off.

But I couldn't.

Because it was the truth.

"Let me know when the meeting is established," I told the Santos brothers. "I think this meeting is concluded."

"Be careful, Maxim," Constantine said quietly. "You're playing with fire. I don't know what your relationship is with your uncle, but he's not a man to be fucked with. He's proven that over the years."

I lifted my head, giving each one of them a final look in the eyes. "And no one knows what I'm made of."

"Well, fuck," Brogan said between clenched teeth. "You were right. She's protecting someone."

CHAPTER 19

 avannah

Fear, regret, and loneliness.

It felt like a lifetime since he'd touched me.

Kissed me.

Fucked me.

Endless hours, one shifting into another.

Another day of being locked inside the room. I'd watched the sun drift high into the sky, fading ever so slowly behind a puff of white clouds. Now twilight was beginning its descent, shadowing the rolling waters of the ocean.

How long was he planning on keeping me here?

My thoughts drifted back and forth from the intense longing that I shouldn't feel to fear and anxiety about Brittany. But I told myself she was safe and maybe, just maybe he wouldn't find her.

I'd heard noises in the day, voices of men who were likely Maxim's soldiers, but I'd been surprised they were roaming inside the house when Maxim was still out. I'd seen them outside, walking the perimeter with weapons in their hands. While the location was private, the view from my window showing hundreds of yards of nothing but beach and water, I suspected given the location Maxim would consider nothing safe enough. Whoever had attacked the resort would try again.

Maria had brought lunch, anger in her eyes as she'd placed the food on the table, leaving quickly. I hadn't bothered to ask questions, knowing that I'd crushed what little trust I'd had with her. As I shifted in the chair, I was reminded of the harsh discipline, my bottom still on fire. Maybe I'd deserved his rough actions, but my acceptance didn't make the trepidation disappear.

The ugliness in the pit of my stomach was a reflection of the gut feeling I'd had since Maxim had left.

He'd have no choice but to kill me. I'd been treated as if I had no understanding of the ways of a mafia organization. But I did. I'd studied everything I could get my hands on in my attempt to do my job to the best of my ability. I'd thought it would help as I transcribed hundreds of hours of conversations, able to decipher the code the men inside the criminal organization used, fearful of being overheard or worse, having their conversations recorded.

While leaders were powerful, providing edicts that could end anyone's life with a single nod, they weren't infallible to acts of treachery. If they'd been made a fool, there were other players ready to take the lead, killing the previous leader in the process. It was a way of life, the only chance at obtaining a promotion.

I knew the players of Maxim's organization, Sergei Sokolov's betrayal as much a surprise to me as it had to the brutal Russian man I'd... that I'd fallen in love with. But I had to remind myself that Sergei hadn't been the target, Maxim had been. What had he told me before? Everyone had a price. I'd learned that the hard way.

My thoughts drifted to Chris, his attempt at protecting me. He'd been like a dog with a bone, obviously pitting himself against Katherine and her orders. I knew why.

Katherine was dirty.

I'd never worked with her before. She'd breezed in and out of our office from time to time, paying compliments when she had no clue what our department had accomplished. I'd heard once upon a time she'd had a fling with the director, but her credentials were topnotch. Plus, I chose never to believe in rumors, which is why I'd taken everything I'd been told about Maxim with a grain of salt and then some. Yes, he was a brooding, dangerous man, but he was highly intelligent, keeping his personal life to himself.

There was little to place my trust in any longer.

I heard a noise and stiffened, refusing to look at the door. I'd changed from jeans and a shirt, opting for a dress instead for the dinner Maxim had insisted on, but my stomach was in knots. After the door was opened, there was no sound for a full thirty seconds. I couldn't stand the anticipation any longer and turned my head.

Maxim's expression was entirely different than I was used to, but I couldn't put my finger on what, if any, emotions were coursing through him. He stood with his hands in his pockets, staring at me.

I shifted in my seat, uncurling my legs. He followed the trail, lust in his eyes. Then he looked away, taking two long strides into the room. "I'm certain you're anxious, Savannah. You have every reason to be. Or should I call you Agent Savannah Parkins of the Atlanta unit of the FBI? You specialize in translations."

I'd known all along he'd discover my identity, but that didn't make it any easier. I was his enemy and nothing else, lying to him about who and what I was.

He walked further into the room, taking several deep breaths. "How many languages do you speak?"

"Several."

"But you're also a trained chef."

"Yes. It just didn't work out."

"I'm curious as to why."

He'd exposed my real identity and he wanted me to answer why I hadn't stayed in the hospitality business? "I have my reasons."

"I'm certain you do." He moved toward the bed, sitting down on the edge. "We have a problem, Savannah Parkins."

The way he said my name, every syllable pronounced was a clear indication of his level of rage. I'd caught the difference in his voice pattern when addressing a man who later turned up dead, washing up near an outdoor café, his body half eaten by a shark. This was his way of threatening without using the words.

I chose my words carefully, my life spiraling to an end. The best I could hope for was keeping my daughter alive. "You have several problems, Maxim, including men who don't trust or respect you, an unknown enemy killing several of your soldiers, and an uncle you can't stand who's likely to take sides with a man who's vying for leadership. I'm the least of your problems."

His eyes lit up from the same fire I'd seen so many times, but there was also a flash of something completely unexpected. Admiration. "Come with me. This won't take long."

There was no malice in his tone but a level of quiet that was just as unnerving. I followed him down the hall to another door. He glanced at my face for a few seconds before opening it.

The shock was instant, and I would have crumpled to the floor had he not wrapped his arm around me, holding me against him. I pressed my hand against my mouth, praying what I was seeing wasn't a mirage.

Tears formed in my eyes instantly, my heart racing from the sight of my little girl sleeping peacefully in a white canopy bed, the warm glow of the light on her dresser highlighting a gorgeous princess haven inside the room. The noise I'd heard. He'd spared no expense at providing everything she could ever want from fluffy stuffed animals to a bookshelf full of books, a toy box brimming with dozens of toys, and I'd bet a closet full of clothes. She was in a fetal position, her arm wrapped around her favorite teddy bear. From what I could tell, there wasn't a scratch on her.

I pressed my hand across my mouth to keep from wailing, no clue what this meant or why he'd do this.

"Relax, Savannah," he whispered. "She's safe and I'll protect her with my life as I will do with you."

"I want to see her. I need to be with her. What did you do to her? You drugged her?"

"I did nothing but collect her from your sister's house and she came willingly when I told her I was taking her to her mommy."

"Jessie. You killed my sister!" I jerked from his hold, turning to face him.

The dim light in the room didn't stop me from studying his face. I was sick inside, terrified of what this would mean.

"Your sister is fine. I have men watching her house to make certain she stays that way."

I opened my mouth, my mind full of questions, but I didn't know where to start.

"Go to her for a few minutes."

I knew he was going to watch me the entire time, but I didn't care. I moved to the bed, easing onto the floor. As soon as I started to stroke her hair, humming her favorite lullaby, she rolled over.

"Mommy!" She was groggy but there was no sign she'd been drugged.

"Hi, baby. Do you like your new bedroom?"

She sat up for a few seconds, glancing at everything before nodding.

"Is dis forever?"

"Well, for now at least. Did you have nice ride here?"

She seemed to notice Maxim standing in the doorway. "He's a scary man but we stopped for ice cream. He let me walk on the beach in bare feet and everything."

"I'll let you in on a little secret. Maxim is a pussycat. I'm curious. Was he barefoot too?"

"Yup! He said he like de sand between his toes."

A lump formed in my throat and as I tipped my head, I was clueless what to think. He'd never stepped on the sand before yet he'd purposely taken my daughter on a walk in bare feet? What was he trying to do to me? To us? Was it his subtle way of telling me I could trust him?

I tickled her tummy until she laughed. "I have a feeling he'll want to take you out for other treats." The thought left a lump in my throat.

"Really?"

"Yes. Why don't you get some rest then you can tell me all about your adventure at Aunt Jessie's house."

"She can't cook," Brittany insisted.

At least I could laugh, continued relief making me shake. He'd brought her here to protect her, to relieve my pain. For information. I had no one else to trust, nowhere to turn. I kissed her forehead, tucking the covers under her neck and making sure teddy was under her arm. "Sleep tight, baby girl. Don't let the bedbugs bite."

Her giggle was exactly what I needed. I felt a tear slipping from my eye and she caught it, wiping her little finger through it.

"Mommy. Why are you crying?"

"Because I'm happy to see you, silly. Now, get some sleep." As I rose to my feet, her happy smile remained. The big bad man had done everything to keep her protected. It was something I'd never forget.

As I turned and walked toward him, I could see a strange layer of emotions on his face. Then he pulled me from the door, closing it softly behind us.

"I don't understand you but thank you," I told him.

"Come downstairs. We'll have a drink. We need to talk."

He'd used her as a bargaining chip to get what he wanted. That's all it was. This wasn't sudden love or an instant family. I was so stupid to care about him, but I couldn't help myself. I had no recourse but to trail behind him, still confused why he'd go to all the trouble to decorate her room if he was going to kill us both. Or maybe he was thinking about keeping her. Oh, God.

He led me into the living room, the bright moon shining through the floor-to-ceiling massive glass doors ominous instead of beautiful. The cold chill coursing through my body was so icy I couldn't stop shivering. I wanted to lash out, to scream at him for putting her life in jeopardy but somewhere inside I knew he was trying to keep her safe. He didn't look at me, concentrating on opening and pouring two glasses of wine.

"Why did you bring her here?"

"Because you missed her and because I need to protect her."

"Protect," I repeated. "Is that really the truth?"

When he turned, he nodded toward one of the chairs. "Sit."

I did as I was told, trying to control my breathing. When I wouldn't take the wine, he put it on the table in front of me. Then he sat down in the chair opposite, crossing his legs.

"Are you going to let me go?"

"It's not as simple as letting you go any longer, Savannah. There are people who want us both dead. The situation is escalating."

His words cut into me, although I'd suspected as much long before I was brought here. "I know."

"Do you understand?"

"Yes, Maxim, I do. I may seem naïve to you, but I know what's going on. I'm your weakness, which is what people in my world wanted."

"Your world. How long have you been listening?" he asked casually.

I'd never be able to explain to anyone, but it felt as if the burden of keeping the secret, the lies from him was suddenly being lifted.

There was no reason not to tell him at this point. "Months."

As he unbuttoned his jacket, I noticed he was wearing a holster, the snap unfastened. He was going to kill me.

"What did you learn?"

"Very little other than background information. You were very careful where you handled business. You swept most rooms for bugs on a regular basis."

"Hmmm… Then how did you learn about the shipment? That is why you were sent in undercover, yes?"

I nodded. My mouth and throat were dry as a bone. "The gym at the resort in Miami. It was my suggestion to have a listening device put inside the room. At first, they thought I was crazy."

His eyes opened wide and he chuckled. Then he looked away. "Clever. You had no business going undercover in my organization. You knew that. How did you know I'd use the gym one day?"

"It's your safe zone, the only place you feel free. I wasn't certain if you'd ever hold a conversation there, but I got lucky, your discussion with Ricardo catching me off guard."

He'd placed his elbow on the arm of the chair, rubbing his jaw as he continued studying me.

"I made a single mistake and it changed everything." He said the words plainly, but with a hint of admiration in his tone.

"Yes," I told him.

"What were the plans once you learned dates, times, and the location?"

"I don't know for certain. That's not in my pay grade. I was to provide information about the shipment only, keeping you off guard, at least that's what I thought."

Maxim cocked his head. "What you thought?"

I moved to the edge of the seat, dropping my head into my hands. "If you're going to kill me, just get it over with. But please don't kill my daughter. She's only four. She's been through so much already. I'll tell you what I know, which is shit since I was lied to."

He said nothing for a little while then sighed. "I'm not going to kill you, Savannah, and I might be many things, but I will never hurt a child. You have my word on that."

"Why? Are you selling me off to the highest bidder instead?" I gave him the full brunt of my fear and anger, snapping my head up to stare into his eyes. I'd once thought they were the most beautiful pair of eyes I'd ever seen, full of life. Now they were as cold as the way I felt inside.

"Don't believe everything you read or are told, Savannah. Have I done terrible things in my life? Absolutely, but perhaps you'd know that better than anyone. And maybe you realize that at the heart of my organization is a business that I'm trying to run."

He was right.

"Did you kill the other agents who attempted to infiltrate your organization?"

"Yes. That is what I must do to stay alive."

"Isn't it you who told me that we all have choices?"

He laughed. "You are correct."

"Fine. Why aren't you going to kill me? I'd like to know."

A wry smile crossed his face. "Because I care about you."

I wasn't expecting what he'd just said, unable to think of a comeback right away. "Why?"

"Do I really need to tell you why, my little wren? Since you entered into my world, I haven't kept my eye on business as I should have been."

I wanted to tell him not to call me that, but I quivered just like I did every time he used the expression. When I looked away, he laughed.

"The passion and affection we've shared is real. Yes, by all rights and to keep my uncle happy and my organization running as it should be, I am required to end your life."

"But?"

"But you're too important to me and I think you feel the same."

"This isn't a fairytale, Maxim. We aren't going to live happily ever after."

"Perhaps not," he said in a husky tone, his pupils retracting from lust.

"Then we really are in danger."

"Yes, both from my enemies and perhaps yours. You were used."

A strangled laugh pushed past my lips. "Yes, by someone I should have been able to trust. Her name is Katherine Helms. The bitch was working for someone other than the FBI."

When he lifted his eyebrows, I looked away. "You knew?" he asked.

"Not until she ordered the termination of my boss. That's what I overheard on the phone just before you burst into my suite after dinner. I didn't want to believe it was her, but she betrayed all of us."

"Yes, but other than large payments dropped in a bank account she established over a year ago, there's no evidence of who she's working for."

"How did you know about her?"

"After I found out who you were, I investigated everyone involved. I only suspected it could be her." He was still so unemotional about everything he said.

"The Colombians?"

"Perhaps."

"Internal. Someone else within your organization you can't trust."

He lifted his glass in a salute. "Very astute of you."

"Damien Pavlov."

He chuckled again. "You were paying attention not just to what was being said but to the inflections of the men talking."

"It's what I do. I can't see your faces, so I listen very carefully to breathing sounds, murmurs that maybe others don't hear because of the ambient noise, but mostly the emphasis placed on certain words. Most people don't know they're doing it. That's how I knew Sergei had betrayed you before you had him killed."

"Jesus." He looked away for a few seconds.

I suddenly had the need for a gulp of wine.

"Your gift makes you a valuable commodity, Savannah. That could also put you in danger. You're certain Katherine ordered a hit on your boss?"

"Yes. She has this little edge in her voice that no one else has. Everything was harried, but I have no doubt."

"Do you know anything else about her?"

Another shiver drifted through me. This time because I was forced to face the fact Maxim had been less deceptive than people I was supposed to trust. Everything was upside down, including the way I felt about Maxim. His ice blue eyes were boring into me, splintering me into a million pieces that could never be put back together. Where I expected to see hate there was something else, a glint, a tiny sliver of love.

I was shocked to my core.

"She had my notes, every scrap of information that I jotted down about you, all the research I did about who and what you are. She knows everything, including about the Brotherhood."

He finally reacted, snarling as he closed his eyes briefly. "What did I say about it, little wren?"

I tried to remember as many details as possible. "You talked to Sergei about it twice. You mentioned two names. Constantine Thorn and Phoenix Diamondis. You talked about quarterly meetings."

"Sergei. Goddamn, the bastard continues to haunt me."

"How did you know he was dirty?"

"I had him tailed," he said, shaking his head. "Maybe not soon enough."

My heart was in my throat. "I don't know if this will make you feel any better, but they used his child against him, threatening to take her away from him."

He issued a low-slung growl. "That's what I suspected."

"Before or after you killed him?" I heard the accusatory tone in my voice, but I had to know how far he'd go.

"I didn't know he had a daughter, Savannah. He didn't tell me, including when I gave him the chance to explain." His voice was filled with more angst than I'd heard before. He cared about his friend deeply.

That's one reason he'd taken good care of Brittany. Guilt.

"Where are they? Are they targets now?"

"No, *malen'kiy krapivnik*. They are being well taken care of. It's my responsibility."

"Just like you're going to take care of my child, my baby?"

"Yes."

I was so frustrated that I almost lost my temper. "She never knew her father. Don't pretend like you care about her only to destroy her again. I won't allow her to become attached to you."

"Tell me about her father."

"There's not much to tell. He was a sexy man I met in a bar. We had a one-night stand that turned into more. He pretended he cared, but he became obsessive, and it turned into abuse. When I found out I was pregnant I ended the relationship, which didn't go over well. Not that he wanted anything to do with her, but I had to get a restraining order as well as go to court to revoke his rights. He finally stopped bothering me. After that, I heard he was killed."

"I'm sorry."

"That's what this life can do to you, Maxim, if you let it. If I have choices, so do you. I want my little girl to have the most normal, boring life she can." I heard the ugliness in my laugh and looked away.

"I will do all I can to give that to her."

"I can't talk about that now. Not with a target on our heads. Did you see who Sergei met with?"

He laughed softly. "A woman and a man, but the video was grainy given the location it was shot. There was no doubt they were Feds."

"My guess is that one of them is Katherine."

"I'll get it for you if you'd like to help."

"I would. Katherine will use everything she collected against you in order to help destroy your empire."

"Yes."

"Who's she working for, Maxim? Is it your uncle? Damien? Viktor? Santiago? Why did she turn? Greed?"

He nodded. "If I'm carted off to prison, that will make it much easier to claim a throne. There has to be more to it. A piece I'm missing."

"Only you know what that could be."

The way he chuckled sliced another chill down my spine. Whoever it was, I had no doubt he'd slaughter everyone involved. While it scared me to death, that's not what terrified me the most.

The thought of losing him did.

He took a deep breath, easing his wine to the table. "Come here."

My fingers still shaking, I placed the crystal stem on the table, moving slowly in his direction. The man continued to surprise me, this time pulling me into his lap.

"What are you going to do, Maxim?"

"It's what *we're* going to do, my *malen'kiy krapivnik*. You're going to provide assistance in obtaining answers. And when we learn the identity of the predator, he will die by my hands for putting your life in jeopardy. No one fucks with my family."

He wrapped his hand around the back of my neck, pulling my head down so he could capture my lips. I'd missed the taste of him, the scent of citrus and sandalwood drifting into every cell in my body. I'd longed for his soft lips pressing against mine, his hot breath skating across my skin.

I'd dreamt of his massive frame over me as he thrust his cock inside, whispering filthy words of what he had planned. Then I'd awakened in a cold sweat, the ugliness of what had occurred swimming back to the surface.

Now, as he held me close, pushing his tongue deep inside, my heartache of not being with him became too much to bear.

He held me more possessively than before, drinking in my essence as the kiss became a roar of passion between us. My core was on fire, my pulse racing, and it felt good to be in his arms. We were never meant to be together, but I doubted we could stand to be apart.

After breaking the moment, we were both breathing heavily.

As he lowered his head, pressing his face against my stomach, I closed my eyes, wrapping my arms around his head.

And for a few minutes, I'd never felt safer.

Or more in love.

* * *

Maxim

"The Colombians will use the misfortune against me," Vladimir said. There was no anger in his voice. He was just making a statement.

"They will try." I'd yet to tell him about the meeting Diego and Dante were in the process of establishing. At this point, I'd decided not to place my trust in anyone. My uncle was an old fool, a man who'd entrusted the wrong people. I moved to the bar, pulling a glass from the shelf.

"There's also unrest in the streets, several customers terrified they'll face a blood war. That's something you need to handle."

"I plan on it."

"The soldiers are antsy, concerned about the loss of product."

I poured us both a drink and smiled. "We'll recover. Any news from Viktor?"

"I've managed to calm him down. He's grateful you tipped him on the arrival of the cops since he's a wanted man in this country. He'll wait for the shipment."

Weren't we all? "Good to know."

He eyed me carefully. "You seem very calm."

"It's amazing what the love of a woman can do for you." I was no fool. I'd kept the news of Savannah's true identity from everyone but Ricardo and the Brotherhood.

"Love? The chef?" He snatched the glass from my hand.

"Yes."

"Isn't she dirty?"

"Only after I fuck her."

He laughed, but I sensed he was angry I was involved with her. "Be careful, my boy. Women can make your life easier, but you might be forced to choose between what's most important to you."

"You were the one who said having a family is vital. I'm interested in creating one of my own, especially since I lost my own parents. I am curious, Uncle. You never mentioned who was responsible for killing my parents." As I waited for his reaction, my gut churned. He was the master of hiding his emotions, but I'd learned from Savannah to pay attention to every nuance.

"Unfortunately, the culprits were never found. I hired men to search but they turned up nothing."

"Well, it's been a long time."

"You're like a son to me, Maxim. You've always been. Your cousins adore you as their brother. Don't forget that."

"I never have." I took a few additional sips then eased my drink to the bar. "It's time to announce your retirement."

He continued to study me, no emotions in his dark eyes. "Yes, I suppose you're right. Once you've settled this issue with the Colombians, it will be done."

"You should be cautious, Uncle. Word on the street is that you have a target on your head."

He seemed surprised. "I have enough security, but I appreciate your concern."

"And Damien?"

The hesitation was as I'd expected.

"You'll be free to do with him what you will. Family comes first."

Family comes first. I'd remember that in the future.

CHAPTER 20

axim

Normal.

Simple.

Happy.

The three words hadn't been in my vocabulary my entire life. I'd never once stared out the window of my uncle's estate in my youth, or from one inside my own house as I'd grown older wishing for something I didn't have.

Until today.

Normal.

I'd promised Savannah I'd give Brittany as normal of a life as possible, yet I had them hidden behind closed doors, fearful they'd be attacked. That was no way for anyone to live, especially a child. I'd come to adore the little girl, appreciating her quiet innocence. She was the spitting image of her mother, precious in every way. I'd never thought about having a family of my own. Now that's exactly what I wanted more than wealth or power.

Three days had passed since bringing the child here, none of which had provided me with acceptable answers. I continued to feel the hum of danger all around me. I'd made certain to be seen, assuming the role of Pakhan while my uncle had remained in his estate, preparing for his retirement.

Or was he?

My mind continued to be a chaotic wreck, something I wasn't used to. It was difficult to concentrate, which could prove to be deadly. Sleep had been nonexistent, my nights spent watching over my girls. I almost laughed at the thought. My girls. I'd called Savannah a possession. She'd become much more than that.

She was my kryptonite.

I'd gone over every computer file, including all the accounting records trying to find why Tony had fallen prey to Santiago. I'd tried to find the holes, the reason I'd been blind enough that I hadn't seen this coming. It was a rookie mistake, something I'd been warned about, yet I'd lost two good men who'd obviously been trying to protect something or someone important. Sergei had died rather than tell me about his own daughter. What kind of man did that make me?

"Good news, Max. The investigation in New Orleans was closed. It would seem a drug deal went bad, the hotel getting in the way and nothing more," Ricardo said in an upbeat voice.

"The Feds accepted that?"

"Since we had nothing to do with the pyrotechnic display, they couldn't pin it on us. They're citing a small cartel located just outside of New Orleans, likely to save face. Who cares? We're back to business as usual."

"You mean except for the millions of dollars we lost, and accounts that are still frozen."

"Yeah, well, there's that." He chuckled and shook his head. "You're stinking rich. You'll recover. However, I need a raise to put up with this shit."

I knew he was trying to bring some levity into the situation given my mood swings. The only person who could make me feel any better was Savannah.

"Uh-huh." What I didn't know was if Katherine was still running a scam from her hiding place. I'd reached out to several men in the FBI who owed me a favor, none of which had any idea she was a turncoat. However, the fact she'd disappeared meant she'd either been taken out as a loose end or was lying in wait. In my mind everything was continuing to unravel, which placed me deeper into the crosshairs with my own men.

"You're really meeting with Emmanuel tomorrow?" Ricardo asked from behind me. "Doing an alliance?"

"The meeting will occur. The alliance depends."

"You like playing with fire, don't you?"

What I wanted was the truth. "It's necessary at this point."

"One day you're going to let me in on your definition of necessary. Do you want me there?"

"In close proximity only. Have at least two other soldiers with you. We're meeting at the Lido at two-thirty."

"Out in public?"

I laughed and turned away from the window. "The perfect place."

"You have balls, my friend. No offense."

"None taken, Ricardo. Where is Damien?"

"Collections."

"You had him tailed?"

"Yeah. He's not dirty as far as I can tell."

When I caught sight of Savannah in the doorway, my cock instantly hardened. "He's dirty. I'm certain of it. Did you bring the sim card?"

He reached into his pocket, grabbing a small plastic box and placing it on my desk. "Here you go. You really think Sergei was being played?"

"It was confirmed. That doesn't make what he did right." When my gaze drifted again, he turned toward the doorway.

"Ah, the lovely bride to be."

"We're not getting married."

"Aren't you? That's what you need, boss. She grounds you even during this mess." His eyes narrowed as he looked at me.

Mess. This was an outrage, a tragedy waiting to happen. Mess was just the tip of the iceberg. "Maybe so, but I won't ruin her life."

He leaned forward. "Take a look into her eyes. She's glancing at you like you're filet mignon on a platter and she's very, very hungry. Then again, if you don't want her, I'd be happy to step in."

"Touch her, my friend, and you learn about Russian punishment."

Snorting, he lifted his eyebrows. "When was the last time you slept or took a night off?"

"I'll do that when this shit is finished."

"You might drop dead before. Take the night off, for fuck's sake. Everything is running smoothly. The resort in New Orleans is back to normal."

"I can't do that. I have business to handle, a new shipment to arrange."

"Which you're not going to do until this shit with the Colombians is settled and our money is flowing again. Period. You know it. I know it. Take the goddamn night off and be with your family."

Family.

There was that word again, the one my uncle had tossed out as if I'd ever felt a part of his family. There was only one reason he'd brought me to the States. To have a successor he could control. But he'd learned quickly that I was a rebellious kid. I rubbed my eyes.

"See, you're fucking exhausted, which means you'll make mistakes."

"Do you want a bullet between your eyes?"

Ricardo laughed. "You wouldn't do that because you need me."

"I can replace you."

"*Riiight.* I'd like to see you try."

I glared at him, giving him the middle finger. "Fine. I'll take the night off but you're here at six a.m. and we're going through every account, every receipt. Every email."

"Jesus Christ. We already did that."

"Yeah, well, we've had our share of men betraying us in the last few months. I think it's worth doing again. Don't you? Or would you prefer to cancel your plans and we can get started tonight?"

He threw his hands up in surrender. "Goddamn. You're a slave driver. It's a deal. I'm still not sure what you think you're going to find."

The answer? Salvation.

"The missing clue." I wanted proof positive that Santiago was behind the shit I'd been through so when I put a bullet in his brain, I'd feel confident in doing so.

Ricardo shook his head. "Like I said. Take the night off."

He didn't yank my chain any longer, heading toward the door, offering a greeting to Savannah.

After grabbing the sim card, I turned my full attention to the gorgeous woman standing in the doorway with her arms folded. There was a quirky smile on her face, but it was good to see her smile at all. I'd watched her with Brittany, the pure joy of seeing happiness that wasn't fake or guarded digging at my heart. That had only made me realize how much in love with her I was.

Love.

I'd never been afraid of anything in my life. I'd faced being stabbed twice, shot three times, almost red lining on a cold slab and nothing had bothered me. The thought of loving another human being scared the fuck out of me.

As I approached, I noticed her lower lip quivering, her hard nipples pressing against the tee shirt she wore. "*Ty videniye krasoty*," I whispered.

"You forget I know what you're saying."

"Yes, but I thought you liked it when I spoke to you in Russian."

"Very much so," she purred and inched closer. "You can whisper sweet nothings into my ear any time."

"Later, my little wren. I thought we'd do something special tonight."

"Oh, yeah?"

"Why not go out for ice cream then settle in to watch a movie tonight."

"As long as it's rated G. If you can handle Disney characters." Shock crossed her face.

It was easy to laugh around her. "I'm certain I might learn something."

"Oh, I know you will. Humanity. Humility. How to relax."

When she laughed, I yanked her against my chest, smacking her bottom several times. Maybe this was what it felt like to be normal. Then I cupped the side of her face, wanting to study her for a few minutes.

"What's wrong?" she asked. "Did something happen?"

"No. I'm just looking at you."

"Are you serious about going out?"

"I am. We'll be fine."

"You continue to surprise me. Brittany would like that." As if on cue, I heard the sound of little feet as they raced down the hallway.

When I bent down, she no longer scrunched up her face, calling me a scary man. "My little *solnechnyy luch.*"

"What did you call me, Max?" she asked, her little voice cutting through my heart.

"His ray of sunshine," Savannah answered for me. I gave her a look, but her sly smile trumped mine.

"How would you like to go for some ice cream?" I'd never had an issue talking to anyone in my life, but I had no idea what to say to a four-year-old with a dazzling smile and a laugh that could melt the heart of the hardest Russian. She'd warmed up to me, but only slightly over the last few days.

"Really?" Her eyes lit up just like her mother's did.

"Yes."

When she threw her arms around me, I was stymied what to do. I took a deep breath, lifting my gaze toward Savannah and for the second time since I'd known her, I saw tears in her eyes. I wrapped my arms around the little girl. And for a few seconds, I felt normal.

"Come on. Let's get going." I gathered Brittany into my arms, making certain the gun was still positioned in the waistband of my jeans.

Ricardo was right. It was time to start enjoying life.

* * *

Savannah

If I had a phone, I would have taken several pictures of Maxim while we were eating ice cream. Brittany had decided that she had to sit on his lap and instead of objecting, Maxim had even allowed her to feed him, including getting ice cream all over his shirt.

"Honey. That's enough. We don't want to spoil dinner," I told her as I pulled the ice cream cup away from her grimy little hands, shoving napkins toward her. Then I caught another glimpse of Maxim's face and couldn't help myself. I started laughing.

"What's so funny?" he asked.

"You should see your face."

When he dragged his tongue around his mouth, Brittany giggled, grabbing a napkin and patting his face. I wasn't expecting his playfulness, especially when he pulled her messy fingers into his mouth. She had a fit of giggles, her eyes lighting up more than I'd seen in a long time.

"You're good with her," I told him.

"It's easy. She's just like her mother. Granted, that will mean trouble later."

"Very funny." I felt a warm blush creep along my jawline from the way he was looking at me. In the last few days, he'd nearly worked himself to death trying to find answers that didn't seem to exist. There'd been no further threats and with no additional information, Maxim had been beside himself. It was good to see him more relaxed.

While Brittany continued toying with what little was left of her ice cream, I couldn't take my eyes off Maxim. He was entirely different, from his more casual look to the light surrounding him. A man shouldn't look so hot in a pair of tight black jeans. My mouth watered at the thought of peeling them off later. The passion we'd shared had seemed endless, but also building a need that I knew at some point could consume us. He was biding his time, waiting for the hammer to fall, and while he remained on edge, he'd done everything in his power to make the time in our gilded cage as pleasurable as possible.

Only we both knew it wouldn't last.

"Mommy. Can we watch a movie when we get back?" My little girl's vocabulary improved every day. She sounded like a miniature adult and that scared me to death. "Yes, but only one. Max is trying to spoil you." I pursed my lips, shaking my head slightly.

"What?" he asked with a grin on his face. "I just wanted to pick up a few that we could watch together."

"I think twenty Disney movies is a bit much."

"Nothing will ever be enough for my girls."

The way he said the words was just as possessive as he'd been with me, as if he was accepting responsibility for a child that wasn't his. A small part of me had already romanticized the situation, hoping that maybe one day she'd consider him her father. That was crazy, so much so that I tried to shut down the thought.

But it remained.

Maybe we could find happiness in a sea of shadows and danger.

Maybe…

"I'm curious. Have you ever been in love?" I knew the question was out of the blue, but I had to know.

He lifted a single eyebrow then tickled Brittany. "Once, or so I thought."

"What happened?"

"My job got in the way."

I leaned across the table, giving him a playful look. "Now, you know I'm not going to let you get away with giving me a cryptic answer. I will keep digging."

He laughed, the sound filtering into my system like a pocket full of bottle rockets. "She betrayed me."

The words were frank, exactly the ones he'd used when finding out who I was. I shrank back, glancing out the large picture window at the soldiers who stood casually by the bulletproof SUV. I still couldn't imagine a life that held the possibility of danger at every turn, but he didn't seem fazed by their constant shadow. Then again, he'd grown up with it.

"She was the niece of another crime syndicate sent in to discover secrets. When I found out, she laughed in my face, calling me a fool. Perhaps I was."

"So, you never trusted anyone again."

"Until you." His eyes bore into mine. There was no malice in them, no hint of retaliation. That no longer surprised me. Our connection was too strong, too... there was no word that summed up what we'd shared, and I'd thought about it more than I should.

"Can you ever trust me again?"

He grabbed the same napkin I'd used on Brittany, wiping her face as he thought about my question. "Trust is earned, Savannah, but I realized during this crisis that there was nothing normal about my world, my reality jaded by something that was destined to collapse."

"That's almost poetic."

The light in his eyes returned. "I'm no poet. I'm no romantic either, but I do know that I can't live without you in my life. You are the only light that's managed to snuff out the darkness. But don't lie to me again. I couldn't take that."

"I won't." It was a simple admission and one I prayed I could keep.

"Because if you do," he whispered carefully, a slight growl to his tone, "I assure you the punishment will fit the crime. I'll keep you chained to my bed."

The heat had risen by a thousand degrees in the little store and I was breathless, my nipples hard as diamonds, my pussy aching.

"You're such a tease. Come on, my little ray of sunshine. We need to get you cleaned up." I eased her from Maxim's lap and could sense him bristling. "I'm just taking her to the bathroom."

He swung his head around, glancing at the hallway. Then he nodded. It was a reminder that I was in a completely different world than what I'd been used to. Or had I been? The ugliness of losing Chris and Katherine's treachery was never far from my mind. How had I been so stupid not to know she was using me?

The bathroom was the last door and as I pushed Brittany inside the women's room, a strange feeling washed over me. Would I ever stop looking over my shoulder? There were two of Maxim's men outside, making certain we weren't interrupted. What I found interesting was that having the soldiers present didn't seem to bother my little girl.

When she was finally chocolate free, I pulled open the door and notice a man standing just inside the emergency door. I took a deep breath, wrapping my arm around Brittany and pulling her backward down the hall.

"Give Maxim a message," he said.

I didn't respond, my heart racing.

"Tell him we're coming for him." He didn't wait for a response, immediately walking outside.

I was shaking as I walked back into the store. As soon as Maxim saw my eyes, he jerked to his feet. "What?"

"Out back. A man."

"Stay right here. Do not move." He kept his voice low, trying not to terrify Brittany. Then he headed toward the hallway, and I watched as he pulled out his phone with one hand, his weapon with another. Fortunately, I'd been able to shield Brittany. I pulled her against the wall, trying not to react. Still, my baby girl knew me far too well.

"What's wrong, Mommy?"

"Nothing, baby. Just a creepy man Max is going to talk to."

"Oh, the one with the ink on his arm?"

I lowered my gaze, staring into her beautiful eyes. That's right. The asshole had a tattoo. Where had I seen it before?

One of the soldiers stormed into the ice cream shop, taking two long strides in our direction. "Ms. Parkins. Come with me." He was smart enough to keep a smile on his face and thank God, Brittany didn't refuse to budge. He used his body as a human shield, hurrying us out the door to the SUV.

After pushing Brittany inside, I glanced behind me. There was no sign of disturbance, but I could feel the pulse of danger all around us, eyes watching everything we did. Shuddering, I climbed inside, pulling Brittany close.

And I prayed nothing would happen to the man I loved.

Maxim

I took off running after the asshole who'd accosted my family, the alleyway behind the store littered with dumpsters and boxes. Whoever he was, the bastard was fast, jetting down the cracked pavement, tossing boxes in my way. But I had rage and adrenaline on my side, jumping over the loose cardboard, shoving other items out of my way. I was gaining on him and when he started to turn, I dropped down, firing off a shot first.

The bullet slammed into his arm, the force making him off balance. That allowed me to gain several yards. Before he had a chance to get off a shot, I tackled him to the ground, slamming his head into the pavement then turning him over.

"Who sent you?"

His mouth was bloody from the fall, but he smiled nonetheless, his dark eyes reflecting amusement. The anger boiled inside of me to the point I shoved my weapon under his chin.

"Talk to me."

He was wearing a hoodie but as I yanked it back, I realized I didn't recognize him. I couldn't waste much time. I had to get my girls to safety. "Who. Sent. You?"

As one of my soldiers raced around the corner, I took a deep breath.

"Go fuck yourself." There was no accent, no indication of ethnicity whatsoever.

There was also no recourse. I pulled the trigger.

When I crawled off, I scanned the perimeter. "Are there more of them?"

Johnny shook his head. "Not that I've seen, sir. The girls are safe."

Fuck. I raked my hand through my hair, wiping blood from my face and onto my jeans. "Get a cleanup crew. I don't want his body discovered."

"Will do. I'll stay with the piece of trash," Johnny told me.

As I headed toward the end of the alley, I kept the weapon in my hand. Only when I moved onto the busy street did I slide it back into position. I didn't need any additional heat at this point. I jogged to the SUV, Marcus immediately opening the door.

"They're okay, boss," he said, but I could tell he was angry as well as shaken. How the fuck did the bastards know where we were?

When I climbed inside, I planted a smile on my face. "Everybody okay?" I wasn't the kind of man to fake how I was feeling, but I managed to sound like nothing was wrong.

"We are just fine, Maxie," Brittany answered. Savannah gave a weak smile but there was terror in her eyes.

"We're going home to watch a movie. Maybe we'll get pizza for dinner." I remained up front, seething from what had occurred.

"Yay!" Brittany exclaimed.

As Marcus headed away from the area, all was quiet for a few minutes.

"He had a message for you," Savannah said quietly.

I turned my head, trying not to react. "Oh, yeah?"

"He said they're coming for you."

As the words sank in, I pulled out my phone, dialing Ricardo. "It's time," I said as soon as he answered.

"What?" Ricardo seemed surprised.

"Gather the troops. The war just started."

axim

I watched as Savannah did her best to act as if nothing was wrong, sliding the movie that we'd picked up before heading to the ice cream store into the DVD player. Brittany was none the wiser, excited as she jumped on the couch, her eyes dancing just like her mother's when she was excited or happy.

Which was rare.

How could I provide a decent life when I had no clue how this damning situation would turn out?

"Are you coming, Max?" Brittany asked with such an innocent voice. I'd been shocked she hadn't said anything about the blood on my clothes, but her mother hadn't been able to take her eyes off my shirt, the terror increasing.

"I will in just a few minutes. I need to talk to some of my employees."

"They're scary just like you."

I couldn't help but laugh. As I headed to the door, Savannah followed.

"Are we safe here?" she asked in a hushed tone.

"Additional soldiers have surrounded the house, manning the street. No one is getting to us."

"Who was he?"

"I don't know. He said nothing," I told her, still uncertain if he'd been a hired gun or just a foot soldier doing his job.

"You killed him."

"I did what I had to do to protect you, both of you."

She shivered visibly and I pulled her into my arms. "This will never be over."

"Oh, it'll be over. That I can promise you."

"Don't make promises you can't keep, Max." She pushed away, running her fingers over the dried blood. "You need to change your shirt."

"I will. Just relax and I'll be back in a few minutes. Okay?"

As her eyes narrowed, she sighed then glanced toward her daughter. "She's happy here."

"I know. I want you to be happy as well." I brushed my fingers through her hair, my anger continuing from the way she was shaking. "I'll do everything in my power to make that happen."

She rose onto her tiptoes, pressing her lips against mine. We remained locked together for a few precious seconds until I eased her away. "Don't die on me."

Chuckling, I broke our connection, heading toward my office, yanking off my shirt in the process. When I entered, Johnny, Marcus, Ricardo, Damien, and four others were already inside the room.

I moved toward Damien, shoving him against the wall. "Did you have anything to do with this?"

For the first time in as long as I could remember, he seemed surprised at my accusation. "Why would I want you killed?"

"Because you want the position of Pakhan."

The other soldiers sucked in their breaths, the tension in the room palpable.

Damien swallowed. "I'm not your enemy, Maxim. Yes, I wanted the position. I won't lie to you, but you have more respect from the men, their loyalty is unquestionable."

I laughed bitterly. If only that were true. "If I find out you aided in this situation in any way, you will die and it won't be painless. Understood?"

He hesitated then lowered his head out of respect. "I vow my allegiance to you, Maxim Nikitin."

I took a deep breath, my instinct telling me he had yet to betray me, other than attempting to yank away loyalties. I'd deal with him later. I backed away, glaring at every man. "I want the city streets swept of all Colombians. Emmanuel Santiago is in town. He is rallying the troops. We will stop him before he has a chance to destroy anything else. Lock down the warehouses, have additional soldiers guarding the resort and nightclubs. Kill anyone who dares deny me. Is that understood?"

My demands were not to be questioned and they knew it.

"What about your uncle?" Ricardo asked.

"He's been warned," I told him. I'd placed a call, providing an update. It was up to Vladimir to handle protecting his family. He certainly hadn't offered to provide any additional security measures for mine. This was nothing but another test.

And I wanted to put a bullet in the man's brain for not caring. If that was the way of the Pakhan, I wanted no part of it.

"You have your orders. I want hourly updates."

The men filed out with the exception of Ricardo. He waited until the others had left. "What do you want me to do?"

"Talk to our informants. I need names."

"Will do. You know everything just escalated."

I laughed bitterly. "We were followed from this house. Tomorrow, I'm taking Savannah and her daughter to my personal safehouse."

"Is that wise? You told me you don't want anyone else knowing the location. You won't have anyone to protect you."

He was right, but at this point I was worried I had no other choice. "It's what I need to do until the meeting with Santiago is concluded."

"I still think you're nuts for seeing him."

"I won't be alone."

After swallowing hard, he took a step away, whatever he was about to say making him anxious. "I just hope this brotherhood of yours comes through for you."

"They will." I headed out of the room, taking the stairs two at a time. As I walked into the bedroom, I stared down at the unmade bed, Savannah's fragrance mixing with the scent of our passion the night before. Goddamn it, I wouldn't lose her.

I yanked on a shirt, grabbing a fresh magazine, slapping it into my Glock. Then I headed downstairs. Every window was bulletproof, the security system the best in the industry. Still, I had a bad feeling I couldn't shake. As I moved into the living room, I remained in the doorway for a few seconds, enjoying the sight of the two girls who'd disrupted my life. They'd brought happiness, something I'd never believed I deserved. No one was going to shatter our glass house. No one.

Savannah looked up as I approached, immediately moving away from Brittany. "I'll be right back, baby. Just getting something to drink. Would you like some milk?"

Brittany nodded, consumed by the colorful movie.

As Savannah pushed me closer to the doorway, I noticed her face was pensive. "I remembered something. I don't know why I didn't before."

"What?"

"That man in the ice cream store had the same tattoo as one I noticed on the agent I went to see."

"What kind?"

She narrowed her eyes as if trying to remember. "It's hard to describe."

"Try."

"It was a symbol in black, but it didn't look like ink."

I snarled. "Come with me. I want to show you something." I led her to my office then moved around the other side of the desk, hitting the space bar on my keyboard.

"What are you doing?" she asked, her voice providing a clear indication of just how nervous she was.

"Just hold on." As I brought up a file I'd put together over the years, searching through several pictures, my chest tightened. Then I found it. "Does it look like this?"

She moved behind me, glancing at the screenshot. "That's it. What does it mean?"

I took a deep breath, my lungs aching immediately from the burn of acid created by the truth. Whoever said truth would set you free was a fool. It was about to bury me.

"It means I shouldn't have concentrated my efforts on one man."

"Talk to me, Max. Don't shut me out on this."

"It's the symbol carved into the skin of men pledging loyalty to the Russian Bratva." I looked her in the eyes.

"I don't understand. Those were your men?"

"No. We don't use it in this country." My words were stilted, my anger raw. Viktor had betrayed all of us. That I hadn't seen it playing out would haunt me. While Santiago had his sights set on coming into Miami, he was concentrating on doing so through product availability, using typical war tactics.

Viktor was using familiarity.

"Go back to Brittany. I need to make a couple phone calls," I told her.

"You're scaring me."

"It's going to be okay." It was going to be anything but okay. "Just go. I will be right there."

She pressed her hand against my cheek, the touch warm and soft, but I was too blinded by anger to respond. She backed away, shaking her head. Then I heard words that shot an arrow to my heart, one that would never heal.

"I love you, Maxim." Her words released the burn, replacing it with something else entirely.

Need threatening to consume me.

She was barely out the door when I dialed Ricardo's number.

"Jesus, Max. I just left," he said, half laughing.

"Yeah? Well, things have changed. I need men to hunt down Viktor Romanoff. If he's anywhere in the country, I want him found."

"Isn't he your uncle's friend or something?"

"Just do it!" There was no time for second guessing.

"Yes, sir. I'll find him."

I immediately dialed Vladimir, getting the man's voicemail. "Viktor is behind this. He'll be coming for you." The words should be enough and I also didn't have the time to track him down.

I took long strides down the hallway, trying to determine the best course of action. When the phone rang, I answered without looking. "Nikitin."

The laugh as soon as I answered it sent a cold shiver down my spine.

"Viktor," I snarled.

"Does that mean you finally pulled off your blinders, bastard child?"

His words were selected on purpose to rile me. I refused to take the bait. "You've been planning this for a long time. Haven't you?"

"I always knew you were smarter than you looked. What a shame your accounts have been frozen and no one wants to work with you."

I was surprised how even my breathing had become. "You had my parents killed."

"Yes."

"Why?" I moved closer to the living room, able to keep an eye on my girls without disturbing them.

"Because it was necessary. Your father was determined to shove me aside when I was the born leader."

What the hell was he talking about? "I will hunt you down, Viktor. And I will take my time dissecting you inch by inch."

He laughed again, the tone indicating he'd already won the war. "Unfortunately, you won't be given the chance. But I will enjoy allowing you to watch as I strip away everything important to you. You took something from me. Now, I'm going to destroy what you covet the most. Family. When I take her and that child from you, they will suffer. And you will watch."

The call was dropped and I used every ounce of control not to throw my head back and roar. Some of what he said made no sense, yet there was no doubt of his savage intentions. I had to get my family to safety now.

When I walked into the room, my phone rang again. This time I glanced at the screen before answering. "Bad timing, Brogan."

"You won't say that after what I tell you."

"What?"

"I took the liberty of checking on that FBI agent. Katherine Helms has ties to the Moscow Bratva."

"Viktor Romanoff." I said the words gruffly enough Savannah glanced toward me, narrowing her eyes.

"They were lovers. It sounds like you already know."

I moved toward the window, staring out at the ocean. "What else did you find?"

"Viktor had been increasing his force. There's talk on the dark web about him launching an attack on several cities. But guess where he's starting?"

"Miami. But that's because it's personal." As I remained unblinking, I noticed lights in the distant sky and sighed. Maybe I should leave the country for a few days. No. If I did, that would mean defeat.

"I've put the others in the Brotherhood on notice. Every city targeted belongs to them."

Fuck.

The information Katherine discovered about the Brotherhood was being used. Jesus Christ. As the lights came closer, I tensed. Then they appeared even closer and I snarled. Within seconds, I realized what was happening, ending the call then turning around quickly.

Savannah sensed something was wrong, gathering Brittany from the couch. I heard the thunderous sound of a helicopter over the noise in the room. There was little time to react. I lunged, tackling them to the floor just as I heard popping sounds.

Boom!

The entire room shook, debris flying immediately from a small missile hit. Panting, I kept my body over theirs, trying to ignore Brittany's screams. Fire erupted in several parts of the room, sections of the ceiling collapsing all around us.

"What's happening?" Savannah asked weakly.

Another spray of bullets was fired, the angle off. I yanked my weapon into my hand, jerking slightly, trying to get off a few shots. We were blocked. Soldiers rushed into the room, several of them firing at the chopper.

"Get them out of here!" I bellowed.

The helicopter swung off, trying to avoid the bullets but the bastard would be back.

"I'm not leaving you," Savannah yelped. "You're bleeding. Brittany. Are you okay? Mommy's right here."

Her words echoed, the agony of hearing them unbearable.

"Boss. We need to get you out of here." The soldier's voice echoed, ringing in my ears.

I crawled them closer to the door, gasping for air. I'd been hit at least once, the pain already blinding. "Come on." I managed to move them into the hallway. At least there were no windows. "Are either one of you hurt?"

Brittany whimpered, her little face ashen. She clung to Savannah, but her eyes were locked onto mine.

Savannah continued to shake as she examined her daughter. "We're fine. You're not."

"I'm okay. Now, listen to me. Stay right here. Stay low. Okay?"

She nodded, blinking several times as tears rolled down her face.

I jerked up, ignoring the pain, lumbering toward the window. As it swung around again, I took aim, firing off several shots in a row. I knew I'd hit it but not with a crippling force. As the rapid gunfire started again, I refused to back down, several of my men joining me.

As I continued shooting, the rage turned to ice in my veins. Seconds later, the helicopter exploded in midair, the fireball lighting up the night. I backed against the wall, gasping for air.

"Jesus Christ," Johnny said. "Are you okay, boss?"

"I'll live. Get us out of here. We're taking every SUV, heading in different directions."

"Got it," he told me. "Where are you going?"

"Somewhere safe. For now." I'd purposely purchased several of the same Escalades, knowing that one day I'd need to use them as decoys. Today was the day. With Viktor using a helicopter, that meant he had full air support, ready to track us at every turn. I returned to the hallway, crouching down, touching Savannah's face. "You're going to need to trust me without reservation, baby. I will get you both to safety but it's going to be treacherous."

"I trust you. Just keep my baby safe." Her words filtered into my mind, elevating the ache, the need for revenge even higher.

"I will." I prayed my promise wasn't in vain. As I pulled Savannah to a standing position, Brittany suddenly attached herself to my legs.

"Don't let my mommy be hurt."

Jesus Christ. I placed my hand on top of her little head and as she peered up at me, my heart melted. "Don't worry. I'm like a superhero."

"Really?"

"You bet." I gathered her into my arms, grabbing Savannah's hand as three of my men remained in front, one in the back. They had their weapons positioned as the door was opened, slowly easing into the night air. There was no way anyone could get through the two dozen men by land, but by air was another story.

Another SUV roared in front of the house, Ricardo tumbling out as soon as the vehicle was in park. "Fuck, boss. You know how to throw a party. Get in." He yanked open the back door, allowing me to rush forward, forcing my girls inside.

"Drive in formation with the other vehicles for a few minutes. Then head to the backroads," I told him then moved to the front.

We both jumped inside, Ricardo scanning the perimeter. "Where to?"

"I'll figure that out. Just drive." As six vehicles rolled down the driveway, the heaviness in my heart increased. Did my uncle know about the treachery before it happened? Had he looked the other way? When I found out, the man might not survive the aftermath.

Within five minutes we were on one of the main roads, every driver maintaining the same speed. I'd drilled the maneuver into them, preparing for an attack of this nature. But this was real. This was brutal.

And this meant living or dying.

Barely two minutes later, Ricardo leaned forward, staring out the windshield. "We have company. Pull over?"

"No, stay the course." I shifted my body so I could look behind me. "Get down on the seat."

Savannah did so without question, covering her daughter's body.

Two helicopters were approaching fast, the open area we were in making us direct targets. But Ricardo knew exactly where to break off, pressing his foot down on the accelerator, the other drivers doing the same. Within seconds, shots were fired, the sound thundering in my ears, but I could still hear Savannah trying to console Brittany, her lilting voice as she sang a lullaby pushing my anxiety to another level. I'd never been so enraged in my life, the horror of deception unlike anything I'd ever felt.

I craned my neck, hissing as the helicopters came closer. Additional shots were fired, one of the SUVs taking a hit. As the vehicle crashed into some trees, I rolled down the window, taking several shots. As one of the choppers veered off, I knew they'd taken a direct hit. It gave Ricardo the distraction he needed, breaking from the formation, heading down another road that thankfully was tree lined.

"Goddamn it!" Ricardo hissed.

"Pull to the side of the road and wait," I commanded.

He did as I ordered, keeping the engine idling. Through the open window, I could still hear the whir of the blades. When they finally faded, I took a deep breath.

"What now?" he asked.

"Head to Surfside. Find a motel."

He glanced over at me, his brow furrowed. "I hope you know what you're doing."

So did I.

Thirty minutes passed without incident. Ricardo knew what to look for. When he found a motel nestled in the trees, he pulled in, driving around to the backside.

"I'll get a room," he told me, immediately climbing out.

"What are we doing?" Savannah asked.

I took a deep breath before answering her. "I'm making certain you're safe."

"Meaning what? What are you going to do?" Savannah sat up, leaning forward in the seat.

"I'm going to kill the bastard responsible."

"You can't. You'll be..." She didn't finish her sentence, taking gulping breaths and returning her gaze to Brittany.

"I'll be fine. Trust me."

"I trust you but no one else. You need medical attention."

"Baby. You know I've been through worse." I pressed my hand against her face, her eyes imploring.

I gritted my teeth, trying to control my anger. When Ricardo returned a few minutes later, he kept his weapon low as he led us to the back of the motel up the stairs to a room.

"I don't like this," he told me after they were ushered inside.

"There's no other choice." I closed the door behind us, immediately closing the drapes. Then I turned to him, keeping my voice low. "I need you to stay here."

"Not a fucking chance. You need protection."

I did something I'd never done before, placing my hand on his shoulder, watching as he slowly lowered his gaze out of surprise. "You need to protect my family with your life. They're all that matters to me. Do you understand?"

There was more discomfort on his face than usual. "What are you going to do?"

"Hunt him down."

"Not by yourself."

"Don't underestimate me, Ricardo. This is important to me."

"Yeah, I see that." He threw a look toward Savannah then sighed. "What if you don't come back?"

Snorting, I refused to think about it. "I will. But if something happens, make certain they're taken care of."

He exhaled, gritting his teeth. "Fine. But you'll owe me big time. I'm thinking a yacht."

"You'll have it, my friend. Just don't let anything happen to them." As I moved closer to Savannah, she started shaking your head.

"I need you to let me see how badly you're injured," she stated, her voice stronger than before.

"There's no time. I'm fine."

"You're still bleeding. You could have internal injuries, bleeding inside."

I couldn't believe she cared so much after all she'd been through. I swiped my thumb through one of the smudges on her cheek. She was scratched and would have a few bruises, but we'd gotten lucky. If I hadn't noticed the helicopter's approach, we wouldn't be standing here. That kept my anger right at the surface. "You need to rest and not worry about me."

"That's not possible. Not after…" She looked away, trying to avoid the tears slipping past her lashes.

"Baby. We'll get through this."

"How. How? You have a monster after you. Viktor?"

I nodded, shifting my gaze to Brittany, her cherub face peering up at me as if I was a savior.

Not a monster.

"This must be done. I don't have any other choices. Ricardo will protect you with his life."

"Goddamn it," she hissed.

"Mommy. You said bad words."

Savannah clenched her fist, pressing it against my chest. "I just…" As she closed her eyes, the tears sliding down both sides of her face, I made several silent promises I intended on keeping.

"I do love you, my little wren."

Her eyes opened wide, several emotions shifting in her haunted eyes.

"You're not leaving me here. Not like this," she said, the defiance sharper than ever.

"I need to do this, baby. This will end tonight."

"But how?"

I wish I had a solid answer. I gripped the back of her neck, pulling her close. As soon as our lips touched, she wrapped her fingers around my shirt, arching her back. I captured her mouth, instantly thrusting my tongue inside. The taste of cherries and cinnamon was a reminder of everything I wanted in life.

She continued to cling to me then pushed away, pressing her hand across her mouth. "I don't want to lose you."

"That's never going to happen." I dropped down, tousling Brittany's hair. "I'll be back, little one. In the meantime, Uncle Ricardo is going to take care of you. Okay?"

The little girl eyed me cautiously then nodded. Then she placed her hand on my cheek. "Maybe not so scary."

I squeezed her hand, bringing her cold fingers to my lips. As I stood, the only thing I wanted to feel any longer was anger, enough so it made me a killing machine. I moved toward the door, turning only once to look back at them. Then I walked out into the darkness.

axim

"If you want me, it will be on my terms," I told Viktor. "Just you and me." I gripped the phone with enough pressure, I was certain the goddamn thing would crack. What did I care at this point? I was shaking from anger, the despair not far behind.

"You think you're a brave man, Maxim Nikitin?"

"Why should you care?"

"I don't. I was curious. You remind me of your father, bold yet stupid." Viktor laughed as he'd done before, still trying to goad me.

"Maybe so, but my father had heart. That's what made him a great leader." I knew little about my father's regime in Russia, Vladimir telling me it was too painful to talk about his brother. Now I wondered if everything he'd told me had been a lie.

Viktor snorted. "Fine. Then we shall meet."

"Come alone."

"Of course. Man to man."

"No soldiers."

"None."

I gave him the address, ending the call and tossing the phone aside. I didn't need it any longer.

The one thing I knew about a power-hungry man was that he couldn't resist the lure of money, greed the mitigating factor in most things. But in this case, Viktor was going off revenge, only I wasn't party to the full reason why. There was only one man who could answer that question.

My uncle.

I was taking a significant chance in playing a game of Russian roulette with a master player, but unless this ended tonight, it was possible Viktor had amassed enough manpower to overrun Miami, and several other cities at the same time.

I'd made a few phone calls. I'd set the stage, planting the lure. Now I had to wait.

But patience wasn't one of my virtues.

I allowed my thoughts to drift back to Savannah, imagining what it would be like to have her in my life on a permanent basis.

If she'd have me.

She'd become more than just the light to my darkness. She'd been able to dig through the festering wounds that had surrounded me for as long as I could remember. Now I knew Viktor was the reason my body and mind were scarred from years of enduring anguish. Maybe it didn't matter why, too many years tamping down the anger felt by a young boy who'd witnessed his parents being slaughtered like cattle.

I remained in the shadows, the LED lights over the arena adding to the dull ache in my head. I tried to concentrate on images of her face, angry at my stupidity. This would end tonight.

One way or the other.

Thirty minutes passed.

Then I heard the slight creak of the metal door as my first guest arrived. Viktor took his time stepping into the light, glancing around the perimeter as if expecting I'd brought a dozen soldiers with me. I hadn't lied. None of my soldiers were here. That wasn't the kind of man I wanted to be.

As he walked forward, I moved from the shadows, keeping my eyes locked on his approach. I had no weapon in my hand, although I'd strategically placed several in close proximity.

He grinned, his nod one of false respect. "You are a brave man but stupid. Like your father."

I remained quiet, studying him intently. As I studied his dark eyes, the anger he exuded was similar to mine. "What is it that you want, Viktor?"

"It should be easy for you to understand. What belongs to me. Everything."

Chuckling, I took two more long strides toward him. "And why would you say that?"

"Because that's what I was promised."

"Hmmm... by my uncle?"

He laughed, narrowing his eyes and staring at me as if I'd grown two heads. "You really have no clue what's going on. Do you?"

I had to admit that being at a disadvantage was unnerving. But I'd play it off as if this was nothing more than a game. "I know exactly what's going on, Viktor. I'd hoped you would put it into your own words."

As he took his time studying the facility, the playroom equipment gleaming in the lights, a smug look crossed his face. "You're more like your father every day, but you didn't know that side of him. He was a vicious, vile man. I once witnessed him carving the intestines of a man who owed him money."

When I said nothing, he snorted.

"If only he'd stayed the savage leader instead of turning soft. He did that the day he met your mother."

I had to admit that for the fucker to bring her up troubled me, but I was smart enough not to show it bothered me. "I didn't know her, Viktor. You made certain of that. Now, let's get to the point as to why. You were a soldier in my father's army. Yes? A friend that he counted on. That he trusted." I walked even closer, repulsed by his choice in cologne.

"Can a thirsty man get a drink in this torture chamber?" he asked, as if this was a social gathering.

"Why not." I pointed toward the bar, watching as he moved to it, selecting scotch.

"I will say you're the spitting image of your mother. She was a beautiful woman, albeit a weakness. If only she would have surrendered to my advances, then maybe I would have allowed her to live. She loved your father too much. Tell me. Is that what Ms. Parkins says to you? That she loves you enough to look past your reprehensible career?"

His efforts of trying to cause a reaction were failing.

However, my rage was increasing.

Before he turned around, I checked my watch. I'd calculated everything carefully, which would help keep me in full control.

When he finally did, it was apparent he anticipated I'd finally react to his goading methods. I was cold as ice, and would remain so. This was no time for emotions.

"How did you like the fact I hired Puerto Rican men?" He laughed as if the joke was still on me.

Little did he know.

"I'm only going to ask this once, Viktor. What did I take from you that's so important, other than your false belief the American Bratva belongs to you?"

He took a few sips, even belching before answering me. The man was an absolute pig. "My only son."

I hadn't been prepared for his answer and by the inflection in his voice, the hint of anger and sadness, I was certain he was telling me the truth. As I tipped my head in his direction, he laughed halfheartedly. Then I knew. "Sergei."

"Yes," he hissed. "You killed him in cold blood."

I racked my brain, trying to figure out how I couldn't have known and why my uncle had never mentioned it. Or did he not know?

As if reading my mind, Viktor continued. "Vladimir promised him so much then gave him nothing."

I hated admitting I had no fucking clue what he was talking about, but if I was to discover the full truth, it had become necessary. "Why don't you explain."

"He was to be the new Pakhan. That was the arrangement made. Then Vladimir was determined to promote you over the rightful heir."

That wasn't possible. Or was it?

I could tell Viktor was studying me intently.

"You really had no clue." He laughed as if I'd just told a joke. "*Glupyy mal'chik.*"

Stupid boy. Maybe I was. I'd been played by my uncle. Why?

"You fucking son of a bitch. You believed that by being Vladimir's friend that your son deserved to be Pakhan?"

His laugh was ready to push me over the edge. "Foolish, foolish boy."

"Then explain what you mean."

While I didn't believe in coincidences, I did buy into karma. As the door was flung open, the metal hitting the wall with a hard thud, I moved closer to one of the tools in the playroom, a weapon within reach.

My uncle walked inside, but he wasn't alone, Damien by his side. "This fucking bullshit stops today," he barked, glowering at the Russian. "The truth needs to be told."

For all the years I'd suspected my uncle had been the reason my parents had been slain, it was beginning to dawn on me that within every family there were ugly secrets, those that eventually found their way up from the sludge and gore to rip apart everything once believed.

"My dear brother," Viktor said, a gleam in his eyes. "I kept your secret."

Brother. There'd been three boys in the family. Fuck. I hadn't noticed the resemblance until now.

"And I kept yours. Then you fucked with my nephew."

"That's because he killed my son!" Viktor's voice boomed in the expansive space.

I stood exactly where I was, although I'd wrapped my hand around one of my weapons. I'd been prepared for almost anything, but this was still shocking. As the two men walked toward each other, I tried to make sense of the situation.

"Your son betrayed our family. He talked to the Feds!" Vladimir insisted. "He deserved to die."

"Just like our brother did."

Brother. I shifted my gaze toward Vladimir, his quick look in my direction confirming the ugliness of what had happened, a power play my parents had lost. I wanted to feel sadness but all I felt was empty inside. I'd lived a lie perpetuated by a man I'd hated most of my life because of his aloofness, his inability to show love of any kind.

That was because Vladimir had felt too guilty to show anything else.

"Let me guess," I interjected. "Viktor was given Russia while you were allowed to come to the promised land, starting a new regime that would eventually be led by your other nephew. But you did something unexpected. You felt sorry for the little boy born to a set of parents who loved each other. You were told to leave me wallowing in an orphanage, but you couldn't do it."

Vladimir's smug look confirmed it.

I took a deep breath, shifting my gaze toward Damien. This wasn't going to end well. Whether or not I trusted Damien was of no consequence at this point.

This would turn into a bloodbath.

The silence in the room was deafening, the tension spiking.

"This ends tonight. My nephew will take over as Pakhan," Vladimir finally said, immediately yanking a gun from behind his back. As soon as he pointed his weapon toward his brother, a loud crash occurred from the side.

Then Viktor's soldiers swarmed in, their weapons pointed at Vladimir. I'd been expecting company, but not so soon.

"Now!" As soon as I roared, the men I trusted the most stepped from the shadows, all with weapons in their hands, several of their soldiers flanking their sides. Viktor's men were easily outnumbered.

"Brother," Constantine said. "I heard you needed some assistance."

"It would appear you do. Or is this just a party?" Phoenix asked, his usual grin crossing his face.

For a few seconds, Viktor was confused, gawking at the members of the Brotherhood. Then realization settled in. "*Vy vse umrete zdes' segodnya,*" he snarled.

You will all die here today.

"I don't think so, Uncle," I told him. "My friends prefer to live."

Vladimir wasn't comforted by the reinforcements, his anger only increasing. "You fucking son of a bitch." He took long strides toward his brother, prepared to take a shot.

That's when I noticed the glint in Viktor's eyes. His brother's reaction had been exactly what he was waiting for. The slight flinch that no one else would notice caught my attention and I reacted without hesitation. Just as he yanked his weapon into his hand, I ripped out mine, leveling it toward Viktor's head. I would only get one shot.

And I took it.

The members of the Brotherhood didn't need to be told what to do. They swarmed Viktor's men, laying down a final line in the sand. As expected, the soldiers dropped their weapons, completely outnumbered.

As Viktor slumped to the floor, I took a deep breath, finally shifting my gaze toward Vladimir.

He slowly dropped to his knees, forced to accept the ugliness of a reality that both he and his brother had tried to hide.

"Why?" I snarled. "Why didn't you tell me?"

Vladimir took several deep breaths. "I have my reasons, a family to protect."

Family. He had another secret to hide.

"*Tebya net dlya menya,*" I told him. You are dead to me.

Whether or not I changed my mind later didn't matter at this point.

As I lifted my gaze toward Damien, I finally took the time to recognize the same eyes my uncle had. Damien was much younger, and he had no idea that as Vladimir's illegitimate son, he'd been brought into a world of hatred and lies.

Then again, I doubted he had any idea who he was or of his importance within the family.

Diego headed in my direction, unable to keep a grin from his face. "You know how to play a game of poker, my friend."

"Did I tell you how much I hate the game in the first place?"

While he started to laugh, my thoughts drifted to the woman I'd taken as my possession. But I no longer wanted her kept in a gilded cage.

I wanted her as my wife, the mother of my children. And they would never be told a lie about their family. They'd never learn of a brother they didn't know they had, or a sister who'd been sent away. We would be a normal family.

The moment I started to walk toward Damien, still uncertain what I wanted to say to him, a slight sound drew my attention, enough so that I swung my head toward Viktor.

But it wasn't soon enough.

I'd always heard the devil wouldn't go down without a fight. As Viktor reared up, roaring like an injured animal, he pointed his weapon in my direction.

Visions of Savannah flashed in front of my eyes, the only good thing that had ever happened to me. That was a split second of vivid color before...

He fired.

* * *

Savannah

. . .

Time.

It held no meaning in a shitty little motel in the middle of a suburb of Miami. Other than that my daughter was hungry, her stomach growling so loudly it had gotten on Ricardo's nerves.

"She needs something to eat," I told him. I'd mentioned it before, and he'd said nothing.

At least he finally looked in my direction. "I will not leave here and there's no room service in this shithole. I checked. Max will be back soon. I promise you."

"You keep promising me, but it's been three hours. Where is he?"

"These things take time."

I glanced at Brittany, thankful she'd fallen asleep. I wanted to laugh, but the heartache was too much. After folding my arms, I paced the floor, staring at patterns in the cheap carpet. By now, I know I'd memorized every one of them.

"You don't know Max as I do, Ms. Parkins."

"For the love of God, call me Savannah. Please."

Ricardo chortled. "I can tell why he likes you."

"What the hell does that mean?" I hated the ugliness in my voice, but my nerves were frazzled. I'd been leered at, shot at, held at gunpoint, and almost blown up. In my mind, I deserved to be a little cranky.

"That means you can handle what he dishes out. Even I have trouble." He turned to face me, leaning against the wall. "You're good for him."

"I don't know any longer."

"He loves you." He seemed shocked at what he'd said, a wry smile crossing his face. "He's a tough man. He'll come back."

"What if he doesn't?"

He hesitated before answering, "He's asked me to make arrangements."

God. Everything was so cut and dry. "How can you do this, Ricardo? How can you live every day of your live as if it might be your last?"

"It's not that bad, Ms.… Savannah. This shit doesn't happen every day."

"But you have enemies that could jump out of the darkness at any time."

"True, but there's usually a line of respect that families don't cross."

Line of respect. He meant criminal families, not blood ties. "And betrayal doesn't happen every day either?"

He narrowed his eyes. "Sergei meant a lot to Max. But Sergei's kid meant more than the oath he took to the Bratva. I kind of understand that now." He glanced toward Brittany.

"What if that happens with Maxim?"

"You don't understand. He's the Pakhan."

"Not from what I understand. His uncle is. And he still might be after tonight."

His smile widened. "I know the old man myself, maybe better than Max does. He's just been testing him."

"No, you're right. I don't get it at all." Lack of trust. Betrayal. Uncertainty. What was I saying? Didn't that occur everywhere, even in the one place I thought it would never happen? What law enforcement community was free of corruption? I doubted there was a truthful answer.

"He'll be back soon. He always keeps his promises."

He continued to say it as if by turning it into a mantra, I'd eventually believe it. When I heard his phone, I jerked up my head, trying to keep from making a sound.

"Yeah?" Ricardo answered. "Shit." When he lifted his gaze in my direction, my stomach coiled into knots.

I shrank back, almost tripping before I eased against the dresser. I knew in my heart he was gone. Oh, God. No. No...

"Understood. I'll handle it," Ricardo said then ended the call.

Handle what? What?

That's when I flew at him, trying to keep quiet but hysteria was increasing, yanking at what was left of my sanity. "What happened? Is he dead? He's dead. Isn't he? Talk to me. Tell me."

"Whoa. Whoa," he told me, trying to push me away.

I reacted badly, but I was terrified. When I slapped him across the face, his eyes opened wide.

"Oh, shit."

He cupped his cheek as he shifted his jaw back and forth. "You do have a mean right hook. Calm down, Savannah."

"Just tell me. Is he dead? I need to know. I *need* to know. I can't remember if I told him I loved him." I was babbling off, no longer realizing what I was saying.

Before he had a chance to calm me down, there was a knock on the door. I immediately backed away, ready to protect my child with my life until I noticed he wasn't reaching for his weapon, just looking into the peephole. Then without hesitation, he unchained and opened the door.

The blur of the image in front of me was from the tears in my eyes. I couldn't process what I was seeing.

Maxim stood in the glow of light, his chiseled features capturing my attention first, the love in his eyes second. "Savannah."

I stood in shock for a few seconds. Then I rushed into his arms.

"You're alive. You're here. You're…"

"Ssshhh… My little wren. I told you I'd be back." As he pulled me off my feet, I wrapped my legs around him, gasping for air.

Then he captured my mouth and stars floated in front of my eyes, the kiss sweeter than anything I'd ever experienced before.

"Jesus, boss. Don't forget about the yacht. I want it fully furnished," Ricardo said from behind us.

As Maxim held me, wrapping his fingers around the back of my neck, our connection changed, morphing into something else.

We'd become one.

CHAPTER 23

 axim

Lido was a beautiful spot overlooking the Atlantic in Miami Beach. It was right on the water, boats of all sizes moored just yards away. As I moved through the main part of the restaurant, I could see all eyes on me from customers as well as most employees. Word had gotten out in less than twelve hours that I was the new Pakhan of the most powerful Bratva on the East Coast.

Their eyes held fear as well as a level of respect. I hadn't fought a war, filling their streets with blood. I hadn't burned down buildings or killed innocent people by doing so. I'd simply fought my way through the ranks, a brutal uncle requiring that I spend more time training, kicking me down if I didn't follow every rule.

I'd hated him for it, blaming him for my parents' murder. But he'd done his best to try to raise me through a haze of guilt, making a promise to his brother, my father, that he'd take care of me. That hadn't come easily or without complications. But here I was, a strong man because of his brutal methods.

The family would survive and thrive once again. Only my uncle would spend his time fishing or playing cards. Whatever old mafia guys did when they retired.

When I headed outside, I was surprised at seeing every member of the Brotherhood at the meeting. Santiago would be overwhelmed but after the near disaster at the playpen, we'd agreed that forming a solid alliance with Emmanuel was in our best interest.

If he played by the rules.

If not, all of us would exact our revenge.

"Mr. Pakhan," Dante greeted me as he held out his hand, a mischievous glint in his eye. "Is that the right title?"

I shook it, shaking my head as I noticed the others either bowing or giving me a salute. "Very funny."

"You didn't think we'd hear about your promotion?" Brogan asked, winking as if this was just another get-together.

"I didn't know it was broadcast." Given the half-consumed drinks on the table, I'd say they'd been here a little while.

Then again, I had arrived late. I'd spent some extra time in bed with my beautiful creature under the guise of comforting her. The passion had been... amazing.

I slipped into a seat, checking my watch. Emmanuel was due in ten minutes. "What about Viktor's soldiers?" I asked, lifting my eyebrows as I waited for the conversation to start.

Within seconds, I had a bourbon in front of me. Constantine laughed. "You have them trained in this city," he said. "I need to do that back home."

I gave him a hard look, snorting under my breath.

"To answer your question," Phoenix started, "my men have rounded up all the stragglers in Philly. The reports were exaggerated. There were three dozen maybe, not very well organized either."

"Same in LA," Dante said. "A few got away, but my men are true hunters."

"All I needed to do was tell the Russian Bratva in New York they had competition. They can handle taking out the trash," Gabriel said as he grinned.

"Good," I told them. There was a lot of cleanup given Viktor had managed to taint a solid portion of my empire including Tony and Sergei. I had a feeling there were a few others I'd need to weed out, but that would come in time.

"It's a good thing we hung around in Miami, huh?" Dante teased.

I figured I had Brogan to thank for that. "You didn't interfere much," I said, unable to keep from grinning.

"That's the first time I've seen you smile," Constantine said, shaking his head.

Diego laughed. "Looks good on you."

"It's the woman," Phoenix said, throwing in a growl to taunt me.

For a few seconds, we enjoyed our drinks. Maybe even each other's company.

"Do you expect retaliation from Moscow?" Gabriel asked.

I shook my head. "Unless there are more family skeletons I don't know about, not for a while. But there will always be snakes ready to strike."

"Amen to that," Diego huffed. "What about Damien? How is he?"

I hadn't expected the man to jump in front of a bullet to save me, his pledged allegiance for real. "He survived the surgery. Unless there are complications, he'll recover."

"He's really Vladimir's son?"

"Yes. But according to my uncle, he was never meant to lead. He'll become my lieutenant when he's fully recovered."

Dante whistled. "I thought our family was fucked up."

"It is," Diego chortled.

Suddenly, Constantine lifted his gaze, nodding behind me. "And so it begins."

I rose to my feet, extending my hand as the single gesture of respect the Colombian would receive from the table. Whether or not the Brotherhood alliance was overpowering for him, I couldn't care less. The fact was that he'd been responsible for thefts of products from each one of us, his sons included.

"I didn't know it was a party," Emmanuel said as he nodded to every man at the table.

"I'd call it more of a wake," Constantine said between clenched teeth.

I threw him a look but couldn't help grinning. "Sit down, Emmanuel. We have a lot to discuss."

"Yes," he said, "we do."

As he did, taking the time to order a drink, I allowed my gaze to shift from one member of the Brotherhood to the other, ending with Constantine, the man who'd created the alliance. I'd spent the time doubting the value of the alliance. I'd been rough and aggressive, an asshole to several of them.

And I'd threatened at least two with bodily harm.

But as I sat here today, forming an entirely different alliance that would prevent innocent lives from being lost, families from grieving for loved ones, I was grateful for their support.

Perhaps I'd make a good leader after all.

* * *

Savannah

One month later

"Why do I have a blindfold on?" I asked Maxim, trying to keep from fidgeting. He'd kept me in the dark, literally, for longer than my patience could tolerate.

"Because I said you're required to wear one. As far as I can remember, you're still following my commands."

"You're a very bad man," I purred, sliding my hand across his thigh, stroking his cock.

"If you don't want me to wreck the car, little wren, I suggest you keep your hands to yourself."

"You are no fun."

He chuckled. "I assure you that when we get to our destination, I'll be a barrel full of laughs."

"Liar. You've never been a barrel full of laughs."

"You so need a spanking."

I wiggled in my seat on purpose, the sting of the one he'd given me the morning before remaining. "I am a very good girl, thank you very much."

"Yes, when you have your hot mouth wrapped around my cock."

Gasping, I feigned shock but was unable to keep from laughing. The last month had been entirely different than the weeks prior. There'd been no explosions, no almost kidnappings, and not a single threat. It had been peaceful, if you could call living in a hotel suite with a four-year-old peaceful. At least Brittany didn't seem to have any residual scars from the ordeal in his house. However, I planned on watching her carefully, prepared to get her professional help if necessary.

In the month since the ordeal, I'd been to the funeral of a good friend, patched things up with my sister, kind of, and had been offered a promotion at the FBI, which I'd turned down. I didn't think the powers that be could tolerate me being the girlfriend of a notorious crime lord while performing my duties. Besides, I still had a bad taste in my mouth because of Katherine's betrayal.

I just wanted time spent with my family. I almost laughed at the thought. I'd never believed I'd see a man like Maxim crawling around on the floor playing horsey with a child. But he'd done that regularly.

I even had a picture to prove it, which I used as blackmail every so often, threatening to show his soldiers. I'd had more than one spanking for that tactic. When I felt the engine slowing down, I almost ripped off the blindfold. "Give me a hint."

"Not a single one. You're going to learn all about patience, my little wren."

"Said by the man who has so much."

"I'm learning."

"Uh-huh."

After he pulled the car to a stop, he hesitated before cutting the engine. "I have news."

"You're going to tell me with a blindfold on."

"I want it out of the way."

"Okay. What is it?"

"The authorities found Katherine's body washed up on a beach. She'd been beaten before she was shot and dumped."

Exhaling, there was no reason for the news to bother me in the least. She was a traitor to her country and the people she'd worked for. But a lump formed in my throat, the brutality of the life forever just below the surface. "She was used like she used me."

"Yes."

"That chapter of my life is over. I'm ready for a new one."

"I am glad to hear you say that." He exited the vehicle and as soon as he opened the door, I gathered a scent of the ocean.

He pulled me out, humming and it shocked the hell out of me. "Come on. Watch your step."

"I could watch it better if you removed the blindfold."

"*Ty neposlushnaya devochka*," he whispered as he nuzzled into my neck.

"You still forget I can understand you. So, I'm a naughty girl, huh?"

"Very much so." A door was opened, and he pushed me inside. There was no other sound, just quiet.

But as he walked me forward, I concentrated on the sound of his footsteps as well as the rapid beating of my heart. Then another sound and the wonderful scent of the ocean popped into my system again.

"I wanted to give you a present," he told me.

"It's not my birthday."

"No, it's not." As soon as he untied the blindfold, letting it fall, he backed away. "But it could be a wedding present."

"Is that a sly way of asking me to marry you?" I blinked several times trying to focus. Then I took a deep breath, the ocean's waters within a few yards. As I turned around to face him, I pressed my hand against my mouth.

"Let's just say I'm not a traditional guy."

Laughing, I moved further into stunning living room. "No, you're not. This is beautiful." While almost empty, the house was exactly like what I'd choose. Though beautiful, it wasn't as lavish as the one Maxim had lived in before the destruction.

"It's yours. Or ours. Depending."

I gave him a heated look before closing the distance, brushing my fingers across his jaw. "You didn't answer me, not technically anyway."

"Repeat the question."

"Is this your way of asking me to marry you?"

"Only if you say yes."

"I'll think about it." I backed away, laughing then moving through the house. The kitchen was bright and airy, the huge deck off the side providing yet another glorious view. When I moved to the bedrooms, the first one I walked inside I knew would belong to Brittany. "This is her room."

Maxim had his hands in his pockets, trailing behind me with a mischievous look on his face. "I thought you'd like it."

I skirted around him, moving to the master bedroom, spinning around in a full circle. "A girl could have many a fantasy inside this room."

He moved closer, leaning against the wall. "It's good they aren't going to be fantasies."

"I don't know," I said in a singsong voice, pushing him gently then moving to other areas of the house. He merely followed me, never interfering, never saying a word. Yet his eyes reflected extreme lust.

When I returned to the deck, planting my hands on the railing, I took another deep breath, shuddering when I felt his presence behind me.

"If this isn't what you want, then I'll understand."

"The house? It's gorgeous."

"Not the house, Savannah. This life."

I slowly turned to face him, cupping both sides of his face as he'd done so often with mine. I'd considered whether or not I could handle the life. But it had never become acceptable to live without Maxim. "There's no other place I'd rather be." As I slowly eased my hands down his shirt, moving to his belt, I narrowed my eyes. "Does this mean I get a decorating allowance?"

"Only if you're good," he grinned. "I thought we'd take Brittany to see the dolphins tomorrow."

"And the sand?"

"Maybe I'll dip my toes into the water as well. Like I said. Only if you're very good."

"I think we've been through this before." I jerked on the leather strap, fighting to yank it free. When I unzipped his trousers, he issued a husky growl.

"You haven't answered my question."

"Repeat the question." As soon as I freed his cock, my core ignited to a thousand degrees. He had that effect on me.

His breathing labored, he reached under my dress, sliding my panties to the side, lifting me with his other arm. I wrapped my legs around his thighs and without hesitation, he thrust the entire length of his cock deep inside my pussy.

"Oh, yes."

"The question is," he breathed, "will you marry me?"

"Only if you're good." I gave him a sly smile and as he started fucking me like the savage he was, I threw my arms around his shoulders, gazing into the pair of eyes I'd fallen in love with the first time I'd seen them.

Then I'd fallen hard for the man, a brutal, powerful beast who'd awakened my senses.

Love wasn't easy, nor was it always kind, but in this case it was right.

And I'd never been happier.

There would always be shadows lurking in the distant corners, enemies threatening to destroy what we'd found in each other, but I trusted that no one could ever break us apart.

If they tried, they'd face my wrath.

Hell hath no fury...

The End

AFTERWORD

Stormy Night Publications would like to thank you for your interest in our books.

If you liked this book (or even if you didn't), we would really appreciate you leaving a review on the site where you purchased it. Reviews provide useful feedback for us and our authors, and this feedback (both positive comments and constructive criticism) allows us to work even harder to make sure we provide the content our customers want to read.

If you would like to check out more books from Stormy Night Publications, if you want to learn more about our company, or if you would like to join our mailing list, please visit our website at:

http://www.stormynightpublications.com

planned to end this arranged marriage before it even began.

But it wasn't Diego waiting for me at the altar.

By all appearances the man who laid claim to me was the mafia heir to whom I'd been promised, but I sensed an entirely different personality, one so electrifying I was swept up by his passion.

A part of me still wanted to escape, but then he took me in his arms and over his knee, laying my deepest, darkest needs bare and then fulfilling them in the most shameful ways imaginable.

Now I'm not just his bride. I'm his completely.

King of Depravity

When Brogan Callahan swept me off my feet, I didn't know he was heir to a powerful Irish mafia family. I didn't find that out until after he'd taken me in his arms… and over his knee.

By the time I learned the truth, I was already his.

I went on the run to escape my father's plans to marry me off, but it turns out the ruthless mob boss he had in mind is the same sinfully sexy bastard who just stripped me bare and claimed me savagely.

He demands my absolute obedience, and yet with each brutal kiss and stinging lash of his belt I feel myself falling ever deeper into the dark abyss of shameful need he's created within me.

At first I wondered if there were bounds to his depravity. Now I hope there aren't…

In my late-night hunt for the perfect pastry, I never expected to be the victim of a brutal attack… or for a brooding, blue-eyed stranger to become my savior, tending to my wounds while easing my fears. The electricity exploded between us, turning into a night of incredible passion.

Only later did I learn that Valentin Vincheti is the heir to the New York Italian mafia empire.

Then he came to take me, and this time he wasn't gentle. I shouldn't have surrendered, but with each savage kiss and stinging stroke of his belt his beautiful seduction became more difficult to resist. But when one of his enemies sets his sights on me, will my secrets put our lives at risk?

Beautiful Obsession

After I was left at the altar, I turned what was meant to be the reception into an epic party. But when a handsome stranger asked me to dance, I wasn't prepared for the passion he ignited.

He told me he was a very bad man, but that only made my heart race faster as I lay bare and bound, my dress discarded and my bottom sore from a spanking, waiting for him to ravage me.

It was supposed to be just one night. No strings. Nothing to entangle me in his dangerous world.

But that was before I became his beautiful obsession…

Beautiful Devil

Kostya Baranov is an infamous assassin, a man capable of incredible savagery, but when I witnessed a mafia hit he didn't silence me with a bullet. He decided to make me his instead.

Taken prisoner and forced to obey or feel the sting of his belt, shameful lust for my captor soon wars with fury at what he has done to me… and what he keeps doing to me with every touch.

But though he may be a beautiful devil, it is my own family's secret which may damn us both.

BOOKS OF THE BENEDETTI EMPIRE SERIES

Cruel Prince

Catherine's father conspired to have my father killed, and that debt to the Benedetti family must be settled. Just as he took something from me, I will take something from him.

His daughter.

She will be mine to punish and ravage, but when she suffers it will not be for his sins.

It will be for my pleasure.

She will beg, but it will be for me to claim her in the most shameful ways imaginable.

She will scream, but it will be because she doesn't think she can bear another climax.

But when she surrenders at last, it will not be to her captor.

It will be to her husband.

Ruthless Prince

Alexandra is a senator's daughter, used to mingling in the company of the rich and powerful, but tonight she will learn that there are men who play by different rules.

Men like me.

I could romance her. I could seduce her and then carry her gently to my bed.

But that can wait. Tonight I'm going to wring one ruthless climax after another from her quivering body with her bottom burning from my belt and her throat sore from screaming.

She will know she is mine before she even knows she is my bride.

Savage Prince

Gillian's father may be a powerful Irish mob boss, but he owes a blood debt to my family, and when I came to collect I didn't ask permission before taking his daughter as payment.

It was not up to him… or to her.

I will make her my bride, but I am not the kind of man who will wait until our wedding night to bare her and claim what belongs to me. She will walk down the aisle wet, well-used, and sore.

Her dress will hide the marks from my belt that taught her the consequences of disobeying her husband, but nothing will hide her blushes as her arousal drips down her thighs with each step.

By the time she says her vows she will already be mine.

BOOKS OF THE MERCILESS KINGS SERIES

King's Captive

Emily Porter saw me kill a man who betrayed my family and she helped put me behind bars. But someone with my connections doesn't stay in prison long, and she is about to learn the hard way that there is a price to pay for crossing the boss of the King dynasty. A very, very painful price...

She's going to cry for me as I blister that beautiful bottom, then she's going to scream for me as I ravage her over and over again, taking her in the most shameful ways she can imagine. But leaving her well-punished and well-used is just the beginning of what I have in store for Emily.

I'm going to make her my bride, and then I'm going to make her mine completely.

King's Hostage

When my life was threatened, Michael King didn't just take matters into his own hands.

He took me.

When he carried me off it was partly to protect me, but mostly it was because he wanted me.

I didn't choose to go with him, but it wasn't up to me. That's why I'm naked, wet, and sore in an opulent Swiss chalet with my bottom still burning from the belt of the infuriatingly sexy mafia boss who brought me here, punished me when I fought him, and then savagely made me his.

We'll return when things are safe in New Orleans, but I won't be going back to my old home.

I belong to him now, and he plans to keep me.

King's Possession

Her father had to be taught what happens when you cross a King, but that isn't why Genevieve Rossi is sore, well-used, and waiting for me to claim her in the only way I haven't already.

She's sore because she thought she could embarrass me in public without being punished.

She's well-used because after I spanked her I wanted more, and I take what I want.

She's waiting for me in my bed because she's my bride, and tonight is our wedding night.

I'm not going to be gentle with her, but when she wakes up tomorrow morning wet and blushing her cheeks won't be crimson because of the shameful things I did to her naked, quivering body.

It will be because she begged for all of them.

King's Toy

Vincenzo King thought I knew something about a man who betrayed him, but that isn't why I'm on my way to New Orleans well-used and sore with my backside still burning from his belt.

When he bared and punished me maybe it was just business, but what came after was not.

It was savage, it was shameful, and it was very, very personal.

I'm his toy now, and not the kind you keep in its box on the shelf.

He's going to play rough with me.

He's going to get me all wet and dirty.

Then he's going to do it all again tomorrow.

King's Demands

Julieta Morales hoped to escape an unwanted marriage, but the moment she got into my car her fate was sealed. She will have a husband, but it won't be the cartel boss her father chose for her.

It will be me.

But I'm not the kind of man who takes his bride gently amid rose petals on her wedding night. She'll learn to satisfy her King's demands with her bottom burning and her hair held in my fist.

She'll promise obedience when she speaks her vows, but she'll be mastered long before then.

King's Temptation

I didn't think I needed Dimitri Kristoff's protection, but it wasn't up to me. With a kingpin from a rival family coming after me, he took charge, took off his belt, and then took what he wanted.

He knows I'm not used to doing as I'm told. He just doesn't care.

The stripes seared across my bare bottom left me sore and sorry, but it was what came after that truly left me shaken. The princess of the King family shouldn't be on her knees for anyone, let alone this Bratva brute who has decided to claim for himself what he was meant to safeguard.

Nobody gave me to him, but I'm his anyway.

Now he's going to make sure I know it.

BOOKS OF THE MAFIA MASTERS SERIES

His as Payment

Caroline Hargrove thinks she is mine because her father owed me a debt, but that isn't why she is sitting in my car beside me with her bottom sore inside and out. She's wet, well-used, and coming with me whether she likes it or not because I decided I want her, and I take what I want.

As a senator's daughter, she probably thought no man would dare lay a hand on her, let alone spank her thoroughly and then claim her beautiful body in the most shameful ways possible.

She was wrong. Very, very wrong. She's going to be mastered, and I won't be gentle about it.

Taken as Collateral

Francesca Alessandro was just meant to be collateral, held captive as a warning to her father, but then she tried to fight me. She ended up sore and soaked as I taught her a lesson with my belt and then screaming with every savage climax as I taught her to obey in a much more shameful way.

She's mine now. Mine to keep. Mine to protect. Mine to use as hard and as often as I please.

Forced to Cooperate

Willow Church is not the first person who tried to put a bullet in me. She's just the first I let live. Now she will pay the price in the most shameful way imaginable. The stripes from my belt will teach her to obey, but what happens to her sore, red bottom after that will teach the real lesson.

She will be used mercilessly, over and over, and every brutal climax will remind her of the humiliating truth: she never even had a chance against me. Her body always knew its master.

Claimed as Revenge

Valencia Rivera became mine the moment her father broke the agreement he made with me. She thought she had a say in the matter, but my belt across her beautiful bottom taught her otherwise and a night spent screaming her surrender into the sheets left her in no doubt she belongs to me.

Using her hard and often will not be all it takes to tame her properly, but it will be a good start…

Made to Beg

Sierra Fox showed up at my door to ask for my protection, and I gave it to her… for a price. She belongs to me now, and I'm going to use her beautiful body as thoroughly as I please. The only thing for her to decide is how sore her cute little bottom will be when I'm through claiming her.

She came to me begging for help, but as her moans and screams grow louder with every brutal climax, we both know it won't be long before she begs me for something far more shameful.

BOOKS OF THE EDGE OF DARKNESS
SERIES

Dark Stranger

On a dark, rainy night, I received a phone call. I shouldn't have answered it… but I did.

The things he says he'll do to me are far from sweet, this man I know only by his voice.

They're so filthy I blush crimson just hearing them… and yet still I answer, my panties always soaked the moment the phone rings. But this isn't going to end when I decide it's gone too far…

I can tell him to leave me alone, but I know it won't keep him away. He's coming for me, and when he does he's going to make me his in all the rough, shameful ways he promised he would.

And I'll be wet and ready for him… whether I want to be or not.

Dark Predator

She thinks I'm seducing her, but this isn't romance. It's something much more shameful.

Eden tried to leave the mafia behind, but someone far more dangerous has set his sights on her.

Me.

She was meant to be my revenge against an old enemy, but I decided to make her mine instead.

She'll moan as my belt lashes her quivering bottom and writhe as I claim her in the filthiest of ways, but that's just the beginning. When I'm done, it won't be just her body that belongs to me.

I'll own her heart and soul too.

BOOKS OF THE DARK OVERTURE SERIES

Indecent Invitation

I shouldn't be here.

My clothes shouldn't be scattered around the room, my bottom shouldn't be sore, and I certainly shouldn't be screaming into the sheets as a ruthless tycoon takes everything he wants from me.

I shouldn't even know Houston Powers at all, but I was in a bad spot and I was made an offer.

A shameful, indecent offer I couldn't refuse.

I was desperate, I needed the money, and I didn't have a choice. Not a real one, anyway.

I'm here because I signed a contract, but I'm his because he made me his.

Illicit Proposition

I should have known better.

His proposition was shameful. So shameful I threw my drink in his face when I heard it.

Then I saw the look in his eyes, and I knew I'd made a mistake.

I fought as he bared me and begged as he spanked me, but it didn't matter. All I could do was moan, scream, and climax helplessly for him as he took everything he wanted from me.

By the time I signed the contract, I was already his.

Unseemly Entanglement

I was warned about Frederick Duvall. I was told he was dangerous. But I never suspected that meeting the billionaire advertising mogul to discuss a business proposition would end with me bent over a table with my dress up and my panties down for a shameful lesson in obedience.

That should have been it. I should have told him what he could do with his offer and his money.

But I didn't.

I could say it was because two million dollars is a lot of cash, but as I stand before him naked, bound, and awaiting the sting of his cane for daring to displease him, I know that's not the truth.

I'm not here because he pays me. I'm here because he owns me.

BOOKS OF THE CLUB DARKNESS SERIES

Bent to His Will

Even the most powerful men in the world know better than to cross me, but Autumn Sutherland thought she could spy on me in my own club and get away with it. Now she must be punished.

She tried to expose me, so she will be exposed. Bare, bound, and helplessly on display, she'll beg for mercy as my strap lashes her quivering bottom and my crop leaves its burning welts on her most intimate spots. Then she'll scream my name as she takes every inch of me, long and hard.

When I am done with her, she won't just be sore and shamefully broken. She will be mine.

Broken by His Hand

Sophia Russo tried to keep away from me, but just thinking about what I would do to her left her panties drenched. She tried to hide it, but I didn't let her. I tore those soaked panties off, spanked her bare little bottom until she had no doubt who owns her, and then took her long and hard.

She begged and screamed as she came for me over and over, but she didn't learn her lesson…

She didn't just come back for more. She thought she could disobey me and get away with it.

This time I'm not just going to punish her. I'm going to break her.

Bound by His Command

Willow danced for the rich and powerful at the world's most exclusive club… until tonight.

Tonight I told her she belongs to me now, and no other man will touch her again.

Tonight I ripped her soaked panties from her beautiful body and taught her to obey with my belt.

Tonight I took her as mine, and I won't be giving her up.

MORE MAFIA AND BILLIONAIRE ROMANCES BY PIPER STONE

Caught

If you're forced to come to an arrangement with someone as dangerous as Jagger Calduchi, it means he's about to take what he wants, and you'll give it to him... even if it's your body.

I got caught snooping where I didn't belong, and Jagger made me an offer I couldn't refuse. A week with him where his rules are the only rules, or his bought and paid for cops take me to jail.

He's going to punish me, train me, and master me completely. When he's used me so shamefully I blush just to think about it, maybe he'll let me go home... or maybe he'll decide to keep me.

Ruthless

Treating a mobster shot by a rival's goons isn't really my forte, but when a man is powerful enough to have a whole wing of a hospital cleared out for his protection, you do as you're told.

To make matters worse, this isn't first time I've met Giovanni Calduchi. It turns out my newest patient is the stern, sexy brute who all but dragged me back to his hotel room a couple of nights ago so he could use my body as he pleased, then showed up at my house the next day, stripped me bare, and spanked me until I was begging him to take me even more roughly and shamefully.

Now, with his enemies likely to be coming after me in order to get to him, all I can do is hope he's as good at keeping me safe as he is at keeping me blushing, sore, and thoroughly satisfied.

Dangerous

I knew Erik Chenault was dangerous the moment I saw him. Everything about him should have warned me away, from the scar on his face to the fact that mobsters call him Blade. But I was drawn like a moth to a flame, and I ended up burnt... and blushing, sore, and thoroughly used.

Now he's taken it upon himself to protect me from men like the ones we both tried to leave in our past. He's going to make me his whether I like it or not... but I think I'm going to like it.

Prey

Within moments of setting eyes on Sophia Waters, I was certain of two things. She was going to learn what happens to bad girls who cheat at cards, and I was going to be the one to teach her.

But there was one thing I didn't know as I reddened that cute little bottom and then took her long and hard and oh so shamefully: I wasn't the only one who didn't come here for a game of cards.

I came to kill a man. It turns out she came to protect him.

Nobody keeps me from my target, but I'm in no rush. Not when I'm enjoying this game of cat and mouse so much. I'll even let her catch me one day, and as she screams my name with each brutal climax she'll finally realize the truth. She was never the hunter. She was always the prey.

Given

Stephanie Michaelson was given to me, and she is mine. The sooner she learns that, the less often her cute little bottom will end up well-punished and sore as she is reminded of her place.

But even as she promises obedience with tears running down her cheeks, I know it isn't the sting of my belt that will truly tame her. It is what comes next that will leave her in no doubt she belongs to me. That part will be long, hard, and shameful... and I will make her beg for all of it.

Dangerous Stranger

I came to Spain hoping to start a new life away from dangerous men, but then I met Rafael Santiago. Now I'm not just caught up in the affairs of a mafia boss, I'm being forced into his car.

When I saw something I shouldn't have, Rafael took me captive, stripped me bare, and punished me until he felt certain I'd told him everything I knew about his organization… which was nothing at all. Then he offered me his protection in return for the right to use me as he pleases.

Now that I belong to him, his plans for me are more shameful than I could have ever imagined.

Indebted

After her father stole from me, I could have left Alessandra Toro in jail for a crime she didn't commit. But I have plans for her. A deal with the judge—the kind only a man like me can arrange—made her my captive, and she will pay her father's debt with her beautiful body.

She will try to run, of course, but it won't be the law that comes after her. It will be me.

The sting of my belt across her quivering bare bottom will teach Alessandra the price of defiance, but it is the far more shameful penance that follows which will truly tame her.

Taken

When Winter O'Brien was given to me, she thought she had a say in the matter. She was wrong.

She is my bride. Mine to claim, mine to punish, and mine to use as shamefully as I please. The sting of my belt on her bare bottom will teach her to obey, but obedience is just the beginning.

I will demand so much more.

Bratva's Captive

I told Chloe Kingstrom that getting close to me would be dangerous, and she should keep her distance. The moment she disobeyed and followed me into that bar, she became mine.

Now my enemies are after her, but it's not what they would do to her she should worry about.

It's what I'm going to do to her.

My belt across her bare backside will teach her obedience, but what comes after will be different.

She's going to blush, beg, and scream with every climax as she's ravaged more thoroughly than she can imagine. Then I'm going to flip her over and claim her in an even more shameful way.

If she's a good girl, I might even let her enjoy it.

Hunted

Hope Gracen was just another target to be tracked down… until I caught her.

When I discovered I'd been lied to, I carried her off.

She'll tell me the truth with her bottom still burning from my belt, but that isn't why she's here.

I took her to protect her. I'm keeping her because she's mine.

Theirs as Payment

Until mere moments ago, I was a doctor heading home after my shift at the hospital. But that was before I was forced into the back seat of an SUV, then bared and spanked for trying to escape.

Now I'm just leverage for the Cabello brothers to use against my father, but it isn't the thought of being held hostage by these brutes that has my heart racing and my whole body quivering.

It is the way they're looking at me…

Like they're about to tear my clothes off and take turns mounting me like wild beasts.

Like they're going to share me, using me in ways more shameful than I can even imagine.

Like they own me.

Ruthless Acquisition

I knew the shameful stakes when I bet against these bastards. I just didn't expect to lose.

Now they've come to collect their winnings.

But they aren't just planning to take a belt to my bare bottom for trying to run and then claim everything they're owed from my naked, helpless body as I blush, beg, and scream for them.

They've acquired me, and they plan to keep me.

Bound by Contract

I knew I was in trouble the moment Gregory Steele called me into his office, but I wasn't expecting to end up stripped bare and bent over his desk for a painful lesson from his belt.

Taking a little bit of money here and there might have gone unnoticed in another organization, but stealing from one of the most powerful mafia bosses on the West Coast has consequences.

It doesn't matter why I did it. The only thing that matters now is what he's going to do to me.

I have no doubt he will use me shamefully, but he didn't make me sign that contract just to show me off with my cheeks blushing and my bottom sore under the scandalous outfit he chose for me.

Now that I'm his, he plans to keep me.

Dangerous Addiction

I went looking for a man working with my enemies. When I found only her instead, I should have just left her alone... or maybe taken what I wanted from her and then left... but I didn't.

I couldn't.

So I carried her off to keep for myself.

She didn't make it easy for me, and that earned her a lesson in obedience. A shameful one.

But as her bare bottom reddens under my punishing hand I can see her arousal dripping down her quivering thighs, and no matter how much she squirms and sobs and begs we both know exactly what she needs, and we both know as soon as this spanking is over I'm going to give it to her.

Hard.

Auction House

When I went undercover to investigate a series of murders with links to Steele Franklin's auction house operation, I expected to be sold for the humiliating use of one of his fellow billionaires.

But he wanted me for himself.

No contract. No agreed upon terms. No say in the matter at all except whether to surrender to his shameful demands without a fight or make him strip me bare and spank me into submission first.

I chose the second option, but as one devastating climax after another is forced from my naked, quivering body, what scares me isn't the thought of him keeping me locked up in a cage forever.

It's knowing he won't need to.

Interrogated

As Liam McGinty's belt lashes my bare backside, it isn't the burning sting or the humiliating awareness that my body's surrender is on full display for this ruthless mobster that shocks me.

It's the fact that this isn't a scene from one of my books.

I almost can't process the fact that I'm really riding in the back of a luxury SUV belonging to the most powerful Irish mafia boss in New York—the man I've written so much about—with my cheeks blushing, my bottom sore inside and out, and my arousal soaking the seat beneath me.

But whether I can process it or not, I'm his captive now.

Maybe he'll let me go when he's gotten the answers he needs and he's used me as he pleases.

Or maybe he'll keep me…

Vow of Seduction

Alexander Durante, Brogan Lancaster, and Daniel Norwood are powerful, dangerous men, but that won't keep them safe from me. Not after they let my brother take the fall for their crimes.

I spent years preparing for my chance at revenge. But things didn't go as planned…

Now I'm naked, bound, and helpless, waiting to be used and punished as these brutes see fit, and yet what's on my mind isn't how to escape all of the shameful things they're going to do to me.

It's whether I even want to…

Brutal Heir

When I went to an author convention, I didn't expect to find myself enjoying a rooftop meal with the sexiest cover model in the business, let alone screaming his name in bed later that night.

I didn't plan to be targeted by assassins, rushed to a helicopter under cover of armed men, and then spirited away to his home country with my bottom still burning from a spanking either, but it turns out there are some really important things I didn't know about Diavolo Montoya…

Like the fact that he's the heir to a notorious crime syndicate.

I should hate him, but even as his prisoner our connection is too intense to ignore, and I'm beginning to realize that what began as a moment of passion is going to end with me as his.

Forever.

Bed of Thorns

Hardened by years spent in prison for a crime he didn't commit, Edmond Montego is no longer the gentle man I remember. When he came for me, he didn't just take me for the very first time.

He claimed my virgin body with a savagery that left me screaming... and he made me beg for it.

I should have run when I had the chance, but with every lash of his belt, every passionate kiss, and every brutal climax, I fell more and more under his spell.

But he has a dark secret, and if we're not careful, we'll lose everything... including our lives.

The Don

Maxwell Powers swept into my life after my father was gunned down, but the moment those piercing blue eyes caught mine I knew he would be doing more than just avenging his old friend.

I haven't seen him since I was a little girl, but that won't keep him from bending me over and belting my bare backside... or from making me scream his name as he claims my virgin body.

He's twice my age, and he's my godfather.

But I know I'll be soaking wet and ready for him tonight...

BOOKS OF THE MISSOULA BAD BOYS SERIES

Phoenix

As a single dad, a battle-scarred Marine, and a smokejumper, my life was complicated enough. Then Wren Tillman showed up in town, full of sass and all but begging for my belt, and what began as a passionate night after I rescued her from a snowstorm quickly became much more.

Her father plans to marry her off for his own gain, but I've claimed her, and I plan to keep her.

She can fight it if she wants, but in her heart she knows she's already mine.

Snake

I left Missoula to serve my country and came back a bitter, broken man. But when Chastity Garrington made my recovery her personal crusade, I decided I had a mission of my own.

Mastering her.

Her task won't be easy, and the fire in her eyes tells me mine won't either. Yet the spark between us is instant, and we both know she'll be wet, sore, and screaming my name soon enough.

But I want more than that.

By the time my body has healed, I plan to have claimed her heart.

backside, then she'll scream my name as she takes every single inch of me.

This naughty girl needs to be put in her place, and I'm going to enjoy every moment of it.

Mustang

I tried to tell him how to run his ranch. Then he took off his belt.

When I heard a rumor about his ranch, I confronted Mustang about it. I thought I could go toe to toe with the big, tough former Marine, but I ended up blushing, sore, and very thoroughly used.

I told her it was going to hurt. I meant it.

Danni Brexton is a hot little number with a sharp tongue and a chip on her shoulder. She's the kind of trouble that needs to be ridden hard and put away wet, but only after a taste of my belt.

It will take more than just a firm hand and a burning bottom to tame this sassy spitfire, but I plan to keep her safe, sound, and screaming my name in bed whether she likes it or not. By the time I'm through with her, there won't be a shadow of a doubt in her mind that she belongs to me.

Nash

When he caught me on his property, he didn't call the police. He just took off his belt.

Nash caught me breaking into his shed while on the run from the mob, and when he demanded answers and obedience I gave him neither. Then he took off his belt and taught me in the most shameful way possible what happens to naughty girls who play games with a big, rough Marine.

She's mine to protect. That doesn't mean I'm going to be gentle with her.

Michelle doesn't just need a place to hide out. She needs a man who will bare her bottom and spank her until she is sore and sobbing whenever she puts herself at risk with reckless defiance, then shove her face into the sheets and make her scream his name with every savage climax.

She'll get all of that from me, and much, much more.

Austin

I offered this brute a ride. I ended up the one being ridden.

The first time I saw Austin, he was hitchhiking. I stopped to give him a lift, but I didn't end up taking this big, rough former Marine wherever he was heading. He was far too busy taking me.

She thought she was in charge. Then I took off my belt.

When Francesca Montgomery pulled up beside me, I didn't know who she was, but I knew what she needed and I gave it to her. Long, hard, and thoroughly, until she was screaming my name as she climaxed over and over with her quivering bare bottom still sporting the marks from my belt.

But someone wants to hurt her, and when someone tries to hurt what's mine, I take it personally.

BOOKS OF THE EAGLE FORCE SERIES

Debt of Honor

Isabella Adams is a brilliant scientist, but her latest discovery has made her a target of Russian assassins. I've been assigned to protect her, and when her reckless behavior puts her in danger she'll learn in the most shameful of ways what it means to be under the command of a Marine.

She can beg and plead as my belt lashes her bare backside, but the only mercy she'll receive is the chance to scream as she climaxes over and over with her well-spanked bottom still burning.

As my past returns to haunt me, it'll take every skill I've mastered to keep her alive.

She may be a national treasure, but she belongs to me now.

Debt of Loyalty

After she was kidnapped in broad daylight, I was hired to bring Willow Cavanaugh home, but as the daughter of a wealthy family she's used to getting what she wants rather than taking orders.

Too bad.

She'll do as she's told or she'll earn herself a stern, shameful reminder of who is in charge, but it will take more than just a well-spanked bare bottom to truly tame this feisty little rich girl.

She'll learn her place over my knee, but it's in my bed that I'll make her mine.

Debt of Sacrifice

When she witnessed a murder, it put Greer McDuff on a brutal cartel's radar… and on mine.

As a former Navy SEAL now serving with the elite Eagle Force, my assignment is to protect her by any means necessary. If that requires a stern reminder of who is in charge with her bottom bare over my knee and then an even more shameful lesson in my bed, then that's what she'll get.

There's just one problem.

The only place I know I can keep her safe is the ranch I left behind and vowed never to return.

Ruthless Monster

When Esme Rawlings looks at me, she sees many things. A ruthless mob boss. A key witness to the latest murder in an ongoing turf war. A guardian angel who saved her from a hitman's bullet.

But when I look at her, I see just one thing.

My mate.

She can investigate me as thoroughly as she feels necessary, prying into every aspect of my family's vast mafia empire, but the only truth she really needs to know about me she will learn tonight with her bare bottom burning and her protests drowned out by her screams of climax.

I take what belongs to me.

Ravenous Predator

Suzette Barker thought she could steal from the most powerful mafia boss in Philadelphia. My belt across her naked backside taught her otherwise, but as tears run down her cheeks and her arousal glistens on her bare thighs, there is something more important she will understand soon.

Kneeling at my feet and demonstrating her remorseful surrender in the most shameful way possible won't bring an end to this, nor will her screams of climax as I take her long and hard. She'll be coming with me and I'll be mounting and savagely rutting her as often as I please.

Not just because she owes me.

Because she's my mate.

Merciless Savage

Christoff Dupree doesn't strike me as the kind of man who woos a woman gently, so when I saw the flowers on my kitchen table I knew it wasn't just a gesture of appreciation for saving his life.

This ruthless mafia boss wasn't seducing me. Those roses mean that I belong to him now.

That I'm his to spank into shameful submission before he mounts me and claims me savagely.

That I'm his mate.

BOOKS OF THE ALPHA BEASTS SERIES

King's Mate

Her scent drew me to her, but something deeper and more powerful told me she was mine. Something that would not be denied. Something that demanded I claim her then and there.

I took her the way a beast takes his mate. Roughly. Savagely. Without mercy or remorse.

She will run, and when she does she will be punished, but it is not me that she fears. Every quivering, desperate climax reminds her that her body knows its master, and that terrifies her.

She knows I am not a gentle king, and she will scream for me as she learns her place.

Beast's Claim

Raven is not one of my kind, but the moment I caught her scent I knew she belonged to me.

She is my mate, and when I claim her it will not be gentle. She can fight me, but her pleas for mercy as she is punished will soon give way to screams of climax as she is mounted and rutted.

By the time I am finished with her, the evidence of her body's surrender will be mingled with my seed as it drips down her bare thighs. But she will be more than just sore and utterly spent.

She will be mine.

Alpha's Mate

I didn't ask Nicolina to be my mate. It was not up to her. An alpha takes what belongs to him.

She will plead for mercy as she is bared and punished for daring to run from me, but her screams as she is claimed and rutted will be those of helpless climax as her body surrenders to its master.

She is mine, and I'm going to make sure she knows it.

Claimed by the Beasts

Though she has done her best to run from it, Scarlet Dumane cannot escape what is in store for her. She has known for years that she is destined to belong not just to one savage beast, but to three, and now the time has come for her to be claimed. Soon her mates will own every inch of her beautiful body, and she will be shared and used as roughly and as often as they please.

Scarlet hid from the disturbing truth about herself, her family, and her town for as long as she could, but now her grandmother's death has finally brought her back home to the bayous of Louisiana and at last she must face her fate, no matter how shameful and terrifying.

She will be a queen, but her mates will be her masters, and defiance will be thoroughly punished. Yet even when she is stripped bare and spanked until she is sobbing, her need for them only grows, and every blush, moan, and quivering climax binds her to them more tightly. But with enemies lurking in the shadows, can she trust her mates to protect her from both man and beast?

Millionaire Daddy

Dominick Asbury is not just a handsome millionaire whose deep voice makes Jenna's tummy flutter whenever they are together, nor is he merely the first man bold enough to strip her bare and spank her hard and thoroughly whenever she has been naughty. He is much more than that.

He is her daddy.

He is the one who punishes her when she's been a bad girl, and he is the one who takes her in his arms afterwards and brings her to one climax after another until she is utterly spent and satisfied.

But something shady is going on behind the scenes at Dominick's company, and when Jenna draws the wrong conclusion from a poorly written article about him and creates an embarrassing public scene, will she end up not only costing them both their jobs but losing her daddy as well?

Conquering Their Mate

For years the Cenzans have cast a menacing eye on Earth, but it still came as a shock to be captured, stripped bare, and claimed as a mate by their leader and his most trusted warriors.

It infuriates me to be punished for the slightest defiance and forced to submit to these alien brutes, but as I'm led naked through the corridors of their ship, my well-punished bare bottom and my helpless arousal both fully on display, I cannot help wondering how long it will be until I'm kneeling at the feet of my mates and begging them take me as shamefully as they please.

Captured and Kept

Since her career was knocked off track in retaliation for her efforts to expose a sinister plot by high-ranking government officials, reporter Danielle Carver has been stuck writing puff pieces in a small town in Oregon. Desperate for a serious story, she sets out to investigate the rumors she's been hearing about mysterious men living in the mountains nearby. But when she secretly follows them back to their remote cabin, the ruggedly handsome beasts don't take kindly to her snooping around, and Dani soon finds herself stripped bare for a painful, humiliating spanking.

Their rough dominance arouses her deeply, and before long she is blushing crimson as they take turns using her beautiful body as thoroughly and shamefully as they please. But when Dani uncovers the true reason for their presence in the area, will more than just her career be at risk?

Taming His Brat

It's been years since Cooper Dawson left her small Texas hometown, but after her stubborn defiance gets her fired from two jobs in a row, she knows something definitely needs to change. What she doesn't expect, however, is for her sharp tongue and arrogant attitude to land her over the knee of a stern, ruggedly sexy cowboy for a painful, embarrassing, and very public spanking.

Rex Sullivan cannot deny being smitten by Cooper, and the fact that she is in desperate need of his belt across her bare backside only makes the war-hardened ex-Marine more determined to tame the beautiful, fiery redhead. It isn't long before she's screaming his name as he shows her just how hard and roughly a cowboy can ride a headstrong filly. But Rex and Cooper both have secrets, and when the demons of their past rear their ugly heads, will their romance be torn apart?

Capturing Their Mate

I thought the Cenzan invaders could never find me here, but I was wrong. Three of the alien brutes came to take me, and before I ever set foot aboard their ship I had already been stripped bare, spanked thoroughly, and claimed more shamefully then I would have ever thought possible.

They have decided that a public example must be made of me, and I will be punished and used in the most humiliating ways imaginable as a warning to anyone who might dare to defy them. But I am no ordinary breeder, and the secrets hidden in my past could change their world... or end it.

Rogue

Tracking down cyborgs is my job, but this time I'm the one being hunted. This rogue machine has spent most of his life locked up, and now that he's on the loose he has plans for me…

He isn't just going to strip me, punish me, and use me. He will take me longer and harder than any human ever could, claiming me so thoroughly that I will be left in no doubt who owns me.

No matter how shamefully I beg and plead, my body will be ravaged again and again with pleasure so intense it terrifies me to even imagine, because that is what he was built to do.

Roughneck

When I took a job on an oil rig to escape my scheming stepfather's efforts to set me up with one of his business cronies, I knew I'd be working with rugged men. What I didn't expect is to find myself bent over a desk, my cheeks soaked with tears and my bare thighs wet for a very different reason, as my well-punished bottom is thoroughly used by a stern, infuriatingly sexy roughneck.

Even though I should have known better than to get sassy with a firm-handed cowboy, let alone a tough-as-nails former Marine, there's no denying that learning the hard way was every bit as hot as it was shameful. But a sore, welted backside is just the start of his plans for me, and no matter how much I blush to admit it, I know I'm going to take everything he gives me and beg for more.

Hunting Their Mate

As far as I'm concerned, the Cenzans will always be the enemy, and there can be no peace while they remain on our planet. I planned to make them pay for invading our world, but I was hunted down and captured by two of their warriors with the help of a battle-hardened former Marine. Now I'm the one who is going to pay, as the three of them punish me, shame me, and share me.

Though the thought of a fellow human taking the side of these alien brutes enrages me, that is far from the worst of it. With every searing stroke of the strap that lands across my bare bottom, with every savage thrust as I am claimed over and over, and with every screaming climax, it is made more clear that it is my own quivering, thoroughly used body which has truly betrayed me.

Primitive

I was sent to this world to help build a new Earth, but I was shocked by what I found here. The men of this planet are not just primitive savages. They are predators, and I am now their prey...

The government lied to all of us. Not all of the creatures who hunted and captured me are aliens. Some of them were human once, specimens transformed in labs into little more than feral beasts.

I fought, but I was thrown over a shoulder and carried off. I ran, but I was caught and punished. Now they are going to claim me, share me, and use me so roughly that when the last screaming climax has been wrung from my naked, helpless body, I wonder if I'll still know my own name.

Harvest

The Centurions conquered Earth long before I was born, but they did not come for our land or our resources. They came for mates, women deemed suitable for breeding. Women like me.

Three of the alien brutes decided to claim me, and when I defied them, they made a public example of me, punishing me so thoroughly and shamefully I might never stop blushing.

But now, as my virgin body is used in every way possible, I'm not sure I want them to stop...

Torched

I work alongside firefighters, so I know how to handle musclebound roughnecks, but Blaise Tompkins is in a league of his own. The night we met, I threw glass of wine in his face, then ended up shoved against the wall with my panties on the floor and my arousal dripping down my thighs, screaming out climax after shameful climax with my well-punished bottom still burning.

I've got a series of arsons to get to the bottom of, and finding out that the infuriatingly sexy brute who spanked me like a naughty little girl will be helping me with the investigation seemed like the last thing I needed, until somebody hurled a rock through my window in an effort to scare me away from the case. Now having a big, strong man around doesn't seem like such a bad idea...

Fertile

The men who hunt me were always brutes, but now lust makes them barely more than beasts.

When they catch me, I know what comes next.

I will fight, but my need to be bred is just as strong as theirs is to breed. When they strip me, punish me, and use me the way I'm meant to be used, my screams will be the screams of climax.

Hostage

I knew going after one of the most powerful mafia bosses in the world would be dangerous, but I didn't anticipate being dragged from my apartment already sore, sorry, and shamefully used.

My captors don't just plan to teach me a lesson and then let me go. They plan to share me, punish me, and claim me so ruthlessly I'll be screaming my submission into the sheets long before they're through with me. They took me as a hostage, but they'll keep me as theirs.

Defiled

I was born to rule, but for her sake I am banished, forced to wander the Earth among mortals. Her virgin body will pay the price for my protection, and it will be a shameful price indeed.

Stripped, punished, and ravaged over and over, she will scream with every savage climax.

She will be defiled, but before I am done with her she will beg to be mine.

Kept

On the run from corrupt men determined to silence me, I sought refuge in his cabin. I ate his food, drank his whiskey, and slept in his bed. But then the big bad bear came home and I learned the hard way that sometimes Goldilocks ends up with her cute little bottom well-used and sore.

He stripped me, spanked me, and ravaged me in the most shameful way possible, but then this rugged brute did something no one else ever has before. He made it clear he plans to keep me...

Auctioned

Twenty years ago the Malzeons saved us when we were at the brink of self-annihilation, but there was a price for their intervention. They demanded humans as servants... and as pets.

Only criminals were supposed to be offered to the aliens for their use, but when I defied Earth's government, asking questions that no one else would dare to ask, I was sold to them at auction.

I was bought by two of their most powerful commanders, rivals who nonetheless plan to share me. I am their property now, and they intend to tame me, train me, and enjoy me thoroughly.

But I have information they need, a secret guarded so zealously that discovering it cost me my freedom, and if they do not act quickly enough both of our worlds will soon be in grave danger.

Hard Ride

When I snuck into Montana Cobalt's house, I was looking for help learning to ride like him, but what I got was his belt across my bare backside. Then with tears still running down my cheeks and arousal dripping onto my thighs, the big brute taught me a much more shameful lesson.

Montana has agreed to train me, but not just for the rodeo. He's going to break me in and put me through my paces, and then he's going to show me what it means to be ridden rough and dirty.

Carnal

For centuries my kind have hidden our feral nature, our brute strength, and our carnal instincts. But this human female is my mate, and nothing will keep me from claiming and ravaging her.

She is mine to tame and protect, and if my belt doesn't teach her to obey then she'll learn in a much more shameful fashion. Either way, her surrender will be as complete as it is inevitable.

Bounty

After I went undercover to take down a mob boss and ended up betrayed, framed, and on the run, Harper Rollins tried to bring me in. But instead of collecting a bounty, she earned herself a hard spanking and then an even rougher lesson that left her cute bottom sore in a very different way.

She's not one to give up without a fight, but that's fine by me. It just means I'll have plenty more chances to welt her beautiful backside and then make her scream her surrender into the sheets.

Beast

Primitive, irresistible need compelled him to claim me, but it was more than mere instinct that drove this alien beast to punish me for my defiance and then ravage me thoroughly and savagely. Every screaming climax was a brand marking me as his, ensuring I never forget who I belong to.

He's strong enough to take what he wants from me, but that's not why I surrendered so easily as he stripped me bare, pushed me up against the wall, and made me his so roughly and shamefully.

It wasn't fear that forced me to submit. It was need.

Gladiator

Xander didn't just win me in the arena. The alien brute claimed me there too, with my punished bottom still burning and my screams of climax almost drowned out by the roar of the crowd.

Almost…

Victory earned him freedom and the right to take me as his mate, but making me truly his will mean more than just spanking me into shameful surrender and then rutting me like a wild beast. Before he carries me off as his prize, the dark truth that brought me here must be exposed at last.

Big Rig

Alexis Harding is used to telling men exactly what she thinks, but she's never had a roughneck like me as a boss before. On my rig, I make the rules and sassy little girls get stripped bare, bent over my desk, and taught their place, first with my belt and then in a much more shameful way.

She'll be sore and sorry long before I'm done with her, but the arousal glistening on her thighs reveals the truth she would rather keep hidden. She needs it rough, and that's how she'll get it.

Warriors

I knew this was a primitive planet when I landed, but nothing could have prepared me for the rough beasts who inhabit it. The sting of their prince's firm hand on my bare bottom taught me my place in his world, but it was what came after that truly demonstrated his mastery over me.

This alien brute has granted me his protection and his help with my mission, but the price was my total submission to both his shameful demands and those of his second in command as well.

But it isn't the savage way they make use of my quivering body that terrifies me the most. What leaves me trembling is the thought that I may never leave this place… because I won't want to.

Owned

With a ruthless, corrupt billionaire after me, Crockett, Dylan, and Wade are just the men I need. Rough men who know how to keep a woman safe… and how to make her scream their names.

But the Hell's Fury MC doesn't do charity work, and their help will come at a price.

A shameful price…

They aren't just going to bare me, punish me, and then do whatever they want with me.

They're going to make me beg for it.

Seized

Delaney Archer got herself mixed up with someone who crossed us, and now she's going to find out just how roughly and shamefully three bad men like us can make use of her beautiful body.

She can plead for mercy, but it won't stop us from stripping her bare and spanking her until she's sore, sobbing, and soaking wet. Our feisty little captive is going to take everything we give her, and she'll be screaming our names with every savage climax long before we're done with her.

Cruel Masters

I thought I understood the risks of going undercover to report on billionaires flaunting their power, but these men didn't send lawyers after me. They're going to deal with me themselves.

Now I'm naked aboard their private plane, my backside already burning from one of their belts, and these three infuriatingly sexy bastards have only just gotten started teaching me my place.

I'm not just going to be punished, shamed, and shared. I'm going to be mastered.

Hard Men

My father's will left his company to me, but the three roughnecks who ran it for him have other ideas. They're owed a debt and they mean to collect on it, but it's not money these brutes want.

It's me.

In return for protection from my father's enemies, I will be theirs to share. But these are hard men, and they don't just intend to punish my defiance and use me as shamefully as they please.

They plan to master me completely.

Rough Ride

As I hear the leather slide through the loops of his pants, I know what comes next. Jake Travers is going to blister my backside. Then he's going to ride me the way only a rodeo champion can.

Plenty of men who thought they could put me in my place have learned the hard way that I was more than they could handle, and when Jake showed up I was sure he would be no different.

I was wrong.

When I pushed him, he bared and spanked me in front of a bar full of people.

I should have let it go at that, but I couldn't.

That's why he's taking off his belt…

Primal Instinct

Ruger Jameson can buy anything he wants, but that's not the reason I'm his to use as he pleases.

He's a former Army Ranger accustomed to having his orders followed, but that's not why I obey him.

He saved my life after our plane crashed, but I'm not on my knees just to thank him properly.

I'm his because my body knows its master.

I do as I'm told because he blisters my bare backside every time I dare to do otherwise.

I'm at his feet because I belong to him and I plan to show it in the most shameful way possible.

Captor

I was supposed to be safe from the lottery. Set apart for a man who would treat me with dignity.

But as I'm probed and examined in the most intimate, shameful ways imaginable while the hulking alien king who just spanked me looks on approvingly, I know one thing for certain.

This brute didn't end up with me by chance. He wanted me, so he found a way to take me.

He'll savor every blush as I stand bare and on display for him, every plea for mercy as he punishes my defiance, and every quivering climax as he slowly masters my virgin body.

I'll be his before he even claims me.

Rough and Dirty

Wrecking my cheating ex's truck with a bat might have made me feel better… if the one I went after had actually belonged to him, instead of to the burly roughneck currently taking off his belt.

Now I'm bent over in a parking lot with my bottom burning as this ruggedly sexy bastard and his two equally brutish friends take turns reddening my ass, and I can tell they're just getting started.

That thought shouldn't excite me, and I certainly shouldn't be imagining all the shameful things these men might do to me. But what I should or shouldn't be thinking doesn't matter anyway.

They can see the arousal glistening on my thighs, and they know I need it rough and dirty...

His to Take

When Zadok Vakan caught me trying to escape his planet with priceless stolen technology, he didn't have me sent to the mines. He made sure I was stripped bare and sold at auction instead.

Then he bought me for himself.

Even as he punishes me for the slightest hint of defiance and then claims me like a beast, indulging every filthy desire his savage nature can conceive, I swear I'll never surrender.

But it doesn't matter.

I'm already his, and we both know it.

Tyrant

When I accepted a lucrative marketing position at his vineyard, Montgomery Wolfe made the terms of my employment clear right from the start. Follow his rules or face the consequences.

That's why I'm bent over his desk, doing my best to hate him as his belt lashes my bare bottom.

I shouldn't give in to this tyrant. I shouldn't yield to his shameful demands.

Yet I can't resist the passion he sets ablaze with every word, every touch, and every brutally possessive kiss, and I know before long my body will surrender to even his darkest needs...

Filthy Rogue

Losing my job to a woman who slept her way to the top was bad enough, and that was before my car broke down as I drove cross country to start over. Having to be rescued by an infuriatingly sexy biker who promptly bared and spanked me for sassing him was just icing on the cake.

After sharing a passionate night, I might have made a teensy mistake in taking cash from his wallet in order to pay the auto mechanic, but I hadn't thought I'd ever see him again…

Then on the first day at my new job, guess who swaggered in with payback on his mind?

He's living proof that the universe really is out to get me… and he's my new boss.

ABOUT PIPER STONE

Amazon Top 150 Internationally Best-Selling Author, Kindle Unlimited All Star Piper Stone writes in several genres. From her worlds of dark mafia, cowboys, and marines to contemporary reverse harem, shifter romance, and science fiction, she attempts to delight readers with a foray into darkness, sensuality, suspense, and always a romantic HEA. When she's not writing, you can find her sipping merlot while she enjoys spending time with her three Golden Retrievers (Indiana Jones, Magnum PI, and Remington Steele) and a husband who relishes creating fabulous food.

Dangerous is Delicious.

* * *

You can find her at:

Website: https://piperstonebooks.com/

Newsletter: https://piperstonebooks.com/newsletter/

Facebook: https://www.facebook.com/authorpiperstone/

Twitter: http://twitter.com/piperstone01

Instagram: http://www.instagram.com/authorpiperstone/

Amazon: http://amazon.com/author/piperstone

BookBub: http://bookbub.com/authors/piper-stone

TikTok: https://www.tiktok.com/@piperstoneauthor

Email: piperstonecreations@gmail.com

Made in the USA
Monee, IL
13 January 2025

76678300R00262